Praise for *Dangerous Depths*

"Colleen Coble uses bold strokes of brilliance to paint a realistic picture of beautiful Hawaii. She then throws in a fast-action plot with plenty of suspense-filled twists to keep us guessing until the very end. *Dangerous Depths* is another winner!"

—Hannah Alexander, author of *Fair Warning* and *Under Suspicion*

"[Coble] captivates readers with her compelling characters. Action-packed . . . Highly recommended!"

—Dianne Burnett, Christianbook.com

"*Dangerous Depths* is a fast-paced adventure, where murder lurks among the hibiscus and bougainvillea. The story gives us a look at island life that goes beyond what tourists see, an exciting world of undersea diving and sunken treasure, plus a tender world of the heart. And there's a scuba-diving dog too!"

—Lorena McCourtney, author of The Ivy Malone Mystery series

"*Dangerous Depths*: exotic locale, delightfully memorable characters, and murder . . . it's classic Colleen at her best. If you want to get swept away, look no further."

—Wanda Dyson, author of the Shefford Case Files suspense series.

"In *Dangerous Depths*, Colleen Coble gives her readers an exotic location, an exciting adventure, and a charming romance. Who could ask for anything more?"

—DeAnna Julie Dodson, author of *In Honor Bound,* *By Love Redeemed,* and *To Grace Surrendered*

"*Dangerous Depths* offers readers the perfect vacation with intriguing dives into blue Hawaii, a peek into mysterious island culture, and the thrill of love's persistent tide. Colleen Coble's latest novel is superb."

—Lois Richer, author of *Shadowed Secrets*

"*Dangerous Depths* is a masterpiece of suspense, romance, and discovery. Colleen Coble delivers exotic intrigue, plunging us into the murky waters of the soul with skill and grace. She is a fabulous writer, giving her readers what they want and so much more! [This book] is not to be missed. Jump right in!"

—Kathryn Mackel, author of *Outriders,*
The Surrogate, and *The Departed*

"In *Dangerous Depths*, Colleen Coble weaves an authentic tale of suspense and romance that will mesmerize! Set in Hawaii and brimming with colorful characters, [she] explores so much more than the bottom of the treacherous Pacific Ocean. Coble will win new fans with this latest installment of the Aloha Reef series."

—Denise Hunter, author of *Finding Faith*

"True to her style, Colleen Coble has written yet another intriguing tale— this time set on the Island of Moloka'i amid myna birds, sunken ships, lost treasures, and . . . murder. Turn on all the lights, pour yourself a cup of coffee, and get comfortable. This third book in the Aloha Reef series is a page-turner from beginning to end."

—Diann Hunt, author of *RV There Yet?*

Dangerous Depths

Dangerous Depths

COLLEEN COBLE

THOMAS NELSON
Since 1798

NASHVILLE   DALLAS   MEXICO CITY   RIO DE JANEIRO   BEIJING

Published in Nashville, Tennessee, by Thomas Nelson. Thomas Nelson is a trademark of Thomas Nelson, Inc.

Thomas Nelson, Inc. titles may be purchased in bulk for educational, business, fund-raising, or sales promotional use. For information, please e-mail SpecialMarkets@ThomasNelson.com.

The New King James Version®, Copyright 1979, 1980, 1982 by Thomas Nelson, Inc., Publishers.

Library of Congress Cataloging-in-Publication Data

Coble, Colleen.
    Dangerous depths / Colleen Coble.
        p. cm.—(Aloha Reef series ; bk. 3)
    ISBN 978-0-7852-6044-8 (pbk.)
    1. Hawaii—Fiction. I. Title.
PS3553.O2285D36 2006
813'.6—dc22

                                                                            2006002561

Printed in the United States of America

07 08 09 10 11 RRD 9 8 7 6 5 4 3

For my son, David,
whose strength and loving heart was the inspiration
for Bane in this book. May you always stand strong and
care for others the way you do now.

Prologue

Koma Hamai sat in the warm Hawaiian sun with his fishing net strung out on the volcanic rock. He muttered an ancient chant as he mended the net with gnarled fingers. Hansen's disease had numbed the nerve endings in his fingers, and net mending was a hard job but one he found satisfying. There was nothing better than seeing something broken become useful again.

The ocean boiled and foamed with blue-green ire as it spent its power on the rocks, then came to lap at his feet with a cooling touch. He heard a sound behind him, back by the fishpond, probably one of the many axis deer that romped the jungle along the edge of the sea. When it came again, the furtiveness of the sound penetrated his contentment.

He stood and turned to investigate. The apparition staring back at him was like nothing else he'd ever seen in this life. From the head to the hips, the thing was round. Dark eyes stared out of a hard helmet, and the rest of its body was covered with some kind of green skin that looked as tough as a lizard's. Koma backed away, forgetting his fishing net, then bolted and ran for his cabin. As he ran, he prayed his ninety-five-year-old legs would run as fast as they did when he was twenty, but with the limp from his broken hip, he knew he'd never outrun the monster. He didn't want to end his life as food for Ku. Surely the thing chasing him was the Hawaiian god who built the first fishpond.

A predatory hiss sounded behind him, and he spared one final glance at the strange being. Ku aimed what looked like a speargun at Koma. He fired. The old man stumbled and the spear barely missed his back. He recovered his balance and ran for his life to his cabin.

Tree branches whipped at his face when he entered the jungle, but he was safe here. He knew these trees and paths the way he knew his one-room cabin in the dark. He paused, sensing no pursuit. He peeked through the leafy canopy and saw the being moving off in the opposite direction. Ku never looked back as he moved off through the trees. Why not follow him to his lair? Koma was able to move without a noise through the jungle. He hurried after Ku along an almost impassable path to a cabin so overgrown with vines it was nearly invisible.

By the time Koma returned to his own cabin, the creature had grown in his mind to a height of fifteen feet and sprouted fangs.

One

Leia Kahale rubbed an aromatic salve of crushed ginger, aloe, and other natural ingredients gently into the deformed hand of the old woman seated in front of her. Hansen's disease was manageable these days, but the scars were not so easily erased. The sight of her grandmother's missing fingers and toes had ceased to make Leia flinch long ago. To her, Ipo Kahale was the most beautiful woman to ever grace Moloka'i's shores.

"That feels much better, Leia," her grandmother said in a hoarse voice. Leprosy had taken her vocal cords as well as her lips and nose, and her words had a flat, toneless quality. "You should have been a doctor."

"My mother agrees with you, *Tûtû*. I thought you had a pact to always take up different sides of the fence." Leia put the salve down and stood. She was nearly a head taller than her grandmother's five feet, and *Tûtû* was practically skin and bones. Leia stepped out from under the shade of the coconut tree to test the pulp of the mulberry bark she was fermenting in wooden tubs of seawater. The odor of fermentation had been the most distasteful part of learning the ancient art of making bark cloth, but now she barely noticed the sour tang. She stirred the mess, then eyed the strips of *tapa*, or *kapa* as the Hawaiian version was called, she'd laid out for the sun's rays to bleach. They could stand some more time in the strong sunshine.

"*Kapa* obsesses you," her grandmother observed when Leia joined her on the garden bench again. "I was never so driven."

"I wish I had your talent for the painting of it."

"Already, you're better than I was, *keiki*, but you try too hard." She nodded toward the pots of fermenting bark. "You're like the unformed cloth, Leia. There is much beauty and power hidden inside you. I grow tired of seeing you shrink back when you should be taking your place in the world. Look forward, *keiki*, not backward." Ipo put her deformed right hand over Leia's smooth brown one.

"I'm finding my way, *Tûtû*. I'm finally doing something I love. No more inhaling antiseptic for me." Leia gave her grandmother a coaxing smile. "I love it here—the quiet that's so profound it's almost a sound, the scent of the sea, the strobe of the lighthouse on the point." Kalaupapa, a small peninsula that jutted off the northern coast of Moloka'i, could be reached only by plane, mule, boat, or a long, strenuous hike down the mountain, but Leia liked it that way. She wasn't hiding here at all, not really. "Besides, I'm needed here. The residents are eager to try my natural remedies."

"It's a good place for those of us who don't want to face the stares of curious strangers. But you deserve more than a dying town filled with aging lepers." Her grandmother caressed Leia's hand with gnarled fingers.

"Like what—breathing smog in San Francisco? Besides, you're wise, not old. Old is just a state of mind. When I watch you, I see the young girl inside," Leia said. Today was going to be a good day. There was no sign of the dementia that often rolled in and took her grandmother away from her. Leia touched the tiny scar on her own lip. "I just want to learn more about making *kapa* from you. I like feeling an important part of this little community."

She turned and looked toward the sea. Her nose twitched as the aroma of the ocean blew in to shore. Smells ministered to her soul—the scent of brine, the rich perfume of the mass of ginger and plumeria outside her clinic, the sharp bite of the ink for the *kapa* she made. Sometimes she wished she could guide herself through life by scent alone. Her garden had been taken over by her hobby. Lengths of *kapa* covered the rocks and tree stumps in the yard, and the wooden shelves attached to the back of the building bowed under the weight of supplies.

She stood and stretched. Usually by this time, her friend Pete Kone had arrived with a dozen teenagers to learn the process of making the bark cloth from her. The art had recently been revived in the Hawaiian community, and Leia taught a cultural class to eager young Hawaiians. "Where is everyone? It's nearly eleven, and no one has come in."

"Pete must be running late again." Her grandmother stood and went to the corner of the cottage, where she peered across the street to the beach. "Just look at your sister. Your mother is going to have a fit when she sees her clothes. She'll have sand all through them."

Leia's cat, Hina, entwined herself around her ankles, then nipped at the speckled polish on her toes. Completely black except for a white spot at her throat, Hina was named after a Hawaiian goddess of the moon, and she carried the attitude of her name-sake—she thought she ruled the family. She roamed the Kalaupapa Peninsula like a small panther. Leia moved her feet out of tempta-tion's way and picked up the cat. She joined her grandmother at the side of the building.

On the beach, Eva lay on her stomach on the sand with her nose nearly touching a *honu*, the Hawaiian green sea turtle. Leia watched her sister mimic the turtle's slow blink and neck roll. Twenty-year-old Eva often took Leia's breath away with her sheer beauty. Her blonde hair, bleached almost white by the sun, topped a face that looked at the world through the almond-shaped eyes of Down syndrome.

"I'll get her." Leia stepped around the side of the building and hurried across the hot sand. Hina clutched her shoulder hard enough to hurt. "Time to come in, Eva." She touched her sister's silky blonde hair. Lost in a world where she was one with the turtle,

Eva didn't respond until Leia took her hand. Her lopsided smile radiated a charm that few could resist. Leia didn't even try.

She helped Eva to her feet, then linked arms with her and turned toward the cottage. The noise of a plane's engines overhead rose over the sound of the surf. Leia squinted against the brilliant sunshine. Shading her eyes with her hand, she gazed at the plane. It surged and rose, then fell once more before rising on the wind again. The engine made a laboring sound, sputtered and whined. A plume of smoke trailed from the engines, then a flash of light superimposed itself on Leia's eyes, and she flinched. Eva shrieked and clapped her hands over her eyes. She began to moan.

"It's okay, sweetie," Leia said, patting her arm. Hina yowled, dug her claws into Leia's arm, and shivered. Leia, riveted, watched the plane.

The aircraft began to spiral in a death dance toward the sea. The silver bird separated from a small form that jettisoned from the cockpit. The puff of a parachute and the sight of the lone survivor floating toward the water galvanized Leia into action. She raced to her shop and picked up the phone. Dead again. The phone service in this part of the island was spotty. She stepped outside again and ran toward the boat.

"I'm coming too!" Eva ran after her.

"Stay here," Leia told her sister, but Eva thrust out her chin and clambered aboard the boat. There was no time to argue with her. She started the engine of the *Eva II*, a twenty-eight-foot Chris-Craft her mother anchored in the bay. Scrambling over the deck, she got Eva into her seat then handed her sister the cat to distract her. She flung herself under the wheel and turned on the engines. Leaving Kalaupapa behind, she opened the throttle to full speed and urged the boat in the direction she'd seen the plane fall.

A sea rescue was always difficult. The reflection of the sun on the water made it hard to see a person in the waves, and she wasn't quite sure where the plane had gone in. A craft might slip under the waves without leaving any wreckage behind as evidence. She stared into the rolling waves. Several times she thought she saw the pilot, but it was only a whitecap bobbing. The Coast Guard might soon appear if there was a boat in the area, but she couldn't count on that.

"Do you see anything, Eva?" Eva could see an ant climbing a monkeypod tree at fifty paces. Her sister had calmed down and was staring across the water.

Eva shook her head. "Did he drown, Leia?" She pushed a wisp of hair from her eyes.

"I hope not." Leia squinted against the glare of sun. A movement caught her attention, and she grabbed a pair of binoculars from where they were stowed in a cabinet. The waves parted, and she caught a glimpse of a face bobbing in the waves. Clad in an orange flight suit and helmet, the man thrashed in the lines of his parachute. He managed to free himself, then ripped off his helmet.

"I see him," Eva said in a singsong voice. She stood and leaned over the side.

"Sit down," Leia said, reaching toward her sister. Eva was leaning over so far that a rogue wave could pull her overboard. With the cat draped around her neck like a shawl, Eva sat on the seat but leaned forward with an eager smile. Leia turned to scan the sea again. Anxiety gnawed at her stomach. She'd lost the pilot in the swells. He had to be close. She cut the engine, and the craft slowed, then slewed to the right. A large swell lifted the boat then dropped it in a trough. A dark head popped up. "There he is." She grabbed the life preserver and heaved it toward the man. "Grab hold!" she shouted.

The pilot turned toward her and moved feebly toward the floating preserver. He looped one arm through the hole, and she began to pull him toward the boat. When he was five feet from the side, Eva screeched.

"It's Bane!" Eva reached over the side toward him.

Leia's pull on the rope slackened at the familiar name, then her gaze traveled to the man in the water. Thick black hair in a military cut framed a Hawaiian face marked by strong bones and a firm, determined chin. The facial hair around his mouth hadn't been there when she'd seen him last, and it gave him the look of a pirate. Exertion had leached some color from his dark complexion, but the eyes above the prominent nose had haunted her sleep for months. The lump that formed in her throat had nothing to do with the danger he was in and everything to do with the threat to her peace of mind he'd caused in the past year.

Bane Oana blinked salt water out of his eyes and flailed in the water. Eva screeched Bane's name again, then Leia found her wits and resumed pulling on the wet rope. Bane helped her by swimming with one hand while hanging on to the life preserver. Within minutes he was alongside the boat. Leia leaned over the side. A wave slapped her in the face, and the warm water soaked her hair. She flinched when he grabbed her wrist but continued to haul him aboard. He collapsed on the deck of the boat.

Eva moved to kneel beside him, but Leia stopped her. "Eva, get my emergency kit," she said, dropping to her knees beside him. "It's in the cabinet." She picked up his hand, and her fingers found the pulse at his wrist. It was too fast, but steady and true. Kind of like the man himself.

He tugged his hand away gently and propped himself on his elbows. "I'm fine. Mind if I borrow your radio? I need to call in the accident." He frowned and glanced around the open water.

Leia pushed him back against the deck. "Just lie still a minute. The plane isn't going anywhere, and neither are you until I check you out." Hina leaped from Eva's shoulders and landed on Bane's chest. He jerked and pushed at the cat, who began to lick his face. Her purr was loud enough for Leia to hear over the boat engine. "She's glad to see you. You're the only one she treats like that."

"How did I get so lucky?" Bane flinched away from Hina's pink tongue. "She's weird all the way around. I know no other cat that will come out on a boat."

"She remembers you," Eva said. She stared at Bane while she twisted a lock of her hair. "Where did you go? I missed you."

Leia busied herself in her first-aid kit so she didn't have to look in Bane's face. How was he going to explain his absence to Eva? Her sister had pestered her with questions since Bane quit coming around. Leia hadn't been able to tell her she'd sent him away with a lie and an attitude that hurt him. Still, the truth would have hurt him more in the end.

"Where did you go?" Eva said again.

Bane cleared his throat, and Leia decided to take pity on him. There would be time for questions later. She plucked Hina from his chest and handed the cat to her sister. "Take care of Hina for me, Eva." She opened Bane's flight suit and slipped the stethoscope inside to listen to his heart. Her finger touched the warm flesh of his chest, and she nearly jerked her hand back. Her cheeks burned, and she avoided his gaze. Her own pulse shot up. The *thump-thump* of his heartbeat in her ears rattled her.

Checking his reflexes, she finally stood and held out her hand to help him to his feet. "You seem to be okay. Other than smelling like a fish."

"I could have told you that ten minutes ago," he grumbled. He stood but continued to hang on to her hand. His gaze examined every inch of her face. "How have you been, Leia?"

"What are you doing here?" Bane had the power to disrupt her life. Even now, she could almost sense the vibrations around her, a warning that her life was about to change.

"It sounds like you're not glad to see me. I thought when I took this assignment—" He dropped her hand and straightened his shoulders.

She didn't answer. Even Eva seemed to sense the tension between them, because she backed away and began to hum to the cat. Leia pointed. "The radio is over there. You'd better call in your accident."

"If it was an accident. I'd say there's something screwy going on." Bane stalked to the VHP radio and grabbed the mic.

She listened as he called the Coast Guard, who patched him through to his boss. Bane had been with the Coast Guard, and she'd heard he resigned his commission and was doing civilian research as an oceanographer. She hoped he hadn't come here planning a reconciliation, because it wasn't going to happen. It couldn't, no matter how much she might want it.

"The controls just weren't responding, Ron," Bane was saying into the mic. "There was a bang like a small bomb, and the plane wallowed like a whale. We need to recover it and see if it was sabotaged." He listened then nodded. "I'll get right on it." When he hung up the radio, his eyes were shadowed with fatigue. "I don't suppose you've overcome your dislike for cell phones?"

She shook her head. "Nope."

He grinned. "I didn't think so. I need to call Kaia and see if she and her dolphin can come sooner than she planned."

"Her dolphin?"

"Yeah, Nani. I've got to recover that plane. I didn't work for months on that equipment to lose it now."

"What are you working on?"

He grinned. "Tony talked me into his pet project. He found a financial backer and roped me into it. So I'm working for his investor, Ron Pimental. He's got a small fleet of research and salvage vessels. I was ready to do something a little different. The thought of seeing you again sweetened the offer."

Tony Romero and Bane had been tight for years. Bane worked at Tony's dive shop before joining the Coast Guard, and the two men were more like brothers than friends. She'd been their younger "sister" until the first time Bane kissed her. She dropped her gaze and began to put her medical kit away. "It doesn't seem your type of job. I never expected you to resign your commission."

"Why? I get to continue mapping the ocean floor, plus I get to dive sunken ships and see the new coral forming. Life doesn't get much better than that."

Life had been better for her before he came back to disrupt it. She looked back at the water half expecting to see his dog's shaggy head. "Where's Ajax? You two are usually joined at the hip."

"He's coming on the ship with Ron."

"Tony has been obsessed with finding that Spanish galleon for years. Who was fool enough to put up good money on this project?"

He grinned. "Your cynicism is showing. I think we have a shot at it. Pimental Salvage has state-of-the-art equipment, and he's got a knack for finding ships. It's a good combo. He should be here in a few hours." He stretched his long legs out in front of him and folded his arms over his chest. "How's your *'ohana*?"

"They're good. I was just visiting with *Tûtû* when I saw your plane go down." She didn't want to make small talk with him. The boat suddenly seemed claustrophobic. "I'm living there now, treating the residents with natural meds."

His dark eyes raked her. "Still hiding?"

"I like it there," she shot back.

"Can we go diving?" Eva asked. "You promised to take me to see the *honu*." She grabbed her sketch pad from the floor. "I drew a picture of one. See?" She thrust the picture under Bane's nose.

Bane studied the sea turtle picture. "You're really talented, Eva. You should go to art school."

The sea turtle looked exactly like the one Eva had been imitating on shore. Eva had a rare talent that often awed Leia. "Great job, Eva. But Bane is too busy to take you diving."

"He said he's never too busy for me!" Eva protested.

"I did, didn't I?" Bane aimed a challenging look at Leia. "When we go diving is up to your sister, Eva. She could have called me months ago and hasn't."

"And I wasn't going to," she muttered.

"Afraid?"

She met his gaze. "You can take her diving any time you like. Just name the day." The last thing she wanted to do was chart the dangerous depths with Bane again, but no one dared call her a coward.

"When are you free?"

Bane knew how much she loved diving—they'd spent years exploring the underwater world. Their love of the wonders in the sea had been their first bond. "Who said anything about me? She's the one who wants to go." She knew he wouldn't be taken in by her bluff. She watched out for Eva in all circumstances.

His smile faded, and he examined her face. He let out a huff, and his lips tightened. "How about tomorrow evening, Eva?"

His gaze told Leia she'd won this round, but the war wasn't over. She felt a tingle down to her toe ring. She had to stay out of his way. He'd forget about her soon enough. Sooner than she'd forget him, unfortunately. She loved him enough to make sure she didn't give in to his charms.

His gaze wandered to the dive boat in the distance moving toward shore, and his gaze sharpened. "Hey, I should go see Tony."

"That's not his boat, but I'll take you to Kaunakakai," she blurted before she thought.

Amusement lifted his lips. "I'm game. I can call Kaia from the shop."

She was always a sucker for Bane's smile.

Two

The appearance of the Aloha Dive Shop didn't live up to its welcoming name. The salt-weathered clapboard structure squatted against the spray of wind and surf at the curl of beach on the south shore of Moloka'i just outside Kaunakakai. Kaunakakai Harbor was the only really safe anchorage on Moloka'i, and nearly all the dive operations were located along the quiet little quay. Hawai'i's barrier reef made the waters calm most seasons and was the perfect haven for marine vessels. Bane Oana was already smiling in anticipation as he strode toward Tony Romero's building.

The thought of seeing Tony helped get his mind off Leia's cool reaction to his appearance. He'd anticipated and dreaded the moment when he'd see her again, and the experience had lived up to all his trepidation. He wanted to be able to greet her as an old friend and not have his heart kick like a whale's fluke, but he wasn't that lucky. One look into her blue eyes, and he was even more determined to find out why she'd broken their engagement. He should have come back sooner, but she'd gone to San Francisco and he'd been on assignment and couldn't get away. This time he wasn't leaving until he knew what had changed her.

He glanced at Leia out of the corner of his eye. Her tanned legs stretched out of her white shorts and had no trouble matching his long stride as they walked from the parking lot to the building. Nearly six feet tall, she could almost look him in the eye. She walked with her shoulders back and her head high, her gaze straight ahead. She'd always been oblivious of her beauty. A thick brown

Dangerous Depths

braid hung over one shoulder, a rope he'd often hefted in his hand and entwined around his arm. He loved the touch of it, the smell of it—a mixture of Hawaiian flowers and herbs. Being around her again made him feel as if he were balancing on the edge of his surfboard with a monster wave at his back. He might surf on to glory or wipe out and have to slink away in humiliation.

Eva clung to his hand, and Bane squeezed her fingers before releasing her in front of the dive shop. He ignored the way the cat kept putting her paw on his arm.

"I'm going to go look for another *honu,*" Eva told him.

He nodded, and she skipped off toward the water. Stepping inside, he glanced around the familiar space. The shelves were crowded with stacks of fins, reef shoes, snorkels, and masks. Racks of postcards and swim goggles crowded the aisles, and displays of T-shirts and bathing suits plastered every available inch of wall space, filling the air with the scent of a mixture of rubber and new clothing. The aroma was as comforting to Bane as old shoes and brought back the memories of working here. Some of the best years of his life had been spent in this place. He suppressed a smile at the way Leia was sniffing the air. He often joked that she had a nose more sensitive than his dog's.

He glanced around the small area, packed with tourists talking to dive instructors. He didn't recognize most of the divemasters. The turnover here tended to be high. Though Moloka'i proclaimed itself to be "the most Hawaiian of the islands," it was also the most quiet. Many who came here looking for work found it to be too rural for their tastes and moved on to the bright lights of O'ahu or Maui. His gaze stopped at the dark head of hair he was looking for. Antonio Romero—Tony to his friends—bent over the cash register as he rang up rental snorkel gear for a family of four. As the family left the counter, he straightened and saw Bane.

Tony's lips parted in a smile that flashed unnaturally white teeth. "Bane! When did you blow into town? Is the research ship here too?" He came around the end of the counter and grabbed Bane. The two men did what Bane called "the man hug," a brief clasp of one hand on a shoulder and one hand in a handshake.

"Just me so far, but the *Pomaik'i* will be here later today. You look healthy and happy. Ready to find that treasure?" Bane nodded toward the doubloon hanging on a gold chain around Tony's neck.

Tony fingered the coin. His smile held even more confidence than usual. He glanced around and lowered his voice. "I'm glad you're here, Bane. I need a friend I can trust. This is it, my friend. We're all going to be rich."

"I think I've heard that one before."

"I'm serious, Bane." Tony dropped his voice and leaned in. "I found an old man out at the leper colony who says he knows where the treasure is buried. He says he knows where to find the ship's remains too."

Leia leaned in. "Koma?" Her lips held a wry twist. "Last week he told Eva he saw Ku coming out of the fishpond."

Tony's bright smile faded. "I believe him," he said in a sullen voice.

"About Ku or the ship?" Leia smiled as if to take the sting out of her jibe.

"We've heard those ship stories for years, Tony," Bane said. "Two years ago you were sure the ship was sunk off Mokapu Island. That was a bust. What makes you so sure this time?"

"This guy says his ancestor helped bury it. If you're so skeptical, why did you hire on to help look?"

Bane didn't answer, not with Leia listening. "If you're so sure it's been buried on land, why do you want to search the ocean floor?"

Tony flushed. "Okay, I admit Koma's story is a little far-fetched, but I want to follow every lead. I want that treasure no matter where it is."

Bane studied his friend's face. The safest course of action was to change the subject. "We've already got problems. I dropped my plane into the drink off Kahi'u Point this morning. Have you mapped that area at all?"

"There's a wreck I dive out there some when the weather is good. The reef is a decent size in sixty feet of water, then if falls off sharp into blue hole. If it's in the deep, you're in trouble."

"My equipment is down there." It was probably trashed now. "Hey, where's that new wife of yours? I'd like to meet her."

Tony nodded in the direction of the bikini display. "Hawking our wares."

Bane raised his eyebrows at the sight of the leggy blonde knitting a minuscule bathing suit. She sat on a stool with a bag of yarn beside her. A frown creased her smooth fair skin. Honey-colored hair rippled down her back to her waist. The pictures he'd seen hadn't done her justice.

"Get your tongue back in your head," Tony said with a grin. "That's the reaction of every man who comes in here. She's good for business." His voice held more than a trace of smugness. Tony motioned to his wife. "Candace, Bane's here."

Candace glanced their way, then put her yarn down and walked over to join them. Her smile was eager, and she held out her hand. Bane shook it. There were no bright lights, no kick of the pulse, and Bane managed to hide his relief that even though she was beautiful up close and personal, he could admire her as he would a painting and feel no real attraction.

He grinned at Tony. "A gorgeous wife who actually knits. Why are you even bothering with a lost treasure that's probably just a myth?"

"I tell him the same thing," Candace said. "I've heard a lot about you. Tony thinks you're some kind of superman. How long do you think it will take to find the treasure so he quits being so obsessed and notices he has a wife?"

He jabbed Tony in the ribs. "In the ten years we've been buddies, I bet we haven't had a single conversation where the subject didn't come up. As far as finding the boat, our chances would have been better if my plane hadn't taken a nosedive into the Pacific. It's going to set us back some."

"How far back?" Tony demanded. "Hurricane season has started. I know the chances of being hit are slim, but that's what we thought about 'Iniki. It would be just my luck to have to worry about the site being mucked up."

"Cool it, Tony. We'll do the best we can." Tony's drive sometimes irritated Bane.

Candace reached under the counter and withdrew a handful of pills, which she gave to Tony. "You forgot your vitamins this morning."

"See how she takes care of me?" Tony grinned. "She and Leia have a lot in common." Tony downed the pills with a swig from the water bottle she handed him. "Thanks, baby. Let's get to diving."

A commotion drew everyone's attention to the front door. Voices raised, something banged, and a projectile of swim goggles flew past Bane's head. Tony spewed out a few choice words and stepped past Bane. Bane followed his friend.

A burly man dressed in khaki shorts and a T-shirt that read Hans Dive Shop stood near the front door. His blond crew cut made his face look even more round, and his bulbous nose and heavy arms made Bane think of Popeye. The guy's eyes were slitted in his red face, and he had his hands fisted on his hips. His eyes squeezed even tighter when he saw Tony. "I've had enough of your tactics, Romero. Play fair, and there's enough to go around. A party of six canceled on me at the last minute, and they just went off with one of your divemasters. I'm sick of it. Back off or you'll be sorry."

Tony crossed his arms over his chest. "Then stop putting oil in my air-fill station, Hans."

The other man sneered. "Having trouble with your air station? How like you to blame someone else, Romero."

"So you admit you sabotaged them?"

"Stuff it." Hans unclenched his fists. "You use people for your own gain." He reached out and yanked on the gold doubloon around Tony's neck. Tony pulled it out of his fingers. "You flaunt this and con people into thinking they might be the ones to help you find that stupid treasure. I've cut my prices to rock bottom, and you still snag all the business."

Divemaster Dirk Forsythe came out of the back room. Six-four and built like a boxer, his size could be intimidating. His thick blond brows lowered as he appraised the situation, then he moved quickly to Tony's side. "Trouble, boss?"

"Nothing I can't handle, Dirk. Hans was just leaving." Tony opened the door and gave Hans a pointed look.

Hans pressed his lips together then stomped to the door. He turned and shot a glance toward Leia. "The kind of company you keep is witness enough of the kind of man you are, Romero. The daughter of a thief and every lowlife who happens to want a job."

Bane sprang toward the door at the slur on Leia's character, but she grabbed his forearm. "Let it go, Bane," she whispered. "He's not worth it."

Several months ago, Leia's dad was working a security shift for the museum on O'ahu when some valuable Hawaiian artifacts went missing. He'd been exonerated from the crime, but he'd lost his job, and people believed what they wanted. Bane pressed his lips together and narrowed his gaze on Tony. "What was all that about? What's his beef with you?"

Tony shrugged. "Hans is no businessman. His dive shop is barely making it. Mine is doing well, and he blames me for his own incompetence. The island can only support one dive shop, and I'm it."

At least one thing Hans said was true: one glimpse of the gold doubloon around Tony's burnished neck had tourists eager to find the mysterious Spanish treasure ship lost somewhere in the deep blue recesses of Hawai'i's waters.

"It's just business," Tony said. "Look, you want to meet the divers I've been working with? We were about to go out to look for the boat today, but we can look for the plane instead. Come with us."

"You're the eternal optimist." Bane glanced at his watch. Ron wouldn't be ready to do anything about recovery until later this afternoon, maybe not until tomorrow morning. "I need to call Kaia first. What about Leia and Eva?"

"We've got room for everyone." Tony smiled and motioned to Dirk, who came toward them. "It's Dirk's fault our ratio of female to male divers has gone from 30 percent to 60 percent."

Dirk grinned and shook Bane's hand. "Don't listen to anything he says. The ladies eye him more than they do me, but Candace makes sure they know he's taken. I am too. Did you hear? I got engaged over the summer. Much to Tony's relief." He jabbed his boss with his elbow. "Even though I told him Candace and I were just friends, he was afraid I was pining for her since he whisked her away."

Candace and Dirk once worked together on O'ahu, and Bane had heard the story of how Tony fell for her at a luau Dirk attended. Candace had come as Dirk's date. "Congratulations," Bane said. "When's the big day?"

"I'll show up whenever Steph tells me to. Wait until you meet her. She's a keeper. I'd say she was prettier than Candace, but Tony would take me down." He grinned, then thrust his hands into the pockets of his denim shorts. "Good to see you again, Bane. I wish I was going diving with you today. I'm on shop duty. You ready to go out fishing again one of these days?"

"You name the day. I want to catch that marlin that got away the last time." Bane had always liked Dirk. In spite of Tony's jibes about the ladies, most men liked Dirk too. Bane took the cordless phone Tony handed him and dialed Kaia's number. Kaia answered right away.

"Hey, sis, can you get here any sooner? I dropped my plane into the water. I wouldn't mind having Nani help me find it."

The pleasure in Kaia's voice dimmed until Bane assured her he was uninjured. "I've got a project to finish up. I don't think I can get there in less than three days."

"Oh well, it was only a thought. I'll figure out something. I just appreciate you bringing her over to help search for the ship. See you soon." He hung up then went outside, where he helped pack up the truck with tanks of oxygen, regulators, weights, and other scuba equipment. They found Eva on her stomach on the dock, staring into the water. She squealed when she found out she was going diving.

Leia had wandered off to talk to Candace. Bane handed the phone back to Tony. "So how are your latest divers working out?"

"They're fine." Tony looked over his shoulder at his wife, but she was fifteen feet away talking to Leia. "Well, except for one. Did I ever tell you about Shaina Levy?"

"The designer from New York? Yeah. What about her?"

"She's here. I've got a big problem." He chewed his bottom lip. "She says her kid is mine. I had lunch with her today, and she's pushing me to get a paternity test."

Bane raised his brows. "Is it possible?"

Tony shrugged. "Maybe. I'd like to know why she waited this long to tell me though."

"Did you ask her that?"

"Yeah. She says the kid, Andi, has some health problems, and she needs financial help now. New York hasn't been good to her lately. I hired her to keep her quiet, but if Candace finds out, there will be fireworks."

"Whoa, buddy, you need to be up front with your wife. Hiding it is going to cause more problems. If she loves you, she'll understand. This all happened before you even met Candace, right?"

"Everything is riding on finding this treasure, Bane. We're living on a shoestring. I can't afford to support some kid I don't even know."

Tony had always been a ladies' man. It was a miracle he hadn't plunged himself into deep trouble before now. "How did she get in touch with you?"

"She saw the ad where I was hiring divers and just showed up. She threatened to tell Candace if I didn't hire her."

"So she knew about the treasure hunt before she contacted you?" Bane asked.

Tony nodded. "Sure. I talked to her about it as much as anyone when we were together."

"Then the first thing you need to do is establish paternity. She might just be out for money she thinks you have or are about to get. The timing seems odd."

"You think so?" Tony's voice was eager. "Maybe the kid isn't even mine."

"There's only one way to find out. Get the test."

Tony's smile faded. "She said she has Andi's DNA profile. She seems confident."

"That doesn't sound good. You're going to have to step up to your responsibilities if the little girl is yours. How old is she?"

"Five."

"How much money does Shaina want?"

"She hasn't said, but if we find the treasure, she wants a share for Andi. I guess I can afford it if we find the ship." Tony gripped Bane's arm. "Find that ship, buddy. I'm counting on you."

"I'll do my best," Bane said.

*B*y the time they got to the boat, the rest of Tony's divers had assembled on the dock. Tony told them about the change in plans, then introduced them—two men and two women whose names ran together in Bane's head as he tried to pay attention.

"I keep telling Jermaine he's going to be the next Michael Jackson," Tony said, nodding toward a young man about twenty-four. Energy seemed to hum along his long limbs in an unseen melody, and he wore a gold guitar clock on a heavy chain around his neck. He was dressed completely in black, even down to his slippers.

Jermaine tossed a mesh bag full of dive gear at Tony. "Not if you have anything to say about it. You think I should stay on this deadbeat island and dive for the rest of my life. But man, I've got to grab the brass ring while it's in reach."

Tony dropped the bag he caught. "You'll make it, Jermaine."

Shaina Levy stepped aboard the boat. Her red hair stuck out around her head like a Brillo pad. "Tony has inspired all of us to follow our dreams. When I get home, I'm going to move to L.A. and get my design business growing. This time away has been good for all of us." She sent a flirtatious glance Tony's way, but he ignored her. Her smile faded, and she bent to rummage in her bag.

Rae and Eric Jardin, a couple in their fifties from Indiana, both nodded at Shaina's words. "We just bought a house here, and Eric is going to open a business in town. Tony has promised to send some clients our way."

Bane grinned. "You try to make out you're a tough guy, Tony, but that mask never holds. You should just give it up and show your soft side all the time."

"Shut up and get in the boat," Tony growled.

Bane chuckled and hopped aboard the forty-six-foot custom-made boat, *Mermaid*, and they headed out to sea.

About an hour later Bane pointed off the bow. "This is close to where my plane went in," Bane said as the boat slowed. "I want to take a look here."

Tony nodded. "If it's here, you're in luck. Out beyond here, there's only blue hole." He instructed the divers to prepare to dive, and the men and women began to shrug into their buoyancy compensators and tanks. One by one, they began to jump into the water.

Bane adjusted his BC, then bit down on his mouthpiece and dropped into the water. The whitecaps caressed him with warm, silken fingers. A brilliant kaleidoscope of fish darted past his mask—butterfly fish chased by yellow tangs, then followed by a flurry of rainbow wrasses. The whirl of color and movement disoriented him for a moment, and he paused, moving his fins slowly in the current as he regained his equilibrium.

Eva swam with him as his buddy. Her eyes were wide with joy behind her mask. It had taken Bane weeks to teach her how to breathe properly with the regulator, but every hour had been worth it to see the pleasure in her face. Bane winked at her, and she winked back, batting both eyes in an awkward imitation. He took her hand, and they followed the line down toward several figures he could see moving along the colonies of lobe coral.

Leia swam past him in leisurely movements to join Tony. The two had buddied up. The pressure built in Bane's ears, and he blew to relieve it. He kicked his fins and dove deeper, checking his gauge as he went down to a hundred feet. Still no sign of his plane. The others were above him at about sixty feet as they explored a coral bed. He tried to stifle his disappointment. It had been a shot in the dark anyway. The ocean was a big haystack, and he was looking for a needle. He and Eva explored for about fifteen minutes before moving to rejoin the group.

He caught a movement out of the side of his mask. Turning his head, he saw a figure shooting to the surface like a torpedo from a submarine. Too fast. The man zoomed up without a pause to decompress. Bane caught a glimpse of his face. Tony. Bane looked around for Leia and found her fifteen yards away. Still holding Eva's hand, he swam to her side and pointed up urgently. She glanced up and saw Tony still shooting up to the surface like a buoy. Her eyes widened. She began to swim up with him. The three of them followed as fast as they dared, pausing occasionally to allow themselves to decompress.

As he neared the surface, he saw Tony floating motionless in the water. Bane put on a burst of speed, kicking out with his fins. As his head broke the surface of the water, his hand touched

Tony's arm. It was flaccid. Leia was right behind him. He spit out his regulator. Tony was floating facedown. Bane rolled him over, his hope plummeting as he saw the blood that bubbled from his nose and mouth. "Tony?" he gasped. He grabbed Tony's limp body and towed him toward the boat. Leia had Tony's other arm, and Eva trailed behind them. He could see Candace sitting on deck braiding her hair. She hadn't noticed her husband was in trouble.

"Help us!" Bane shouted at her. She turned her head then sprang to her feet. "It's Tony."

"Tony?" Her mouth gaped, and she put her hand up to cover it.

"Hurry," Bane panted. A wave slapped him in the face, and the salty spray filled his mouth.

Candace came partway down the steps and grabbed Tony's arm. "Tony," she cried as they hauled him onboard. "What's wrong with him? He has to be okay." She crouched by his side and touched his face.

"Let Leia take a look." Bane scooted back and put his arm around Eva. Candace moved back a few inches, but her gaze stayed on Tony. Leia knelt by Tony's side. Eva's shoulders trembled, and Bane squeezed her arm reassuringly. She stuck two fingers in her mouth and sucked on them.

Leia pressed her fingers on Tony's neck, then lifted his lids and peered into his eyes. "Call for the Coast Guard to get over here!" she told Candace. She began CPR. The next few minutes passed in a blur, but when it was all over, Bane knew Tony Romero would never flash his famous white smile again.

A weeping Candace, Tony's body, and the rest of the divers were loaded onto the Coast Guard boat that had been in the area, but Bane and Leia stayed behind to bring the boat back. Bane pulled Leia aside and pointed to Tony's gear still heaped on the deck of the *Mermaid*. "What happened to his weight belt?" It wasn't among his things.

Leia seemed as confused as Bane. "He wouldn't just drop it off. We both saw him trying to slow his ascent. You want to go back down and try to find it?"

"I was thinking the same thing," he said grimly.

Three

Leia hovered at about forty feet below the surface. A school of highfin chubs congregated along the underground cave entrance in front of her, and she swam in the midst of them as they nosed around her curiously. Bane's bright halogen light joined hers to penetrate the inner reaches of the cave. The beam illuminated a sleeping reef tip. She saw the eagerness in Bane's eyes. He'd be back. Cave exploration was his favorite pastime.

They turned in unison and swam down past the opening. She kept an eye on her computer to make sure she didn't go too deep. The rest of the divers had been exploring the reef along here when Tony shot toward the surface. Leia paused to let her light probe a mass of antler coral. A school of bright yellow tang scattered from her gloved hand as she gently moved the coral out of the way to probe at the sand under it. Tony had been right here before his ascent. His weight belt should be on the sandy bottom fairly close.

The currents were strong around Moloka'i, but the belt shouldn't have gone far. Leia swung her light around, and the powerful beam caught a moray eel peering from behind a rock. She moved her light onto a mass of finger coral. Bane swooped in beside her and examined the coral but came up empty-handed. They searched the seafloor until their air began to run out. She turned to motion Bane it was time to go up and saw him and Eva swimming away. She followed, then realized he'd found his plane, down about a hundred feet.

He made a triumphant gesture with his fist. She smiled and jabbed her finger toward the surface. About twenty feet from the top, Bane grabbed her arm and pointed toward two dark shadows looming toward them. Tiger sharks. Tigers accounted for most shark attacks in Hawaiian waters. A burst of bubbles escaped as she exhaled. The tigers veered at the bubbles, but they circled and came back for another look.

Eva had seen them too. She started to swim toward the boat, but Leia grabbed her arm and held her tight. She thrashed to free herself, her blue eyes wide with terror. Leia embraced her, patting her back for comfort until her sister calmed. Bane grabbed his octopus regulator and purged it. The sharks turned at the explosion of bubbles and with a flick of their tails vanished into the dark blue water. Leia finned toward the boat as fast as she could go, Eva at her side. Bane was right behind them. Her head broke the surface, and she struck out for the boat. No matter how often she dived, seeing a shark always unnerved her.

Leia kept an eye out for any approaching shark fins until her sister was aboard the boat, then climbed the steps herself just ahead of Bane. She shrugged out of her tank and unzipped her wet suit, rolling it down to her waist. "I thought sure we'd find his weight belt. It has to be down there somewhere," she told him. "But at least you found your plane. We need to mark it with a buoy."

Bane unzipped his wet suit and peeled it off. "I'll call it in. The Coast Guard is right over there." He nodded toward the cutter anchored about half a mile away. "Something doesn't smell right, Leia. Tony wouldn't die at the surface just from losing his weight belt. He was a smart diver and would have exhaled to prevent his lungs from exploding, but he was dead when I got to him. I think something else happened to him down there. And now we can't even find the weight belt. It doesn't add up. It should have dropped right to the seafloor. It's too heavy for a marine animal to carry off."

"We need to have an autopsy and see what killed him. From

the blood, I'd guess his lungs ruptured. But he knew to exhale as he ascended."

Bane rubbed his chin. "Maybe I'm jumping at shadows. I'd say something happened on the seabed to disorient him enough that he held his breath. Or maybe he just had some kind of stroke or seizure down there."

"But where is his weight belt?" Leia tried to imagine a scenario where Tony was disoriented enough to shed his weight belt, but she couldn't come up with anything that worked. The wind brushed her exposed flesh, and she shivered as chicken skin pebbled her arm. Her stomach growled. Bane's answered with its own low rumble.

"Got anything to eat? Diving always makes me hungry enough to chew a gecko."

"Check the small pouch of my backpack." She watched Bane unzip the pocket and rummage inside. She grinned at his snort of disgust when he found her stash.

"What is this?" He read the label. "Fried nori? What kind of food is that for a hungry man? It looks like something your cat chucked up."

"I like trying new things. It's fried seaweed seasoned with a little chili pepper. It's the newest thing from Japan. And it's not fattening. You look like you've gained a few pounds since I saw you last."

He tossed her backpack aside, and she nearly laughed at his narrowed eyes and tight mouth. She rolled her eyes instead. She'd rather have him believe she found him unappealing than for him to know her pulse throbbed like her boat's engine at full throttle. "Try the nori. It's good."

"I don't have any choice. I could eat Hina if I had a fire." He glared at the cat.

Eva frowned and pulled the cat closer to her. "You can't eat Hina. She's part of our family."

Bane's mouth relaxed in a smile. "I'll make do with the seaweed.

Hina is probably old and tough anyway." He dropped into a seat and began to shovel handfuls of nori into his mouth. His eyes widened.

"Not bad, is it?" Leia didn't try to keep the satisfaction from her voice. She took off her wet suit and pulled on shorts and a top over her wet swimsuit. She squeezed the water from her braid and toweled it dry.

"You love to be right." He offered her the bag, and she took a handful of the chips. "Let's head back to shore and see how Candace is doing. How do you think she'll handle this?"

"She's a strong woman, but this would shake anyone." Leia went to the helm and started the engine. "Tony was larger than life, and they were still newlyweds. It's going to be hard for everyone who knew him. Okay with you if we stop by the peninsula a minute to drop off Hina?"

"Sure."

She pointed the boat toward shore. "What about the search? Will you and his partner continue it?"

"Ron has a lot invested in this search already. He won't want to give it up now. But it won't be the same without Tony." He pressed his fingers to his eyes and turned away.

She reached out to touch his rigid shoulder, but drew back. Her eyes stung, and she blinked rapidly. She'd finished with crying years ago, and as much as she liked Tony, she wasn't about to start again now. Tears accomplished nothing except a headache. She'd learned that at age six. Gritting her teeth, she stared ahead at the sea.

Riding high on its bow, the craft cut through the waves toward the peninsula. The swells around Moloka'i moved under the boat and made for a choppy ride. They reached the dock, and Bane stepped up to toss a rope over the moorings. She averted her gaze from his strong brown legs and back. She grabbed her backpack and towel. Eva took Hina in her arms. Five other boats ranging from yachts to fishing boats bobbed in the harbor.

"Hang on, let me get this stable." Bane pulled the rope tight, then leaped to the dock. He extended his hand.

Leia moved out of the way and let Eva take her place. While Bane helped her sister to the dock, Leia stepped ashore by herself. A cluster of men and women on the beach caught her eye. "What's going on?" She nodded toward the crowd milling along the shore. Raised voices rumbled with an undercurrent of excitement.

Bane took the backpack from her unresisting hand. "Beats me. Let's see." He led the way down the gray boards of the pier to the beach. "Maybe a monk seal has come ashore."

"Maybe." The seals were endangered, but they sometimes lumbered to shore and sunned themselves on the golden sand. Eva held tightly to Leia's hand as they walked along the sand. The crowd parted in front of her, and she peered through the opening. Her confident step faltered when she saw Pete Kone in the middle of the crowd. His hands planted on his hips, Pete seemed to be barring anyone from coming near a roped-off section of beach. About thirty-five, Pete was a well-known figure on the island. His passion was teaching young Hawaiians about the old ways, from fishing to hula to crafts. His influence had helped her decide to learn to make the *kapa*.

"Stay back," he shouted at the crowd. "The police are on their way. I've called the DLNR as well."

The Department of Land and Natural Resources involvement meant whatever had Pete in a stew was big. Leia put Eva's hand in Bane's. "Wait here." She approached Pete. "What's going on, Pete?"

His dark eyes registered her presence. "Leia, just who I need. A doctor could give an opinion on this." He took her arm and ushered her past a line of men who stood shoulder to shoulder around an area cordoned off by yellow rope.

She didn't bother pointing out she wasn't really a doctor. Most of the islanders seemed to forget she'd stopped shy of her residency. Several long white objects lay half buried in the sand. The closest one was mostly exposed to the sun, and Leia squinted to make out what it was. She caught her breath. "Bones? Where did they come from?" The remains looked pitiful in the sand.

"We don't know yet. I think they're human. Can you tell?"

Leia knelt on the hot sand and touched the smooth surface of the bone closest to her. "This one looks like a tibia. Definitely human." The bones looked old and weathered by surf and sand. Bones were revered among her people. The *mana* of a chief was said to be in his bones, and in the old days, when a chief was defeated, his successor took possession of the skeleton to gain his rival's power. By Hawaiian custom, these remains would need to remain buried to preserve what *mana* was left in them and to keep them from an enemy's power. She had a length of *kapa* she could donate for the burial.

She stood and dusted the sand from her hands. "How did they get here?"

"They washed up in last night's surge."

"You've been out here all day?" This discovery was probably why he never showed up with her students today.

He nodded. "This could be a huge find." His voice was hushed with suppressed excitement.

"Any artifacts to help date the remains?" Leia glanced around and saw many more bones strewn about.

"Look here." He showed her a *lā'au pālau* that was used by the ancient Hawaiians as a weapon. The three-foot-long club had a stone mounted on the end and shark's teeth embedded in the handle. "I think the surge last night uncovered a Hawaiian boat or burial spot of some kind. I want the DLNR to look into it." He seemed to finally look at her. "You've been diving. Were you with Tony? I heard about his death. I'm sorry."

"Yes, Bane and I are on our way to see Candace."

"Bane is here?" His gaze went past her to Bane. A flicker of an eye showed his interest. "I should have known he wouldn't miss the festival." His eyes gleamed.

The two men were friends and professional rivals at the same time. Both had a passion for cave exploration and playing the ukulele, and neither liked to lose to the other, though they respected each other as men. Leia never understood the complexities of their relationship. It was like watching two jungle cats circle each other before deciding to be friends.

"Let me know what you learn about these remains, Pete. I'd better get back. We want to see if there is any news about what happened to Tony." She hurried back to Bane and Eva.

Bane listened as she told him about the bones. "I wonder if it's a hoax. There's no likely spot for the surge to uncover bones. Could Pete be staging something for attention?"

"What is it with you two? One minute you're listening to his advice, and the next second you're trying to one-up him."

Bane was looking out over the water. "The ukulele festival is coming up. Think I can beat him?"

"You didn't hear a word I said, did you?" She sighed. "Winning a ukulele festival isn't the most important thing in life."

His white teeth flashed in a wide grin. "I live to win."

That was Bane's problem—he was so caught up in the notion that everything depended on him that he never relaxed enough to enjoy life. It was admirable to be dependable, but Bane took the trait to an extreme. The world wouldn't come to an end if he failed at something.

She took Eva's hand. "It's getting late. If we're going to see Candace, we'd better get moving." And then she was going to go home and forget Bane Oana. If she could.

They left the cat patrolling the beach and got back in the boat. No one said much as they rounded the eastern side of the island and headed to town. Leia nodded toward the parking area beside the dock as they approached. "I keep my car in the lot to use when I come to town. We can take it." They docked and headed toward the car.

"Want me to drive?" Bane jogged to catch up with her.

"I don't let other people drive my car."

"You let me drive your car once."

"And you wrecked it. That taught me a lesson." She made the mistake of looking at him. His grin made it hard to stay mad at him.

"It wasn't my fault!"

"You ever hear of defensive driving? You drive like you do everything else—full steam ahead with your eyes on the goal."

"You just like being in control."

"That's a pot calling the kettle black." Eva began to hum, and Leia looked down at her sister. "What's wrong, sweetie?"

"Don't yell at Bane. He'll go away, and I won't get to go dive anymore." Eva stuck her fingers in her mouth again.

Leia pulled Eva's hand down with a gentle touch and shook her head. Eva winced and rubbed her wet fingers against her shorts. Leia patted her arm, and Eva's face cleared. "Bane isn't going anywhere, are you, Bane?"

He shook his head. "Not when I get to take the prettiest girl in town diving." He smiled at Eva, then his gaze shot to Leia.

The trip to the Romero house only took ten minutes, but Bane's larger-than-life presence in her small car was like being caged with a tiger shark. He was every bit as sleek and dangerous to her peace of mind as the big fish. She parked in front of the Romero house behind Dirk's green army jeep.

The plantation-style home sat in a grove of palm trees. Though modest, the pale pink-and-white color scheme reminded Leia of a frothy glass of pink guava juice. They stepped past the mass of welcoming flowers at the road. Candace's green thumb showed in the banks of ginger and hibiscus that bloomed along the walk.

Leia's steps dragged as she walked to the front door. There would be no boisterous Tony flinging open the door to greet them. Her throat thickened, but she went to the door and pressed the doorbell with a steady finger. She could hear a murmur of voices beyond the door, then heavy footsteps approached and the door swung open.

Dirk's shoulders filled the doorway. He didn't wear his usual smile. "Come on in. Candace is in the living room. The doctor wanted to give her a sedative, but she wouldn't take it. See if you can get her to listen, Leia."

"I'll try." She stepped past Dirk with Eva and Bane on her heels. They kicked off their slippers at the door, as was the Hawaiian custom, and went down the hall. She knew the way. This home had been filled with light, laughter, and good friends. The somber tone now made the place unfamiliar. The cool tile floor felt good against her bare feet. Without the usual aroma of cappuccino candles that Candace normally burned, the air smelled stale and lifeless. Candace lay curled on the sofa with her eyes closed. Someone had drawn curtains over the wall of windows, blocking out the view of the garden.

"Oh, good, she's asleep," Dirk said. "She's been crying so much, her eyes are practically swollen shut." His voice was a whisper, but it sounded loud in the room.

"I'm not asleep." Candace sat up. "I was just resting my eyes for a minute." She rubbed her swollen face. "I still can't believe it, you know?" Her face crumpled again, and she hugged herself.

Leia sat beside her on the sofa and slipped her arm around her. "I'm so sorry, Candace. Tony was a great guy."

"Yes, he was. I don't know what I'm going to do. I don't know anything at all about running a dive shop, but it's the only income we have."

"Doesn't Tony have some insurance?" Bane asked.

Candace shook her head. "Only enough to bury him. I told him we needed it now that we were going to—" She looked down at her hands.

"Going to what?" Leia had a sick feeling she might know what Candace was about to say. She glanced at the young widow's flat stomach.

"We're going to have a baby," Candace whispered. "I just told Tony yesterday. He was so happy." She buried her face against Leia's neck. "We were going to wait a few weeks to tell anyone."

Candace's hot tears trickled down Leia's skin. At a loss for words, Leia just hugged the woman. No comforting words could change what had happened. The way Candace trembled made Leia feel weak. She drew away. "I can help out with the administrative part of the business a few hours a week. I can work around my clinic hours. You won't have to pay me."

Candace raised her head. "Oh, Leia, would you really? Just until I get the hang of things? I never paid any attention when Tony tried to show me the books. I don't know what to do." She gazed up at Bane. "What about the search for the galleon? Are you and Ron going to go ahead with it?"

Bane shifted from one foot to the other. "I haven't talked to Ron yet, so I can't speak for him. But I plan to stay. If we can find it, the money from the discovery will set you up for a long while. It's the least I can do for Tony." Bane's voice was husky.

Candace was wilting against Leia by the minute. "Lie down and try to sleep," Leia told the grieving widow.

Candace nodded. "Maybe that would be best. I'm so tired." She stood.

"I'll call you tomorrow," Leia promised. "If you need anything, just call." No one said anything as Candace went down the hall.

"I wish she had family here," Dirk said.

"What about her parents?" Bane asked.

Leia shook her head. "They're dead. They died in a house fire about three years ago along with her twin sister."

"Any other siblings?"

Leia shook her head. "I don't think so. I've never heard her say anything about it."

"I'll do everything I can to make sure she's provided for," Bane said, his voice grim.

Leia didn't doubt that he would. The caretaker of the world, that was Bane Oana. Sometimes it irritated her beyond measure, but right now she wanted to hug him for it. Candace would need all the help she could get.

four

The research vessel *Pomaik'i* floated about a mile off Kalaupapa Peninsula. There was no place Bane would rather be than standing on the bow of a ship with the throb of the engines radiating up his legs. The wind was in his face as he stood on the metal deck with his feet planted apart and surveyed the whitecaps just off the bow. Ajax, his Irish setter, lay at his feet. The dog whimpered at the whine of the crane that labored on deck.

His boss, Ron Pimental, joined him at the railing. About forty, he reminded Bane of one of the many mynah birds on the islands—slicked-down black hair and rapid, jerky movements. He was in constant motion, which accounted for his thin frame. He popped a handful of unsalted peanuts into his mouth. "They're raising the plane now. Good job finding it so quickly."

"I want to know what happened to it." Bane refused Ron's offer of peanuts and watched the boom crane lift the plane. The waves churned white foam as the plane neared the top of the water. Flotsam from the bottom boiled to the surface around the aircraft, and Bane leaned over the railing to watch. He itched to find the cause.

"We owe it to Tony," Ron agreed. "I want to find the ship now more than ever. I'll see Tony's widow gets her share, of course."

"Candace will be glad to hear that. She could use the money." Bane hadn't slept much last night. He knew Tony would expect him to help his widow. He turned as footsteps clanged on the metal deck, and one of the technicians, Logan Masters, joined them.

"Ron, there's something on our new sonar you need to see." Logan's red hair was a punctuation above a freckled face. He could have passed as a stand-in for Rugrats character Chuckie Finster minus the glasses.

"In a minute." Ron turned back to the plane. "Bane, do you think there's a chance Westerfield Salvage has gotten wind of what our equipment can do? Could they have planted an explosive device to bring you down?"

"I suspected sabotage from the first. I heard a bang that almost sounded like a small bomb before I lost control. Do you think Westerfield is capable of doing something like that? What would be the point?"

"Sam Westerfield is capable of anything." Ron tossed a peanut shell into the water, then cocked his head like a bird. "He particularly likes to humiliate me. If he finds the wreck before we do, he'd get his papers filed first to arrest the shipwreck, and we'd be out in the cold. If he had an inkling of how advanced this new equipment is, he'd do anything to remove it from our arsenal of search options."

"What makes you think he knows about the new seafloor scanner we developed?" Bane wanted to know.

"Nothing I do ever goes unnoticed by him for long. I've never figured out how he finds out my business, but he always does. I suppose one of my men is on his payroll." Ron sighed heavily.

The crane lifted the aircraft fully out of the water, and the runoff rained a small waterfall back into the ocean. "Is there a history with the two of you or just professional rivalry?" Bane asked. He didn't know much about his boss yet. Ron was good at what he did, and his reputation in the business was impeccable. The only rumbling Bane had heard before he took the job was that Ron never forgot a grievance.

"We were partners once," Ron admitted. "I headed up the business, but Sam was never one to take orders. He started his own company, which was fine. What wasn't so fine was that he stabbed me in the back and lied to a major client, who took his business to Westerfield. I would never trust him again." He drummed his fingers on the railing. "What do you think of the equipment? Is it all we hoped it would be?"

"Unfortunately, I wasn't able to really test it fully, but the preliminary stuff I got back looked like it might be everything we'd dreamed of. We got some awesome imagery before the plane went down—3-D quality stuff, like looking at a top-notch video game."

Ron frowned. "And now it's waterlogged. Can we salvage any of it?"

"Maybe. Most of it was in waterproof housing. I'll have to test it out. We might not need it for this job, though. Tony mentioned an old man who lives out on the peninsula who claims the treasure is buried there. He also says he knows where the boat sank."

"Sir, about the images on sonar," the technician put in again.

"All right, Logan, we're coming," Ron said.

The men followed Logan to the deck room that housed the scientific equipment. Ajax padded close behind. The room reeked of electronics and new plastic from the meteorological and oceanographic equipment that crowded the space. Banks of computerized equipment lined the room—from bathymetric equipment like shallow- and deepwater echo sounders to multiple computer stations used to collate the data. The men stepped to the swath bathymetric sonar system. The system was capable of hydrographic charting and seafloor acoustic backscatter imaging in water depths of 50 to 20,000 meters. It was Bane's own design, and he grew fonder of the device on every mission. There was something sexy about a machine that performed perfectly and had great graphics.

"Look here." Logan jabbed a finger at the image on the computer screen. "There's something under where we found the plane. Could be a rock formation, but it's too symmetrical. I think it's a sunken ship."

Bane sat at the computer and transferred the data so it showed up as an oblique view of colored bathymetry, a 3-D image that allowed him to assess the area, though not with the detail of the equipment he'd been testing. "Looks promising," he said.

Reeking of peanuts, Ron leaned over his shoulder and pointed. "That looks like it could be a fallen mast."

In the old days, the only way to find a sunken ship was to stumble onto it in a dive, which was about as likely as a New Yorker stumbling across a mermaid. Now sophisticated sonar could pinpoint likely spots in living color. The truth of the matter still required visual confirmation, and Bane's adrenaline surged at the thought. "It might be just a rock formation, but there's only one way to find out. We'll have to go down and take a look." He glanced at his watch. "We've got another couple of hours of daylight. Let's get suited up."

"You were down twice today, bailed from a plane crash, and lost a friend," Ron observed. "We've only got a little daylight left. Are you sure you're up to it?"

Bane glanced at his watch. Nearly five. Was it only early this morning he'd arrived on Moloka'i? The day's events had piled onto each other. "I'm fine." Ron's reminder brought the aches and pains in his back and legs into focus. Bane felt like an old man, but he was intrigued by what he saw on the screen. And his mind kept going back to Candace's fearful confessions about the future. He owed it to Tony to do what he could for his widow.

"I'll go with you." Ron followed him to the deck, and they both pulled on wet suits. Ajax nosed Bane's gear and barked. "You want to go, boy?" The dog barked again, and Bane opened his bag and grabbed the dog's snuba gear: a specially made harness with hose and enclosed bubble around his head.

Ron's mouth gaped. "You're kidding me, right? He doesn't really dive."

"He loves it. He can go down around twelve feet or so." Bane finished fastening Ajax's vest. "Watch." The dog took a flying leap off the end of the boat and into the water. He disappeared from view moments later.

"And I thought I'd seen everything." Ron shook his head. A boatswain helped them into their air tanks, and they jumped into the water.

Bane was too tired to enjoy the colorful show this time. He finned his way down, using a portable GPS device to pinpoint the exact location of the image on his equipment. Ajax joined him, paddling his big paws and looking around with a doggy smile. Bane's fatigue lifted just watching the dog, and he refocused on the job at hand. Bane paused when he realized the site was the same one he and Leia had explored while looking for Tony's weight belt. Coral often grew on a shipwreck, creating a seemingly natural reef that was hard to detect as artificial. This particular bed spread out over the area, stopping at a blue hole that dropped off into the abyss.

He left Ajax exploring a school of wrasses. Diving deeper than the dog could go, he snapped pictures of the banks of bright coral and the outline of the seabed. It extended back to the cave he had wanted to explore. Down here, it was difficult to see the full scope of the site. They'd have to do some excavation. Maybe the cave would be the place to start so they didn't disturb the coral unless they had to. Bane was adamant about preserving and reviving the ocean's coral reefs, and he wasn't willing to toss that away for a sunken ship of dubious value.

He motioned toward the cave, and Ron swam with him to the opening. Bane's powerful halogen light probed the recesses. Good, the sharks were gone now. They were only reef tips and not really dangerous normally, but invading their lair might rile them enough to attack. He entered the cave. The sides were about forty feet apart, and the ceiling zoomed over them about twenty feet up. Lichen and shrimp clung to the cave's surfaces. His small shovel clanked against the side of the cave as they entered. Bane checked his dive computer. He still had another forty-five minutes, long enough to dig a little. His beam swept the sides and ceiling of the cave. He fumbled with his shovel and finally got it in hand, then began to dig at a long symmetrical line on the seafloor. Digging underwater was never his favorite pastime.

Ron joined him. Bane kept checking his computer as the minutes slipped away. They went down through silt until his shovel brought up something he recognized. He touched Ron's arm, then hefted the palm-sized cannonball in his hand. Bingo. They'd struck pay dirt. Ron's grin was wide. He took the cannonball and rolled it around in his hands. Jabbing his thumb up, he swam toward the cave opening with the artifact still in his hand. Bane glanced around, reluctant to leave. He had another ten minutes of bottom time. Ron paused at the mouth of the cave and motioned him energetically. Bane shrugged and swam to join him. Further exploration would have to wait for another day.

He wished Tony were alive. This ship was old—old enough to have seventeenth-century cannonballs. It just might be Tony's Spanish galleon.

A mass of red-and-white ginger flanked the front door of the Kahale home. The embrace of its sweet scent eased the tension in Leia's shoulders. Candace's grief had sapped her energy like cold water drained her body temperature. A movement to her right caught Leia's attention, and she turned to see her mother, Ingrid, and her cousin, Malia.

"You're just in time to help," Malia called. She wore her long, dark hair swooped to one side and draped over her left shoulder. A white orchid nestled behind her right ear because she was unmarried, and a mass of orchids, plumeria, and ginger lay around her where she sat on the grass making leis. Malia was tiny and petite, a classic Hawaiian beauty, and Leia towered over her.

Leia detoured from the path to join them under the shade of a giant monkeypod tree. Eva lay on her back on the grass and watched Hina stalk a gecko. Leia picked up a finished ginger lei and draped it over her neck, inhaling the heady fragrance, before dropping to the soft grass next to Malia. "You look almost done. Are these for the hula festival in O'ahu?" Malia's leis were renowned in the islands and commanded a premium price. Her shell leis rivaled those sold on Ni'ihau and sold for hundreds of dollars.

Malia nodded, her gaze lingering on Leia's face. "What's wrong?"

"I take it you didn't hear the news? Tony Romero died on a dive today."

"Aloha no!" Malia said. She put down her lei.

Ingrid patted Leia's arm. "Eva told me. Are you doing okay? Tony's been your friend a long time."

Leia had been damming up how she felt, but at the touch of her mother's hand, she wanted to burrow into Ingrid's lap and inhale her familiar plumeria scent. She knew better than to give in. Her mother didn't hold with obvious shows of weakness, which would have surprised most of Ingrid's patients. As chief of staff at the tiny Moloka'i hospital, Ingrid was warm and understanding, but as a mother, she kept herself aloof.

Leia shrugged, and her mother's hand fell away. "Candace is a mess, of course. Maybe the autopsy will show what happened. The funny thing is that his weight belt is missing. It should have been on the seafloor, but it's nowhere to be found."

"What does that mean?" Her mother picked up the twelve-inch-long lei needle and began to slide orchid blossoms onto it.

Leia took a spare needle and began to thread it through a blossom. "I'm not sure. It seems odd, that's all."

Malia's gaze sharpened. "Odd as in strange or odd as in suspicious? Are you thinking it might not have been an accident?"

"Oh, no, nothing like that. Everyone liked Tony. I can't imagine someone wanting to hurt—" She stopped, remembering the threats from Hans.

"What?" Malia demanded.

"Do you know Aberg Hans?"

Malia nodded. "Vaguely. He owns the other dive shop."

"He came into Tony's shop just before we went out. He was mad that Tony was taking all the island's clients. He claimed Tony was using his treasure-hunting spiel to run him out of business."

"Was he?" Ingrid asked in a quiet voice.

Her mother always did that to her. She was the voice of reason when Leia wanted to jump to conclusions. Ingrid's medical training, unlike her own, made Leia analyze everything. "Maybe. Tony had a way of making people believe in his dream."

"Did you see *Tûtû*?" Malia asked.

Leia nodded. "She's doing well." She kept her eye on her mother's forehead. When a slight frown creased the fair Scandinavian skin, Leia held her breath.

"I suppose you pushed more of your herbal preparations on her?"

"The scars are fading." Leia squared her shoulders and met her mother's gaze.

"You're wasting your medical training, Leia. Why can't you see it? Two more years of residency, and you'd have been a full-fledged doctor."

"Why can't you see I'm not cut out for filling out insurance forms and seeing patients in ten-minute segments like cattle?" Leia fired back. "I tried it your way for months, Mama. I felt like I was turning into someone I didn't know or like. And I couldn't stand the smells of antiseptic and drugs. That's not how God wanted us to live."

"You didn't give it a fair try. I know San Francisco wasn't what you were used to, but I pulled every imaginable string to get you that opportunity, and you threw it away. It was one of the most sought-after residency programs in the country."

"I'm not like you," Leia said. "I have Dad's Hawaiian blood in me too. I just want to be who I am inside. I want to learn the old ways before it's all gone."

"Making paper cloth. What good is that? You can do better, Leia."

Leia's gaze shot to her cousin, but Malia didn't seem to take offense at Ingrid's denigration of Hawaiian arts. Maybe because she was actually making a living at her leis while Leia scraped by on what little she could sell her cloth for and the tiny payments she got from the patients at Kalaupapa. If not for the chance to live in a house her father owned, she'd never make it.

Her mother's gaze touched the scar on Leia's lip, and Leia had to resist an impulse to cover it with her hand. Her mother wanted only what was best for her—she knew that. She'd known it when she was six years old, when Ingrid had taken her to the hospital for yet another operation for her cleft lip. No tears had leaked from Leia's eyes since that day, and she vowed never to cry again. She was strong enough to be her own person.

She watched her mother stand and go to the house. Nearly six feet tall and still blonde and graceful, she had always seemed to Leia to be a throwback to some Valkyrie, maybe Brunhild herself. All her life Leia had tried to live up to her mother's expectations. Leia often thought of the verse in Revelation of being lukewarm. That's how she felt—lukewarm. Neither Hawaiian nor Swedish but something in the middle. Neither a success nor a failure but always a disappointment. Since the medical school fiasco, she had become all the more determined to prove to her mother that she was capable of choosing her own path.

Malia winced. "You've riled her again."

"You brought up Tûtû," Leia pointed out.

"Sorry. I didn't think it would reopen the subject of your chosen profession."

"Bane showed up today too," Leia blurted, watching her cousin's face.

"His plane fell into the water," Eva said, sitting up. "We saved him."

Malia was beginning to smile. Leia dropped her gaze. "He's with Pimental Salvage now, the company that Tony had gone into partnership with to find the Spanish galleon he always talked about."

"Bane Oana. What a yummy man. Did you talk to him?"

"I had no choice. We plucked him out of the water, like Eva said."

"You two belong together. God has opened the door again. Don't let him get away this time."

"Nothing has changed. He is still too rigid and structured. I hate being put in a box." Besides, she didn't want to run the risk of Bane figuring out the real reason she'd broken off the engagement.

A school of wrasses sensed the movements and darted away. The tiny earthquakes, barely large enough to disturb the current, vibrated along the seafloor and moved through the sea cave. Ripples of tiny waves from the swarms—several quakes back-to-back—caused the sleeping shark to awaken and escape the enclosed space with a flick of its tail. The swarms finally subsided and left no evidence of their activity except for a tiny crack that opened on the seabed, right under the garden of lobe coral. The crack was barely a quarter of an inch across, but it stretched along the seafloor more than a hundred feet before it petered out at the edge of the abyss. A moray eel poked its head out from under a rock and grabbed a wrasse that got too close. Life and death resumed its usual placid rate.

five

Leia still wasn't used to living alone. She'd lived at home until she went to school and then endured six years of sloppy roommates and late-night parties when she wanted to study. The luxury of having all her clothes lined up neatly in her own closet wasn't something she took for granted yet. Though it was only a small, one-bedroom cottage, it was all hers, thanks to her father's generosity. He couldn't live in it anyway. The only people who lived in Kalaupapa were those with Hansen's disease and those like her who worked in the little clinic down the street.

She sat on the lanai with her Bible. Her gaze drifted across the yard to the distant water. She opened her Bible and tried to focus on the passage she was reading, but capturing her wandering thoughts was difficult lately, especially when she tried to read her Bible. Ever since she'd given up the idea of being a doctor and come home, she and God hadn't been on the best of terms.

She should work on her *tapa* for a bit. Maybe that would clear her head. She shut her Bible and moved to the garden. The pungent odor of fermenting bark welcomed her. She plunged her hand into the glutinous mess and extracted a clump. She laid the fermented bark on a stone anvil and picked up the *kua kuku*, a round beater that had been her grandmother's. Her muscles coiled and released as she swung the tool and beat the *tapa*. The ball of fermented bark began to flatten and spread. The sound of her *kua kuku* striking the stone reminded her of buoys offshore the day she'd told Bane she was breaking their engagement. She pounded harder with the *kua kuku*. She didn't want to remember the hurt in his eyes when she refused to answer his questions. But how could she tell him the truth? He was an honorable man. He would have said he would marry her anyway.

The day he began talking about the children they would have, the death knell for their relationship sounded. Her unease blossomed into full-fledged panic before she'd finally gone in for genetic testing. She shut her eyes and threw all her strength behind her arm. Anything to block out the memory of sitting in that doctor's office and hearing the verdict. A verdict that had doomed the love between her and Bane. If only he hadn't come back into her life today.

She opened her eyes again and wiped the tears that had rolled down her cheeks. A movement caught her eye under a large banyan tree in her backyard. She squinted, not sure if it was branches moving in the wind or someone standing in her backyard. The movement came again, and she realized it was a man staring at the house.

The hair on the back of her neck rose. A rash of burglaries around Moloka'i had been all over the papers, but she had nothing of value. Anyone looking at the peeling paint on the house would know she didn't have anything worth stealing, and Kalaupapa wasn't exactly teeming with wealthy residents. Most subsisted near the poverty level. She put down her tool and started toward the man to find out what he wanted. He took off running, evidently realizing he'd been spotted.

She charged across the backyard. "Hey, you there!" The man vanished into the jungle that touched the back of the property. She jogged to the tree line and stared into the tangle of vegetation. Adrenaline pumped through her veins, and every nerve ending tingled with something that she told herself was caution, not fear. Prudence said not to go into the forest alone, but what if he got away and just came back when she was sleeping? She would much prefer to face an adversary in the daylight when she could see him.

She should call the police. She went back to the lanai and picked up the phone. No dial tone. The phone service in town had been spotty lately.

Leia stepped back outside, and Hina ran past her legs. The cat dashed into the trees. "Hina, come back here!" She ran after the cat, but stopped at the edge of the thick growth. She heard nothing. Maybe the guy was gone. She turned to retrace her steps when she heard Hina yowl. The distress in the cat's cry made her turn and plunge into the forest. She wasn't afraid, she told herself. Holding her hands in front of her in the jujitsu pose, she took a step into the trees, then another one. Her breathing was loud in her ears. Everything in her screamed for her to go back, but she would not be ruled by fear. Besides, Hina needed her. The cat cried out again, seemingly in pain.

Leia started to call out, but she didn't want to give away her position in case the man was the cause of her cat's distress. Stopping near a palm tree, she listened, but there was no sound but the soughing of the wind in the treetops. She forced herself on. There was a clearing out this way and a small cabin Koma said was inhabited by Ku. She smiled at the thought of the old man's insistent claim.

The trees parted, and she stepped into the clearing. She heard a sound, and something came at her. She dove, her chest slamming into the dirt. Hina landed on her back. Leia lay on the ground with her heart punching against her ribs. "You just cost me a year of my life, you bad kitty." She rolled over and grabbed the cat. All Hina's fur stood up, and her eyes were huge. Something had frightened her badly. Leia ran her hands over Hina but didn't find any sign of injury. She got to her feet, held Hina under one arm, and dusted her clothes before looking around the clearing.

Her feet carried her closer to the cabin, even though alarm bells were beginning to go off in her head. The cabin had a closed, secretive feel with its tightly shuttered windows and bolted door.

The sound of her shallow gasps filled her ears, and she forced herself to take deeper breaths. Thick vines crawled up the sides in a suffocating mass. She knocked on the door, an unpainted surface that looked as though someone had hewn it with an ax. The rough prick of the wood against her knuckles made her feel more in control.

Her touch caused the door to swing inward a few inches, creaking, and she noticed the latch was broken, almost as though someone had forced it open. She pushed the door open a few more inches. "Is anyone home?" Keeping her hand on the side of the door, she opened it the rest of the way and stepped inside.

The dirty windows let in only a bare minimum of light. Leia waited until her eyes adjusted to the dimness. Once she could see, she let her gaze sweep the room as she moved across the floor. A sudden flurry of movement made her jump, but it was just a family of mongooses who raced for the safety of an old sleeping bag heaped in a corner. A battered Coleman cooler stood open in the middle of the room. She glanced inside but only saw a dirty plastic bag that looked as though it had been chewed by the mongooses.

Another sleeping bag lay on the other side of the cooler. If Ku lived here, he ate and slept like any other human. She squinted in the dim light at a heap of clothing in another corner. Approaching it, she realized it wasn't clothing but diving gear. The deep-sea suit was state-of-the-art and looked like it hadn't been here long. Nothing had chewed on it or disturbed it.

She hefted the helmet in her hand. Could this be Koma's Ku? He'd never left the leper colony, so the sight of a deep-sea diver might look like an ancient god. She would have to show it to him and see if the creature he saw might have been an ordinary diver. Dropping the helmet back onto the suit, she turned to go. Something about this place made chicken skin rise along her back and arms, and she couldn't leave the cabin behind too soon.

*E*va sat on the bench and pawed through the stuff in her Big Bird backpack for a Take 5 candy bar. She opened the wrapping and bit into it as she watched the children playing on the schoolyard. She wished she wasn't too old to still go to school, even if the kids had been mean to her sometimes. It was more fun than working at ARC, the Association of Retarded Citizens. She liked the thought of being a citizen, but she hated it when people called her retarded, especially when her mother was around. Her mother's eyes got all squinty and sad. Eva didn't like it when her mom was sad.

Work was over for the day though, and she could go home and watch *Home Alone* as she did most afternoons. She was supposed to go right home after work, but she was reluctant to leave the sunshine. Her sister and her cousin might be at the house, and they were usually doing boring stuff like making leis or *kapa*. Eva had tried to get interested in both, but her thick fingers couldn't seem to make the pretty things. She stuffed her candy wrapper into the backpack and saw a man walk across the grass toward her. Hotshot had said he'd meet her here, but she thought maybe he'd forgotten. His smile always made her happy, and he was smiling now.

"I brought you a present," he said. He held out his hand. A pocketknife inlaid with red coral lay in his palm.

Eva clapped her hands together. "For me?"

"I saw it and thought you'd like it. It has a *honu* on it, see?" He pointed out the tiny bone turtle on the handle.

She gently picked it up out of his hand. That was one thing she liked about Hotshot—he never acted like she was damaged. Her mother wouldn't let her touch a knife in the kitchen. "Do I get to keep it?" The knife felt good in her hand—smooth and strong.

"Yep, it's all yours. Hey, you want to go for a shave ice?" He held out his hand to help her up.

"I brought money." She clutched the Roxy wallet Leia had gotten her for her birthday. It had a red hibiscus on the front. Red was Eva's favorite color.

"It's my treat." He was smiling as he watched her.

Hotshot's eyes always made her feel like her feet were too big or something, and she didn't know why. He was an interesting person and had been places like Alaska and Mexico. She liked to hear him talk about all the things he'd seen. She walked beside him as he led the way to the shave-ice stand.

"Your dad seems kind of quiet lately. Is he all right?" Hotshot took her arm and guided her through the trees. "Let's go this way. We don't want anyone to see us and make you go home."

She nodded and moved the way he indicated. No way did she want someone butting in. She clutched the knife in her hand. "He's been sad since he got fired. It wasn't his fault though. I don't know why the thief had to break into my dad's museum. It's mean to take things."

"We all know it wasn't his fault. You're a good daughter to be so concerned about him. The sleds he makes are very interesting. I'd like to look at one."

"I could take you to his workshop and show you." She nearly bounced on the balls of her feet.

"Maybe you could get one and bring it to me to look at. I wouldn't want to bother your dad."

"I could do that. I'll do it tomorrow."

"You go buy the ices, and I'll wait here." Hotshot gave her some cash and stepped back into the trees.

Eva swelled with pride that he trusted her with his money. She hurried to the stand with it clutched in her hand.

The cemetery overlook offered a great view of Maui and Lana'i across the channel. The warm breeze, heavy with the scent of the wood rose that climbed the crumbling brick walls, riffled Leia's hair, and she craned her neck to catch a bit of fragrant air on her face. Everyone on the island had turned out for Tony's funeral, and she half expected the building's walls to bulge and burst any minute.

She hadn't seen Bane in three days, and she told herself she wasn't watching for him as she scanned the sea of faces around the casket suspended over the hole. She hoped he was dealing okay with Tony's death. Candace stood shaking hands and receiving consoling hugs as the mourners filed past her. Dark circles ringed her eyes, and she hadn't bothered with makeup—not that it mattered, Leia thought, gazing into Candace's lovely, haunted face.

Leia was in line with the other divers who had gone down with Tony the day he died. She eyed the fifty-something couple in front of her and mentally composed a question.

"I can't believe he's dead." Rae shifted from one slippered foot to the other. "He had such an impact on us. I still keep expecting to hear his big laugh and see him on the boat with the wind in his face."

"The police have been talking to everyone who was there when Tony died," Eric blurted. "You don't think they suspect murder, do you? I don't see how it could be anything but a weird accident."

Leia forgot her question. "I had a message from Detective Ono in Maui on my answering machine several days ago and called him back, but he was out. I haven't heard back from him."

"With a name like that, I bet the detective gets teased a lot," Shaina said. "Doesn't *ono* mean *delicious?*"

"Or fish." Rae smiled. "Maybe that's why he's such a jokester," Rae said. "He was more interested in telling jokes than asking me questions."

"He's an *oh no*, all right," Jermaine said, standing behind Leia. "He called me too, but I'm not staying on the island while he takes his time figuring it out. I've got a singing gig in Vegas next month. This is my big break to escape this dullsville island. Tony was a great guy and all, but I can't miss out on it because he was murdered. He'd want me to go."

Why do you say *murdered*? Did the cop say the death was suspicious?" Leia asked. She had always liked Jermaine. He was about Eva's age and had gone to school with her. Eva had adored him ever since he'd defended her in a schoolyard bullying session.

"He's acting like it." Jermaine fingered the gold clock guitar around his neck.

"That's ludicrous." Shaina Levy bit her lip, and her voice rose. "Ono is just a small-town bureaucrat trying to act important. It was an accident."

"I can't imagine the investigation would take long. It seemed to clearly be an accident," Rae Jardin said. She tugged self-consciously at the red shirt she wore that did nothing for her short, plump figure.

Leia wondered if she realized it was an insult to wear red to an Italian funeral. Probably not, she decided. The couple was too nice to deliberately show disrespect to the dead. "I suppose I'd better try Detective Ono again when I can get to a phone."

"You can use my cell," Eric said, tugging the clip free from his belt. "I have a plan where there's no roaming charge."

"*Mahalo no*. I hate cell phones. They cause acoustic neuroma," Leia said.

Eric's mouth dropped. "What on earth is that? Are you sure?" He glanced at the phone in his hand, then clipped it back on his belt.

"It's suspicious but not proven," Leia admitted. "Acoustic neuroma is a rare type of cancer that develops in the nerves near the inner ear. Better safe than sorry. Besides, the call will wait until this is over." She caught sight of Bane's familiar dark head. Her initial reaction was to hunch down out of sight, but she forced herself to stand still.

She watched him embrace Candace and murmur a few words of condolence. Leia's fingers curled into her palms, and she told herself not to be a child. Still, Candace was a widow now, and it would be natural for her to turn to Tony's best friend for comfort.

Bane was a free man, and Leia had no claim on him anymore—if she ever had. She'd thought she was emotionally free of him too, but his sudden reappearance on the island had shown her how foolish that belief had been. Seeing him again was like free-falling off a cliff into a bottomless blue hole.

Dirk Forsythe joined them. "Can I cut in? I need to get back to the shop, and the line looks an hour long."

"Sure." Shaina stepped back to allow him to crowd in behind Leia.

At nearly six-four, he towered over everyone but Leia. He'd always made her think of a blond Sylvester Stallone, and she expected him to drop to the ground and start doing one-armed push-ups any minute. He turned his languorous, heavy-lidded gaze on Shaina, and the other woman became visibly flustered. Leia had to bite her lip hard to keep from warning the woman that Dirk's attention was merely polite. He talked about his fiancée back on O'ahu all the time, and no woman seemed to tempt him to stray. She admired that.

"How's Candace doing?" Leia asked him. Maybe she could distract him long enough for Shaina to recover her wits. Dirk was too attractive for his own good. He didn't seem to have any idea how he made a woman's heart go pitter-patter.

Dirk shrugged. "You'd know that better than me. I'm sure she'll be fine. The dive shop is worth some money, and it's booming with business."

"I meant emotionally," she said dryly. Men could be so obtuse. "They were newlyweds. I thought maybe you'd checked on her."

"Tony's parents are in town. I didn't want to intrude. Besides, I thought I'd be able to help more by keeping things running smoothly at the shop. I'll do all I can to help, of course."

"I'm sure she's thankful you're doing that." Her gaze wandered to Bane again as he moved past Candace and turned to go. Her gaze met his, and he half raised his hand, then came toward her.

"I suppose you've all gotten calls from Ono?" Bane's gaze swept the group again as everyone nodded. "You realize we're all going to be under suspicion if Tony's death is deemed a murder, don't you?"

Shaina straightened, and her bushy hair bounced as she shook her finger at him. "That's the most ridiculous thing I've ever heard. Tony was our friend. None of us would hurt him."

"I wish I'd been down there," Dirk said. "Maybe I could have saved him."

Bane colored slightly. "It all happened so fast. You know how it is underwater. None of us saw anything suspicious."

Leia examined the faces of the other divers. Could one of them be a murderer? "The police have to know it couldn't have been one of us," she said. "Anyone could have seen the dive boat out there and realized he was down. Another diver could have attacked him."

"Who was his buddy?" Jermaine demanded.

"I was," Leia said. "But I was looking at the coral, and he signaled that he'd be right back, then he swam into the cave."

"He knew better than to go into a cave alone," Rae said.

"Apparently not," Dirk said. "Then what happened, Leia?"

"I don't know. I just remember Bane pointing to Tony shooting to the surface. We all swam up and found out what happened. I never saw a thing."

"No divers you didn't recognize or any other kind of disturbance?" Bane asked.

She shook her head. "Nothing. This isn't your problem, Bane," Leia told him. "You always think it's your job to take care of everything. Let the police handle it."

"Tony was my best friend. He gave me a job when I needed to help support my family, he pulled me from the waves when I got knocked from the boat and hit my head on the side—he would expect me to be there for his family. I'm not going to turn my back on him now."

"I'm not asking you to. But let Ono handle it."

"He can use all the help he can get. I know Tony better than he does. He won't turn down any leads I can come up with."

Leia knew he was right about that. Murder wasn't an everyday occurrence on the tiny island. "I'll see what Dr. Kapuy has to say. He would have looked at Tony's body before it was sent to Honolulu for the autopsy." She was next in line to talk to Candace. The person ahead of her stepped away, and Leia moved up to face the young widow. "I'm so sorry," she murmured. She embraced Candace, and the other woman clung to her.

"I don't know what I'm going to do without him," Candace whispered in her ear.

"Are you doing okay? Any cramps or anything?"

Candace wiped her eyes. Her eyes were so red and swollen they looked painful. "I'm fine physically. I have to tell his parents about the baby."

"They'll be thrilled." Leia's gaze went down the line to where Alfredo and Carlotta Romero stood. Carlotta had wailed her misery at the funeral, and Alfredo had taken her from the church. She stood sobbing against her husband's shoulder and kept mopping at her face with a soggy handkerchief.

"I don't think so. They never thought I was good enough for Tony. Working in Hollywood tainted me in their eyes. They'll probably wonder if the baby is even Tony's." Tears welled in Candace's eyes again. Tony always bragged that she could have made it big in the movies if she hadn't married him, but Leia didn't think Candace had enough drive or a hard enough edge to get to the big time. She'd done a few commercials, most notably one for Nike. Leia had seen it a few times, and Candace had done a good job, but she was no Julia Roberts. And she hadn't acted in years. Her last job had been as a receptionist for a security company on O'ahu.

"Having a baby will change everything," Leia told her. "Tony's parents won't want to alienate you or their grandchild."

"They've taken charge of everything this week. Alfredo pulled strings to get the autopsy completed and Tony's body released right away. But they haven't said two words to me."

Bane touched her arm. "They'll come around when they hear the news. A new baby is like witnessing the creation of the world."

Hearing the profound thought, Leia glanced up at him. Sometimes his almost poetic way with words surprised her. "When will the results of the autopsy be back?"

"Another week or so," Candace said.

Leia squeezed her hand. "I'd better move along. The line is getting longer." As she moved away, she caught sight of Aberg Hans. She hadn't expected him to show his face. He stood off to one side, his eyes wide and uncertain as though he might bolt for his car any minute. Leia moved toward him. He saw her coming and looked away. She stopped in front of him. "I'm a little surprised to see you here, Aberg," she told him.

"I'm here to pay my respects just like all of you. Tony and I had our professional differences, but I wouldn't hurt him," he said. "I know that's what people think."

"You threatened him just before he died," she pointed out. "It sounds like you'd sabotaged his air tanks too."

His gaze fell. "That's a lie. I never did anything to his equipment." His voice wavered.

From the way he shuffled around and wouldn't meet her gaze, his guilt was not in question. "Were you diving in the area, Aberg?"

His head jerked up, and he began to glower. "I don't have to answer any questions. I'm just here to pay my respects. If you'll excuse me, I need to get in line." He stalked off. Instead of getting in line, he vanished through the door to the outside. Leia wondered why he'd even come.

Six

Life moved at a sluggish pace in Kaunakakai. On the southern shore of Moloka'i, it was the largest of the tiny burgs that had sprung up around the pineapple and sugarcane trade in the old days. With no buildings over three stories, no traffic—or traffic lights, for that matter—it was Bane's favorite town in all the Hawaiian islands. No nightclubs or fast food, just a friendly little town full of native Hawaiians. Bane wouldn't mind living here someday.

He stopped at the tiny police station and answered the detective's questions about Tony's death, though he didn't feel he had anything helpful to offer. When he was done, he drove through town in his rental car and headed for the wharf. Ajax sat beside him with his head hanging out the window. Bane wasn't sure where Hans Dive Shop was located, but it had to be here somewhere. Aberg's appearance at Tony's funeral yesterday had raised more questions in his mind.

Bane parked. "Stay here, boy. Keep watch." Ajax whined but stayed where he was. Bane walked past the few boats bobbing in the harbor waves. The ferry was just offshore, having disgorged its few visitors onto the island, and now chugged its way back across the waves toward Lana'i.

He saw a boat with the dive shop's name painted on the side and paused to see if anyone was aboard. He wanted to find Hans himself. The deck looked deserted, and it was after three, so most likely the day's diving was done. The trade winds blew along Moloka'i with greater ferocity than the other islands, and the unprotected waters took the brunt, churning up large swells outside the reef. Most of the divemasters would be hawking wares in their stores by now.

He passed Tony's shop. It had a large Closed sign in the window. Aberg Hans was probably rejoicing today at the prospect of a larger clientele. He wouldn't be so happy when Bane was done with him. Bane couldn't believe the man had the nerve to show up at the funeral. Luckily, Candace hadn't seen him. Bane continued on and was nearly at the end of the harbor when he spotted a small, clapboard building with Hans Dive Shop on a wooden sign over the door. Through the open door, he could see Hans standing behind a counter. He was smiling at a young woman buying something.

Bane stepped inside the shop and got in line behind the woman. He caught a whiff of the coconut in her suntan lotion. It was doubtful Hans would recognize him. The other day the dive operator had been too intent on yelling at Tony. He glanced around and saw only one other employee, who was outside rinsing salt water off scuba gear. Perfect. The woman took her bag and exited the shop.

"What can I do for you?" Hans asked. His skin was red and sunburned under his blond crew cut. "You want to schedule a dive?"

"I was in the Aloha Dive Shop when you arrived the other day."

Hans reddened even more. "I was sorry to hear about Tony."

He decided to go for a sympathetic attitude. "It sounded like the two of you have had problems in the past, though I know Tony could be a steamroller."

Hans huffed. "A steamroller, that's pretty accurate. He didn't care who he hurt as long as he found that stupid ship. I doubt there even is a ship. He was obsessed."

"Did it really hurt your business?" Bane put just a touch of skepticism in his voice.

Hans invented a few choice words Bane had never heard. "He was about to bankrupt me. He had ads plastered everywhere about the treasure. That's all my clients wanted to talk about, if I got them

as far as going out with me instead of Tony. No one was interested
in the fish or coral I could show them."

"It sounds like you had cause to dislike him."

"I hated his guts." Hans narrowed his eyes. "But I didn't kill
him, if that's what you're thinking."

"I didn't say that. You have any idea who might have wanted to
hurt him?"

"We weren't friends, you know? Besides, I thought it was an
accident."

"Apparently the police suspect foul play. I heard him accuse
you of putting oil in his air-filling station. That doesn't sound too
dangerous."

"It's not. It just makes the air taste bad." Hans held up his
hands. "But I didn't say I did it."

Bane nodded. "It sounds more like something a kid would do,
not a business owner." Aberg looked away. Bane pretended not to
notice.

"Well, I don't like the way he acts, like customers will get something extra by diving with him." Aberg was grinding his teeth and
looking toward the door. He inhaled a deep, ragged breath. "I just
wanted him to play fair. He had plenty of enemies though."

"Who?" As far as Bane knew, everyone liked Tony. He was a
friendly guy and could always be counted on to help a friend.

Hans just frowned and didn't answer. Still, Bane had to admit
to himself that a prank like putting oil in the air-filling station was
a far cry from murder. All the oil would do was make the air taste
like diesel fuel and cause customers to leave. "Were you diving in
that area?"

Hans hesitated, and his gaze fell. "Yeah," he mumbled. "But I
never saw Tony or any of his divers. It's a big ocean."

He was there. Bane examined Hans's face again. "Maybe one of
your divers saw something. Could I get a list of who all was out
there that day?"

Hans's jaw hardened, and he shook his head. "No way. You're not harassing the few customers I have." He folded his arms over his chest. "Look, I have work to do. I had nothing to do with Tony's death, okay?"

Bane could tell he wasn't going to get anything else out of the man. "If you think of something that might help, give me a call."

"I told you—I didn't see anything."

"Here's my business card if you think of anything else."

"Keep it." Hans pulled his hands away to keep from touching the card. "I don't want to see your face again in my shop. Just leave me alone."

Bane put his card away and backed out of the shop. That had been a bust. He wasn't totally convinced of Hans's innocence. Hans had been at the site when Tony died, and that was suspicious in itself. If Bane could only get hold of the man's client list. He exited the shop and nearly bowled over Leia. As she teetered on the sidewalk, he grabbed her arms and steadied her. "What are you doing here?"

"I might ask you the same thing," she said.

She didn't pull away immediately but stood looking up at him. Her dark blue eyes, so like her mother's, had always fascinated him. The slant, the length of her lashes, the admiration he always found in her gaze could get addicting. Her arms felt cold, as though she'd had her car's AC blowing full blast. The chill was in sharp contrast to the warmth he felt in his hands, a heat that seemed to grow from contact with her. The chemistry between them had only increased with the time away.

He dropped his hands and stepped back. "I wanted to ask Hans a few questions."

"So did I."

"You told me to leave it to the police," he pointed out.

A flush ran up her neck and landed on her cheeks. "I stopped by the police station to answer their questions. Since I was here, I thought I might drop in. I tried to talk to Hans yesterday, but he walked away. I hoped he might be more forthcoming on his own turf."

Bane took her arm again and moved away from the building with her. "He was at the dive site. He just admitted it to me."

She pulled her arm loose and stood looking back at the dive shop. "You think he had anything to do with Tony's death?"

"I don't know. He said he didn't see Tony down there, but it's mighty suspicious that he was in the area. I think we should tell the police."

"I need to call Detective Ono back anyway. I can tell him then."

"How about some dinner first? I know it's a little early, but I'm starved."

"I guess that would be okay. I'm hungry too."

"Your enthusiasm is overwhelming," he said dryly.

She rubbed her arms. "What did you expect, Bane?" She rubbed her forehead, and her voice thickened. "I'm an adult. I can choose the path that's best for me." She turned her head away.

She began to walk away, and he caught at her arm. "Let's not fight," he said.

"You think you know what's best for everyone, that if you keep everyone in a neat little box they won't hurt you. I want more than that from a relationship. We're not compatible, Bane."

He shifted and looked away. "If you're talking about our argument about you going to San Francisco, I was proved right. You hated it, just like I thought you would. But I've always felt there was something more to our breakup, Leia. You handed my ring back with some rehearsed line about how we weren't right for one another. I don't get it." Things had been strained when she left for San Francisco. He'd flown out to see her a month later, and she'd given him back his ring. He still didn't understand why.

"Maybe I was wrong, but I needed you to support me, and instead you sounded just as controlling as my mother. All my life she's hovered over me like a mother *nene*. I wanted more than that from you." She yanked her arm out of his grasp and walked away. "Let me know if you ever decide you're not God," she said over her shoulder.

He watched her braid sway against her back and the way the sun caught the blonde highlights like strands of liquid gold. Squashing the poetic imagery, he stared as she got into her Neon and slammed the door without looking back at him. The strains of Amy Hanaiali'i Gilliom's "Paluahua" floated out the window, and he wished he could leave Leia as easily as she'd left him.

*L*eia was more sad than angry as she drove to Dr. Kapuy's office. Bane meant well, she had no doubt of that. But he wasn't her big brother; he was supposed to have been the man who loved her. She'd had enough of being told what to do growing up. She didn't want a despot for a husband. Bane didn't mean to be that way either. He just thought the world sat on his shoulders. His mother's desertion when he was a child had left a deep need in him to keep his world controlled and unchanged.

She parked and walked into Dr. Kapuy's office. The color scheme of beige walls that ran down to meet with beige carpet was meant to be restful, but it only succeeded in making her feel half alive. The odor of antiseptic assaulted her nose, and she nearly turned around and left, but she forced herself to approach the receptionist, who told her the doctor might have a few minutes to spare if she could wait a bit.

Leia snagged a scuba magazine from the rack and settled onto the brown sofa. Two women sitting in the waiting room looked at her. One leaned over to the other and whispered. Leia knew they were talking about her, but she raised her head and stared them down until their whispers stopped. She flipped through the pages but didn't really notice what she was seeing. She put down the magazine as Dr. Kapuy entered the waiting room, a faint cinnamon scent coming into the room with him.

He took the cinnamon toothpick out of his mouth. "Leia, what a pleasant surprise. Have you come to your senses about finishing your residency yet?" His voice was as gruff as a truck driver's.

She stood and took his hand. "Not yet, Doc." The doctor had always reminded her of a Hawaiian monk seal. His weathered face was plump and lined with deep creases, and a huge mustache dwarfed his round face. He was bald as well and had deep wrinkles on his scalp just like the seal.

He shook his head. "Such a waste. You're still vegetating at Kalaupapa with your *kapa* hobby, eh?"

Dr. Kapuy had taken her under his wing, helped her get into college, and sent her encouraging e-mails all through med school. He had a right to question her. She nodded. "I'm getting rather good at it."

"Ah, Leia, I still have hopes for you. I could get you back into a good internship if you'd just let me."

"Now you sound like my mother. Tell me about an internship in homeopathy and I might be interested." She followed him down the hall to his office, a small room stuffed with medical journals. A silver-framed picture of his wife, Alema, sat on the bookshelf behind his desk. She'd been dead for fifteen years now, but as far as Leia knew, the doctor had never considered remarrying.

He stared at her over the bulge of his nose. "I actually heard about a residency in natural medicine recently. It's in Honolulu. If you're interested, I'll get the information for you."

"I might be. I'd like to look at it anyway."

He settled his bulk into the well-worn leather chair and steepled his fingers together. "What brings you to see me if it's not a request for help to get back into residency?"

"You examined Tony Romero. I wondered if you could tell me what you found?"

He dropped his hands. "What's your interest in it?"

"I was there when he came up dead. The police are acting like it was murder."

Dr. Kapuy quirked an eyebrow. "I really shouldn't be talking about it. You should speak to Detective Ono."

She saw the gleam in his eye and kept quiet. What the doctor should do and what he did do were often miles apart. When he didn't say anything more for a few moments, she prompted him gently. "His weight belt was missing. Did the detective tell you that?"

He frowned. "No, he didn't. I was just told to examine him and run toxicology tests before sending him on to Honolulu for the autopsy."

"So there's no real evidence yet that he was murdered."

"I didn't say that." He sighed and pulled one pudgy ankle up onto his knee. "I know Tony. He was an expert diver. I suspect he ingested something or was poisoned in some way that caused respiratory failure. If he'd just been unconscious, he would have exhaled naturally as he came up."

"So he should have exhaled even while unconscious, but it appeared that he didn't and his lungs burst. What could cause that?" Her mind raced through the different drugs she'd studied in school.

The doctor pursed his lips. "I suspect he may have been injected with a sedative that depressed his respiration. Tony wouldn't have been able to exhale. A pulmonary embolism would have resulted. I found blood on his nostrils."

She nodded. "It looked like a pulmonary embolism when he came up. I knew he was too experienced to forget to exhale, even if he was shooting to the top."

"Good girl. You haven't forgotten all your training yet. The autopsy showed evidence of a fish meal in his stomach. It's possible he ingested tetrodotoxin. I'm not sure what caused it, but something kept him from exhaling."

"Puffer fish," she said. "I don't think he would have done that. He had a close call with puffer fish once before in sushi. I've never seen him eat it since. Which do you suspect?"

Dr. Kapuy's dark eyes were bright with interest. "We won't

know for sure until toxicology comes back, but I told Detective Ono my suspicions."

"Which is why he's telling us all not to leave the island until the investigation is finished. I doubt it's a puffer fish though, and aren't narcotics controlled? How hard would it be for someone to steal Demerol or some other narcotic?"

"Narcotics are kept in a locked cabinet and inventoried. Detective Ono has asked for the hospital to check stock. We'll see if there's anything missing." He glanced at his watch. "I hate to run away, but I have an appointment. Let me know if you hear anything. I'm interested in the case too."

"*Mahalo*, Dr. Kapuy." She rose and went to the door. The drugs that he suspected weren't easy to obtain. For a moment, her mother's face rose in her mind, but she pushed it away. Her mother would be the last person to murder Tony Romero.

Seven

Leia, Eva, and Malia worked quietly in Leia's backyard. Malia's mother, Luana, had joined them, her head bent over a fine white piece of *kapa*. Still in her late forties, Leia's aunt was nearly as round as she was tall. Dressed in a muumuu and slippers, she looked like any other Hawaiian resident, but she had a warmth that drew everyone to her.

Leia examined the marks in the cloth she was working on and sighed with satisfaction. Using her grandmother's *kua kuku*, she had reproduced the same watermark that appeared in the *kapa* her grandmother made years ago. The texture and color had turned out to her satisfaction as well.

"You're looking content," Luana said. "Malia told me Bane has come back."

"I'm just in a good mood, Auntie. Why does it have to be Bane? A more aggravating man never walked the earth."

Luana smiled. "You only feel that way because you're still in love with him."

If only her own mother cared enough to talk to her like this. Leia bent her head over the cloth again. She was ready to begin painting the designs. "Bane is in the past. He's here to do a job, that's all."

"You know I'm right. You need to both say you're sorry and kiss and make up."

The idea of kissing Bane brought back feelings Leia didn't want to explore. She looked away from her aunt's astute stare. "I had to do what I did. He should have understood."

Malia shook her head. "None of us thought you should give it all up, Leia. Why take it out on Bane when you don't hold it against the rest of us? You have to admit it sounded nuts to give up your career to make bark cloth and administer herbs."

Eva began to hum and fidget. "Don't fight," she muttered with a worried frown. "You'll scare Hina."

"Sorry, Eva. We're not arguing. We're just—discussing." Leia smiled, then turned around and ruffled her sister's hair. "Want a snack?" Food always distracted Eva.

"Do you have Cheetos?"

"Sure do. Just for you. They're in the kitchen cabinet."

Eva started toward the house, then stopped. "Pua was in my dream last night," she said, referring to their grandmother's pet goose. "She built a nest in the big tree behind Koma's house."

"Pua doesn't fly into trees," Leia pointed out.

"I know, but she was there anyway." Eva went on to the cottage.

Eva and her dreams. Leia gave her sister an indulgent smile then turned back to Malia. "If I can win the *kapa* trophy at the festival, maybe Mama will take my talent seriously. Pete thinks I have a chance."

Her aunt answered her instead. "Never sell your *kapa*, Leia. It's too precious to be sold. So what does your future hold? You can't keep hiding on the peninsula. What do you really want out of life?"

Leia looked down at her hands. "Dr. Kapuy gave me some information about a natural-medicine residency in Honolulu. I'm thinking about it."

Malia gave a tiny gasp. "Really? That's wonderful, Leia."

"Mama will have a fit, but at least she'd see I'm going to follow my own path."

"Are you sure you're not going that direction just to aggravate your mother?" her aunt asked in a quiet voice.

Leia's first reaction was to deny her aunt's comment, but she finally shrugged. "Maybe. I'm not sure anymore why I became interested in natural medicine. Mama's hostility to it might have had something to do with it in the beginning, but not now."

Malia nodded. "Your mother isn't capable of the love you want from her. You need to face it. Just take the job and follow your heart."

"It will take a lot of time away from my *kapa*. And I'd have to leave Moloka'i. My patients are depending on me here. I hate to leave them."

"You cling too much to the past, Leia. I think that's why you love *kapa*," Malia said.

Leia bristled. "You make flower leis. How is that different from what I do?"

"I make a living at it. Leis are used for everything here. *Kapa* isn't used for anything but display and ceremony." Leia touched the scar on her lip, and Malia's gaze touched it. "Clinging to the past won't make your scar go away. You're beautiful, why can't you see that? The scar is gone."

"You're perfect. You don't know what it's like to live with stares," Leia said. Malia exchanged a long look with her mother, and Leia realized this was something the two had talked about privately.

"There are no stares now, Leia." Malia's gaze locked on Leia. "That's the real reason you broke up with Bane, isn't it?"

"What?" Leia dropped her hand.

"You're afraid, Leia. Afraid to marry and have children." Malia lowered her voice as she leaned forward, her long hair falling over her shoulder. "Admit it."

Leia should have known she couldn't keep anything from Malia for long. Her gaze connected with her aunt's, and she saw compassion on Luana's face. "I studied genetics, Malia. With Eva and I both being born with birth defects, I knew how likely it was for me to pass on that gene to my children. I didn't want to inflict that on another child." *Tell her.*

"At least you're admitting it. I was getting tired of the subterfuge.

You used Bane's objection to your giving up your career as an excuse, didn't you?"

"Maybe I did. Things were strained when I left for San Francisco. Once I got away and thought about things, I knew it wasn't working." She resisted the urge to tell her cousin the whole truth.

Luana's voice was heavy. "Your mother has a lot to answer for. She's made you believe you don't deserve love. Something is broken in her. All the wanting in the world won't change it. All you can do is let it go."

"I wish it were that easy."

"You can't force love. Or ignore it forever." Malia studied her face. "I know you, Leia. You love Bane. There's more to your break-up than a vague fear. There has to be."

The silence stretched out between them. *Tell her.* Leia rubbed her forehead. "It's more than vague, Malia. I consulted a geneticist. There's a strong chance that any child of mine would have the cleft lip, maybe a cleft palate too."

Malia put her hand to her mouth. "Did you tell your parents?"

"No, why would I?" Leia didn't want to talk about it anymore. "It's time to go out to *Tûtû's*. She'll be glad to see us. She's making pineapple boats."

They stood, and her aunt embraced her. "I have to get back home. I'll be praying for you, Leia. Remember, God is in this, even when you can't see his hand."

Leia sank into her aunt's embrace and inhaled the white ginger scent she wore. Why couldn't her own mother love her as her auntie did? She pulled away and kissed her aunt's soft cheek. "Thanks, Auntie."

Eva had wandered close enough to hear. "I love pineapple boats. Can Hina come too?"

"Sure." Leia put her paints away, and they went to Leia's motorbike. Malia and her mother got into the sidecar, and Eva climbed on behind Leia. She drove through thick mangroves to a small, quaint cottage overgrown with red jade vines, their crimson lobes nearly covering the surface of the west wall. More flowers choked the yard, so many that it was hard to distinguish one plant from another: ginger, hibiscus, orchids, and proteas vied for space in the tiny yard. Bougainvillea rambled over the picket fence, and a bromeliads splashed a bright canvas of color by a monkeypod tree. The heady mixture of fragrances was nearly overpowering. She parked and they hurried to the front of the house.

Leia opened the screen door. "*Tûtû,* we're here." She stepped into the cool darkness of the cottage. For someone who loved flowers and spent every moment in her garden, it always amazed Leia that her grandmother kept heavy drapes pulled all the time. She said she didn't want the sun to fade her furniture, but Leia thought it was her grandmother's way of hiding her deformity from tourists. The interior smelled closed up and musty, though her grandmother kept everything spotless.

Eva ran past Leia as their grandmother came through the doorway to the kitchen. "*Tûtû!* We've come to visit you."

"I see that, *keiki.*" With one arm around Eva, Ipo Kahale advanced to embrace Leia and Malia. She wore a muumuu, but rubber boots clad her feet. "Would you like some *kope*? I just made a fresh pot."

She tried not to look at her grandmother's feet. Since the dementia problems, *Tûtû* often chose unusual combinations to wear. "I'd love a cup." They followed their grandmother to the warm kitchen. Most homes didn't have air-conditioning, but with the curtains drawn, the trade winds had a hard time cooling the interior.

Ipo poured three cups of coffee and handed Leia and Malia each a cup. "Let's go outside and sit in the garden. Koma is coming to join us for pineapple boats, and he should be along shortly."

"Good. I wanted to talk to him." Leia followed her grandmother out to the garden. Malia flung herself onto the soft grass and picked a hibiscus blossom to tuck behind her ear. A loud honk came from the side yard, then Pua, her grandmother's Hawaiian *nene*, came running to meet them. The goose honked again and rushed to Leia. She plucked a flower to feed Pua, and the *nene* gobbled it up. *Nenes* were the only native geese left on Hawaii, and they had only recently been brought back from the edge of extinction. Leia loved to watch Pua waddle through the tall grasses and paddle in the pond. The goose had been a part of the family for ages. At twenty-five now, Pua wasn't as spry as she used to be. Leia sat on the grass by her sister and let Pua sit beside her. The *nene* put her head on Leia's lap.

Her grandmother went to the picnic table and cut pineapples in two, then scooped out the fruit and began to chop it for the dessert. In spite of her deformed fingers, she managed the knife efficiently. Leia knew better than to try to help her grandmother.

"What do you want to talk to Koma about?" her grandmother asked.

"He's lived here a long time, hasn't he?"

"All his life. His parents lived here before him, and Koma contracted the disease by the time he was five." She nodded toward the jungle. "Here he comes now."

Leia turned to see Koma moving slowly through the tangled vines that drooped from the *'ohi'a* trees. He'd broken his hip several months ago, right after her father lost his job, and he still wasn't fully recovered. Watching his limp, she wished she could do something to fix it, but he surely must be ninety by now. He carried the characteristic marks of Hansen's disease—missing eyebrows, deformed nose that almost made him look like a lion, lumpy ear lobes, and clublike fingers. He sang a tuneless song as he walked, leaning on his hand-carved cane. His leathery face brightened when he saw the girls. "Ah, my *keikis*, I hoped you'd be here. I wanted to tell you about seeing Ku." He steadied himself on his cane, then lowered his bulk into the chair.

Leia sighed inwardly at the vacant look in his eyes. At least he was talkative. Sometimes he stared into space and said nothing. "I wonder if you might tell me some stories of the old days."

He dropped his hand and smiled. "Many people ask me about the old days. No one wants to hear what an old man is doing now." Pua tried to nibble on his toes, and he bent to rub the goose's head.

"Who else has asked you about the old days?"

"The diving man wanted to know all about my childhood." Koma straightened and stroked Eva's hair with his deformed fingers as she leaned her head against his knee.

Tony said he'd talked to Koma. Leia leaned forward. "I'd like to hear too. Did your parents tell you a story about buried treasure?"

Koma noticed Hina. "That nasty cat," he said. "Why did you bring her? She doesn't like me, and she scares the birds."

"She likes you fine," Leia soothed. "What can you tell me about the treasure?" She doubted she was going to get anything out of Koma today. He seemed almost secretive rather than vacant.

"Your *tūtū* is the real treasure," he said. "She always invites an old man like me to come eat. I would starve if it weren't for Ipo."

"You said you saw Ku," Eva pressed. "Did he have big teeth and claws?" She made a pretend roar and swiped in the air like a cat.

Koma patted her head. "Nothing like that. He carried the shovel he used to dig the fishpond."

"Shovel?" Leia stifled a giggle. "Where did you see him?"

"In the mangroves by the fishpond. He lives in the cabin nearby."

The one Leia had seen. Moloka'i had once boasted nearly seventy-five fishponds, dug out by the ancient Hawaiians to raise fish. Most of them had fallen into disrepair and only three had been restored. As far as Leia knew, there were no fishponds in this area; most were on the south shore, and Koma wasn't strong enough to have climbed out of the valley. He refused to ride in cars or boats, and to go to another area, he could only have walked. She hadn't looked around outside the cabin much that day. Maybe she should go back.

She grabbed her purse and pulled out a page she'd torn from a scuba magazine. "Did Ku look like this?" She showed him the picture of the deep-sea diver in high-tech equipment.

Koma put up his hand to hide his eyes. "It's *kapu* to look on one of the gods."

Leia suppressed a sigh. "Please, just look at it, Koma. I think Ku might just have been a special kind of diver."

"Get it away from me." His voice was high with stress.

Leia received a warning glance from her grandmother. She couldn't push him. He was too old and frail. "That's fine, Koma. We won't talk about it anymore," she soothed.

"Maybe Ku was looking for the treasure," Malia said.

Koma's hand stilled on Eva's head. "He was in the wrong place. The treasure isn't by the fishpond. It is in my *'ohi'a* tree. It's the original one, you know. Pele herself turned 'Ohi'a into a tree when he refused to marry her. That's why it's the largest in the forest. 'Ohi'a guards the treasure now."

Leia had heard the story many times. She knew which tree he meant. The big canopy tree dwarfed the others in the forest. "Can you show me the treasure?"

Koma's forehead wrinkled, and he shook his head. "My father told me something terrible would happen if anyone dug up the treasure. I'm the caretaker."

"What happens when you die then?" Ipo put in. "You have no children. The treasure will be lost forever."

Koma's crooked smile faded. "I don't know. My father said to pass it on to my own son someday. I have no son to tell." He looked like he might cry, then his gaze lingered on Leia. His smile came again. "I will show you," he said. He rose and beckoned to Leia. "Come. This won't take long."

"I want to come too," Eva said, scrambling to her feet.

Malia grabbed Eva's arm. "Hush, Eva, you have to stay with me. *Tûtû* needs someone to turn the crank on the ice-cream churn."

Eva's eyes widened. "You said I'm too slow. Can I really?" She turned to ask her grandmother.

"*'Ae*," her grandmother said. "But you must follow my instructions." She waved off Leia and Koma.

Leia followed the old man through the jungle of vines tangled with morning glory. She matched her steps to his, but he didn't seem disposed to carry on a conversation. He muttered to himself and stared into the recess of the trees. Leia started to ask him more questions about the treasure, then decided she'd better not push her luck. If he got upset, he'd order her back to her grandmother's.

They came to a clearing filled with wild ginger and the spicy scent of turmeric. Koma paused and wiped the perspiration from his forehead. He turned to her with his mouth open as though he were about to speak. Leia heard a muffled *whump*, then saw his mouth go slack. His eyes rolled back in his head, and one clublike hand pawed at her arm.

She grabbed his forearm. "Koma, what's wrong?" His mouth worked, and then he sagged against her. She smelled a familiar coppery odor, and her hand swiped something warm and sticky on his back. She eased him to the ground and rolled him over. A tiny hole spurting blood bloomed in his back. She leaned forward and put the heel of her hand against the wound to slow down the flow of blood.

"No time, no time. Talk to your *tûtû*," he gasped. His body went limp.

Leia touched his neck and felt for a pulse. Nothing. She ran her hand over his forehead and touched his thin hair. The back of her neck prickled, and she craned her neck to scan the clearing. He'd been shot, and the killer was probably watching her now.

Eight

Perspiration dripped down Bane's forehead, and he wiped it with his forearm. When they'd discovered traces of powder and the remains of a small bomb under the landing gear, he knew he was right—someone had sabotaged his plane. It was only by God's grace that he was still alive. Ron needed to know about this. With Ajax following him, he went in search of his boss, and found Ron poring over printouts of the last magnetic scan of the seafloor.

Ron's smile was full of satisfaction. "I still can't quite believe we've found it. The cannonballs mean the rest of the ship is down there somewhere. When news hits about what we've found, we're going to have every treasure hunter in the world breathing down our necks. Good job hiring Tony's divers to help us look."

"We'll have salvage rights," Bane pointed out. "I assume you've already applied."

Ron nodded. "Like pirates care. We'll post a guard, but they'll try to sneak in underwater. You and I both know there's no keeping a lid on this once the media get wind of it. I'd like to make as much progress as we can before Westerfield Salvage moves in. Sam Westerfield is a blight on the earth. It's like he has some kind of inner radar that can detect whatever I've found."

Bane eyed his boss's face. "The plane was sabotaged," he said quietly. "I found what was left of the bomb."

Ron's smile faded, and his lips thinned. "Westerfield," he spat.

"Maybe. There's no way to know for sure. The bomb components are pretty generic. Gunpowder, steel pipe."

"Of course it's Westerfield. No one else is trying to horn in on my missions. Well, this time I beat him anyway." Ron huffed.

"We need to cement our find, announce it to the papers so no one else can take credit. I'd suggest we get back down there and get more proof. The cannonballs are great, but we need more." Bane opened his locker and pulled out his diving gear. "If Westerfield did sabotage that plane, he must be insane. I can't believe he'd go this far to steal your finds."

Ron took his wet suit from his locker. "I didn't tell you the whole story. There were too many people around." He sat on a bench and looked out over the water. "I married his sister. She died in a waterskiing accident. He's never forgiven me for her death."

Ajax whined and bumped Bane's hand with his nose. "I'm getting your stuff too." He pulled out the dog's snuba gear and began to get Ajax ready. "That must have been terrible. Why would he blame you?"

"I was driving the boat. He swore he'd make me pay, and he knows how important my work is to me." Ron adjusted the tanks on his back and reached for his mask. "He's working on some similar equipment too. If he can get a patent first, we'll be out of luck."

Ron's work was his consuming passion. Anyone who disrupted that rocked his world. His voice was dispassionate even as he told about the death of his wife. Bane could see how her brother might get the wrong idea. Bane watched the dog jump in, then bit down on his mouthpiece and held on to his mask as he went over the side. The warm water enveloped him. He paused and adjusted his regulator, then finned his way down. He passed Ajax on the way, and the dog had a smile on his face. Baskets dropped by the crew on deck sank past him. They were attached to the winch in case the men found anything worth hauling to the surface.

The throb of the engines faded from Bane's ears as he dove toward the bottom. He followed Ron's scuffed and worn fins to the coral bed. Bane's gaze scanned the seafloor for any artifacts churned up by the current. An inquisitive triggerfish peered into his mask, then zipped away. A *honu*, the Hawaiian green sea turtle, paused nearby while half a dozen surgeonfish nibbled algae from its back. The *honu* turned to look at him, then swam in lazy strokes to the surface. Ajax struggled to dive deeper, but he couldn't manage it and turned to follow the sea turtle.

Bane's attention wandered to the cave. He wondered what secrets lay inside. Ron expected his help, but he felt drawn to the mouth of the cave. He finned over to the opening and shone his light inside. No sharks today, though the bright beam picked up a garden of colorful sponges attached to the walls and ceiling of the cave. A squid oozed away from his probing light into a rocky crevice. He itched to explore farther. The cardinal rule of cave diving was never to go in alone. Tony had broken that mandate and died for his trouble. Bane paused and glanced back at Ron. His boss would never agree to give up digging to go caving.

Bane couldn't bring himself to leave. He stayed near the mouth and swept his light inside. The cave stretched back farther than his light could reach. Entering just a few feet wouldn't hurt. He advanced, careful to keep the opening in sight. Translucent shrimp occupied one corner. This was stupid and dangerous, especially at this depth. He needed to get out of here and get to work.

A noise, or maybe a sensation, enveloped him—it sounded like a boat engine revving up and going over him. The rumble began to dissipate, then another started. Earthquake? Just in case, he swam out of the cave and joined Ron. Ron seemed not to notice the sound. Bane touched his arm, and Ron looked up. His eyes narrowed as the sound seemed to grow then fade again.

Bane looked down and saw a crack widening along the seabed. The sound came again, and he realized it had to be an earthquake swarm. He grabbed Ron's arm and pointed at the crack, which continued to expand. The sound intensified and seemed to surround him until he wanted to clap his hands over his ears and shoot for the surface. He saw the same panic on Ron's face. The crevice spread out as it ran toward the abyss. Then another crack developed, this one running perpendicular to the first. The rumbling noise filled his head until he couldn't think. The seafloor began to crumble and fall over the side, where it disappeared into the bottomless ocean of blue hole. He felt as if he were falling with it, though he knew he was still safely swimming at about a hundred feet.

Ron had a viselike grip on Bane's arm, but Bane barely noticed. He turned to look at the cave he'd just exited. The entrance still yawned, but a rock slide down the face had left a pile of stones to the side. He turned back to look over the side of the drop-off into the deep. He and Ron watched as the crumbling of the seabed finally slowed. It stopped about twenty feet from where Ron had been working. The water swirled with debris, and the visibility had dropped to about fifty feet.

Bane extricated himself from Ron's grip, then swam to the edge to peer over the side. He couldn't see much, but he knew he'd never see bottom even with great visibility. Eddies of dirt motes danced in front of his mask. He shook his head and rejoined Ron, who was examining the crack. When he glanced up at Bane, lines were etched in his forehead, and his eyes behind the mask were slitted. He pointed up, and Bane nodded.

They swam upward, pausing several times to decompress. Ajax joined them near the surface. When they finally reached the surface, Bane spat out his regulator and turned to face his boss. "Earthquake swarms."

Water ran in rivulets down Ron's face. He spat out his mouthpiece and raised his mask. "We're going to have to move fast. If we get another series of quakes, the ship and all we've worked for will go right over the edge."

Not only would they lose the ship, all Ron's investment in the search would be wasted. Bane nodded. "Let's get our divers organized for tomorrow. We can't let it slip away, not now when we're so close."

*L*eia crouched behind Koma's body. Her skin prickled as her gaze searched the jungle tangle of *'ohi'a* and koa trees. She strained her ears to hear something—anything, a footfall or a snapped twig. But all that came to her was a hawk screeching overhead as it dove to seize a honeycreeper.

She prayed for poor Koma, though he was past help.

She needed to get the police out here. Who would want to kill an old man? She wondered if it could have been a poacher out hunting a black buck or an eland antelope. It happened, especially in remote areas. The forest was rich with pheasant and wild turkey as well. Her muscles felt like lead as the minutes ticked by while she watched and listened. She didn't like this feeling, and it wasn't getting her anywhere. She was not going to cower here in fear. She got to her feet and dashed toward the tangle of foliage. The normal aroma of vegetation sharpened her senses. Fighting her way through lianas—huge, woody vines—and ferns, she fought back the panic that choked her throat. She wouldn't run. If she broke her concentration, the fear would overtake her. She lost a slipper but didn't pause to retrieve it.

Leia broke through the forest tangle into the clearing where her grandmother's house stood. She glanced back, but the smooth green leaves merely swayed in the trade winds without parting for an attacker. She kicked off her other slipper, then ran for the house. She burst through the back gate and nearly stumbled.

Malia rose from her chair in the garden. "Leia, you're as pale as an orchid. What's happened?"

"Koma. Shot," Leia gasped and clasped her arms around herself. She couldn't believe she'd come so close to total, mindless panic.

"Shot?" Malia lifted an eyebrow as if she was waiting for the punch line.

Leia nodded. "He's dead. Call the police." She ignored her

cousin's gasp and headed for the hose that lay curled like a giant snake along the side of the house. She needed to wash the blood off her hands.

Her grandmother followed her. "Koma? How can that be? Who would want to harm him?" Her gaze went to the blood running off Leia's hands in the stream of water from the hose.

"It might have been a hunter's stray bullet." Leia turned toward the door. "We have to call the police."

"I'll call." Malia dialed the phone. She paused with it in her hand. "You should sit down. You look like you're going to pass out."

"I'm fine. Just a little shaky." She glanced around. "Where's Eva?"

"Napping in the grass." Her cousin nodded toward Eva, who lay on a soft mat of grass under a hao tree covered with white blossoms.

Leia relinquished the rising fear that her sister was in the forest somewhere with a madman. Eva had always been her responsibility, but on days like today, that duty weighed heavily. She'd been right beside Koma and was unable to do anything to protect him. Tears burned the back of her eyes, and she tuned out the drone of Malia's voice as she explained to the policeman what had happened.

"Leia?"

Leia jumped at the sound of her cousin's voice. Malia was holding out her cell phone. "Detective Ono wants to talk to you."

Leia shook her head. "Not on the cell phone. I'll tell him about it when he gets here."

Malia sighed. "My cousin won't use a cell phone. Okay, I'll tell her." She clicked off the phone. "He's on his way. He said not to disturb the body and to stay in the house until he got here."

"I'll get Eva." Leia hadn't thought how exposed they were in the yard. She ran to awaken her sister.

Eva always woke up smiling, and today was no exception. "I had a dream, Leia."

"I hope it was a nice one." Leia took Eva's hand and led her toward the house. She paused long enough to grab the tray of pineapple.

"It was scary. Bane was in a hole."

The family had learned over the years not to discount her dreams. They often held a grain of truth to them. "What kind of hole?" Leia murmured, wondering what Detective Ono would make of her witnessing two murders in less than a week.

"I don't know, but he was really stuck. And he couldn't breathe. Then he saw the stars and followed them out. Can we call him and make sure he's okay?"

"Sure." They reached the safety of the house. Leia locked the door behind them and rushed toward the phone on the wall in the kitchen. Her hands trembled as she dialed Bane's cell number. When she got only his voice mail, something inside cracked and broke. She'd visualized digging up the roots of the love she'd had for Bane just like the Hawai'i Invasive Species Council worked at digging out fountain grass. Her efforts hadn't done any more good than theirs.

*L*eia picked up the slipper she'd kicked off. "I lost my slipper," she said.

"We're following the trail of the slippers? Is that anything like bread crumbs?" Detective Ono guffawed, and the other two policemen laughed.

Ono's laughter struck an incongruous chord in Leia. The situation was too serious for jokes. She exchanged a glance with Malia, who hovered protectively near her elbow.

He must have caught their expressions, because he sobered and took out a notepad. "Did you see or hear anything before or after the shooting?"

Leia thought for a moment, hoping to dredge up some small memory that would help. She finally shook her head. "Nothing unusual. Normal bird noises, the wind in the trees, that kind of thing. I heard a funny sound from in front of me that I know now was the gun firing. Then Koma slumped. It took me a few seconds to figure out what had happened." She stooped to retrieve her second slipper and put them both on.

"Why were you together? Where were you going?"

She hesitated. Should she talk about the treasure? Ono caught her delay and turned a questioning gaze toward her. He needed to know, she decided, just in case it was connected to Tony's death as well. "Koma claimed he was the caretaker of the treasure from the Spanish galleon Tony was searching for. I thought he was delusional, especially when he talked about seeing Ku." She told him about her find at the cabin. "But maybe he really did know something, and he was killed for it."

Ono shook his head. "For what purpose? If he knew where the treasure was, wouldn't the killer want Koma to tell him?"

Some sleuth she was. "I guess you're right." She stopped. "His body is in the middle of the clearing." She didn't want to go in there again.

Ono held up a hand and took out his gun. "I'll handle this, Pilgrim," he said in a bad John Wayne imitation.

What a goofball. Leia found a log and started to sit down. "Not there," Malia said. "The haiku trees are too close."

The hairy ovaries of the haiku flowers made her break out in hives, so Leia was grateful her cousin had been quick to point out the danger. Leia nodded and selected another log. Malia joined her. Insects buzzed around her in a pleasant background noise that made the horror of the day's events fade a bit. "I wish I could have reached Bane."

"He'll call. You know how spotty cell-phone coverage is on the island." Malia reached down and plucked a blossom. "The way you long for him now says a lot."

Leia didn't answer. Bane's strength and levelheaded assessment would be welcome about now, and that was the only reason she wanted him. She could see Ono through the brush as he knelt around Koma's body and examined the ground for evidence. Now that she thought about it, the shooter had to have been standing near where she now sat. She rose and began to study the foliage on the ground.

"What are you doing?" Malia asked.

"I thought the shooter might have dropped something." A glint of white caught her eye, and she saw three cigarette butts under a huge anthurium leaf. She started to pick them up, then thought better of it. Detective Ono would want to retrieve them to save any DNA on them. She called to him, and he joined her and Malia.

He knelt beside the butts and picked them up with gloved fingers, then dropped them into a paper bag. "Good job, Pilgrim," he said, still in John Wayne mode. "I'll have them tested for DNA. Whoever dropped them was standing right here." He pointed out an area where the foliage had been flattened. "This is recent."

Leia glanced around, a feeling of unease running along her back. Did the man just now leave, or was he still out there watching to see what they'd found? She moved to a nearby bush, startling a mynah bird. The bird squawked and dropped something from its beak. She caught a bright flash of metal. She knelt, and the bird dropped the trinket and flew away with an indignant squawk.

"What is it?" Ono stooped to join her.

Leia didn't touch it. "I think it's a watch. The band is broken."

Ono picked it up with his gloved hand and turned it over. "A common Casio. Kmart sells them by the thousands." He squinted. "Though this one has the initials JR on the back."

"Why would a cheap watch be engraved?"

Ono's grin was sly. "Maybe a girl thought she could impress him with an engraved gift."

"You think it belongs to whoever shot Koma?"

He dropped the watch into another bag. "It's not rusted or wet. I'd say it was dropped today."

Leia's neck prickled again. "I hope it was an accident."

Ono waggled his eyebrow. "Looks like premeditated murder to me, Pilgrim. The bullet is a high-powered 30-06. Not your usual hunting gun."

Murder. Such an ugly word. Leia shivered and settled back on the log.

Nine

Bane's cell phone beeped as he lay on his bunk in the belly of the boat with Ajax sleeping beside him. He had a message. Odd that he hadn't heard it ring. He must have been in a dead spot. When Leia's voice came to his ear, his fingers tightened on the phone. He could hear the stress in her voice as she told him Koma had been killed, and he sat up on the bunk. Ajax lifted his head and looked at him.

The research ship anchored off the Kalaupapa Peninsula. He called his dog to come with him, then took the small skiff from the boat to shore and docked it. He hurried to Leia's grandmother's cottage. Bane went toward the door, and Ipo's *nene* came running to meet him. Ajax cowered from the goose. Pua squawked, and Bane reached down to rub her head. "Ajax, you're a big baby. Pua won't hurt you." The goose waddled away after a moment, and he stepped to the door. Before he could knock, Eva opened the screen.

Her lopsided smile burst out when she saw him. *"Pehea 'oe?"*

"I'm fine," he said. "It's all of you I'm worried about."

"I dreamed you were trapped in a hole and couldn't get out." Her bright blue eyes skimmed over his face. "Then you followed the stars out."

For a moment, he thought of the deep blue hole of the abyss he'd peered into. "Don't worry, I'm fine. Where are Malia and your sister?"

"Malia is talking to the policeman. Leia told me I had to stay here with *Tûtû.*"

Dangerous Depths

He listened but heard no voices. "Are they outside? Where is your *tûtû?*"

"She's fixing tea. Leia took the policeman to find Koma." Her eyebrows came together. "He got shot."

"I heard about that."

She hugged him. "You want some mango tea?"

He hugged her back, then released her. "I'd better go help your sister. But save me some tea."

"We're going to have pineapple boats too. So don't be late."

She seemed to have forgotten the dead man, and Bane patted her arm. He wished he could focus on the good in life the way Eva did. Sunshine seemed to follow her around. He started toward the door, but Ipo began to sing in her monotone voice. Hesitating in the doorway, he sighed and shut the door. Ipo usually only sang when the clouds rolled in. He wasn't sure he should leave Eva here alone with her grandmother. Though she was twenty, her mind was like a child's, and she was easily frightened.

Eva's smile began to falter. "*Tûtû* is singing. She won't know who I am. I hate it when she forgets my name." Tears flooded her eyes.

"Maybe it will pass soon. I'll go check on her. Why don't you get Ajax some water?" He patted her shoulder, and they went into the kitchen.

Ipo sat at the wooden table. Most of the white paint on it was scuffed and worn. She stared at the wall and sang in a surprisingly melodious voice. When she got to the final stanza of "Ka Uluwehi o Ke Kai," a traditional hula tune, she stood and began to sway. In her day, Ipo had been a hula dancer of great renown on the islands. Hula had originated on Moloka'i, and it still boasted exceptional dancers. He could still see traces of her grace in the fluid movements.

"Ipo?" He stepped to her side and touched her hand. She ignored him and continued to sing and sway. "It's Bane." She pulled the hand he touched away and moved into the center of the kitchen.

"*Tûtû*, I'm hungry," Eva said. She placed herself directly in front of her grandmother, but Ipo danced around her grand-daughter. Her voice grew louder, and she closed her eyes. Eva looked at Bane. "She forgot me again."

The pathos in her voice touched Bane. Though he felt an urgency to see Leia and find out what had happened, he didn't dare leave Ipo and Eva like this with a shooter in the forest. He went to the refrigerator. "I think I'll take some tea after all," he said. "Would you like some mango tea, Ipo?"

The older woman dropped her arms from over her head. "Loose tea in the treasure chest," she said in a wooden voice.

Bane sighed. She was still lost in the clouds and talking nonsense. He grabbed three glasses from the cupboard and dumped ice into them, then poured the mango tea. He took Ipo's hand. "Here, why don't you sit down and have some tea with us? It's nearly eight o'clock. Leia will be back soon."

"Pieces of eight, pieces of eight," she chanted. "Tea in the treasure chest and don't be late."

He frowned. Was it possible she might know something about the treasure? Maybe she'd heard people talking so much about it that it had lodged in her mind and was coming out like this now. That had to be it. She would surely have told someone if she knew anything. He took a sip of tea. He wished she did know. It would make his job a lot easier.

Darkness had descended and it seemed even darker in the forest. Ono closed the body bag, and several other men lifted the body onto a stretcher. "We've got everything all zipped up." He grinned. He paused and stared at her from under dark eyebrows. "Watch your step, Pilgrim. Two killings in four days, and you're around for both. I'm beginning to wonder about you."

"Me?" She shook her head. "Two killings, you said. Are you sure Tony was murdered?"

He hesitated, his walrus mustache twitching. "Not totally, no. But the autopsy should come back shortly. And we found some drugs missing at the hospital, so we think they were stolen by someone who had access to it there. Did your mother know Tony well?" He slipped in the question with a studied casualness.

Leia put her hand to her mouth. "You surely wouldn't suspect my mother. She had nothing to gain by Tony's death. She knew him, yes, just as my whole family knew and loved him. You're going in the wrong direction."

He pretended to jog his head from side to side. "As long as I don't get whiplash." He smiled. "What can you tell me about Aberg Hans? You were there when he came into the dive shop."

The tension in her shoulders eased. "He seemed mad enough to do anything. He told Tony he'd better back off or he would be sorry."

He touched his lips with his forefinger. "But he has no access to the drugs as far as we know. Does your mother know Hans?"

"I doubt she's ever met him. My mother is focused on her patients. She's a healer, not a killer."

"What about Tony's wife? Any trouble there?"

She shook her head. "They were newlyweds and very happy. She's going to have a baby."

He raised his brows. "I hadn't heard that. At least she'll have a bit of him left."

Leia gave him credit for a pinch of compassion. "I hope the baby will help heal the discord between her and Tony's parents." Too late she realized she should have kept her mouth shut.

He raised his brows. "Caught you, Pilgrim. She didn't like Tony's parents?"

"She liked them fine. They thought Tony married beneath him." "Did he?"

"Of course not! Candace may not have had the Italian pedigree they would have liked, but she loved Tony."

"How did he meet her?"

"Dirk introduced them. She was on the island shooting a commercial. She'd been working as a receptionist for a security company when she got called for the job. It was filmed on a boat, and she knew Dirk from working with him on O'ahu. She put him in touch with the producer, and Tony captained the boat. It was love at first sight." She smiled at the memory of Tony's instant infatuation. Candace had been just as bad.

He put his notepad away. "That's all for now. I'll give you a call if I think of any more questions. *Mahalo*." He nodded to Leia and Malia, then tromped off in the wake of the men bearing Koma from the clearing.

"Let's get out of here." Malia linked arms with Leia, and they followed the path back to their grandmother's.

"How weird that he would ask questions about my mother." Leia couldn't get the detective's suspicions out of her head.

"He has to ask those things. No one could seriously suspect your mother." Malia's voice was unconcerned.

As they approached the house, the sound of *Tûtû's* singing came to her ears. "Oh, no," Leia groaned. "*Tûtû* is having a bad day." Ajax came to greet her, and she patted his head.

"Our parents are going to have to make a decision soon," Malia said. "I've talked to my mother about having her live with us, but my father is against it. He and *Tûtû* have been at odds so long, I think neither of them know how to mend the breach. He's never forgiven her for giving the coffee plantation to Uncle Makoni."

"Someone needs to bring her home to live with them," Leia said. "I think it's outrageous that Mama is so against it. She would hate to live in a home herself, so you'd think she would consider how *Tûtû* feels."

"I've tried talking to my dad too. He says my mother doesn't have time to care for *Tûtû*. I've offered to stay with *Tûtû* during the day, but my father is against that as well. He says Uncle Makoni can do it."

Even Malia's family wasn't perfect. Leia sometimes forgot that. "We could share the responsibility. Or maybe I could move in with *Tûtû*."

"That would be fine until you had to go to work," Malia pointed out. "But I could help you. Most of my job is done at home anyway. I can string leis anywhere. *Tûtû* could help me."

"We'll think about it." Leia dreaded confronting her mother. Her mother had formed her ideas decades ago, then slapped a permanent coat of shellac on them. She opened the door and stepped into the dark house. If Leia moved in, the first thing to go would be the curtains. She stopped when her gaze met Bane's, and Malia nearly bumped into her.

He rose from the sofa with a fan of cards in his hand. "We were just playing Go Fish. Eva was whopping me. Are you all right?"

She wanted to run into his arms, and it was only by a thin string that she managed to hang on to her composure. "I've had better days," she said, raising her voice over the sound of her grandmother's singing. *Tûtû* rocked in her chair and stared at the wall as she sang.

"What did Detective Ono have to say?"

"He found bullet casings, cigarette butts, and footprints. And a watch someone dropped."

"He thinks Leia might be in danger," Malia put in. She glanced at her watch. "My parents should be home. I'd better call them and tell them what happened." She went toward the kitchen. "I'll call your parents too."

Bane's gaze focused on Leia. "Does he think the shooter was aiming for you?"

"Of course not. He's just looking at the fact I was nearby when Tony was killed, and now Koma. It's coincidence though."

"Maybe. Maybe not." Bane put down his cards and came toward her. He rested his hands on her shoulders. "I've got an idea. We need some extra help diving. An earthquake swarm ripped a crack in the seabed close to the wreck. We have to move fast or the site may slide off into the abyss. You're an expert diver. Ron will pay you well, and I can watch out for you."

"I've got responsibilities at the clinic," she protested. "And I've offered to help Candace as well."

"It wouldn't be long—just until the police wrap up this investigation. No one will harm you out on the boat. Besides, if Candace realizes we're so close to finding the treasure, she'll want you to go. She could use the money."

She thought about it a minute. "Now might be a good time to take a few days off from work. I'd like to find the treasure for Candace's sake." She told herself her excitement about the dive had nothing to do with the fact that she felt alive in Bane's presence and wanted to bask in his attention.

The stars shone like pearls in a blue-velvet sky. Leia inhaled the scent of the sea deep into her lungs and felt its power relax her muscles. Malia's father had agreed to let her take *Tûtû* home with her tonight while Leia and Bane went to get Candace's permission for Leia to help with the dive.

"I need to stop by the ship and drop off Ajax. Do you mind?"

She shook her head. "I was glad to see him when I got to *Tûtû's*."

"You're not fooling me. I know, you hoped he'd run off by now." Bane's grin told her he was aware of her distaste for the canine. "I don't know what you have against poor Ajax."

The dog thrust his head between them and whined at the sound of his name. Leia leaned down and rubbed his head. "Oh, you mean you've never noticed how he acts like we're all here to serve his every whim? You spoil him terribly. Human food, filtered water, a featherbed." She shook her head. "You're a mess, Bane Oana. That dog has gotten you wrapped around his finger, er, paw, in just a year. He was a spoiled puppy when I last saw him, and now he's even worse." She gave Ajax a final pat. She actually liked the dog, but Bane didn't seem to realize Ajax was a dog and not his child.

"You just don't like the competition."

She crossed her eyes at him, thankful he couldn't see her silly gesture in the dark night. "I thought Ajax would have forgotten me." Hina was struggling to get to the dog, but Leia kept a firm grip on her. The cat eventually gave up and settled into a nap.

"I doubt it. You're unforgettable." His voice took on a husky tone, and he reached over and grasped her hand.

The touch of his warm hand sent a shock along her arms. It was a perfect night for romance. The heady scent of the sea mingled with Bane's cologne. She needed to be careful. It would be easy to drop her guard on a night like this. She withdrew her hand, feeling a stab of regret. She didn't want to hurt him, but it had to be this way. She saw him hunch his shoulders over the boat's controls. She turned her gaze away.

He didn't say anything more until he moored at the big research vessel. "I discovered my plane had been sabotaged. I forgot to tell you."

"A bomb?"

"Yep. I found the traces. Ron is sure it's his ex–brother-in-law, Sam Westerfield. I guess the guy blames him for the accident that killed Ron's wife."

"Sam Westerfield? My dad can't stand him. He was the one who implicated *Makua* in the robbery. He is on the board at the museum and insisted my father had to know more than he was telling. Even when the police exonerated him, Westerfield kept pointing fingers. My father won't be happy to hear he's here."

"Sounds like no one much likes him."

"Could this guy be behind Tony's death too?"

Bane didn't answer for a moment. "I wouldn't think so, but I have to admit I never even considered it. Ron says Westerfield wants to find the galleon, and the ship is worth millions. That's massive stakes. If you add revenge into the mix, it's a killer motive. I'll say something to Ron." Bane stood and began to climb the ladder to the ship. "You want to come aboard?"

"Sure, why not?" She followed him onto the deck. Hina had been sleeping in her arms, but she raised her head and looked around.

A crew member with red hair stood in the doorway. He backed away when he saw the cat. Hina stalked toward him with her tail in the air. "Uh, I've got work to do." He vanished through the doorway.

"I'd guess Logan is scared of cats too, just like Ajax," Bane said. "Come here, boy," he said in a coaxing voice. "You can stay in my quarters."

Leia stifled a giggle. No wonder that dog was the most spoiled animal on the face of the earth. Purring, Hina reached out her paw and touched Bane on the arm as if he were calling for her. Ajax's claws clicked on the deck as he raced to slobber over his owner. Hina hissed. She let out a yowl that would have raised Neptune from the deep. She arched her back, her tail lashing in the air, then with a last yowl, leaped onto Ajax's back. The dog yelped and dashed for Bane's legs.

He soothed him. "It's okay. The bad cat won't hurt you." He was grinning, and his gaze met Leia's. "Those two are like oil and water. What's wrong with this picture? The dog should be terrorizing the cat, not the other way around."

He was like a kid with that dog. Whenever he had children, he would be a great dad. Her smile faded. She watched while Bane fed Ajax, then they got back in the boat with Hina and headed to shore. They were both quiet. Leia wondered what Bane was thinking about as he stared out over the dark waters. She always got the impression that Bane was holding something of himself back. There was an invisible wall around him. He wanted to be the one to take care of everyone else, but it somehow made him aloof. She'd always wondered if he thought he wasn't allowed to show any weaknesses.

Nothing more was said between them as they docked and walked to Candace's house. The lights spilled out of the big plantation house. The driveway was empty, but Leia assumed Candace's car was in the garage. As they approached the door, she could hear music drifting out the open window. Candace was a huge fan of Paul McCartney and played his songs all the time. Through the open curtains, she could see Candace in a nightgown. Her eyes closed, she was dancing in the middle of the floor. Swaying and weaving with the music, she seemed to be talking to herself.

"You think she's okay?" Leia whispered.

"You'd better go in alone. She's ready for bed," Bane said. "I'll wait in the car. She wouldn't want anyone but a woman to see her like that."

She respected the way he kept his eyes averted from the spectacle of Candace in the flimsy nightgown. Leia pressed the buzzer and waited. No response. She tried the handle and found the door unlocked. "Hello? Candace, it's Leia." There was still no answer, so she stepped inside and went down the hallway.

Candace was still lost in her music and dance. Leia's gaze went to the coffee table where two glasses and a bottle of scotch sat. Even from here, she could smell the reek of the alcohol. She grimaced and stepped across Candace's discarded slippers and clothing on the floor. She touched Candace's arm. "Candace, are you all right?"

Candace looked back at her with glassy eyes. "Leia," she slurred. "Come dance with me."

"You need a smoothie to counteract the effects of that alcohol," Leia said, guiding the other woman to a nearby chair. "Wait here." She went into the kitchen and opened the refrigerator. She dumped ice, a banana, and some fresh pineapple into the blender and turned it on. What was Candace thinking to be drinking while she was pregnant? Leia pressed her lips together as she poured the smoothie into a glass. Carrying it into the living room, she found Candace curled up on the sofa with her eyes closed. "Here, Candace, drink this." She lifted her friend and held the glass to her lips. Candace barely opened her eyes, but she managed to sip the smoothie.

Leia watched her, and in a few minutes, Candace began to look a little more alert. "You can't do this again," Leia said. "You have to think about the baby."

Candace sat up straighter. "Tony would have made such a good fa—father. I'll make a terrible mother."

"You'll be fine." Leia smoothed Candace's hair back from her forehead. "Look at the way you baby your flowers. You'll be a great mother. It will be hard, but I'll be here for you, and so will the rest of your friends."

Candace clutched Leia's hands. "You think so? I haven't been around kids much. I—I'm scared to do this by myself."

"I think it will come naturally to you. But you have to take care of yourself. No more alcohol. It's bad for the baby."

Fresh tears filled Candace's eyes. "Is it really? I haven't been to the doctor yet. Do you think I hurt the baby?"

"You're going to be fine. Your baby is going to be fine. But you have to go see the doctor and let him tell you how to care for yourself." Candace nodded and Leia let her lean back against the sofa again, then forced a few more sips of the drink down her. "I'll be right back," she told Candace before she went to tell Bane she needed to stay here.

Bane was leaning against the trunk of the car with his arms folded over his chest. "Is she okay?"

"Not really. She's been drinking. I think I should stay with her tonight. *Mahalo* for bringing me over."

"I'll come by and get you for work in the morning. You're stranded here."

"What time?"

"About eight?"

"You know, don't bother. I want to get my mom's boat anyway. I'll have Malia get me. Don't look for me before ten." She laced her fingers together and wished she knew what to say to him. He'd been a rock for her today.

"Okay."

"Well, good night." The words were barely out of her mouth when he stepped toward her and leaned down. His lips brushed hers, and the unfamiliar facial hair tickled her lip. Inhaling the masculine scent of him was like the most potent drug. Without a conscious movement, she found herself grasping his shirt and kissing him back. When she realized what she'd done, she jerked away. Dropping her hands, she whirled and ran for the house. Bane's soft laughter floated after her on the wind.

Ten

ane waved at his sister, who sat at the helm of a thirty-foot Chris-Craft. She waved back and cut the engine. The boat slewed sideways as it slowed near the *Pomaik'i*. He went down to the boarding platform to greet her. It was only then he noticed the dolphin zipping through the water beside her boat. Nani leaped from the water, rolled in the air, and splashed down. The spray arced through the air and drenched him in a warm salt bath.

"Hey, you did that on purpose! No fish for you, Nani." The dolphin chattered from the water, and he could have sworn she was smiling. Her exuberance brought a smile to his lips. "Did you tell her to do that?"

"Nope," Kaia said, climbing aboard the platform. "She is just trying to show how excited she is to see you."

"Here, I'll share the excitement with you." He hugged her tight, trying to transfer as much moisture from his shirt to her red tank top.

"Ew, *mahalo nui loa*." She hugged him back, then stepped away and looked up into his face "You've lost weight. Are you okay?"

"Sure. I've just been too busy to eat."

"You get on a new project like this, and you get obsessed." She shook her head, then linked arms with him. They went up to the deck of the research vessel. Kaia stepped to the salon, where she rummaged in the cooler and got a Pepsi.

"Don't let Leia see you drink that. She'll be on your case about how bad sugar is for you." He probably shouldn't have said anything about Leia. Kaia wanted to see everyone married now that she was happily settled. Mano was just as bad. Bane was the oldest and would be the last to enter matrimony.

Kaia stopped with the can halfway to her lips. "Leia is back? You never said a word."

"She chucked her career and came back here. She's making *kapa* now and working in the little clinic on Kalaupapa administering alternative treatments to the residents."

She looked at him with a sharp gaze. "I can see her doing that. I never saw her as a traditional doctor. I hope you didn't say 'I told you so.'"

His sister knew him too well. "I didn't expect her to hate it so much she'd quit. But I did talk her into helping out on the project."

"Is that all you've talked her into? Is romance blooming again?"

"Easy, tiger. Don't go pushing me." He grinned. "How's *Makuahine*? And *Tûtû-man*."

She shot him a droll look. "I guess I'll let you change the subject. They're fine. Grandfather wants to come over for the ukulele festival. Have you been practicing?"

"Not yet, but I will. Are you still happily married?"

She smiled. "I think Jesse is relieved all the fuss is over, and I have to admit I feel the same. Now we're just an old married couple." She patted her stomach. "And baby makes three."

Bane grinned. "I'm going to spoil that kid rotten. You look great."

Kaia sipped her soda. "I feel good too, other than the morning sickness. So what do you have planned for Nani? I can only stay for the weekend, then I need to get back home, but Nani can stay as long as you need her. I have to write up a massive report on the progress with Nani to apply for some new funding."

"We're looking for a Spanish galleon down here. We've found some artifacts. Twenty feet or so from the site where we found the cannonballs, the ocean floor drops off. I was hoping Nani could go down with a camera and see what's there. We've got a minisub we can take down too, but Nani can maneuver into smaller places."

"I'm sure she'll love the work."

"There's something else. There have been some earthquakes in the area. Part of the shelf we're examining went over the edge. I hope we have time to get it all out."

"You should call Annie and ask about activity."

Annie was Mano's fiancée. A top-notch volcanologist, she worked at the Hawaii Volcano Observatory. "Great idea. I'll call her now." He dug his cell phone out of his pocket and found her stored number. No signal. He walked to the deck and tried again, finally getting a signal, though it was weak. "Annie, it's Bane." The signal was still poor, so he stepped a few feet to the port. Kaia followed him.

Annie's soft voice was full of welcome. "Hey, Bane. Mano and I were just talking about you."

"Mano is there? Tell him I'm on Moloka'i and could use some dive help. He's still looking for a job, and I've got one for him."

"Moloka'i?" Her tone turned sharp. "We've been having some earthquake swarms off the north shore."

"That's why I'm calling. I found a crack right where I'm working, and the last quake sheared off some of the seabed into the deep. How serious is it?"

"No way of knowing for sure, but the quakes have been increasing in frequency and strength. We're scrambling to get some scientists out there to check it out. We may have another seamount developing like Lo'ihi. In fact, I was planning on coming there myself. I think I can talk Mano into coming."

"Kaia is here too. We'll make it a family affair. Let me know when you're arriving, and we'll pick you up." He clicked his phone off and dropped it back into his pocket. "They're both coming." He told his sister what Annie had said. "We're going to have to watch that fissure. If it starts spewing lava, we're in trouble."

"I wish I could dive with you." She chewed on her lip. "Diving isn't recommended while pregnant."

"Don't worry about it. We've got a good crew." He turned at

the sound of a motor craft and shaded his eyes with his hand. "Here comes Leia now." He tried to keep the pleasure from his voice, but he saw his sister's smile as she followed him to the rail.

Leia handed a backpack up to him. Kaia met her on deck, and the two hugged. "You look great," Leia said.

"I feel great. A little morning sickness, that's all. Got any concoctions to help with that?"

"I sure do. I'll bring it to you."

He listened to them chatter before deciding he needed to interrupt and get to work. "Hey, we're not finding the galleon up here. You ready to suit up?"

"I'll swim while you dive," Kaia said. She grabbed her satchel. "I'll change into my swimsuit in the head."

Leia had a pair of drawstring shorts over her one-piece swimsuit. She shucked the shorts and pulled her leopard wet suit out of her bag, then began to tug it onto her slim figure. Bane turned away to get into his own gear. She'd run from him last night—but she'd also kissed him back. Did she still find him attractive, or was that special something between them only on his part? He couldn't decide, but he wasn't giving up without a fight.

Diving a few feet down the sea cliffs, Kaia looked like a mermaid with her long hair flowing out behind her. Kaia smiled at her from behind her mask, and Leia smiled back. Maybe having Kaia here would help ease the strain between her and Bane. Ajax had on his miniature diving gear, and he would stay close to Kaia.

Emitting her little sounds, Nani's gray body cut through the water around Kaia like a torpedo. Ajax was more awkward, but his enjoyment could be seen through the mask. Leia reached out and grabbed the dolphin's dorsal fin as she zoomed close. Nani slowed and pulled her through the water. The warm rush of silken water through her hair and over her face brought a feeling of euphoria.

Leia had never swum with a dolphin before. Seeing the intelligence and humor in Nani's eyes was like looking into the face of a close friend. Leia ran her gloved hands over the dolphin's body in a last caress, then turned to examine the crack Bane was pointing out. She was sure it wasn't there the last time she dived here. She looked around to get her bearings and recognized the cave to her left and the mound of coral growing here. This was the place. But there had been no large crack, and wasn't there more seafloor?

She swam to the edge of the abyss and looked down. The sharp drop-off intrigued her, and she squinted through her mask at the area below her. A bed of seaweed caught her attention. Was that *Hypnea musciformis?* The rogue seaweed had been introduced to Hawai'i over thirty years ago and spread rampantly. All divers in Moloka'i were asked to be on the lookout for it and to report any outbreaks here. She motioned to Nani. The dolphin approached, and Leia grabbed hold of Nani's dorsal fin again. She jabbed her thumb down, and the dolphin flipped her tail and dove. The water rushed past Leia's ears, and she felt a terrifying sense of vertigo. She checked her dive computer and saw she was nearly to two hundred feet. The seaweed was right in front of her. It looked like the *Hypnea musciformis.*

Leia released Nani and clipped a bit of the seaweed to take back. She was too deep and knew she had to get back to a more shallow depth, but the coral formations here entranced her. To avoid nitrogen narcosis, she inhaled and exhaled slowly and paid attention to her surroundings. The underwater sea cliffs continued down as far as she could see. There was no bottom here. But there was an interesting ledge that jutted out. She floated just above it. The ledge was nearly as long as a football field and about a hundred feet wide. It held the most beautiful coral garden she'd ever seen. Lobe coral massed against the back sea cliff, and red cauliflower coral grew in profusion. The fish in the area had found it too, as schools of bright yellow tangs and striped butterfly fish darted around her.

She stared with a sense of wonder and growing euphoria. A peacock grouper, speckled in bright blue, swam close to take a look at her. The fish seemed to glow with iridescent colors. She wanted to reach out and touch it. If only she could live down here among this beauty. She realized she was grinning hugely when an explosion of bubbles escaped her mouthpiece. She clamped her teeth back down on her mouthpiece, but her lips felt numb. Leia knew she should go back up. The others didn't know where she'd gone, but she didn't want to leave. This place was magical.

Her gaze swept the ledge, and she saw the outline of what looked like the hull of a boat. The beauty of it dazzled her even more. Could she have found the galleon they were looking for? She should go up and get Bane, but she couldn't bring herself to leave. She tried to read on her dive computer, but she found it hard to focus her eyes. Only gradually did she become aware that her ears were ringing, and the sense of euphoria began to slip. She was narced, she realized sluggishly. Nitrogen narcosis. She needed to surface, but her muscles didn't want to obey.

Nani bumped her nostrum against her hand, and Leia managed to fasten her gaze on the dolphin. She told herself to grab hold, and she reached out with numb fingers. Had she managed to grab Nani? Yes, there was the resilient stability of the dolphin's body. She wrapped her fingers around the dolphin's fin, and Nani began to pull her up. Were they going too fast? Leia couldn't tell. She watched the sea cliffs move past as in a kaleidoscope. She could only trust the dolphin.

They reached the top of the drop-off. Leia paused to try to get her bearings, but her brain still wasn't thinking clearly. It would take a while for the narcosis to wear off. Nani pulled her toward Bane and Kaia. They were separated by about forty feet and seemed to be looking around. Probably for her, she realized with a dull sense of shame. They were both going to scold her when they got to the top. And she deserved it. She'd broken a cardinal rule of diving by going off alone. She hadn't realized how quickly she could become narced. If not for Nani, she would probably have died down there. She could only thank God he'd kept the dolphin close.

Bane turned and saw her, and even from this distance, she could see the rigidity in his body relax. An explosion of bubbles escaped from his mouth, and she knew she was in for it. The way she felt right now, she would welcome a chewing out. At least it meant she was alive to hear it.

*E*va dragged the *he'e holua* sled behind her on the grass. It was heavier than it looked. She'd watched *Makua* show it to clients. He stood and balanced on it as it raced down a slope. She hoped Hotshot wasn't going to take up the sport. Her father said it was very dangerous, and she didn't want anything to happen to her new friend.

His car was waiting where he'd said it would be—in the alley behind the drugstore. He got out to help her when he saw her lugging the sled. "I didn't realize it was quite so big. That's a real beauty." He ran his hands over the lines of the sled, then turned it upside down and examined the rail.

"My father makes the great lava sleds." She knew this because newspapers called all the time. "The only one who makes better sleds is Tom Stone. This is *Makua's* personal one, but he never uses it."

Hotshot pulled on pieces of it, but they didn't move. The sled was one solid piece. "You're right, it's a beauty. I hear Tom Stone makes secret compartments on his sleds for wallets and keys and stuff. Does your dad do that?"

"No." Why did he look disappointed? Did he think it should be bigger? It would be hard to balance on such a narrow thing. She didn't think she could do it. "I have to get it back before my dad gets back. He went to get his hair cut. I wasn't supposed to go anywhere."

"I could take you part of the way home. You brought this a long way. I should have met you closer to your house."

She knew he was ashamed to be seen with her, but that was okay. Lots of people didn't like her to hang around. At least Hotshot wanted to be her friend. She'd told her best friend, Lani, about Hotshot, and Lani hadn't believed her, even when she'd shown her the pocketknife. They weren't talking right now. Lani should know Eva didn't lie. Maybe she'd ask Hotshot if they could meet Lani for a shave ice. Then they could be friends again. Before she could ask him, he looked around like he was afraid someone was watching.

"You didn't tell anyone about me, did you?"

She couldn't lie. "Just my best friend, Lani." As he began to scowl, she hurried to explain. "It's okay, she didn't believe me anyway."

He grabbed her arm. "What did you tell her?"

"Just that I had a friend named Hotshot who was a man and not a little kid. And that you gave me a pocketknife." She forced herself not to cry out, but her arm hurt.

"Such a silly name for me."

He let go. He was smiling again, and Eva found she could breathe. "All the kids call you that. It's because of what a hotshot you are in basketball."

"Do you even know my real name?"

She searched her memory. She'd heard it once, but it eluded her. "I can't remember," she said, hanging her head.

"That's okay, Eva. It's better that way."

Eleven

Leia still shivered on the deck of the research boat, even though Bane had wrapped a thin blanket around her shoulders. She couldn't stop her teeth from chattering, though the salt-laden trade wind was warm.

Bane paced the deck in front of her as she huddled on the bench. His short black hair, as thick as fountain grass, still held droplets of water. He barked orders at the staff preparing the small manned sub. Leia could see the tension in his shoulders. "I'm sorry," she said. "I know going off by myself was stupid. I won't do it again, okay?"

Before he could answer, the roar of a small speedboat caught his attention. Bane turned to face the water, his hand shading his eyes. "It's Pete Kone. I wonder what he wants?"

With the blanket still around her shoulders, Leia stood and joined him at the railing. "Be nice," she murmured.

"I'm always nice to Pete, except when he beats me."

Pete's boat reached the larger craft. He cut the engine and threw a rope to Bane, who caught it with one hand and tied it up. Pete clambered aboard. Dressed in shorts and a green aloha shirt, he wasn't smiling. Leia wondered if the bones he'd found had been identified.

Bane lifted his hand in greeting. "Hey, Pete, what's up?"

"You all need to stop whatever you're doing." He thrust a paper at Bane, who took it and began to read.

"We're just looking for an old sunken ship."

"You remember the bones that washed up on shore? The OHA

asked the courts for an injunction to stop any excavation until we determine if this is the site of Hawaiian burials."

The Office of Hawaiian Affairs fiercely protected the Hawaiian culture and its artifacts. "They must be sure the bones are Hawaiian," Leia said.

Bane balled up the paper and tossed it to the deck. "There are no native Hawaiians buried out here. We're looking for a Spanish galleon."

"That may be what you're looking for, but there's more than that out here. The bones belong to a Hawaiian chieftain."

"How do you know that?" Leia strove to keep her voice calm and even. She narrowed her eyes in a warning gaze at Bane. *Let me handle him*, her gaze told him.

"We had an expert on Hawaiian history look at the *lā'au pālau* that was found with the bones. He confirmed the club dated from at least as far back as 1850."

Bane huffed, but his voice stayed calm. "How does he suppose it survived all that time underwater?"

Pete hesitated. "We're not sure about that yet, but we'll figure it out. In the meantime, you all have to move away from this area."

"I just found the galleon," Leia said. If Pete would listen to anyone, it would be her. "It can't have anything to do with your site because it's about two hundred feet down on a shelf. Any surge across the shelf would just send things into the abyss, so the remains can't be from the area where we'll be digging."

Pete's lips softened. "You actually did it. Too bad Tony isn't here to see the day." He rubbed his forehead. "I'm sorry, but it doesn't change anything. We can't take the chance. This is really important, Leia. Surely you see that. You too, Bane."

Bane spoke up. "I understand that, but we're not harming the bones. There have been earthquakes in the area. The ship's location is precarious. We may not have much time." Bane leaned against the rail. "How about if we compromise? We won't go down unless there is an OHA diver along. He can watch what we're doing and make sure we're not hauling out any Hawaiian artifacts. Doing anything to harm our heritage is the last thing we'd want to do. You know that, Pete. It's important to us too."

Pete began to shake his head. "Your boss is out to make money, not preserve Hawaiian artifacts. If you two were the only ones involved, it might be different. We're friends, guys, and I don't want to be the bad guy here, but I just can't risk it."

Bane held out his hand. "Pete, you have my word. We'll watch the site carefully. The galleon is part of Hawaii's history too."

Pete gripped Bane's hand. "I don't want to argue with you, Bane. The OHA has already filed, and the court has issued a stop-work order. I'm sorry."

"Can we go down in the sub and just look at it?"

Pete sighed and shrugged. "As long as that's all you do. No diving or excavation." He managed a smile. "You ready for the competition, Bane? I'm going to win this time. I've got a real honey of a new ukulele."

"You just might do that. I haven't had much time to practice."

"Don't try to waffle about it now—when I beat you, I want the full glory." This time Pete's grin was full-blown.

Bane grinned too. "I think I'd better get to practicing."

Leia would never understand men. How could they be at each other's throats over the dive and then turn around and joke about a competition? She watched Pete turn and go back down the ladder to his boat. Moments later, his engine roared to life, and he putted away with a careless wave at them.

Bane gave a heavy sigh. "I don't know how I'm going to break this news to Ron."

The boss was in the equipment room charting the next step. "We'd better tell him."

Kaia held up her hands. "You two are on your own."

"Coward," Leia said.

Dangerous Depths

"You bet. I hate shouting." Kaia shuddered, then grinned.

Bane scooped up the wadded paper and went toward the door. Leia followed Bane and Ajax to the equipment room. The odor of electronic equipment burned her eyes. This room needed more ventilation. Ron was sitting absorbed in front of a twenty-one-inch flat-screen monitor. He didn't seem to notice they'd stepped into the room. Another technician sat at a different screen.

"We've got trouble, boss." Bane spread out the crinkled notice. "Read it and weep."

"What's this?" Ron frowned, then his gaze finally left the monitor. His gaze skimmed the top of the paper. "From OHA?" He smoothed the paper and began to read. His next breath was a quick intake. "They can't do this!"

"I think they just did."

Ron stood and paced the small room. "We have to figure out a way around this. We're so close. Our luck so far hasn't been good. First the plane sabotage, and now this."

"Speaking of the sabotage, what's the status of that?" Bane asked.

Ron shrugged. "We can't prove who did it, though we both know it was Westerfield. Since there's nothing we can do about it, I'm just having the equipment dried out and rebuilt." He began to reread the notice Bane handed him. He made a sound of disgust.

"We can appeal the decision," Leia pointed out.

Ron shook his head. "And we will, but with the earthquakes, I doubt we have much time. We need to get on it right away." He tossed the paper into the chair he'd vacated. "We'll just pull away from this site. It will take them time to gather together divers for a proper expedition. We can take the minisub in from a distance, get out and do our work, then leave undetected."

Bane frowned. "We'd be breaking the law. I'm not cool with that. Pete said we could take the minisub down to take a look, but no excavation." Leia could see from the glower on Ron's face that he wasn't happy with that option. "I care about our heritage too,

Ron. If there's a chance a Hawaiian burial site is down there, I'm not going to disturb it."

Ron slammed his hand against the doorjamb. "There has to be a way! I'm not getting this close to lose it all now."

"Let me try to talk to Pete again," Leia offered. "I have a feeling he was just the messenger and wasn't totally behind this ruling. We just have to be careful."

"That will take time too. In the meantime, we're going down there." Ron set his jaw and went back to his computer. "We're about ready to dive. Is the minisub in the water?"

"Yeah." Bane joined him at the monitor. "You see anything?"

"Yeah, I see what she said. It's as clear as rain once I knew where to look." Ron's finger circled the anomaly on the screen. "It's right here." He glanced back at Leia. "Good work, Leia. We never would have found it."

"I don't think I'm ready to go down again," Leia said. She clasped her hands on her forearms.

"We don't expect you to," Ron said with an airy wave of his hand. "The sub only holds two men. Bane and I will take a look to see how we can best handle the excavation. It's too late to do much work right now."

Bane shot her a quick look. "We can only look, Ron. No excavation without permission. We're not going to break the law." Ron grunted but didn't answer.

"I'll get dressed and go see Pete after you're back up," Leia said. "It can't hurt to try again." She saw the displeasure on Bane's face. She tilted her chin up and stared him down. He had no claims on her.

*B*ane barely registered the hiss of air above his head, but his tongue noticed the stale, canned taste of it. He maneuvered the controls of the minisub and peered through the window at the surreal world outside. The dying light barely penetrated at this depth, but the bright headlamps of the sub picked out the details: an octopus uncoiled its arms from a rock and zoomed away in a spray of ink, a puffer fish peered in the window at them then lumbered away, and a hammerhead shark cruised its terrain.

Ron fiddled with his screen settings, and the picture from the camera mounted outside zoomed into focus. Bane was too busy handling the sub to see what the camera was picking up, but he heard Ron whistle. "What is it?" he asked.

Ron jabbed a finger at the screen. "There she is!"

Bane saw it then and caught his breath. A Spanish galleon, the stuff of dreams and legends. Coral encased her, but it only showed more clearly the shape of her bow, and the way her masts had broken and fallen as she'd sunk. God was good to let him see this in his lifetime.

Ron leaned closer to the screen and studied the image. "Can you deploy the shovel?"

"No excavation, Ron."

"Get out of the way." Ron shouldered him aside. He fiddled with the controls, and the mechanical shovel extended from the sub. It had five claws to take samples of the seabed and was about a foot wide. He maneuvered it to the man-made reef and then plunged it through lobe coral and into the dirt.

"Careful! We don't want to harm the galleon or the coral. I think you should stop. This is stupid." When Ron didn't answer, Bane leaned forward and watched the claw pick up some samples. Ron retracted the arm and deposited the sample in the hold, then got the equipment into place again for another go. He moved the claw back and forth for nearly an hour, picking up samples from all over the reef. More and more night predators began to come out: sharks, barracuda, squid, moray eels. The water was alive with hungry marine life looking for prey. At least he was inside, away from the daily cycle of life and death playing out in front of him.

Ron stood and stretched. "That's enough for now. I'm eager to see what we've got. Let's surface and take a look."

"Aye, aye, Captain." Bane adjusted the controls, and the sub began to rise. An inquisitive tiger shark followed the sub as it surfaced. The sub bobbed to the top of the waves about fifty feet from the ship. A few minutes later, they heard the clang of the winch retrieving the sub, then they rose alongside the boat. Moments later, a crewman rapped on the window, and Bane released the pressure and opened the door. The fresh air tasted great.

Leia and Kaia were waiting outside. Leia had a bottle of water for each of them in her hands. She handed it to them as they stepped onto the deck. "I'm usually parched after a ride in that dry air."

"*Mahalo.*" Bane accepted the water and uncapped it, then took a long swig. The cold, wet liquid soothed his dry throat.

"Did you find it?" Leia's voice was a little too casual.

"You weren't narced as badly as we thought. We found what you did. You found it. Ron got some samples." Her smile beamed, and he looked away, nodding toward the men unloading the cargo from the vessel. "Let's see what we've got."

"It's nearly eight o'clock. Aren't you hungry?" Kaia demanded. "I'm starved."

"The whole thing has turned my stomach."

The women followed Bane and Ron to the trays that held their illegal booty. "Get me a sieve," Ron ordered Logan.

The technician nodded and went below. He came back a few minutes later with a large sieve, two feet square. Ron took it and the small shovel the man had brought him and began to move the dripping-wet mixture onto the sieve. Bane took it, and with great care, began to sift the debris into buckets. He frowned when two round, encrusted objects lay open to his gaze. He picked one up and rubbed it. Caked-on mud began to loosen, and the round, flat object looked familiar.

"It's a gold doubloon," Ron murmured. He picked it out of Bane's palm. "We've found her for sure."

Twelve

Darkness blanketed the water, but moonlight glimmered on the whitecaps. Leia left the research vessel behind and aimed her boat toward the lights along the quay. Even though it was late, Pete would likely be jogging along the shore. He ran every evening about this time.

She had docked the boat and started toward the town lights when she saw Pete's familiar form running toward her. "Pete, is that you?" she called. The figure slowed, and the man raised his hand. The restaurant lights illuminated his face, and she relaxed when she saw he was smiling.

"You're just getting back?" he asked.

"They took the sub down. I waited until they got back. It's there, Pete. Look." She showed him one of the gold doubloons.

He picked it up and turned it over in his fingers. "I never would have guessed it would actually be found. You're sure?"

"This proves it."

He looked up with a frown. "I told Bane there was to be no excavation. How did they get this?"

Too late she realized her error, but she wasn't going to lie to him. "They found it down on the shelf I told you about. They didn't disturb anything."

"We can't take any chances, Leia. The possibility of an ancient burial site is big—huge. If I'm right, this could be as big as the Kawaihae Cave discovery on the Big Island."

"And your ticket to fame," she said.

His smile faded. "That's hardly fair. You've always been with me on the importance of preserving our culture. Since when did money get to be so important to you?"

"I don't care abut the money," she protested. "The shipwreck is part of our culture too. Our culture didn't end when the Europeans came."

"It was the beginning of the end."

The slap at her own heritage made her straighten. "All cultures have a part in what the islands became. Look at me—I'm a mongrel myself. Most people who call themselves Hawaiian have mixed blood. Even you, Pete. You've got some Japanese blood in your lineage. We can't discard part of what makes us Hawaiian."

He flushed and looked away. "I didn't mean to sound so judgmental. Look, let's not argue. This will all work out. Be patient."

"I'd like you to see if you can withdraw the injunction. There's a cave down there. That's probably where your artifacts are located. This ledge where we found the ship has nothing to do with your site. Please trust me."

"It's not in my hands."

She stopped and put her hand on his arm. "I'm going to be too busy to teach for a few days."

"Why? You can't dive on the wreck. I have nearly fifteen students lined up for you next week. Will you be back by then?"

"I don't know." She tried not to let his impatient tone bother her. She wasn't his employee. "I want to help Candace, and I have some personal business to take care of."

"Let me know if you're going to make it back in time. If you can't do the class, I'll see if I can get someone to take your place, if you'll give me the key to your house."

Everything in her tightened. He was acting like he was in charge. It was her house, her life. "I don't loan out my supplies. Whoever you find will have to use their own facilities."

"What's got into you? I thought this was important to you."

"It is. But people are more important than even our heritage. Candace needs me."

"I really need to use your shop, Leia. You have the supplies, and there's nowhere else to take the kids. Would you disappoint the children because you're mad at me?

Leia sighed. Maybe he had a point. The kids loved to come. She dug in her purse for her key. "Here. Just don't let them mess up my stuff." Lifting her hand, she walked away before he could say anything that made her regret giving him the key.

She found her car in the lot and drove to her parents' house. Her mother's car, a Buick Park Avenue that had replaced the Lexus her mother loved, was parked in the driveway. Leia pulled her Neon behind her mother's car and shut off the engine. Lights shone through the sweeping expanse of windows that looked out on the water. Though they'd had to downsize the house and move off the beach after *Makua* lost his job, her mother had insisted on still living where she could see the water. Ingrid would notice the lights of her car and wonder why she wasn't coming in, but Leia couldn't seem to force herself to move. The encounter would be about as pleasant as a meeting with a hungry tiger shark.

A shadow moved, then lingered at the window. She'd been spotted. She had to go in now. The door was unlocked, as usual, so she opened it and stepped inside. Though the house was a step down from the mansion on the beach her parents had sold a year ago, this house still didn't have the homey feel of the cottage in the jungle where Leia and her sister had grown up. She walked through the tiled hallway, past walls that matched the color of the floors. Her mother preferred the stark look of bare walls. Minimalist, she called it. Cold and unwelcoming, Leia dubbed it. She found her mother in the living room. Done in shades of gray, the room always made Leia shiver, even with all the lamps shining. The room's furniture had no sloping, comfortable lines, just sharp, boxy edges that looked stiff and uninviting.

Her mother put down the magazine she was reading, a crisp copy of *Architectural Digest*. She narrowed her eyes. "I was beginning to think you weren't coming in."

Leia glanced around. "Where's Eva?"

"I sent her to bed early. She didn't come right home from work today. Let me tell your father you're here. He's still in the shop." Ingrid rose in a graceful motion and went to the intercom on the wall. "Akoni, Leia is here."

Leia's father's voice blared back through the speakers. "I'll be right there." Leia warmed at the pleasure in her father's voice. She needed him here. He would be her support, even if he wasn't sure what the right course of action should be.

"Want some mango tea?"

Leia shook her head. "Later. I haven't eaten yet." She heard her father's heavy tread in the hall and tried not to show her relief. Sometimes when she looked at her mother, she felt the same way she did when she was praying—unworthy, and hopeless of making anyone proud. The difference was that she knew God loved her in spite of her failings. She wasn't so sure about her mother. Malia said Ingrid wasn't capable of love. Maybe she was right, though Ingrid showed love in other ways. The car parked outside was a gift from her mother, and the boat she used had been bought with her mother's money. Leia had accepted it all, so what did that make her?

"Makua." Leia went to hug her father. At nearly six feet tall to his five feet nine, she towered over him just as her mother did. But he was bulky, and his massive arms squashed her to his barrel chest. She inhaled the scent of him: a mixture of wood dust, coconut, and spicy cologne. He made her feel safe and protected. He'd give his life for her, and she knew it.

"Where have you been? You've been neglecting your old man."

She kissed his cheek, then wiped away the *'ohi'a* dust that had transferred from his whiskers to her nose. Since his dishonor, he'd taken up building sleds for the ancient Hawaiian sport of *he'e holua,* or lava sledding. The sport wasn't popular yet, but he believed it would be. She'd watched a competition once, but the men racing down a hardened lava slope at breakneck speed on something that looked like a ladder lashed together with coconut fiber terrified her. She kept imagining what they'd look like if they fell onto the lava at that speed. Leia thought he buried himself in the woodshop to avoid facing the censure among the islanders.

"I've been a bad daughter." She released him and stepped back. "I spent the night with Candace last night. She had a little too much to drink."

"You're a perfect daughter." He started to sit on the pale gray damask armchair, then intercepted a pointed glance from his wife directed at his dirty clothing. Selecting a wooden rocker he'd built instead, he leaned back and propped one leg on the other.

"Candace was drinking?" Her mother's voice was stiff with disapproval. "I thought she was pregnant."

"She is. I scolded her this morning and gave her some homeopathics to counteract the hangover. She promised not to do it again. She's hurting."

"That's no excuse. She increases her chances of giving birth to a child with a birth defect. I hope you, of all people, impressed on her the importance of abstaining."

"I did, yes." Leia managed to keep her hand from wandering to the scar on her lip, but she felt her mother's gaze touch it.

"Where have you been all evening?" her father asked.

"I took some time off to dive with Bane, but we're held up by an injunction OHA has slapped on us. I went to see Pete to try to sort it out, but he wouldn't budge. I finally gave up since I had something pressing to talk to you both about."

"Oh?" Her mother took a sip of her mango iced tea. "That sounds rather ominous."

Leia wet her lips. "It's about *Tûtû*. She's been very confused lately, as I'm sure you know."

"I know." Her father moved his head in a weary wag. "I think she's getting worse."

"I'm sure of it too." Leia glanced at her mother, then back to her father's face. "I think she shouldn't be living alone any longer. Something has to be done."

Her father plucked a strip of coconut twine from his shorts. "I don't want to move her into a home."

Leia kept her gaze on her father. "I had another idea. I'm going to move in with her."

"You will do no such thing!" Her mother stood and put her glass of tea on the glass-topped table. "I blame your grandmother for your ridiculous obsession with that paper cloth and for throwing away your career. Paper cloth! Is there anything less relevant to real life?"

Leia wondered if her mother might be jealous of the closeness Leia shared with her grandmother. She rejected the idea. Her mother always seemed so self-sufficient, jealousy didn't seem possible. "You're consumed by your work as well."

"I'm not consumed, I'm merely interested. I can leave it at my office. You put in way too many hours at that little clinic for a pittance, and then spend your off time working on an outdated hobby. You'll never have anything at this rate." Ingrid's voice softened. "I want only what's best for you, Leia. You have your head so up in the clouds that you never seem to see the chasms yawning under your feet. As your mother, it's my duty to protect you. I can't let you do this. I'll begin to look for a place for her."

Leia shook her head. "I'm going to try it for a few weeks and see how it goes. Malia said she would stay with Tûtû during the day when I'm gone. At some point, we likely will have no choice but to put her in a nursing home for her own safety, but she's not bad enough yet."

"I don't like it. Ipo will just require more and more of your time. You'll never break free." Ingrid clasped her hands together. Her gaze went past Leia, and she frowned. "Eva, you're supposed to be in bed."

Leia turned to see her sister. She had her fingers in her mouth and was humming. "Aloha, *keiki*. I've missed you."

Eva took her fingers out of her mouth. Her eyes were huge in her face. "Don't go in your shop, Leia. I dreamed it was broken."

"Broken?" Leia tried not to smile. "You mean the roof or what?"

Eva's forehead wrinkled. "I don't remember. But it was scary. I don't want you to go there."

"I'm sure it's fine. Want me to read you a story before you go back to sleep?"

Eva began to smile, and she nodded. "Will you read *Green Eggs and Ham*?"

"Okay. You go on up, and I'll be right there," Leia told her. She ran from the room, and Leia turned back to her mother. She wet her lips. "There's something else I need to talk to you about. This involves you, Mama."

Her mother sat back down slowly on the edge of the chair. "All right, I'm listening."

"Have the police been to see you about Tony's death?"

Her mother's eyes widened. "Whatever for? I didn't even know he'd died until Eva told me. Why would you think they'd be coming to see me?"

"Yesterday after Koma was killed, Detective Ono asked me how well you knew Tony. They suspect he was injected with a narcotic that depressed his breathing. And some narcotics are missing from the hospital."

Her mother didn't say anything at first. She took a sip of her tea. "So that explains why there was an inventory of the controlled substances."

Her mother was handling it better than Leia had thought she would. "Ono asked if I'd ever heard you and Tony fighting."

"I suppose you told him about the disagreement we had over the lease on the building." Her mother gave a heavy sigh. "Really, Leia, you should learn to hold your tongue. I'm sure he'll be around to see me."

"I didn't tell him. I'd forgotten." In fact, Leia hadn't even remembered her mother owned the building Tony leased for his shop. They'd argued over her mother's decision to raise the rent, and the disagreement had gotten heated.

Her mother began to smile. "You're a good daughter. The last thing I need is for my patients to hear that I'm under suspicion for murder. It would be the final death knell for my practice." The glance she sent toward her husband held a trace of censure.

Her father interrupted. "No one who knows you would suspect you of killing anyone."

Her mother's frosty smile thawed. "Spoken like a devoted husband. Maybe I'll fix you a good dinner after all."

"How easy would it be for someone to steal the drugs?" her father asked.

"Very difficult. Access is limited and everything has to be signed for. We track inventory on the computer and then do a periodic visual check. It would have to be someone who worked at the hospital."

Leia tried to think of everyone who worked at the hospital that she knew. She couldn't see any of them doing something like this. "Maybe even an orderly who got access to a key?"

"Maybe, but we watch that kind of thing pretty closely. You have to have two people go to get out controlled substances to verify what was taken. Maybe the murderer bought it over the black market."

"Since some is missing from the hospital, I would think it was stolen from there."

"Well, it's not my worry."

In spite of her mother's assertions, Leia could see the unease on her mother's face, and it fueled her own anxiety. Surely the police wouldn't focus on her mother.

After diving with Kaia and Nani all day, Bane took Kaia to Kaunakakai so she could call Jesse without using up her cell minutes. He sat on a lava rock on the beach with his ukulele in his hands. His fingers picked out the traditional tunes without conscious thought. While he might not beat Pete this year, he would give him a run for his money.

A host of giggling children ran past. One boy around six stopped to listen to Bane. Bane motioned him to come closer and showed him how to strum the instrument. When the boy tired of the game, Bane ruffled the child's hair and gave him a handful of macadamia nuts. He watched wistfully as the child ran off with his booty clutched in his pudgy fist. Kids generally gravitated to him, and he thought he'd make a good father. At least he liked to think that was true. He might never find out.

He stopped by a small hut and ordered a rainbow shave ice with macadamia-nut ice cream on the bottom. Taking the treat with him, he started toward his car, then noticed a van that said Westerfield Salvage on it. Sam was here? Maybe Ron wasn't so paranoid after all. Bane stepped closer to the van. He'd met Sam Westerfield once, before taking the job with Ron. He couldn't be missed in a crowd. He resembled Mr. T, only instead of heavy gold chains, the leather necklace he wore held a mammoth shark tooth, which nestled in the *V* of his aloha shirt. Matching shorts covered his meaty thighs, and he would have looked more at home on a wrestling mat than strolling across the parking lot of a Hawaiian beach.

His gaze touched Bane. "Bane Oana. I wasn't expecting to see you here."

"Sam. I didn't know you were on the island." He kept his tone even. No sense in getting Westerfield's back up.

"Yeah, I got to town yesterday. I hear there's an interesting find out near Elephant Rock." He grinned and revealed a gold-capped tooth.

"You're a little late to get in on the action. We already have salvage rights."

"I heard there's been a snafu. Maybe I could help smooth the way if you cut me in on the action."

"I think we can handle it."

Sam's smile faded, and he looked sour. "This is too big a find for Ron to handle by himself. I have the heavy equipment he needs."

"We have our own equipment, *mahalo*. Why are you talking to me anyway? Ron is the owner. I'm not the one to ask."

"But you have influence over him. You could persuade him of the wisdom of letting me help you."

Bane's shave ice was melting. Enough of Sam's hypocrisy. "Sorry, I can't help you," he said. He walked away and tried not to imagine a knife thrust in his back.

Thirteen

The boat passed by the Moloka'i Lighthouse on the tip of the peninsula, framed by the soaring sea cliffs. The tallest U.S.-owned lighthouse in the Pacific, the sight of the grand beacon never failed to thrill Leia. The sea glimmered as blue as lapis lazuli in the bright morning sunshine. The boat passed the boundary of the Pelekunu Preserve. The lowland rain forest held a mystique for her. For one thing, access was forbidden, and she'd never taken well to anyone telling her what she couldn't do. It also held one of Hawai'i's last free-flowing streams, and the tallest sea cliffs in the world.

She enjoyed a last look at the jungle, then headed in to shore. She checked in at the clinic and made sure she wasn't needed, then went toward her cottage. Pete had called and said he left her key under the pot of ginger by the front door. It was right where he'd said it would be. She pushed open the door and stopped. The place was a mess. Bottles of dye had been spilled on her work table and onto the floor, her cupboard doors stood open, and all kinds of supplies were off the shelves and on the floor.

She marched to the phone and punched in Pete's number. As soon as he answered, she didn't even say *aloha.* "The least you could have done is not let the kids trash my house," she barked.

"Leia? What are you talking about?"

"My cottage. It's a disaster, Pete. How could you leave it in this shape?" Her voice rose.

"It was spotless when we left. I know how picky you are."

"There's dye everywhere. Nearly everything is off the shelves. I hardly call that spotless."

"I didn't leave it like that. Maybe someone broke in."

That stopped her. It was possible with all that had been going on. "Maybe," she said.

"You shouldn't jump to conclusions, Leia." Pete's voice was sharp.

"Sorry, Pete."

"You can make it up to me. I want to show you something. Will you be there for a while?"

"Just long enough to clean up, then I'm going to my grandmother's."

"If you're not at home, I'll come find you there. You won't believe it." He sounded excited.

She hung up, opened the door to let Hina in, and set to work. An hour later, she had everything in order. She packed a small bag, found her sketchbook, and took the motorbike to her grandmother's.

She heard *Tûtû* before she saw her. The strains of "Makaha" carried through the jungle. The incongruity of her grandmother singing a surfing song made her recall that *Tûtû* was young once. The songs she sang reminded her of the days when she was as slim and lovely as Malia and just as graceful. Leia pushed away the pang of sadness. She grabbed a bag of *'ohelo* berries she'd brought for the goose, then opened the door and got out. Pua waddled to meet her, and Hina jumped down. Pua nipped at the cat's tail, and Hina spat at the goose. The two had an uneasy truce that wasn't always respected.

Squawking for a treat, the *nene* bumped her head against Leia's leg. "I didn't forget you." Leia dumped some berries in her palm and extended her hand to Pua. The goose honked, then gobbled up the berries. She looked up as if to ask if there were any more. "That's it, girl. You're on your own now." Pua followed Leia as she moved away from the cycle. "You have to stay out here," she said, patting the goose a final time.

Pua hissed, and Leia drew back her fingers. The temperamental *nene* had never nipped her, but she was taking no chances. "See if I bring you anything again." She left Pua at the edge of the driveway voicing her displeasure, then joined her grandmother in the garden. She kissed *Tūtū's* soft, wrinkled cheek, but the older woman continued to sing without looking up. Her grandmother wore earmuffs and a bathing suit.

Leia sighed. She might as well unpack. Once she was occupying the spare room, her grandmother wouldn't kick her out. Maybe she would be lucid again, and Leia would be able to coax her into putting on some clothes. She went to her cycle to get her suitcase. A pickup truck pulled in behind her. She shielded her eyes with her hand and recognized Bane's thick, dark hair on the passenger side. Something inside her leaped in response, but she squelched it.

He thanked the Kalaupapa resident who'd given him a ride, held the door open for Ajax, then slammed the door behind him. Leia raised her hand in greeting. "Aloha," she said.

"Kaia was a little tired after diving today, so I dropped her off back at the ship to rest for a while and decided to come check on you." He glanced toward her grandmother. "She's bad today. Can I do anything?" The dog whined and leaned against his leg.

Her eyes stung at the sympathy in his voice. "I don't think there's anything anyone can do. She'll come out of it soon."

He took her suitcase from her. "Are you sure this is wise?"

"I'm worried about her. If we're not careful, she's going to wander off into the Pelekunu Preserve and never be seen again." She nodded to the edge of the encroaching jungle. "I'd be happier if we could get her to leave here, but she won't go without a fight." Hawaiians revered their elderly. The thought of forcing her grandmother into a home made Leia shudder.

Before Bane could answer, a tan SUV pulled up to the edge of the driveway and parked. Pete got out carrying a small box. He wore a blue shirt that said WELA KA HOA!, which meant "Strike while the iron is hot." His smile faltered when he saw Bane, but he quickly recovered and approached them. "Aloha," he said, raising his hand. "I was told I could find you here." He rubbed Ajax's ears, and the dog groveled.

"Ajax, you traitor," Bane said, but he was smiling.

Leia nodded toward the box in Pete's hands. "Hey, Pete. What you got there?" Pua waddled to meet Pete, craning her neck to see what he carried. He stepped around the goose, but she scurried after him. "Pua is wondering if you've brought her some fruit."

Pete's smile widened. "I found this *kapa* cloth in my grand-mother's attic, and I wondered what you could tell me about it." He extended the box to her.

Leia took the box and caught her breath. "It's gorgeous." She carried the box to the picnic table where her grandmother sat singing. Setting it down, she carefully lifted the precious cloth from the box, and the aroma of sandalwood and plumeria embedded in the cloth drifted to her nose. Whoever had made this beautiful piece was a *kupuna* of the art that Leia was still trying to learn. The golden-rod and black colors were still vibrant on the snow-white cloth. There were a few blemishes because of the age, but it was still lovely.

She ran her hand over the soft cloth. "I think it's a ceremonial robe. Look at the *Ukanipo*—the shark god—design. This is a real treasure." *Kapa* cloth was highly prized and was still even used for bartering. She suppressed her own covetous thoughts.

"How much do you suppose it's worth? I know it's damaged." Pete touched a hole in the fabric.

"Several thousand dollars at least." Leia put her hand over the hole. "This is not much damage considering the age. It's lovely."

Her grandmother stopped singing. She reached out to touch the beautiful cloth. "That reminds me, I still haven't found my great-grandmother's *kapa* bedcovering. You must see it, Leia."

Her grandmother had never mentioned any *kapa* bedcovering before. Was she still befuddled? Leia took her grandmother's hand and thanked God that the clouds had lifted. Smiling with relief, she pressed her lips to her grandmother's hand. "Aloha, *Tûtû.* I've come to stay with you for a while."

"*A'ole loa!* I can get along just fine on my own." Her grandmother frowned and pulled her hand away. "Your mother can't be happy about this. You belong in her *haole* world, not here."

"I'm not a *haole, Tûtû.*" Leia's gaze met Bane's, and she looked away from the sympathy in his face.

Her grandmother dismissed her words with a wave of her hand. "You've been raised by a *haole,* and you'll always be one. Your father should never have married her. I knew from the first moment I laid eyes on her that she was wrong for my Akoni. He should have married the girl I had picked for him. Beautiful Pela. She came to see me last week, and she's still as lovely."

"Did she?" Leia glanced at Bane and gave a slight shake of her head. Pela had died five years ago.

Her grandmother stood and went to Pete. "Who are you, young man? Are you chasing after my granddaughter? You'd do better to find someone of pure blood."

Leia knew her mouth was dangling, and she shut it. She blinked back tears. Grief swamped her. Her grandmother had been Leia's supporter when she was growing up—she couldn't bear it if the illness changed that. "It's me, *Tûtû.* It's Leia."

"I'm not blind, *keiki.*" Ipo's voice was still sharp.

Pete patted her arm. "I'm a friend of Leia's. The cloth belongs to me. Do you recognize the family pattern?"

"Maybe." *Tûtû* touched the cloth again. "Where is my *kapa* cloth, Leia? Did you steal it while I wasn't looking? I don't want you here. There are too many valuable things in the house. I can't trust you."

Leia looked away from the sympathy she saw in the men's eyes. "You can trust me, *Tûtû.* I wouldn't take anything of yours." Ajax whined and licked her hand.

Her grandmother put her finger to her lips in a shushing

motion. "You're just like your mother. She was always sneaking around here looking for treasures. She talked me out of the little jade whale I loved so much. I didn't want to give it to her, but she kept hammering me until I couldn't think."

Leia knew the figurine her grandmother meant. Her mother loved it. Ipo's eyes filled with tears, and Leia tried to embrace her, but her grandmother waved her away. Leia wanted to run away, to hide her shame from the two men watching, but she couldn't. *Tûtû* needed her—she just didn't know it.

Bane put his arm around Ipo, but she didn't brush him away. Her white head nestled comfortably against Bane's shoulder, and she gave him a coquettish smile. "You remind me of my husband, God rest his soul. What did you say your name was?"

Was she confusing Bane with Pete? Leia exchanged puzzled glances with the men. "You know Bane, *Tûtû*. He and I were engaged once." A wave of heat touched her cheeks when she said the word *engaged*, and Bane's chin jerked up so that his eyes locked with hers. She wondered what he really felt now. Did he care at all, or had all those feelings burned up in their final conflagration?

Her grandmother waggled her finger at Leia. "You *haoles* are flighty. You take after your mother."

"She's not a *haole*, *Tûtû*," Bane said. "She's got more Hawaiian in her than the majority of those who call themselves native. Look at her—she looks like a Hawaiian princess."

Her grandmother snorted. "She's got blue eyes. No Hawaiian ever had blue eyes." She patted Bane's arm. "I want to go inside. Can I lean on your arm? My legs don't seem to want to work right. I need to find that *kapa*."

Leia watched her grandmother walk away still muttering about the cloth. Pete took his box of cloth and beat a hasty retreat. She didn't blame him. What had she gotten herself into? Her grandmother needed more care than Leia could give her. She sighed and followed them.

Ipo leaned heavily on Bane's arm. Her hands gripped his forearm in a hold that was almost painful, and he wondered where she got the strength. The dog trotted after them. "You hurt Leia's feelings, *Tûtû*," he chided.

She paused in the hall and let go of his arm. "I said nothing to the *keiki* but the truth. She's too sensitive."

"She's your granddaughter who loves you and tries to help you in every way she can. You should be ashamed of yourself." Bane knew he shouldn't be talking to an elder so frankly, but seeing the pain in Leia's eyes compelled him. She'd done nothing to warrant her grandmother's censure. "It's not her fault your son married a *haole*. Leia loves her Hawaiian heritage."

"Perhaps you're right." Ipo looked suddenly tired, though her dark eyes sparkled with more alertness than they'd possessed only a few minutes earlier. "I need to find someone to trust," she muttered. "Where's my granddaughter? Where's Leia?"

Maybe she was less clearheaded than he'd thought. He grabbed a bathrobe hanging on a hook on the wall and helped her slip it on. "You can trust Leia. And me. What do you need?"

"I must get the *kapa* to a safe place. It's not safe now." She plucked at her sleeve in a fretful motion.

"Where is the cloth? I'll get it for you." He suspected there was no *kapa*. Leia joined them, and he saw the doubt on her face at her grandmother's mention of the cloth.

They moved on into the living room. Bane stopped and stared. The entire house was topsy-turvy. He gaped at upended drawers, their brightly colored contents juxtaposed against the dull brown carpet. Cushions had been pulled from the sofa and chairs. The doorway to Ipo's bedroom stood open, and he could see more devastation in that room. Through the large archway to the kitchen, he saw cabinet doors ajar. Ajax began to growl, and his hackles raised.

"*Tûtû*, did you do this?" Leia asked, her voice quivering.

"Who has been here?" Ipo demanded. "Or was this your handi-
work, Leia? Are you trying to find the *kapa*?"

"I haven't even been inside, *Tûtû*." Leia walked down the hall.
"Hey, the back door is open. Someone's been in here."

Bane situated Ipo in a chair, then went to join Leia. Muddy
footprints mixed with bits of crushed grass and debris came from
outside and went down the hall, where they disappeared into the
master bedroom. "These weren't made by your grandmother. It
looks like they're about a size 12 man's shoe."

Leia rubbed her arms. "It almost looks like the person was
searching for something. Someone trashed my house too."

"Maybe it's just a series of random break-ins," Bane said. He
and Leia went to her grandmother's bedroom and began to pick up
the clothing dumped on the floor.

The phone rang on Ipo's bedside table, and Leia answered it.
Bane could hear Eva's excited voice through the receiver. Leia spoke
in a soothing voice. "I'm fine, Eva. I know you said not to go to the
cottage. You were right about it being messed up, but I'm okay."
She spoke a little longer to her sister, then hung up. "Eva and her
dreams. She dreamed something happened to my house. Strange,
isn't it?" She began to put things away.

Bane sorted through the discarded clothing. Did Ipo still wear
any of this? The muumuu looked ancient.

"Bane, look at this." Leia was holding a brooch. "It's a diamond-
and-sapphire brooch. Why didn't whoever it was take this? My
mother told me once that it was worth several thousand dollars."

"We'd better call the police before we straighten anything else
up. This is weird." He plucked the phone from his pocket and
dialed 911 to report the break-in. The dispatcher promised to send
out an officer, and Bane hung up.

"There's more, Bane." Leia held out a small teak box with the
lid open to reveal rumpled hundred-dollar bills. "This was in plain
sight with the lid up."

"It seems our intruder was after something specific. I wish we could count on your grandmother to know what was missing."

"In her lucid moments, she would know, but I don't think we can believe anything she says today. We're going to have to figure this out ourselves."

"It's obvious they weren't after cash." He closed the lid of the box and set it on the dresser.

"Could it have anything to do with Koma?" Her eyes widened as her gaze connected with his.

Bane tore himself away before he drowned in her big blue eyes. "What could Koma have to do with it?"

"I may be totally off base, but Koma told me to talk to my *tûtû*. Those were his last words. He said he wanted to show me where the treasure was, but I thought I'd just get another of his stories. What if it wasn't? What if he really knew where it was—and now *tûtû* is the only one who knows? She could be in danger too."

"Leia," Bane began, "this place is isolated, and even if someone drove by, they couldn't see the house for all the trees. No one would hear you if you yelled for help. I think you and your *tûtû* need to go back to your dad's place, at least until we figure out what's going on."

Ipo wandered in as he finished, and she was shaking her head. "I'm not leaving my home. Make him leave me alone, Leia." She covered her face with her hands and began to cry—a pitiful sound that plucked at his heartstrings. He was a sucker for elderly people. Bane sighed. "How about if I stay too? I don't want you two women out here alone."

Ipo didn't seem to hear him. She continued to wail, and Ajax whined. Leia finally went to her grandmother and put her arms around her. Ipo allowed Leia's embrace this time, and Leia managed to calm her. "I'm sure we'll be fine," Leia said to Bane. "You don't have to stay. We're going to the village luau tonight, and there will be lots of people there. My parents are coming too."

"I'm either staying or you're going to your dad's. Those are your only choices." He folded his arms over his chest. "Whoever broke in has no fear. He did it in broad daylight."

"We don't know that. *Tûtû* was so confused earlier, and maybe she awoke to the mess and it disoriented her."

He shook his head. "The mud on the carpet was still wet. Whoever it was, he hasn't been gone long. Your arrival may have frightened him off. Besides, your house was vandalized too." He stood looking down at her and had to resist a powerful impulse to kiss her. She looked so vulnerable, so frightened. No doubt she wouldn't welcome his embrace.

Once Eva talked to Leia and knew she was okay, Eva got out her colored pencils and paper. Her best friend, Lani, looked over her shoulder. Lani was so pretty, with the dark hair Eva had always wanted. She had Down's too, but she was a year older than Eva and sometimes tried to pretend she was smarter. Eva didn't think she was, though she loved Lani just like a sister.

"I'm bored," Lani said. "You said your friend Hotshot might come. He is just made up, isn't he? He's not real."

"The boys told you they play basketball with him." Eva tried not to let her friend bother her. Lani just hadn't seen Hotshot before, and she was jealous. "He's real." Her gaze touched on the woods that lined the park. "There he is!" She jumped to her feet, and her pencils scattered over the grass. She knelt and tried to grab them up, but they kept escaping her thick fingers. If only she had slim, pretty fingers like Leia and Malia instead of these short, stubby things.

Lani stood with her mouth dangling as Hotshot came toward them. He stopped when he saw Lani, and his smile faded. Eva got up from the ground. She didn't want to make him mad, but she wanted her two friends to meet. She stuck her fingers in her mouth, then remembered she wasn't supposed to do that. She pulled her hand down and put it in the pocket of her shorts. "Hi, Hotshot," she said.

He acted like he didn't know her and walked on past her. Tears filled Eva's eyes. "He's mad at me," she said.

"I wouldn't care. He's old," Lani said. "I think he's scary. You shouldn't go anywhere with him."

"He's my friend. He was just mad you were here." Eva resolved to make it up to Hotshot somehow.

fourteen

Her grandmother calmed down as evening fell. "We must go to
the luau," she told Leia and Bane. "I promised Jenny I'd bring
sesame-cabbage salad. I made it yesterday and it's all ready."

Leia had been hoping to talk her grandmother out of the party
in town, but at least the clouds in Ipo's head had parted. She heard
the crunch of tires on gravel outside and looked out the window.
Bane's brother stepped out of the village van that delivered people
to various areas of the peninsula. "Mano is here," she told Bane.

"He thought he'd be in time for the luau." Bane smiled and
went to the door. Ajax began to bark and ran out first.

Leia followed Bane outside as Mano came striding through the
yard. He held the hand of a diminutive Asian girl who wore a smile
that could light up a room. The young woman knelt and threw her
arms around Ajax's neck. While she wasn't exactly beautiful, she
had a charm that made Leia instantly warm to her.

"You must be Annie," Leia said, stepping out to meet her.
"I'm Leia."

"I get a hug before we get on with the introductions." Mano's
beefy arms enveloped Leia in a tight embrace. "It's been too long."

Bane was taller and thinner than his brother, with long, sleek
limbs. Mano looked more fully Hawaiian with his massive arms, broad
chest, and muscular legs. Hugging him was like being swallowed up by
a bear. Leia had always felt comfortable around Mano. He fully
approved of her, which seemed to be a rare occurrence in her life.

"I want to meet your fiancée." Leia turned to the young woman.

"I've heard all about you, Annie. I thought you'd be wearing a Wonder Woman outfit." She extended her hand and Annie took it.

Annie stood, and Ajax went to greet Mano. "Whatever these Oana men tell you, cut it in half and you might get close to the truth." Annie's smile was friendly. "Kaia will meet us in town."

Leia released Annie's hand. "I've been eager to talk to you about the earthquake swarms happening just offshore. Do we have a problem?"

Annie nodded. "It's looking pretty serious, Leia. The swarms are increasing. We may actually have an event brewing."

"An event? Are we talking a major earthquake?"

"It's too soon to tell, but there's something happening, maybe a new magma chamber forming."

"We found the treasure ship. An earthquake or eruption could destroy it."

"It might be an earthquake, but my gut tells me a new seamount is forming that's getting ready to spew. Hawai'i might be gaining another island that will merge with Moloka'i."

Leia suspected it might be true, but she'd hoped she was wrong. "If lava starts pouring out, the water will be too hot to work and too murky with ash to see. It will gum up our equipment too."

"I'd suggest you work fast. Don't quote me, but I wouldn't be surprised if we see an eruption in the next week or so."

Leia gasped. She hadn't expected news of this magnitude. All her bright hopes of making a huge discovery began to fade. There was no way they could excavate the ship in that time. "Is there any way to tell for sure how much time we have?"

Annie shook her head, and her dark eyes were full of regret. "*Aloha no.* Predicting lava flow is like trying to surf the pipeline— it takes all your expertise and you still wipe out a lot. I've been wrong as often as I've been right. So you might have longer than I just said, but I think it's coming. I'd like to get down there and take a look. Have you seen any rocks tossed up through the cracks?"

Leia shook her head. "Not that I noticed."

"I can probably tell once I get down there. My boss said I can stay as long as I like if the captain of the ship will allow me to use his facilities as a base. I brought some portable equipment, and I want to put in some GPS recorders along the seafloor. They will tell us if there is any movement or thrust."

Leia grew more and more impressed with the tiny woman's knowledge and expertise. She could only hope and pray Annie was wrong about how long they had.

The Kalaupapa luau was in full swing when they arrived. Tiki lights flickered, and the citronella had so far managed to repel the mosquitoes. Leia's father had brought his drums, and the Oana family had promised some hula demonstrations later in the evening.

Bane found Leia talking to Kaia by the stone fountain. Ajax lay at Kaia's feet. The *kapa* skirt Leia wore reached her knees, and her white top glowed in the soft lights strung around the perimeter of the garden. He knew he was staring and tried to stop, but she took his breath away. He wanted to quote "She Walks in Beauty Like the Night" by Lord Byron, but she'd laugh if she even realized he read poetry.

"We should probably mingle. Shaina Levy looks lonely over there." He indicated the woman who sat alone on a stone bench. She kept looking into the jungle as though she expected Tarzan to come swinging out of the trees any minute. If someone made a loud noise, she'd likely run screaming from the place.

Besides, he was interested in finding out more about her. Bane took Leia's arm and guided her toward the seated woman. For once, Leia didn't pull away. "Listen, there's something about Shaina I haven't told anyone. She claims Tony is her little girl's father. Tony was worried about it."

"Does Candace know?"

"Not when I spoke to Tony. I don't know if Shaina has told her yet or not. Maybe we can find out." He led the way to join Shaina.

"Hi, Shaina, are you enjoying yourself?" Leia asked. She stood looking down at the other woman with a smile that Bane thought would prompt anyone to unload their burdens.

Shaina's smile seemed forced. "Of course. I wanted to attend a luau while I was here, but I never expected to get to come to one as authentic as this." A cell phone chirped, and she fumbled in her purse. "Excuse me a minute." She flipped it open and answered it. "Andi, is something wrong?" She hunched over the phone with tense shoulders.

Bane could hear a young voice on the other end, but he couldn't make out what was said.

"I'm trying to get the money together," Shaina was saying softly. "I'll be home as soon as I do. Don't worry, this will all be over soon. Listen, I've got to go." She listened a moment. "I know it's hard, baby, but hang in there. I love you." She clicked off the phone and dropped it back into her purse. "Sorry about that. My five-year-old daughter is staying with my mom and getting tired of it."

Leia's attention went back to Shaina. "I'm sure she's fun to have around."

This time Shaina's smile was genuine. "She's a great kid! She's been sick a lot, but she rarely complains."

"What's wrong with her?"

Shaina's smile faded. "She has muscular dystrophy. It's been hard to squeak by with all the medical costs. My insurance premiums are through the roof. I'm here trying to drum up some new business for my new line of clothing. If I can get some accounts, I want to move her into a house near a school in New York that caters to children like her."

New York? She'd said something earlier about L.A. Bane noticed the way she stared earnestly into Leia's face as though trying to convince her of her sincerity.

"This trip sure turned into a nightmare for you," Leia said. "I

wouldn't think there would be much business you could connect
with here on Moloka'i. It doesn't have the tourism like O'ahu or
Mau'i have. What made you come here?"

Trust a woman to hone in on shopping facts. Bane hadn't even
thought of that. He watched Shaina drop her gaze.

She recovered her aplomb. "Well, I was working on accounts
on O'ahu, but the opportunity came up to check out the island
here. I hadn't realized there were so few shops until I got here." Her
gaze shifted away. "I decided to take up Tony's offer of a job while
I was here."

Tony had talked like she'd forced him into offering her a job.
Bane watched her. "Did you know anyone here? It makes for a
lonely adventure when you don't have anyone to share it with."

She didn't meet his gaze. "No, no one. I'd always wanted to see
this island though, and there was no time like the present."

"Look, I guess I should be honest with you," Bane said. "Tony
told me about your claims that he was Andi's father."

Shaina's eyes widened. "I didn't think anyone knew but
Candace," she mumbled.

"You told Candace?"

She nodded. "How did you know?"

"He mentioned it before his last dive. But he thought Candace
didn't know."

"She called me a liar." Shaina lifted her chin and gave a slight
toss of her head. "She just doesn't want to face the facts. And I'm
not leaving until I get something for Andi. I have to have help."
Her dark eyes held a feverish light.

Bane's gaze wandered to Leia, and he saw from her expression
that she shared his suspicions.

Fifteen

Leia's father and uncle sat at the drums; their thumping rhythm like a drug in Leia's limbs. She knew Kaia and Malia felt the same way. Hula was as much a part of them as their hair color and blood type. "Let's dance," she called out.

"I'm ready." Bane came toward her.

He'd changed into a *malo*, a loincloth covered with strips of *kapa* that hung to midthigh. A necklace of shark teeth hung around his neck, and leis of shark teeth and leaves circled his ankles and wrists. Mano was dressed like Bane, but she barely noticed him. Leia realized she was staring at Bane and dropped her gaze. Her heartbeat resounded with the throb of the drums.

The two men began a *hula ku'i Moloka'i*. It made Leia breathless just to watch. Ajax barked and ran around the dancers. Leia called him to her and put her arm around his neck to quiet him. Their thumping feet and chants choreographed with the thrusting, aggressive movements of their arms and necks and the guttural battle chant. Leia had to hang on to Ajax's collar to keep him from joining the hula. She watched in rapt attention as their dance told the story of a group of fishermen who encountered a sea monster. The men were glistening with perspiration when they finished. Leia and Kaia jumped to their feet and cheered. Annie clapped in a sedate manner, but the pride on her face spoke volumes.

"Whew, I have to sit down," Mano said. "My blood-sugar levels haven't been very stable lately. Exercise makes it worse."

Annie got him some water, then the women lined up to take the place of the men. Akoni and her uncle Makoni changed the rhythm of the drums to a more mellow pace. The women had begun to sing "Aloha Ku'u Pua" when Ipo stepped up to the line. "You're wearing my *pau*," she said to Leia. "I need it back if I'm going to dance." *Tûtû* folded her arms over her chest.

Leia looked down at her *pau*. She'd made the *kapa* hula skirt just two weeks ago. Her grandmother had never seen this one. Leia had another skirt in her bedroom at *Tûtû's*, though it would never encircle her grandmother's girth. But maybe a walk would clear her grandmother's head. She motioned to the other women to go ahead with the dance, then took her grandmother's arm. "I think your *pau* is at home. Let's go look for it."

Her mother half rose as if to go with her, but Leia shook her head, and her mother sank back into her seat. Leia led her grandmother to the shuttle. *Tûtû* didn't speak during the short drive to the cottage. Leia thanked the driver and led her grandmother down the hall to her room. Leia kept hula memorabilia her grandmother had given her in the closet. Pictures of her father from babyhood through adulthood hung on the walls and adorned every surface of the battered dresser. The room still held the hint of the sandalwood incense her father was so fond of, even now.

"Where's my *pau*?" *Tûtû* asked in a fretful voice. She glanced around and her eyes began to clear. She looked out the open window toward the beach and cocked her head as if she heard the hula chants. "Leia, we should be out serving our guests. We don't have time to be inside." She started toward the door, then a picture caught her eye. It was of a young Akoni dressed in hula garb. "He was twenty-seven here," she said, picking it up. "Your grandfather was a *kupuna* that put other dancers to shame."

"Isn't that *Makua*?" Leia took the picture from her grandmother and stared at it. She'd always thought the young man in the picture was her father. Studying it now, she could see the differences. Her *tûtû-man* had a little broader nose, and his mouth was wider than her father's.

"I need to give you the *kapa*," her grandmother said. "The treasure needs guarding now that Koma is dead."

Leia jerked her head up, and she stared at her grandmother. She expected to see *Tûtû* looking bewildered again, but the dark eyes regarding her were clear and bright. "What treasure?" she asked. "Koma told me to talk to you about it. Do you know where he buried it?"

Her grandmother nodded. "I'm not sure I can find it again. Tomorrow we'll go look."

Tomorrow her grandmother might be singing again. "Can you describe the location to me?"

"It's easier to take you. We'll get up and go first thing in the morning. The treasure needs to be safeguarded. Legend says that the day it's uncovered, the sea will open up. We have to protect it."

Leia knew her grandmother might not be this clearheaded again. "Could we go now? Bane could go with us and carry a torch."

"I hate the dark." Ipo looked out the window into the night. "And our friends will think it rude for us to leave them. We've already been in here much too long. Tomorrow is soon enough."

Her voice was firm, and her jaw was set in the familiar way that told Leia there was no swaying her. She suppressed a sigh. "All right, *Tûtû*. But do you suppose you could draw me a map?"

"I told you it mustn't be dug up. What if the map fell into the wrong hands? We can't run the risk. I know what you're thinking— you think you can get the treasure for yourself. I should take Malia there, not you. You're just out for what you can get."

Leia saw the clouds rolling across her grandmother's consciousness again. She took Ipo's hand. "Let's get you something to drink."

The last embers of the fire glowed red deep in the ashes. Bane sat on the bench by the fountain and felt a deep sense of contentment. Ajax's head was heavy on his foot, but the heat and weight added to his comfort. The women were singing a soft Hawaiian lullaby to Eva, who leaned against Leia's chest. The girl's eyes closed as her older sister smoothed her hair and planted a kiss on top of her head. The remaining guests awaited the final ferry of the night, which would take them back to Kaunakakai. Akoni and Ingrid lingered near the fire on a blanket. Bane heard Ingrid demanding to go home earlier in the evening, but her husband had prevailed, and they stayed. Bane felt as drowsy as Eva.

Jermaine stirred and threw a stick in the fire, then glanced at Leia's father. "Hey, Akoni, I heard you used to work for Bishop Museum. Were you working there when the Karshmer Cave fiasco went down?"

"Karshmer Cave? What was that about?" Shaina asked. "I've heard of the Forbes Cave thing, where they turned over the priceless relics to Hui Malama without authorization. Is this the same thing?"

Akoni took a sip of his drink. "The museum had some priceless artifacts—including human remains—that had been recovered from Loke Lau Caves on Moloka'i. The museum held them for several years, but native organizations wanted to rebury them, just as they did the Forbes Cave remains. Bishop Museum wasn't going to allow that, which saddened me. The artifacts disappeared one night. We lost an irreplaceable part of our culture."

"What went missing?" Jermaine asked.

"Some wooden gourds, a *kapa* depicting the death of Captain Cook, hand-carved wooden bowls with *nene* figures on the outside, and several *lā'au pālau*. And the bones of course."

"Why did some people want to rebury them?" Rae Jardin asked.

"Their spirits are not at rest if they're not buried. The power of our ancestors is in their bones. They are not to be some profane display for tourists to ogle." Akoni's voice was sharp. "The people are our grandparents. They deserve to rest in peace."

"What do you think happened to them?" Jermaine wanted to know.

Akoni shrugged. Behind him, the horn of the arriving ferry split the air. "We'd like to think a native Hawaiian group reburied them, but no one knows. The pieces could have been sold on the black market for millions of dollars. All we know is that they're gone. I doubt we'll ever see them again."

"Sam Westerfield claimed you stole the pieces yourself," Bane said, catching the surprise in Leia's eyes at his boldness. "Did you suspect he might have taken them? Rumor was he wanted to buy them."

"I'd rather not talk about Westerfield," Akoni said. With an abrupt movement, he threw a stick on the fire.

"And I'm sick of hearing about it," Ingrid said. "The fiasco has ruined our lives. People gawk at us and think my husband had something to do with the theft. Let's not talk about it anymore." She tugged on Akoni's arm. "I'm tired. Get your youngest daughter and let's go home."

Akoni nodded and rose. He gently shook Eva. "Time to go home, *keiki.*" She murmured but didn't stir as her head lolled against Leia's shoulder. He finally succeeded in rousing his daughter. She leaned against her *makua* as he led her to the boat. "Call us if you need anything," he told Leia. She nodded.

The ferry pulled away with the last of the guests, and Bane and Leia were left alone in the moonlight. He took her hand and squeezed it. She didn't pull away, which emboldened him to slip his arm around her and inhale the familiar plumeria fragrance of her hair.

She went still. He wondered if she could hear his heart pounding like the drum her father had played. He turned her and pulled her against his chest, then leaned his chin on the top of her head. She stood like that for a minute, then began to withdraw. He put his fingers under her chin and tipped her head up to look down into her face. Having her in his arms was sweet torture. Her lips parted, and he could see the fear in her eyes.

"I should get *Tûtû* home." Her sweet breath whispered over his face.

He rubbed his thumb over her chin. "I've missed you, Leia. I'd like to start over."

She inhaled and stepped away. "I don't think so, Bane. It's over between us. You know it too."

"But why? I've never understood that. Not fully. I know you were mad when I tried to talk you out of going to San Francisco, but I only wanted what was best for you. That couldn't have been enough to result in this." He ran his hand through his hair. He wanted to tell her he was afraid, but what kind of admission was that to the woman he loved? He needed to show strength and courage. "Would you pray about it?" he asked.

Her only answer was to turn and head back toward *Tûtû*.

Leia put her hands on her hot cheeks. She hadn't been sure she could resist Bane's nearness without telling him she still loved him. If only she could tear out the roots of her love for him. He wanted children, and that wasn't something she could give him. It was better he thought she didn't love him. Besides, even after dating him for months, she still found him an enigma. She wasn't sure who he really was at the core. He was a good man—she knew that much. He shared her faith and cared about people. But she always felt he had on a mask and was afraid to let her in to see his real heart.

She sat on the edge of the bed and read her Bible. Or tried to read it. Hina batted at her toes from under the bed. Nights like this made her question the decision she'd made not to marry. The Scriptures should have soothed her, but lately she felt so alone. If only she could figure out how to get over being mad at God. The overhead fan thumped the air, and the crickets chirped outside her window in a cacophony that pushed back the edges of the darkness. These normal noises should have subdued the sudden prickle along her arms and back, but they didn't. She felt as though someone was watching her. She told herself she had an overactive imagination, but her gaze swept the room and landed on the open window. She got up to shut it and saw a shadow flitting through the moonlight under a large monkeypod tree.

She shrank back against the wall, then stepped to the doorway and flicked off her bedroom light. The warm, fragrant breeze blew in her face as she peered out the window again. She held her breath and scanned the yard and surrounding jungle. There. The movement came again. It wasn't an animal or a branch blown by the breeze. The movement was too deliberate for that. She shivered. There was something sinister in the silhouette's skulking movements. No one lived out this way, and the village was five miles east of here. It was no casual walker out for a stroll. The area was too dangerous, and hiking was discouraged. Anyone walking here at night was asking for an injury. Could it be Bane?

Leia went to the door and stepped into the dark hallway. She listened for a moment to the grandfather clock ticking in the living room. The rhythmic sound of Bane's breathing came from the vicinity of the couch. He seemed to be asleep. She peeked into her grandmother's bedroom, then relaxed when she saw *Tûtû's* serene face, her eyes closed and the sheet rising and falling in a peaceful way.

Whoever was out there was up to no good purpose. Leia could feel it. She knew Bane would have her hide if she investigated alone. She tiptoed down the hall and stood looking down at him asleep on the sofa. A shaft of moonlight illuminated his face, and she felt a wave of love swamp her. She savored the feeling for a moment, then touched his shoulder. "Bane."

His eyes opened instantly, and he sat up. Ajax awoke as well and began to growl. "What's wrong? Has *Tûtû* wandered off?"

"No, she's fine. But someone is in the jungle watching the

house. I saw a shadow moving." Talking about it made the fear rise up and flutter in her chest so her voice came out like a squeak on the final word. She realized she didn't want to go out there. But she would. "Let's go see who it is," she found herself saying.

"You stay inside. Let me check." He swung his legs off the sofa and went toward the back door. Ajax followed him.

She followed him. "I'm going too."

"Someone should stay with your grandmother." He rummaged in his backpack and brought out a flashlight.

"She's asleep."

He sighed and opened the back door quietly. "You're the most hardheaded woman I know. Stay behind me."

"Do we need a weapon?"

"What do you have in mind? Your grandmother's butcher knife? I can handle it."

"Don't turn the flashlight on yet. The intruder will see it."

He nodded, and they moved past the mass of orchids and around a large bougainvillea. "I saw the shadow just outside my window," she whispered. Her bare feet were drenched in cool moisture from the grass. Ajax pressed close to her legs. She thought vaguely of cane spiders and wished she'd taken time to stick her feet into slippers. They stepped into the coolness of the jungle. A light touch on her shoulder nearly made her scream until she realized she was wrestling with a passion-flower vine. She thrust the plant away and scurried to catch up with Bane, who had stopped three paces ahead of her.

He had his head cocked to one side and was listening. Ajax growled softly. Leia paused and listened too but could hear nothing other than the crickets and the sound of the nearby stream rushing over the rocks. An owl hooted overhead, and she clutched his arm. "What is it?"

"I thought I heard a thrashing in the brush." He stepped around a log.

She tried to follow him and slipped on the wet bark, banging her shin. She suppressed a moan and decided she should have listened to him and stayed in the house. Maybe she had brought them both on a wild-goose chase. Her imagination could have been playing tricks on her.

Bane flipped on his flashlight. The sudden illumination made her blink. "He'll see us!"

"There's no one here now. But there was. Look." He pointed to a depression in the soft mat of leaves. "Someone was standing here for quite a while." The flashlight shone on scattered cigarette butts. One was still smoldering. "He probably saw us coming."

"But what could he want? Someone's already been in the house. I don't get it."

"I don't either, but we need to find out."

She hadn't had a chance to talk to him about what her grandmother had said. "You remember Koma said to talk to my grandmother? She told me tonight that she knew where the treasure was. I tried to get her to take me tonight, but she didn't want to do it until morning."

"You know how fuzzy she was tonight. I wouldn't take anything she said too seriously."

"No, she was clear about this. I think she really knows something. If she does, she might be in real danger, Bane." Suddenly cold, she rubbed her arms.

He put his arm around her. "I'm here, Leia. I won't let anything happen to your grandmother or to you."

Leaning against him, she believed he meant what he said. "But you can't be here every minute. We're so remote out here. I'm not sure any of us should stay at the cottage."

"You want to go to your mom's tonight?"

She hesitated, then shook her head. "*Tûtû* is already sleeping. I don't want to disturb her. But we'd better think about it tomorrow. We're dealing with a bold person. They ransacked her house in the middle of the day and skulked around at night even though we're with her now. A person like that sounds desperate, and desperate people are dangerous."

Bane dropped his arm from her shoulder but took possession of her hand. They turned and started back to the house. "I'll stay up tonight and keep watch."

"I hate for you to do that. It's midnight, and daylight is a long way off. Wake me in a couple of hours and I'll take a turn."

"A little thing like you wouldn't scare him off."

"Little! Look at me." She smiled in the darkness. He always knew the right thing to say.

"You get some rest," he said as they stepped into the house.

"Wake me," she told him again. He didn't answer, and she knew he was going to be bullheaded about it. She'd just set her alarm. She went to her room and set the clock, then lay back on the pillow. The walk had made her hot. She relished the fan's movement. Moonlight spilled in the open window, and the breeze touched her heated body. She heard a rustle from her bedroom closet and froze. Her throat closed. She heard the tick of the clock over the sound of her ragged breath. Should she run to get Bane or investigate?

She'd look pretty foolish if it was only Hina in there. Glancing around for a weapon, she saw nothing that would work. Her slippers were just thin rubber, and she wished she had her hiking boots handy. Then she spied her grandfather's *lā'au pālau* hanging in a wooden rack on the wall. She took it out. Moving stealthily, she advanced to the closet. Putting her hand on the doorknob, she hesitated. Should she yell when she flung it open or just do it quietly? Her grandmother was a heavy sleeper, so maybe she wouldn't awaken.

Hefting the bat to her shoulder, she planted her feet wide and held on with one hand. Her other hand twisted the knob and flung the door open as she uttered a war cry. "Aiiaa!" Hina rushed past her, squalling at the top of her lungs. Leia giggled, and she slumped in relief. But the hair on the back of her neck still stood at attention. She felt a presence, a noiseless something from inside the closet.

Then she heard another scrabble in the back of the closet. She backed away with the club held high, then a dark figure rushed her. She swung the *lā'au pālau*, connecting with the person's mid-section. A muffled *umph* told her she'd inflicted some damage. But it wasn't enough, because the intruder brushed by her, knocking her out of the way. She fell back against the nightstand. It toppled and sent the lamp crashing to the floor. She heard Ajax begin to bark. The figure flitted by the window, blocking the moonlight, then the door to the hallway opened, and he fled. She heard Bane's heavy footsteps pound down the hall, then a crash. Ajax was growling ferociously. The man yelped. She ran to the door and peered into the hall. Bane was picking himself up off the floor, but the other man gained his feet first and disappeared into the kitchen with Ajax on his heels. Moments later, the back door crashed open and slammed shut again. Ajax's bark was frantic.

Leia ran to Bane. "Are you okay?"

He was shaking his head as if to clear it. "Only my pride is hurt."

He started to go toward the back door, but she held him back. "It's useless in the dark. We already found that out. We need to call the police again." She called to the dog, then stepped to her grandmother's doorway and peeked inside. *Tūtū* sat up and looked at her with a vacant stare, then fell back against the pillow and rolled over. Her eyes closed, and her breathing evened out.

"At least she's okay," Bane said. "The guy must have sneaked back around while we were outside. He's after something."

"It has to be the treasure. That's the only thing that makes sense." She went to phone the police. Her grandmother knew something. If only Leia could figure out what it was.

Sixteen

Every muscle in Bane's body ached this morning. After dancing, traipsing through the woods, and then colliding with the intruder, as well as getting no sleep, he felt wasted. The police hadn't left until about an hour ago. He splashed cold water on his face, then swiped it with a towel and went out into the hallway. Rounding the corner, he collided with Leia. Ajax got up from the floor by the door to greet him.

"Sorry," Leia said. Her gaze searched his face. "You look exhausted."

"I could use some coffee."

"I just put it on."

He sniffed. "I could eat a horse." He glanced at Hina, who was winding her body through his legs. "Or a cat." Her purr was loud enough to be a chain saw.

"*Tûtû* is making taro hash browns and eggs."

"How is she this morning?" Hina's tongue felt like wet sandpaper. He slid his toes out of her reach.

"Still bright. She said she'd take us to the treasure after breakfast."

He knew better than to let himself believe it, but the muscles in his stomach tightened anyway. "I wonder if I should call Ron."

"I wouldn't do that yet. Let's see if there's anything to her claim. I'd hate to humiliate her."

He had started to pull out his cell phone, but he put it back. "Yeah, okay. I wasn't thinking about that."

"She has so little dignity left."

He examined her face. "You look beat too."

"I'm a little tired. *Tûtû* is the only lively one." Her smile held a trace of wistfulness. "She'll likely outwalk us both. Let's see what she knows." He untangled his feet from Hina, then touched Leia's arm, and she went before him down the hall to the kitchen.

She sniffed. "That smells wonderful, *Tûtû*. We're hungry."

"*Aloha kakah'aka*," she said in the traditional morning greeting. "Sit down, eat." Ipo bustled toward them with a huge white apron wrapped around her. The ties went around her twice, and she'd tied them in the front. She plunked down the plates of food.

Bane pulled the chair out for Ipo. "Sit down, *Tûtû*. You've worked hard all morning."

"You take care of yourself, and let me handle breakfast." Ipo went to the refrigerator and took out a pitcher of juice. She poured it into three mismatched glasses and placed them on the table before finally sitting down.

Bane sipped the strawberry-guava nectar. "Um, good." He took a big gulp of the sweet juice. He could drink a gallon of the stuff. "So where are we going today?"

She gave him a pained look. "You shall see. But not until after breakfast."

"Playing hard to get, huh?" He winked at Leia, who returned his smile. She still looked a little wan. Her eyes were red, and he wondered if she'd been crying. But that didn't make sense. Unless her grandmother had been mean to her again. He knew it was a symptom of Ipo's illness that her sweet nature sometimes turned on a dime, and she forgot how much she loved her family, but it was wearing. He shot Leia a questioning look, but she turned her head away.

"I shall take you only," Ipo announced. "I told Leia she must stay here. I cannot trust the treasure to a *haole*." She turned a smile toward her granddaughter. "I don't wish to hurt you, *keiki*, but I must be careful about this and think clearly."

So that was the reason for Leia's turned-down mouth. "Leia

must come too," he said firmly. "She is your kin. Koma was going to show her. He trusted her to pass it on to future generations."

Ipo hesitated. "I had forgotten," she murmured. "Perhaps it will be acceptable."

"You can trust me, *Tûtû*," Leia said. "I want only to help you." She leaned forward and put her hand over her grandmother's. "Think, *Tûtû*, and you will remember how close we have been."

Ipo patted it with her other hand. "I know I am sometimes hard on you, Leia. You may go with us." She said the words as a queen bestowing a boon on a subject.

"Thank you, *Tûtû*." Leia's eyes grew luminous, and she sniffed and bent her head. Picking up the serving spoon, she began to ladle food onto her plate.

Bane decided not to say anything else about it in case Ipo changed her mind again. "You slept through all the commotion last night." Leia's head came up, and she gave it a slight shake. He sent her a quizzical look. In his opinion, Ipo needed to know about the danger so she could be on her guard. "An intruder was in the house."

Ipo's fork paused halfway to her open mouth. She closed her mouth and put down her food. "Intruder? Did you catch him?"

"Nope, he was too wily for me. But your granddaughter thumped him with your son's bat. You should have heard her war cry." He grinned at the way Leia ducked her head and blushed. The high color in her face made her blue eyes even brighter.

Ipo straightened in her chair. "In my day, I would have chased off any intruder who dared to come here. Now I must depend on the kindness of others." She took a bite of food and looked away.

The old woman was proud. Bane didn't know how to answer her, so he finished his breakfast in silence. He carried his plate to the sink, then squirted a drop of dish soap into his plate and washed up his utensils.

"How domestic," Leia said, elbowing him aside.

"Now aren't you sorry you broke my heart?" He grinned and put his dishes in the drainer, then leaned back against the counter.

"I might have had second thoughts if I'd realized I'd have a live-in maid."

He was close enough to study the pink lobes of her ears that peeked out from the upswept sides of her hair. He leaned forward and whispered in those cute ears. "I have unplumbed depths of talents. You should reconsider."

His all-out assault had the desired result: a tide of color swept up her neck and cheeks. She turned and faced him. "I don't want to talk about it."

His smile faded. "I think we should talk about it. Pray about it together."

"I told you, we're not right for each other."

"But you haven't told me why." If he had a reason, maybe he could help her deal with it.

She looked away. "That's not important."

He struggled to keep his voice even. Losing his temper wouldn't help. "It is to me."

She looked over his shoulder. "*Tûtû*, are you ready to go?"

"Let me get my walking stick." Ipo moved toward the hallway.

"This discussion isn't over," Bane whispered to Leia. Leia ignored him as she followed her grandmother. He sighed and went after the women. Ajax followed him.

*L*eia wished she hadn't made a vow never to cry again, because the release of tears would be welcome about now. She knew she was reacting to the fear and stress of the past twenty-four hours, but Bane's flirtation with her wasn't helping matters. She stood in the haven of her room for a few minutes and clutched Kanda, the stuffed bear Bane had given her for her last birthday, to her chest

for comfort. If only she could go back to that time, back to before
she knew there was no future.

She reluctantly put down her bear and joined the others at the
door. Pua came squawking to meet them when they stepped outside
into the yard. She rubbed the goose's head and fed her a handful of
berries she'd filched from her grandmother's refrigerator. Pua honked
in appreciation and gobbled up the treat. Ajax kept a safe distance.

"Get out of here, Pua, you've had enough." Her grandmother
shooed the *nene* away. Pua honked in protest but waddled away
toward the backyard.

"Where are we going, *Tûtû*?" Leia fell in behind her grandmother, who walked slowly with her hand on Bane's arm.

"To the fishpond." *Tûtû* marched forward as though she knew
exactly where she was going.

Leia almost stopped. There were no fishponds in this area. Bane
glanced over his shoulder, and she saw the same awareness in his
face. He gave a shrug and kept walking. Her earlier hope began to
fade. She'd thought her grandmother was clearheaded today, but
now she wasn't so sure. Bane jerked his head slightly as though to
urge her forward. She sighed and stepped out after them. It was
going to be a wild-goose chase, so they should take Pua along.

She batted a large frond from a fern out of her face. An irate
insect buzzed out. Leia swatted it away and plodded after Bane and
Ipo. How far could her grandmother go in this jungle? It was slow-
going with Bane taking care to help the older woman over rough
ground and fallen trees. It was hotter here with the trees blocking
out the trade winds and the moisture rising from the plants in an
early morning mist. The humidity caused jungle scents to be more
pronounced: the heavy fragrance of the red ginger that grew here in
profusion and the light scent of lime that hung from the shrubs
that snatched at her shorts as she passed.

Ipo paused and looked around. Her confused frown cleared, and
she pointed at two monkeypods whose branches were growing

together, leaving an arch underneath. "I remember this—it's through here, I'm sure. Koma called it the wedding arch." Her grandmother sounded almost girlish.

For the first time, Leia wondered if her grandmother had feelings for Koma. She'd been morose and irritable since his murder. Of course, she was that way sometimes anyway. But Koma and Ipo had been friends a long time, probably sixty years or more. Leia looked at her grandmother with new compassion.

Ipo was walking with more spryness now, leaving the security of Bane's arm in her eagerness to get to her destination. Bane jogged to catch her. "Don't try to go by yourself, *Tûtû.* I don't want you to fall."

Ipo paused, her breath coming in sharp gasps. "I think I should sit down." She held out her hand, and Bane guided her to a fallen log and helped her settle onto it.

"Are you all right?" Leia rushed to her grandmother's side and knelt beside her. The thick canopy of leaves overhead blocked out the light. She suddenly realized there was no sound here. Not even the hum of insects or the call of a mynah bird. The quiet felt eerie, almost sinister. She shivered.

"I'm fine, *keiki,* just fine." Ipo raised her hands and cupped them around Leia's face. "You're a good girl, Leia."

Her real grandmother was back. Leia wanted to bury her face in the folds of Ipo's skirt and forget the harsh words her grandmother had lashed her with. If only she could keep her grandmother just like this, her own sweet self.

Ipo dropped her hands and looked through the arch toward where the forest darkened even more. "We have to go. I hate that place. I'd forgotten how much I hated it. It's haunted and evil." She lowered her voice. "People die there. We must be careful." Her eyes emptied of light.

Leia sent a silent plea in her gaze to Bane, who stood watching quietly, though she knew there was nothing he could do to prevent this. Even prayer hadn't been able to hold off the confusion that swirled in and took her grandmother away. She wanted to grab

Tûtû and shake her until her eyes cleared, to hold on to every moment of lucidity, every crumb of love that still fell her way. If only her grandmother's disease was something fleshly she could fight, instead of a faceless enemy that kidnapped the grandmother she knew and loved and left this empty shell behind.

Bane seemed to feel her despair, because he put his hand on her shoulder and squeezed. "She'll be okay again soon." Ajax pressed against Leia too.

Leia stood and rubbed the dog's ears. "But for how long?" Her voice was low and raspy. "Each time her lucid moments are shorter. I feel so helpless."

He didn't answer right away. "Accepting God's will sometimes is hard. I think we all struggle with it. Why was Eva born with Down syndrome? Why do babies sometimes die? Why do mothers leave their children? We're full of questions sometimes. There aren't any easy answers." He fell silent again. "Those things shape us and make us who we are. They make us stronger."

"And less trusting," she said. She had felt the weight of his suspicion sometimes when they were engaged and knew he wondered if she would leave him without a word. It was another nail in the coffin of their relationship. "God scares me. You never know what he might do." She put her hand to her mouth, uncertain if she'd actually said the words. From the comprehension on Bane's face, she knew she had blurted them out. She realized her anger was at the core of the lackluster worship she'd managed lately.

He nodded. "I can understand that. I've been like that a time or two in my life. The last time was when we broke up." He grinned, a sideways smile that didn't reach his eyes.

"I don't want to talk about us." She stood and clasped her hands together to keep them from shaking. "What do we do now that *Tûtû* is obviously not going to lead us to the treasure?"

"We could look around I guess." He glanced at Ipo, who had begun to sing. Her dull voice echoed in the treetops and reverberated through the clearing. "Come along, *Tûtû*, let's go for a walk." He helped her to her feet, and she continued to sing as they walked along the faint path between the trees. "She said something about a fishpond. Are there any legends of ancient fishponds in this area?"

"I've never heard of any. How far are we from the ocean here? The ponds would have to be near the water."

"Unless they're so old, the water receded and land filled in." Still helping Ipo along, Bane studied the jungle. He stopped and cocked his head. "Listen. Is that water?"

Leia tipped her head to the side and strained to hear. Sure enough, the tinkle of water on rocks came to her ears. "I think it's that way," she said, pointing to the north.

"That would be the direction of the ocean." His voice rose, and he started off in the direction from which she'd heard the sound.

They passed through a stand of mangrove trees and entered a lovely meadow sparkling with wildflowers and sunshine. A brook rushed over rocks, creating the noise that had drawn them. There was a bowl-shaped depression in the middle of the area. The opposite side was lined with rocks, some of them loosened and fallen into a heap.

"I'd say we found the fishpond," Bane remarked, his voice deep with satisfaction.

"Where do we even look?" She didn't want to go into the trees again. She felt safe here, secluded from prying eyes. In the jungle, she had felt as though someone was peering at them, especially in that place of utter quiet. Her grandmother gave a soft sigh and began to fall. "Bane!" Leia leaped to try to catch *Tûtû*, but Bane was there first. He caught Ipo in his arms and eased her to the ground. Leia knelt beside her grandmother and felt the carotid artery for a pulse. "Her pulse is thready. We need to get her to the hospital."

Bane whipped out his cell phone and looked at it. He groaned. "No signal."

"I'm not leaving you here alone," Leia said. "Can we carry her out?"

"We'll have to." Bane lifted Ipo in his arms and started for the path.

Seventeen

heck my cell phone and see if we have a signal yet," Bane
panted. His muscles burned from the strain. Though Ipo
didn't weigh more than a hundred pounds, she was hard to carry as
a deadweight. He labored to pull air into his lungs as he rested a few
minutes while Leia dug his cell phone out of his shirt pocket. At
least she wasn't refusing to use it.

"Still no signal." Leia snapped it closed. She pressed her fingers
against her grandmother's neck. "Her pulse is still weak, and she has
dyspnea. Shortness of breath," she amended when he raised his eyebrows. "Classic signs of a myocardial infarction."

At least he knew that meant heart attack. "Let's get going
again." Bane picked up Ipo and followed Leia along the path with
renewed urgency. "How much farther?"

"Not far. Just through the trees. I'm going to run and call the
clinic." She put on a burst of speed and disappeared through the
monkeypod trees. Ajax ran after her. A few moments later, he heard
the slam of the front door. The sound encouraged him. His arms
and back aching, he hurried through the last of the trees and broke
through the jungle into Ipo's backyard. Pua honked and waddled to
meet them. He'd never seen a more welcome sight. Nearly groaning under the weight, he labored the last few feet to the house.

Leia was coming back through as he reached the door. "I called
the clinic. They'll be ready for her. They have a defibrillator unit too."

He nodded. "Open the backseat door to your grandmother's
car," he gasped. She ran to the car and flung open the door. The

stale odor of disuse rushed out. Nearly losing his grip on Ipo, he managed to get her on the seat then gently laid her down.

"I'll get in back with her," Leia said. She tossed him the keys and scrambled inside and slapped the door behind her.

Bane ran to the driver's side. "Stay here, boy," he told the dog. He started the engine and tromped on the gas. The car tires spit gravel as he accelerated out of the driveway. "How's she doing?"

"I think she's had a heart attack." Leia's gaze met his in the rearview mirror. "Pray, Bane. She has to make it."

"I've been praying the whole time." He pressed harder on the accelerator. They reached the edge of town, and he drove past the town sign that read Peace to All Who Enter. He hoped the mantra worked for Ipo. "Where is the clinic?"

"That building." She leaned over the back of the seat and pointed to a small white building.

Bane parked and flung open his door. He grabbed Ipo's arms and managed to get her upright. Putting his hands under her arms, he started to lift her from the car. His muscles screamed in protest. He gritted his teeth and kept on going.

"She's coming to!" Leia put her hand on his arm. "Wait a minute, let her sit up."

He steadied Ipo on the backseat. She was blinking her eyes, but she didn't seem to be aware of her surroundings. "Any water?"

Leia nodded. "In the trunk." He tossed Leia the keys, and she ran to get the water. When she returned, he held the bottle to Ipo's lips.

She managed to take a sip, then coughed and waved it away. "Don't fuss. I'm fine."

"*Tûtû*, you are not fine." Leia peered at her watch. "You've been unconscious for nearly forty-five minutes. We're taking you to the clinic."

Ipo folded her hands over her chest. "I'm not going in, Leia."

"You have to go. A nurse needs to check you out, and we'll need to transport you to the hospital."

"Take me home." Ipo thrust out her chin.

Bane's gaze met Leia's. Short of manhandling Ipo into the building, he didn't know what to do. He saw the same helplessness he felt reflected on Leia's face. Looking back at Ipo, he saw she was getting more color in her face.

Leia took her grandmother's pulse. "Let me see if the nurse will come out here." She jogged to the clinic and disappeared inside. A few moments later she and the nurse came hurrying back to the car. The nurse took Ipo's blood pressure first. Ipo flinched as the blood-pressure cuff expanded. The nurse listened through the stethoscope, then pulled it down around her neck. "Your pressure is a little low. You really need to be in the hospital where a doctor can check you out."

"You're the only doctor I need. I'm tired, Leia." Ipo's voice was querulous. "Take me home so I can rest."

Leia sighed. "Let's wait on the helicopter and see if the technicians can convince her," she whispered to Bane and the nurse. "At least she's lucid."

"I'm not deaf—or dead yet. I can hear you. And they're not talking me into going either." Ipo took the water bottle from Bane's hand and sipped it. "We need to go back to find the treasure. Or did we get it already?"

"No, we didn't. But you're in no shape to go traipsing through the jungle." Bane shut the door and got in the car. Leia thanked the nurse, then went around and got in beside her grandmother in the back. By the time they got back to Ipo's house, she was acting her normal self. She talked with Leia about making *kapa* and was telling her where to gather special berries to make dye. He didn't know what to think. One thing was sure—they weren't finding the treasure today.

Tûtû insisted Leia cancel the arrival of the helicopter, and she reluctantly agreed. Her grandmother seemed fine now, and no one could force her into going in for treatment. Ipo agreed to tell her doctor about it at her visit later in the week, and Leia had to be content with that promise. Malia arrived to spend some time with their grandmother.

"You're sure you'll be okay? I promised Candace I'd stop by the dive shop while Kaia is out sightseeing with Mano and Annie," Leia said.

"Go, go," Malia said. "We'll be fine. Leave Ajax with us. He'll protect us."

They took Leia's bike to the pier and took the boat around to Kaunakakai, where they got Leia's car. There was a familiar van outside the dive shop when they pulled up. "Hans is here." Leia nodded toward the lettering on the side of the van. "He's got a lot of nerve to bother her." She jumped out and ran toward the front door. She heard shouting as she neared the door and put on an extra burst of speed. Before she could enter, the door flew open, and Aberg Hans barreled through. His face was even redder than usual, but he was smiling. He paused when he saw Bane behind her. Anger flashed over his face, and he brushed past Leia.

Bane blocked his escape. "What are you doing here?"

"I don't see a badge on your chest. It's none of your business." Hans tried to go around him, but Bane sidestepped into his path again. "Get out of my way, Oana. This doesn't concern you."

Candace came to the door. Her eyes were red, and her cheeks were wet. "He came to tell me he's bought the building."

"What?" Leia and Bane said in unison.

Hans was smiling again. "I want you out by next week. It belongs to me now, and I'm going to bulldoze it down myself." His voice was ripe with satisfaction.

Leia directed a glance at Bane. "How could my mother do such a thing?"

A worried frown crouched between his eyes. "Is she in financial trouble?"

Candace leaned her head against the wall. "If she'd only told me it was for sale, I would have gone to the bank and tried to get a loan."

"Look," Bane said to Hans. "Let her buy it from you. Have a heart. She has to have a way to raise her baby by herself."

Hans laughed. "I don't think so. I heard you found the treasure ship. That will see to her needs. I've got all I want." He stepped past Bane, and this time Bane didn't block him. The big man strode to the van and drove off.

As the sound of the motor faded, Candace wilted even more. "What am I going to do?" She put her face in her hands.

Leia embraced her. "Maybe we can find you another building."

"You know how impossible it is to find a waterfront—and how expensive." She shook her head. "It's over." Candace wilted against the doorjamb.

Leia led her friend inside and made her sit down. Bane went to fix them all a cup of coffee. "I haven't wanted to pry about your finances, but do you need any money?" She had a little set aside, not much, but enough to buy some groceries.

"I've got enough for now, but it won't last long." Candace tossed a tissue onto the counter, where it joined several other wadded ones. She put on a brave smile.

Money never lasted long here, not with the costs of living in Hawai'i. "Well, if you need some help, I'll be glad to share what I have."

"You're so sweet, Leia. But don't worry about me."

A request that would be hard to grant. Leia curled her fingers into her palms. Tony's death and Candace's plight was yet another reason to wonder why God acted the way he sometimes did. What was the use of all these trials? "Let's go talk to my mother," she said to Bane.

She simmered in silence as they drove to her parents' house. Ingrid had to have been planning this when they talked last. A sale like that didn't happen overnight. What could have possessed her mother to do it?

Ingrid met them at the door. "Leia, Bane, what a nice surprise."
Her smile vanished. "Is something wrong?"

"Why did you sell the Aloha Dive Shop building to Aberg
Hans?" Leia's voice vibrated with fury. "I didn't even know you
knew him."

Her mother turned and went down the hall to the living room.
Leia and Bane followed. A light floral scent from the candle on the
hall table permeated the air, confirming how her mother was all
about possessing the right image, not real substance. "How could
you?" Leia demanded. "That was all Candace had."

"It was a business decision. He offered me more than anyone
else would pay. She can relocate to somewhere else."

"Where? Mama, she's pregnant, alone, and scared. This will
crush her."

"Always looking back and never forward, isn't that right, Leia?
You always think with your heart and not your head. My invest-
ments are what have paid for the boat you use and the car you
drive. Before you question my judgment, remember that you all
rely on me for food to eat and a roof over your heads."

It was all Leia could do not to physically flinch. "You always
extract a price for your generosity, don't you? You give, then expect
us all to kowtow to your demands."

"What demands? Is it unreasonable to want you to live up to
your potential?" Her mother spread out her hands with the palms
up. "You could have been the best doctor in the country, Leia."

"It's not what I want, Mama! I can't be the perfect daughter you
always wanted." Leia touched the scar on her lip. "I can't control who
I am inside. I don't trust drugs, scalpels, and anesthetics. I want to help
the body heal naturally. Why is it so wrong to pursue my own path?"

"It's another way you look back, Leia, another way of not facing the future and the reality of modern life." Her mother turned
with a jerky movement. "I'm done, Leia. Do whatever you want,
but don't come crying to me to pick up the pieces."

Leia flushed hot then went cold. Her auntie was right—her mother wasn't capable of unconditional love. "Very well, Mama. Sell the building, stick the money in the bank. I don't think it will make you happy. And certainly none of us can. We can't live up to your expectations." Her fingers were cold as she dug in the pocket of her shorts. "Here, you can have the keys to the car and the boat."

Her mother waved away the keys. "The car was your gradua-tion gift."

"And the boat is my gift to you from this minute on." Her father spoke from the doorway. "What's going on here, Ingrid?"

"Just your daughter being unappreciative as usual."

Leia had never been so happy to see her father. He stepped next to her and put his arm around her. She sagged against his bulk and wished she could disappear under his arm. "It's fine, *Makua*. Mama and I have finally come to an understanding. I won't expect her to love me, and she won't expect me to be perfect."

Akoni turned to his wife. "What have you been saying to Leia?" he demanded.

"Let's end this discussion right now. I'm going to make some tea. Anyone want any? Bane?" Ingrid's smile was brittle as she turned to Bane.

He shook his head. Leia's gaze met his, and she looked away from the sympathy in his eyes.

The sun was just barely peeking over the edge of the horizon. Bane stepped outside while Ajax did his business. He watched the mist rise in the warmth of the morning. Ipo was clear-eyed this morning and was happily gathering orchids in the garden to make leis with Malia.

Leia slung her backpack over her shoulder. "Call me if you need me," she told Malia.

Malia tried to hand her a cell phone, but Leia pushed it away. "It would be so much easier if you'd take my cell phone."

"I can call on the ship-to-shore phone."

Bane grinned. "Give it up, Malia. Call my cell if you need anything, and I'll relay the message. We'll leave Ajax with you." He scribbled the number on a piece of paper and handed it to her. She stuffed it in her purse and waved them off.

"How are we going to do anything today if Ron tells us the court hasn't intervened? OHA has forbidden us to excavate, and they'll have boats out guarding the site by now. What if they have sonar to watch for underwater intrusion?"

Bane had been wondering the same thing. "I suppose Ron will have a plan. He generally does, and he knows we won't go down without permission."

"Have you heard if his appeal to the courts has done any good?"

"No, but I'm sure we'll find out when we get there." He glanced at her out of the corner of his eye. She was like a warm tropical breeze blowing over the sea. He remembered the day his mother left in a vivid motion picture that played over and over in his mind. He, Mano, and Kaia had been playing in the tree house by the lagoon. He had taken a Cup of Gold flower to his mother with pride. She always smelled of ginger and sunshine. She took the huge flower and stuck it in her hair. It covered nearly the whole side of her head, and the fragrance of it enveloped him when she leaned down to hug him. "You're my poet, Bane. Don't ever change."

He'd promised he wouldn't, but when he woke up the next morning, she and Kaia were gone. She'd left the flower he'd given her behind, and he knew then that a poet would never win the heart of a princess. And the responsibility for his brother had fallen on his skinny shoulders. He'd sworn to broaden them enough to make sure he and Mano were never hurt like that again. He couldn't let his guard down, ever.

He became aware that Leia was staring at him. "What?"

"You seem almost dreamy. What were you thinking about?"

For a crazy minute, he wondered what she would say if he told her she looked as beautiful as the sea. The words stayed clamped behind his teeth. He nodded toward the deck of the ship. "Looks like they're all waiting on us. You took too long on your makeup."

She punched him in the arm, then undid her seat belt and grabbed her satchel of gear. "I don't wear makeup and you know it."

"You don't need it." She looked at him with surprise in her eyes, and he looked away. No woman respected a soft side. He needed to remember that. "You seem to have recovered from the break with your mom."

She frowned. "It's been coming a long time. Now I understand there's something broken in her. It's freeing, actually. I don't have to worry about pleasing her anymore, now that I know it's not possible."

"I'm sorry." He wanted to tell her his love was as limitless as the sea, but the words wouldn't come.

"Don't be. I'm fine." She straightened her shoulders. "Let's go. I'm eager to see what's down there now."

"Are you sure you'll be okay? I don't want you getting narced again."

"I'm fine. We'll need to do this in short hops. Do you think Annie is right, and we might be getting ready to deal with a new seamount?"

"She might be. The crack was definitely widening. She brought along some equipment to test the water. Maybe that will tell her more." He had swum near the seamount offshore the Big Island. It was very unpleasant with underground hissing and popping that was so loud it was hard to think. And the water was nasty—too warm and filled with ash that made visibility poor.

"I guess we're going to find out." She walked ahead of him to the boat. Kaia stood with Mano and Annie at the edge of the dock. The divers Tony had hired were already in the boat.

"I thought we were going to have to drag you both out of bed," Mano said. "Let's get this show on the road."

They climbed into the smaller craft that would take them out to the research ship. The steward guided the boat out on the choppy waves. He loved the sea—the smell of it, the feel and taste of the salt in the air. God was good that he had allowed Bane to do what he loved and get paid for it.

He glanced at Leia with her face in the wind as well. Her eyes were bright, and he knew she felt the same way he did about the ocean. The ship anchored above the site where they'd found the Spanish galleon. They all boarded the ship. Bane turned to find Ron. "I thought we'd be anchored a ways from the site. What gives?" he asked Ron.

Ron smiled, but the impression was that of a shark on the prowl. "Judge Hapo is a friend of mine. He saw the merit of my claim and has lifted the injunction for now. It still has to go to court, but until it does, we can proceed here. I've got Trimix gas in the tanks, so we're all set."

The boat pitched and yawed with the high surf, and he planted his feet apart to maintain his balance. "If Annie is right, we may not have much time anyway. There may be a volcanic event brewing."

Ron's gaze turned to Annie, who clung to the railing. "Really? There hasn't been an active volcano in this area for centuries."

"That could change." Annie's voice was soft but full of quiet authority that made everyone look at her as she stood beside Mano and surveyed the area. "We've been recording earthquake swarms right here of the frequency and magnitude that preceded the last event at Mauna Loa. I'm going to take samples and check it out. But don't get your hopes set on excavating this wreck. You need to stay smart about it."

Silence greeted her words. Something lurked under the choppy seas, but was it fame and fortune or a nightmarish scene out of Dante's *Inferno*? They needed to go down, but he knew none of them really wanted to do it.

"Let's get down there now, then." Ron began to pull on his wet suit. The rest of the crew hurriedly began to prepare for the dive. They trooped down to the platform near the water. Nani performed a leap off the bow of the ship and splashed Shaina as she was preparing to jump into the water. The dolphin rose and chattered in an agitated manner.

"Sounds like she has something she wants to say." Kaia opened the backpack she'd brought down and grabbed the hydrophone contraption she used to communicate with Nani. "You remember how to use this?"

"Sure."

She handed it to Bane. "You handle it. I need to leave tomorrow, and you'll be on your own with her."

He nodded and dropped the communication device into the water. He typed, "Hello, Nani." The hydrophone picked up a series of clicks, then the computer display read: DANGER HOT. He looked up at his sister. "This doesn't sound good. Is she serious?"

"I'm sure she is." Kaia's gaze met Annie's. "Annie, could you call the observatory and see what they're picking up?"

"I was just about to do that." Annie went to her satchel and dug out her cell phone.

Leia's blue eyes were wide as she stepped close to Bane. "Do you think it's safe to go down?" She tipped a wide smile his way and fingered the tiny scar on her lip.

"I hope so. We haven't even begun to figure out this thing. It would be a huge disappointment to have come this far only to have it all fall apart just as we're about to investigate. What do you think? You tend to run tilting at windmills with no help."

"I don't like to be a scaredy-cat," she admitted.

"It comes from being the oldest. We older siblings grow up believing we have to handle things. You take it to extremes though. It's okay to lean on someone once in awhile. Like me, for instance."

She looked away, and he wondered what she was thinking. When he stood outside with her after the luau, the electricity bounding between them had been enough to power the Molokai'i Lighthouse.

Annie interrupted his thoughts by shoving a printout in his

face. "There has been a huge swarm of quakes overnight. They tried to call me, but I was out of range. Fawn says to be careful. It might be hot down there."

Bane winced. "We'd better not all go down. I'll check it out, and if it's safe, we'll take a team down."

"You can't go alone." Leia pulled her face mask down and went to the exit ramp.

"I'm going too." Annie followed her. "I need samples."

"You're not going into danger without me," Mano objected.

"Well, I'm not going down." Jermaine folded his arms over his chest.

"Count me out," Shaina said. "Volcanoes scare me."

"*Ho'olohe.* Just let me go take a look by myself. We don't all need to be in danger."

"Give it up, Bane," Leia said. "We're going." She went into the water, and her bubbles rose to the surface.

He shook his head and got into his gear. Holding on to his mask, Bane jumped into the water. The warm waves welcomed him in a salty bath. Nani brushed against him, and he grabbed her dorsal fin and dove with her. At least he could get there before the rest and check out the level of danger. He located the mound of lobe coral to orient himself to his location. The water temperature seemed to stay level, and he took encouragement from the fact until he noticed how few fish were here.

He passed the cave but didn't spare it a glance today with his focus on the state of the developing cracks. He located the one that ran from the cave toward the drop-off, then swam along it. It seemed to have stayed the same width. He noticed a crack that veered off from it and decided to follow it. Nani followed along beside him, but she was showing signs of agitation: rolling over in the water, darting in front of him as though to bar his advance. He knew the danger must be along this crack, so he slowed his speed and peered ahead as far as he could see.

The water began to feel warmer. The clear visibility dropped to less than fifty feet, then to less than thirty. He checked his dive computer. He was at about sixty feet.

Then he saw it—a red glow deep in the billowing pillow lava. The soft, cushiony-looking mounds would be anything but soft if he dared to touch them. Annie was right. An eruption had begun down here. There was no telling how long it would be before the eruption spread and endangered the site where the sunken ship sat. Ron wouldn't like this.

Bane turned and swam back the way he'd come. He reached the mother crack and decided to follow it down into the abyss a short distance. Nani followed him, but she was still distressed. He pressed on anyway. He had to know what the conditions were. Checking his dive computer, he monitored his mental state as he dove past one hundred feet, then one hundred fifty. He could see the ledge ahead, but something more ominous caught his attention. Another red glow in the distance, on the same level as the ship.

Staying at about one hundred fifty feet, he swam above the ship and over to the red glow. It was about fifty feet beyond the ship. Much too close to allow them to work safely. Ron wouldn't be happy. He had turned to rejoin the others when he saw the opening to a cave. He approached it and shone his powerful halogen light inside. It was mammoth, opening to about fifty feet in diameter. Interesting varieties of coral enticed him farther in. Nani zoomed around him. She bumped him with her nostrum and blocked his path. He patted her and started to rise.

From out of the darkness at the back of the cave, another diver emerged into Bane's light. Bane blinked, not sure he was really seeing a person. Then he saw the knife in the diver's hand. The man might not mean any harm. He smiled and lifted his hand in greeting. The diver came at him with the knife. Bane kicked out with his fins and managed to move enough to get out of the way. The diver came at him again, his green eyes behind the mask dark with menace. but

Nani dove between them. She torpedoed into the diver's stomach, and the knife dropped to the cave bottom. The diver was doubled over, struggling to suck in air through his regulator.

Nani came close, and Bane grabbed her dorsal fin. With a final glance at the man who was beginning to recover from Nani's blow and swim away, he allowed the dolphin to pull him up to safety. She swam to where Leia was helping Annie take samples. Bane released Nani's dorsal fin. He touched Annie on the arm, and Leia saw him. She shook her finger at him, and he could see the worry in her face. At a touch on his shoulder, Bane turned to see Mano. His brother squeezed his shoulder in a tight grip, and Bane knew Mano had been looking for him.

Bane motioned to the women and Mano to follow him. He took them to the site of the eruption. Annie and Mano began to take samples, and from their swift, efficient movements, he realized they might be in more danger than he'd realized. Could this slight eruption turn to something more? It was hot down here, and getting hotter.

Eighteen

Leia had never been so close to molten lava. When visiting the Big Island, she had never managed to walk out to Kilauea and look at the lava flow. Today's experience had been surreal.

"Any idea why someone would attack you?" Mano asked Bane. "What could be in the cave? And where did he come from? There's no boat up here waiting for him."

"I wonder if he was just narced and paranoid. Maybe he'd gone deeper than he expected, like Leia did the other day." Bane's voice was impatient. "Or maybe he wanted any treasure for himself."

Ron scowled. "No one is taking that ship away from me. The eruption isn't bad enough to overheat the water by the ship yet, you said. I want to get down there and get it out while we can."

"We don't even know there is a treasure on the ship," Leia said. "Legend says the treasure was removed and buried somewhere on the island, and an old man I knew claimed his ancestors buried it on land. You could be putting lives in danger for nothing. I'm not going down again." Leia watched Ron's face to see if she was getting through.

He shrugged. "Even if that's true, the ship itself is of value, and we have only a small window of time to preserve it. We're too close to give up now." He looked at Bane.

"You'll be fine. Annie here can monitor the eruption and let us know when it's too dangerous to go down. I've got deep-sea diving gear on its way, but the Trimix will work in the meantime if you don't stay down too long."

Annie shook her head. "It's too dangerous *now*. The earthquakes haven't slowed. We had a large swarm just this morning. I think a big event is imminent. My advice is to not go down there anymore, no matter where the treasure really is."

Ron growled. "If the treasure had been taken off the ship and buried, surely someone would have come back for it."

"There are places on Moloka'i where no one goes and access is forbidden. I don't find it implausible that it's still buried somewhere on the island." Leia should have expected his argument.

"Does anyone know more about this legend?" Ron squinted his eyes and looked at the water.

"The only one I heard talk about it is dead now. Someone shot him a few days ago." Leia wondered how Koma's death fit in. All the pieces of the puzzle had to fit in somehow.

"Convenient," Ron said. "No one knows who shot him?"

She shook her head. "I was with him, and the shot came out of the blue. He said he was taking me to the treasure."

Ron eyes brightened. "Did you believe him?"

"He saw Ku the week before, so I wasn't holding my breath."

"Great. He sounds like a crackpot." Ron rubbed his eyes. "I want that ship. Not just the gold, but the artifacts. I can't give it up with it being right under us." He looked to Bane. "Hang with me on this, Bane. I'll go down with you. We'll keep an eye on the eruption. Just one good dive. That's all I ask. We can haul up some artifacts even if we don't find a treasure of gold doubloons. I'll give you a twenty-five percent share in whatever we find in addition to the salary I'm paying you."

Bane was tempted—Leia could see it on his face. "Don't go, Bane," she said softly. "It's too dangerous. I don't want you down there when an eruption starts."

"She's right," Mano said. "Annie and I have lived through an eruption. You don't want to experience it."

Bane chewed on his lip, then finally nodded at Ron. "One dive, and that's all. Get us some deep-sea gear here, and we'll go down tomorrow."

Ron's relieved smile came, and he clapped his hand on Bane's back. "You won't regret it, my friend. I'll make it worth your while."

"I'm doing it for friendship, Ron, not for money. My twenty-five percent goes to Candace. But one dive is all I'm doing."

Ron nodded and went toward the control room. Leia tried to hide her disappointment. She'd thought Bane would take her wishes into account, but why had she even thought he might? He didn't owe her anything, not anymore.

"I've got to get back to work," she told Bane. "Can someone run me to shore? I've got to run the shop today while Dirk takes a group out on a dive." They had a week before they had to shut it down, and she was going to help Candace milk every dime out of it.

"I'll take you," Bane said. "I need to drop Kaia at the airport anyway. She has to get back today."

"I want to stay here and tabulate this data. Do you think Ron will mind?" Annie asked.

"I'm sure he'll want to know what's going on. There's all kinds of equipment and computers in the control room. Make yourself at home." Bane helped Leia into the boat, then joined her there. He went to the helm. "Eva ought to be out here with us. It doesn't feel right not to have her here. She likes to steer."

"She's working today. She'll be sorry she missed you." Leia watched him fiddle with the controls before he got the engine started. They cruised the tops of the waves, and Nani followed them for a while, then turned back to the research boat. Leia decided she would go to Koma's cabin and look around. If she could find a lead to the treasure on land, maybe Bane wouldn't dive in dangerous conditions. She'd check out Koma's cabin, then talk to her grandmother again. Maybe she would draw them a map this time. Leia had about an hour before she had to be at the dive shop. She glanced at Bane. Best not to tell him though.

ynahs screamed from the treetops over Leia's head as she followed the sound of the waterfall by Koma's house through groves of coconut, lauhala, and banana trees. Insects hummed near her head, and she batted them away after a quick glance at her watch. She needed to hurry. She'd stopped by her grandmother's cottage to check on *Tûtû*, but Malia and Ajax had everything under control.

Koma's cabin had always seemed to her like the one belonging to the witch in *Hansel and Gretel*. When she was a little girl, she used to have nightmares for several days following a visit here. Even now, she suppressed a shudder as she approached the structure. It hunkered in the woods like a malevolent scorpion. The hipped roof reminded her of the humped back of a beetle, and the shuttered windows looked like two half-closed eyes. She shook her head at her fanciful thoughts. It was an old cabin, nothing more. There was nothing to fear here.

Leia tried the door and found it unlocked. The sounds around her seemed loud, and even her breathing was harsh and labored. She stepped inside the dimly lit, one-room cabin. Koma didn't have much of a kitchen—just a cabinet at the back of the room with a sink that held a hand pump to the water catchment in the back. She felt like a Peeping Tom as she advanced into the house. The air smelled stale and musty and held a hint of tobacco from the spittoon by the easy chair.

The room was cluttered with old Hawaiian memorabilia from bouncing hula girls to old movie posters of the Elvis movies made here. A stack of books sat beside the chair, and she glanced at the titles. They were all about the old Hawaiian kingdom. A small cot was pushed against one wall. She peered under it but found nothing except dust bunnies, a whole nest of them. If she were Koma, where would she hide her most prized possessions? Surely not here. He loved the jungle. This place was where he came when he was finally too tired to roam the wilderness.

She didn't really know why she was here. Maybe she'd hoped to find a treasure map with a giant *X*. She smiled at the thought. She stepped out the back door and found several old pails for cleaning—not that it looked like they'd been used much. They held cobwebs and the remains of some spider's meal. She suppressed a shudder and stepped off the back stoop into the yard. A frayed yard chair sat beside a firepit. Koma had spent a lot of time out here. She looked around the yard, trying to see where he might hide something. Her gaze stopped on the old banyan tree at the edge of the jungle. Koma had told her stories about this tree. He loved it.

She approached the massive tree, its aerial roots now massive, intertangled trunks so thick it was hard to see between them. Tipping her head back, she gazed into the branches loaded with leaves and birds. Koma used to climb this tree every day and sit and meditate, he'd told her. She glanced at her shorts. She'd get her legs scratched, but she couldn't leave without at least climbing to the platform she could see the tip of.

She kicked off her slippers, then wedged her foot into the crook of the tree and heaved herself up. Once on the first branch, the climbing became easier, and her fingertips soon touched the lip of the platform. When she at last stood on the platform and looked down into the surrounding yard and jungle, she felt like Tarzan. She glanced around the platform and saw that an old wooden chest was nailed to the tree.

Could it be the treasure? Her pulse skipped, and she rushed to throw open the lid. Inside lay a jumble of bones, and she shrank back and slammed the lid. It had to be something from Koma's weird religion. She didn't know what kind of bones they were, and she didn't want to know. Who knew what animals he'd sacrificed? This had been a waste of time. She was preparing to descend the tree when she heard voices below her. She shrank back. Who else would be exploring Koma's property? She dropped to her knees and peered down through the branches. The murmur of voices grew louder, but she didn't recognize them. They stopped about ten feet from the tree. She hoped they wouldn't see her slippers at the base of the tree. Their voices carried in the clear air. Leia could see their heads through the leafy cover beneath her, but their backs were to her and she couldn't identify them.

"I thought sure she'd come this way. We must have lost her somewhere. Old Koma might have told her something. We're getting nowhere by ourselves."

"I'll grab her tonight." The second man's voice was high and whiny.

"That's what you said last night," the first man growled.

"Yeah, well, she had the guy staying there. I wasn't going to tackle him. He's ex-military."

Bane. They were talking about her and Bane. Leia put her hand over her mouth. Last night had been an attempt to kidnap her. Fear rose in a wave, and she fought it back. She had to figure out who these men were and what they wanted. Did they think Koma told her where the treasure was? If so, how could she convince them she knew nothing?

After dropping Kaia at the airport, Bane drove back toward the harbor. He saw the dive shop up ahead and decided to stop by for a minute. He told himself he really needed to check on Candace. Tony would expect it of him, especially now that she was being tossed out of the business on her ear. He didn't see Leia's little Neon parked in the lot, though there were several other cars. Maybe someone had dropped her off. She should have been here half an hour ago. He pulled into the first available slot and shut off the engine. The dirt road had left a scum of red dust on his rented pickup, and he made a mental note to get it washed after work tonight. The place was nearly deserted, and he saw only one customer perusing the display of swim masks on the shelves.

Candace was looking out the window on the door. She chewed her lip. "I was hoping you were Leia," she said.

"Isn't she here?"

Dirk lifted one eyebrow. "We were just wondering what happened to her. She's late, and I've got a group to take out on a dive in about fifteen minutes."

"She left for here two hours ago." Bane thought of last night's intruder. "There was someone lurking around Ipo's last night. I hope she's all right."

"It's not like her," Candace said. "She's generally early, not late. I don't like it. I wish she'd carry a cell phone."

"You have her grandmother's number?" Bane realized he didn't.

Candace shook her head. "She just moved out there, and we haven't updated her file yet."

"We could call her mother, but I'd hate to worry her if Leia has only had a flat or something simple like that." Candace looked past Bane's shoulder, and the worried creases on her forehead eased. "There she is."

Bane turned to see Leia running to the door. She glanced over her shoulder as though she was afraid someone was following her. The door stuck, and she practically fell into the shop when it finally opened. She caught herself, then her gaze collided with Bane's. Her face was white, and a smudge of dirt marred her cheek. She rushed to join them.

"What's wrong?" Bane took her arm and helped her to the chair, where she sat and caught her breath.

She glanced up at Bane. "I went to Koma's cabin," she began.

"By yourself? Why didn't you ask me to go along?"

She tilted her chin up. "I wasn't afraid."

He sighed. "You never are when you should have more sense. The man was killed, Leia. We still don't know why."

She nodded, then gulped. "I was in the tree, and two men came by. I overheard them talking. One of them was the one outside

Tûtû's house last night. They were planning on grabbing me and asking me where the treasure is. They think Koma told me!"

Candace gasped, and Dirk grabbed a bottle of water from the little fridge under the counter. "You look like you need a drink," he said.

Bane mentally slapped himself. He should have thought of that. He was the one who loved Leia, and he hadn't even stopped to think of how upset she must be. "You want me to take you home?" he asked.

Leia stiffened. "I'm fine." She pushed the water away. She moved so that Bane's hand dropped from her shoulder.

He stuck his hand in the pocket of his shorts. He wished he could figure out what was eating her. "Did you get a look at the men?"

"Just a glimpse. I didn't recognize them. I told Malia to be careful with *Tûtû*. If they're watching the house, I don't want my grandmother in danger."

"We don't want you in danger either. What makes them think Koma told you anything?" Candace asked.

"I wish I knew. Koma said he was going to show it to me just before he got shot."

"Did he give you any hint of where it was?" Candace uncapped a bottle of water and took a swig.

"No, but—" She clamped her lips together and looked away.

"But?" Candace prompted.

"Nothing." Leia slumped back against the chair and fingered her upper lip.

"Hey, I have to go," Dirk said, glancing at his watch. "I'm already late. I'm taking a group out along the barrier reef." He chucked Leia under the chin. "Keep a stiff upper lip, babe."

Leia smiled. "Have a good dive, Dirk. I'll hold down the fort here."

"Are you sure you're up to it?" Candace asked. "You're still pale."

"It was just a shock to find out someone was looking for me."

She licked her lips and slanted a glance up at Bane. "Um, are you still staying at *Tûtû*'s house?"

At last she was asking him for something. "You're not staying there without me. Candace, would you call Detective Ono and tell him what happened to Leia? He'll probably want to talk to her."

"I called him from *Tûtû*'s house. He said he'd meet me here," Leia said.

"I think you and your grandmother should move in with your parents for now."

Leia sighed. "You're right, but *Tûtû* will never agree. Besides, I'm not living under my mother's roof again."

"Her safety is more important than your issues with Ingrid."

"Of course it is," she mumbled, looking away. "But all she has now is her dignity, Bane. How can I take that from her? If she wanted to go, I'd take her, but I'm not staying there myself."

"You already know she's not well. That spell with her heart or whatever it was showed us that. She's so remote. What if she has another attack? Put aside your differences with your mother."

She inhaled, then blew her breath out. "All right, I'll call my father. He can break the news to my mother. But I'm not going to stay there. Don't ask me to do that." She rubbed her forehead. "I don't know how I'll tell *Tûtû*."

He knew better than to argue with her. "Where will you stay?"

"In my cottage. Or maybe I can stay with Candace." She glanced at her friend, who nodded.

"Once we find out who is behind this—or find the treasure ourselves, it will be safe to go back," Bane said.

"Are you still going to try to find the treasure? You really think it's buried somewhere near Koma's house?" Candace asked. "It would solve a lot of problems if you could find it. You probably haven't heard this, but Shaina has filed for a paternity test to be done. If Tony really did father her child, I'm in even more trouble than I thought."

"Candace, I'm so sorry." Leia put her arm around Candace, and the other woman wilted against her.

Though Candace was still beautiful, the past days had left their toll in the dark circles under her eyes. Bane wished he could promise he'd find the treasure. "We haven't given up yet," he told her. He directed his next question to Leia. "Did Koma have any friends?"

"Just my grandmother. Oh, and one other man. Paulo Niau. I think he's ninety-five. He used to run the general store in town, and Koma worked for him years ago. They played *konane* together regularly."

Bane had never played the ancient Hawaiian board game that was similar to checkers and chess, but he'd seen older natives playing it. "How could he have told Paulo anything while playing *konane*? You're not supposed to talk."

She smiled. "Maybe they broke the rules. It's worth talking to him, I guess."

The door to the shop opened, and Detective Ono stepped inside. He was smiling in his usual genial way. "What's this I hear about some men wanting to kidnap you, Pilgrim?" He winked at Bane. "I might try it myself if it wasn't for my wife and the frying pan she's liable to hit me with."

Leia began to smile, and Bane knew she was finally getting over the shock of the afternoon. He listened to her tell the detective about the men. Ono jotted notes in his pocket notebook, then put it away. "Do you have any leads on Koma's death?" Bane asked.

The detective shook his head. "Some poachers were shooting birds in the area. We found some bloody remains a few yards from Koma's body. I was beginning to suspect it was a hunting accident until Leia told me her story. Now I just don't know. I'll check it out though." He looked at Leia. "You're sure you didn't recognize the men?"

She shook her head. "I couldn't see them well enough to be able to tell who they were. Only the tops of their heads."

"Maybe you should have made a noise so they'd look up." He laughed.

Ono smiled, but Leia frowned. "I'm not some flighty female, Detective. This is more serious than you seem to think. Bane ran off an intruder last night, and now we find I was the target. I don't want me or my grandmother to end up like Koma."

Ono held up his hands. "*Kala mai ia'u.* I meant no offense." He smiled again. "I'll see what I can find out."

"Another thing—a man attacked Bane underwater with a knife just this morning."

Ono shook his head. "Why didn't you call me?"

"It was on the water. We called the Coast Guard. They've probably notified your office by now," Bane said.

"I'd better get back then," Ono said. He whistled as he sauntered out the door.

"He won't find anything," Leia said, her voice thick with disgust.

"How about dinner when you get off work, and then we can run out and talk to Paulo?" He ignored Candace's knowing smile and kept his gaze focused on Leia's face. *Say yes, say yes,* he thought.

"I guess that would be okay."

He controlled his elation. She just wanted his help, he reminded himself. That was all. But if he could just get under the shell she'd erected and find out what went wrong between them, maybe the next date would be different. Tonight might be his one shot at the truth.

Nineteen

Leia dusted the counters of the dive shop, then emptied the trash. The afternoon had dragged by, and she gazed longingly out the window at the surf pounding the rocky shore. She'd rather be out on the water than stuck here inside with the scent of rubber swim fins. The shop had been dead too. Even dealing with tourists who didn't know what equipment they needed would be preferable to this silence.

She heard the crunch of gravel through the open window and looked up to see Pete Kone getting off his Harley. Her gaze went to his hands to see if he was carrying a new court order, but they were empty.

He shoved open the door with effort and stepped into the shop. "Aloha, Leia. I was hoping I'd find you here."

"Any more news on your bones?" She came around the counter to greet him.

His dark eyes shone with enthusiasm, and he nodded. "More bones washed up this morning. And more ancient tools. We've definitely got a site out there of something big."

"Any ideas what it might be? How would the bodies get into the ocean, and then wash ashore?"

"We know that the ocean has covered over at least one burial cave in this area. I suspect it might be close to where you've been diving. A storm surge could have washed the bones out of a cave."

She studied his face. "You don't seem angry that your injunction was stopped."

He shrugged. "You care about our history. Bane does too. I

don't think you'd willingly allow any damage. So what about it—did you see anything down there that might hold the bones?"

"There is a cave." She bit her lip. "It may not matter for any of us, Pete. A seamount is forming. I saw the lava with my own eyes. It's getting too dangerous to even go down."

Pete stared, his eyes growing wide. He sighed. "Maybe Pele is protecting the dead in her own way—keeping them from desecration—but I'd hoped to find the cave and seal it with an explosion from further erosion. We don't want these bones exhumed by the sea."

She'd always known Pete adhered closely to the old ways, but she hadn't realized he took it so far as to believe in the ancient gods. At least her parents had made sure she learned about the one true God, even if she wasn't sure she could trust him anymore. "God may be protecting them," she corrected.

The smile Pete flashed was full of amusement. "You don't really know where you fit, do you, Leia? A little of your dad's Hawaiian beliefs, a little of your mom's Swedish stoicism, and none of the passion for our spiritual heritage from either. This land belongs to us, not the *haoles*. Pele will protect her people from the rape of the land."

He'd put his finger close to the truth about her beliefs, but she refused to let him rile her. "Well, Pele hasn't done such a good job of that in the past. I'm as Hawaiian as you are, Pete. Your grandmother was Asian. Pele didn't stop the kingdom from being ripped from us." She stopped short of telling him he was praying to the wrong god. He was smart enough that he would get her inference.

"I went to church with my aunt a few times. Who wants to follow a god who passively submits to whatever comes his way? I want a warrior, a god who will help me fight this battle." He turned toward the door. "Keep your eyes open for a cave and let me know if you find it. I know you love our history too, Leia. You won't want it destroyed any more than I do."

He was right about that. She felt a connection with her culture and her people with an ache that went clear to the bone. Could the

cave above the sunken ship hold a burial site? Though she knew it
wasn't safe, she longed to find out. Pete was right—it needed to be
sealed off for protection from the sea. Maybe God would use the
volcano to do just that, but if not, she owed it to her heritage to
help take care of it.

"Where are we going?" Leia shouted over the sound of the
wind. He was captaining her boat.

Bane grinned and shook his head. "I'm not telling," he shouted
back. He'd spent all afternoon making the arrangements. It hadn't
been easy to get a beach dinner catered. She stuck her tongue out
at him, and his grin widened. This was going to be a great evening,
he could feel it. The wind whipped her hair around, and a long
strand touched his face. He focused his thoughts and drummed his
fingers on the steering wheel. No talking just yet, he reminded himself. They'd have a nice dinner, and he'd woo her again. Once she'd
mellowed, maybe he could get her to open up about the real reason
she'd broken their engagement.

"Did you hear the news?" he asked. "I called Ono to check on
the investigation, and he said they'd found the missing drugs at the
hospital. The initial inventory was wrong. If the toxicology report
comes back with that in Tony's blood, the murderer had to have
gotten it somewhere else. Your mother is off the hook."

She closed her eyes. "Thank God," she said. For the first time
in quite a while, she realized she meant it. She shut off the engine,
and he dropped the anchor overboard. "Here we are," he said.

She looked around at the deserted beach. "What do you mean,
here we are. I thought we were going for dinner."

"We are." He nodded toward the beach. "Our restaurant,
madam."

A smile teased the corners of her lips. "What a romantic idea.
Did you come up with it yourself, or did Kaia suggest it?"

"It was all hatched in my own brain." He hopped out of the boat, and they strolled to a table covered with a white tablecloth. The server in the van parked by the sand waved to him and began to haul out the food. Pleasure suffused her face with color. She squeezed his fingers. The pink-and-white sundress she wore fitted her figure perfectly and showed off her shoulders and arms. He could barely take his eyes off her.

The warm caress of the trade winds was like a touch of heaven. He seated her at the table. The server brought drinks and rolls, and the entertainment arrived. Within a few minutes the live entertainment—three singers and a bevy of hula dancers—began to perform. The sound of the slack-key guitars set the mood, and he could see Leia relaxing.

She fingered the tiny, adorable scar on her lip, but her eyes smiled at him. "I'm impressed," she said. "This is wonderful. But, Bane—"

He held up his hand. "No buts. We're going to forget our past for a little while and just enjoy the evening."

"I think you're expecting too much of tonight. This was just supposed to be dinner." She stirred the lemon in her iced tea and didn't look at him.

He knew he should wait until they'd eaten, but the words burst out before he could clamp them back. "I want to know what happened, Leia. Why did you break our engagement? I know you still care about me, so what is it? Let's fix it and build a future."

She still wasn't meeting his gaze, and the color had leached from her cheeks. She sat back and sighed. "We get along better when we're not talking about us and the future. Do you remember that time we stopped at Kepuhi Bay and we had the whole beach to ourselves?"

This wasn't going to be easy. "Why do you always look back, Leia? The future is much more exciting than the past."

She bit her thumbnail, then put her hands in her lap. "I'm afraid, okay? I never know what the future is going to bring. There's always some new trial that seems to come along. The past is safer."

He leaned across the table and took her hand. "We can weather anything if we have each other to lean on. We'll build a family together."

She exhaled. "There will be no family. I don't want any kids, Bane," she said softly.

"You'll be a better mother than your mom. You shouldn't worry."

A frown crouched between her blue eyes. "You're misunderstanding me, Bane. It's not because of my mother. I don't want kids."

He opened his mouth, but no words came to mind. He'd always wanted a bunch of kids running around. Her blunt statement altered everything. "No kids?" he finally managed. "You seem to love kids." He felt like he was floundering in uncharted waters. This wasn't going according to the script in his head.

"This isn't easy." She sighed and rubbed her forehead. "I lied to you, okay? Our final argument had nothing to do with you taking charge. I've always liked the way you try to take care of me. I just didn't want to tell you the real reason, so I picked a fight."

"I—I don't understand." A sour taste came to his mouth. "How could you lie to me?" He realized he was raising his voice and made an attempt to lower it. "You know I hate lies."

"I know." She wet her lips. "Birth defects run in our family. I won't put a child through what I went through."

"You don't have any defects," he blurted. "You're beautiful and perfect."

She touched the faint scar on her lip. "This wasn't a cat scratch like I told you. I was born with a cleft lip. I had half a dozen surgeries by the time I was five. And Eva has Down's as well as a cleft lip. I don't want to bring a damaged child into the world. And don't think we can adopt. I've thought it all out. Adoption is as much of a gamble as having my own baby. So no kids, not ever. Do you understand now?"

He stared at her. "Damaged? You are looking at it wrong. Sure, Eva has special needs, but she's a joy to be around. Don't you feel her wonder and excitement when you examine an anthill with her?

God has her here for a purpose. Who are you to say she's damaged?"
He was having a hard time holding on to his temper. "And what
about your life? Do you enjoy it less because you have a tiny scar?"
He stopped and stared into her face. "You moved to Kalaupapa,
right in the midst of lepers. Do you think they have no significance
because they were once called unclean? You've got a skewed version
of what makes life worthwhile, Leia. Accept the gift of life God and
your parents gave you and be grateful for it."

She kept a steady gaze into his eyes. "I'm not changing my mind,
Bane. I won't give you children. And if you can sway me later, don't.
I'm not ever having children. That's not negotiable."

"Have you talked to your pastor about this?"

"Why? My mind is made up. You don't know what it's like
to have your earliest memories be those of hospitals and pain.
That's why I fear the future. You never know what God is going
to allow to come." She looked away. "I don't mean to sound
whiny. I'm grateful for my life. But my mother has never let me
forget I was less than perfect. And it was my father's fault in her
eyes, of course. No one in her family had ever had a birth defect.
I couldn't stand it if you someday blamed me for any problems
our child might have."

"I'm not like your mother," he protested. "I could love any
child, regardless of the problems." But could he? A vision of the
various birth defects he'd seen over the years flashed through his
mind: missing fingers, retardation, muscular dystrophy. He wouldn't
accept something like that easily. He knew himself well enough to
know that he'd fight to try to control it, to fix it. Did he have the
right to risk putting a child through something like that? Maybe
Leia was right. And if she was, would he someday blame her for
their childlessness? He was going to have to consider how he
really felt.

The rest of the dinner had been quiet, and Leia wanted other people around so she suggested they head back to the peninsula. They docked the boat in Kalaupapa, and she was the first one off the deck. "Let's check on *Tûtû* and Malia. Malia was going to start packing up our grandmother's things for the move home tomorrow. I'd like to see how *Tûtû* is taking it." She led the way to her bike. He got on behind her and put his hands on her waist. Maybe this idea had been a mistake. The mint scent of his breath on her neck gave her a delicious shiver.

His voice in her ear vibrated with anger. "I never took you for a coward, Leia."

She frowned and started the bike. "We'd better go."

"You're afraid of really living. You think God is supposed to lay your life out neatly without any pain. Did you ever stop to think that you're the person you are now—strong, brave, capable—because of the things you've faced?"

"I want more for a child," she said stiffly. She was tempted to put her hands over her ears and hum like Eva. Bane could be so argumentative. "You think you have all the answers, but you haven't gone through what I have." She started off with a jerky movement and putted down the road.

His voice in her ear didn't let up. "And you haven't experienced what I have. You grew up with both parents, while I was raised by my grandfather."

"I know you didn't have it easy either. I'm not asking you to give up your dream of children, Bane. That's why I broke the engagement. Find someone else. Someone perfect who can give you perfect children."

He was silent so long she realized he wasn't going to answer. What was he thinking? She wasn't sure she wanted to know. He wouldn't give up his dream for her, no man would. She didn't want him to sacrifice himself that way, and that's what marrying her would be—a sacrifice. Bane Oana was born to be a dad. He took care of everyone around him, his brother and sister, his friends. He deserved a whole and perfect mate. And she wanted that for him— she really did. Or at least she did when she had her jealousy under control.

Twenty

When they entered Ipo's cottage, *Tûtû* was clear-eyed and interested in talking about the treasure. Bane tried to keep his excitement in check. "Can you tell us where it is?"

Ipo nodded. "It's time for you to find the treasure. Look for a mango tree on the north side of the fishpond. Just to the right of there is what's left of a giant tree trunk. Count off fifty feet to the west and then dig. The treasure is there." She grabbed Leia's hand. "But watch that no one sees you."

"I will," Leia promised. She glanced at Bane. "Want to go out looking for it? There's a full moon tonight."

"Can I eat first? I barely touched my dinner." He rubbed Ajax's head. "You're hungry, too, aren't you, boy?" The dog woofed in agreement.

"I'll see what I can find." Leia stood. "You need my help getting ready for bed, *Tûtû*?"

"I'll get her tucked in," Malia said. "Go feed Bane. We've got most everything she wants packed up. We'll go in the morning." She assisted Ipo to her bedroom.

Bane followed Leia to the kitchen. "Maybe I should cook. You might try something weird on me."

Though he was trying to joke with her, he realized he still couldn't look at her. It would take some time to process what she'd told him.

"Too late. I've been wanting to try a recipe for *gon lo mein*. It has oyster sauce in it."

He curled his lip. "Gag a maggot. That doesn't sound like something I'd want to try."

"Live a little! You never know—you might like it. Remember the broccoli casserole I fixed that you thought you'd hate? It was on our second date."

"That was a fluke. You always think I'll like it if I just try it. I don't know why you have to try new recipes. I like my tried-and-true favorites. Spam with hash browns, macaroni and cheese, teribeef sandwiches, *huli huli* chicken. Normal stuff."

"This is normal."

"For who? Not for me." He rummaged in the refrigerator past little dishes of leftover casserole that were beginning to sprout colonies of mold, half-eaten containers of yogurt, and carrots that had begun to lose their color. Even Ajax turned up his nose at the yogurt, the only edible thing in the refrigerator. "There's nothing good in here. I don't think you'll find the stuff you need to make that lo mein thing."

"I brought it a while back." She went to the cupboard and pulled down some cans, then stepped to the back porch and brought in a bag of frozen vegetables from the freezer. "Trust me, it will be good."

"I don't have much choice," he grumbled. "Can you leave the oyster stuff out of mine?"

She lowered her brows and shot him a look. "No. Just sit down and be quiet."

He grinned. "Taking charge, are we?" Pulling out a chair at the table, he plunked down on it and stretched out his long legs.

She worked in silence, and Bane couldn't think of carrying on a conversation. Leia finished the meal preparations and set it in front of him. "See what you think."

He took a bite. "It's better than I expected," he admitted. He dropped a bite on the floor to Ajax, who snatched it up. "Ajax agrees." He began to shovel the food into his mouth. "Do you think we're really going to find anything at the fishpond?"

Her shoulders tensed. "Not really, I guess. I wish we would. I'm ready for this all to be over."

Maybe it was all over. Between them anyway. He clenched his teeth at the thought. No, he wasn't ready to let it go. He loved Leia, and he was going to have to figure out a way to make this work.

*E*va peered out her window into the moonlight. She felt funny tonight, like there were bugs crawling on her skin. When the bad dream woke her, she wanted to go find her mother, but Mama got mad when Eva told her about her dreams. She said to think nice thoughts and go to sleep, not wake her up. It was hard to think nice thoughts when there had been a monster under her bed.

The scary part was that the monster seemed to want to eat Leia. Eva hugged herself and tried not to cry. It was very late so she knew she couldn't call her sister. Leia wouldn't care, but she might wake up *Tûtû*. Eva wanted her sister though. Leia was the one person who never made Eva feel stupid. She couldn't let anything happen to Leia. Eva looked at the phone again. She had to call her sister.

*T*he moonlight whispered around Leia and Bane as they retraced their steps to the grove where they'd found the fishpond. The moonlight illuminated the clearing like a giant lamp. "Do you think we're going to find anything?" Leia asked Bane, who was holding back a large frond to allow her to pass. He carried a shovel in his other hand.

He shrugged and let the branch fall back into place. "Maybe. At any rate, we'll have an adventure."

She stopped. "Listen. Do you hear something?" It almost sounded like someone chopping something. A rhythmic *thwack* resounded in the forest.

"I hear it. It sounds like it's coming from the fishpond area." He put his hand on her forearm. "Hang on, let me check it out."

"I'll go with you." She fell into step beside him.

"I know better than to argue with you."

She couldn't hide her smile. "Smart man." He took her hand, and she let him keep it a few minutes. The warm pressure of his fingers made her forget all the reasons she couldn't be with him, all the things she'd told herself in the night about why she could never marry. She made a show of moving a branch out of the way so she could pull her hand out of his grasp. He didn't try to take it again, and she wasn't sure whether to be relieved or not.

The sound was just beyond the last stand of trees. Bane held out his arm. "Wait, let's not just bust through and startle whoever it is." He parted the branches to look into the clearing.

Leia peeked through the leafy window with him. A man with a shovel bent over the ground. Holes had been dug all over the clearing, and some still gaped open while others had been backfilled. "What's he doing?" she whispered.

"I'd say he's looking for the treasure." Bane's voice was grim.

"How would he know where to look?" Leia had visions of someone skulking outside the house listening to all their conversations.

"Maybe he got it out of Koma."

She'd rather believe that. "Can you tell who it is?"

"He's too far off. Let's go around to the other side and see if we can get a glimpse of his face. Try not to make any noise."

She nodded, and they crept through the jungle, moving north. "At least he's not digging where *Tûtû* told us to," she whispered when they finally stood with the ocean to their backs. She could hear the sound of the surf in the distance.

"Listen! Someone else is coming." Bane grabbed her arm and dragged her down into the foliage.

Leia held her breath as someone passed by. She peeked out from behind the fronds and saw a familiar form. She tightened her fingers on Bane's muscular forearm. Bending close, she whispered in his ear. "It's Jermaine." He nodded, and they stood and crept forward again. Peeking through the leaves again, she watched as Jermaine approached the figure in the clearing. The two spoke in tones too low to make out words.

She was beginning to think it was an accidental meeting until the man they'd seen digging stepped back and lifted his shovel. Before they could react, he whacked Jermaine in the neck with it. Even from here, she could see the blood spray out from Jermaine's neck. "He's severed his carotid artery." She didn't bother to lower her voice.

She jerked away from Bane's restraining hand, then parted the foliage and barreled into the clearing. "You there, get away from him!"

The man's face was startled as he stared at them with vivid green eyes. Dropping his shovel, he disappeared into the forest. Bane shouted and ran after him with the shovel they'd brought from Ipo's while Leia went to help Jermaine. He was still conscious, but just barely. His lips moved, but she couldn't make out the words. "Don't try to talk. We'll get you help." She pressed the heel of her hand against his neck, but blood continued to spurt. She needed a cloth or something, but she had nothing. Crouching over Jermaine, she used both hands and applied as much pressure as she dared. "Bane!" she yelled. "Hurry!"

She couldn't do this alone. Praying for God to help her, she worked on the young man. The blood flow began to taper, and she thought maybe she was going to be successful in saving him.

"Made a mistake," Jermaine whispered. "Should have known." His eyes rolled back in his head, and the blood flow slowed, then stopped.

"Jermaine?" Leia pressed her fingertips against his neck. No pulse. Her hands fell to her sides.

Bane reached her side. He was breathing hard and perspiring. "He got away." He knelt by her side and looked down at Jermaine's sightless eyes. He reached down and closed the young man's lids.

"I'm sorry." He slipped his arm around her shoulders and hugged her to him.

She pulled away. "I need to wash my hands." The coppery smell of the blood nearly made her gag.

"The water is close. Let's go get you cleaned up."

He took her hand, not seeming to mind the gore on it. This time she didn't pull away. His strength was all that kept her putting one foot in front of the other. He pulled branches out of their path and led her to the beach. The fresh scent of the sea purged her lungs of the blood's pungent odor. She ran forward, up to her knees in the rolling waves. Plunging her hands into the warm water, she washed the gore in the cleansing power of the ocean.

"Now what?" Leia asked.

She was looking to Bane for answers, and he wasn't sure he had any. "I wish this lousy cell phone would work. We need to report what happened right away, but I hate to leave without checking out the site your grandmother said to dig. We can't do anything for Jermaine anyway, so I'd like to dig at the site first."

He'd expected shock and censure, but she nodded. "I'm so tired of this. I just want to get to the bottom of it. It shouldn't take long to dig a hole and see if there's anything there."

"I left the shovel in the clearing. Let's go." He took her hand and helped her through the rough terrain back to where they'd left Jermaine. When they stepped back into the open meadow, his eyes went to where they'd left the young man's body. He froze. "Jermaine's body—it's gone!" He dropped her hand and ran to the spot. Surely this was where they'd left him. He took in the matted, bloodstained grass. His head came up, and he gazed around the clearing. Jermaine's body had vanished.

Leia was still standing where he'd left her. Her eyes were wide, and she had her hand to her mouth. "I don't like this, Bane. Whoever killed him is still here. He's taken the body. What if he's watching us now? We need to get out of here."

He glanced around. "I think he's gone now. Go sit by that big tree. Climb it, if you're game, and watch for anyone coming while I dig the hole." She nodded, and a bit of the shock left her face. She hurried to the large monkeypod tree he indicated and began to scramble into its twisted branches. "All clear?" he asked her.

She nodded. "I don't see anything. It's getting too dark. The moon is coming out, but it's still hard to see very far."

He grabbed the shovel that he'd dropped into a thick clump of ti. Striding to the big mango tree to the north of the fishpond, he found the remains of the tree trunk just where Ipo had said. Fifty feet took him to a small rise that was covered in wild orchids. Thrusting the shovel into the fertile ground, he uprooted the plants and laid them to one side so he could replant them when he was done. It was hard digging in slippers, and he wished he had his hiking boots. He pressed on, bringing up the moist earth in heavy shovelfuls. About two feet down, the shovel struck something. His excitement surged, but he told himself it could just be a rock. He began to dig around the obstruction. If it was a rock, it was a large one.

He dropped to his knees and began to feel with his hands. The rough surface had regular grooves in it, like a wooden chest. "I think I've found it!" he yelled to Leia.

"I'm coming," she called.

He heard her feet thump on the ground, but he didn't turn. When Leia joined him, they both began to scoop out dirt with their hands. It was fully dark now, but moonbeams illuminated the hole enough to keep working. Sweat trickled down his back and soaked his T-shirt. "I think we've almost got it loose." He struggled with a tree root that had entangled the box until he succeeded in breaking its grip. The large chest lay exposed. "Can you help me lift it out of the hole?"

"I think so." Leia got her fingers under the end of the chest and began to lift. "It's heavy, but I think I can do it."

He hefted his end, and they succeeded in maneuvering the

cumbersome object out of the hole and onto the solid ground. "Open it," Leia said, her voice hushed. He nodded and tried to lift the lid. It was locked.

He seized the shovel and stood. "Stand back." He hit the lock with the back of the shovel, again and again, until it broke. "You want to do the honors?" His smile felt huge as Leia reached toward the lid.

She touched it. "I'm almost scared," she whispered. They stared at each other, then she lifted the lid to reveal a small jumble of jewelry and gold coins. She frowned. "I expected more," she said.

The jewelry and gold coins barely covered the bottom of the chest. Bane had reached to pick up a coin when he felt something hard dig into his back.

"Step away from the chest," a cold male voice said. "Don't turn around." A burlap bag was thrust into Bane's hands. "Put the stuff in the bag and don't try anything, or I'll shoot you both. The girl-friend can help too."

Bane's anger rose, but he didn't dare turn and attack. Not with Leia here. They both began to drop handfuls of jewelry and coins into the bag. He felt keen regret as precious rings, brooches, and coins went through his fingers and into the bag. To come so close and now lose it left a bad taste on his tongue. Maybe he could over-come this guy. His thoughts raced to find a way out. His fingers scraped the bottom of the wooden chest, and he got the last pieces into the bag.

"Where's the rest of it?"

"That's all there is."

The man swore, and the gun dug deeper into Bane's back. "Drop the bag behind you. Don't turn around, either one of you."

There went his idea to hit the guy with the bag when he handed it to him. Bane eased the burlap bag to the ground behind him. If only he still had the shovel at his fingertips, but he had nothing, no weapon other than his bare hands.

"Count to one hundred before you turn around, or your girl-friend gets a bullet to the head," the gruff voice warned. "Start counting."

Bane curled his fingers into his palms. If only Leia weren't here, he would whirl and jump the guy. It was foolhardy to try it, he knew. The hard gun dug in again, and he began to count. "One, two, three . . ."

"Keep counting."

The gun was removed, and he heard a soft *umph* and the sound of footsteps running away. "Fifteen, sixteen, seventeen . . ." He stopped and turned cautiously. There was no one there. Leia was gone too.

T he man's hand smelled of onions as he kept it clasped over her nose and mouth. Leia struggled to free herself, but the man kept an iron grip on her and dragged her behind the other man. Her captor paused, and his grip slackened. Leia bit down on the finger closest to her mouth. His stifled scream sounded like a snort, and he turned her loose. She darted into the thick vegetation to her right.

Leia dived under a thick bush. The moon hid its face behind a bank of clouds. On both sides of her, the jungle was alive with sound: crickets chirped, tree frogs croaked a deep bass melody, and some larger animal thrashed through the underbrush. Probably a deer, she told herself. She could hear the men whispering as they searched for her, and she held her breath. The sound of their voices faded, and she prayed they were giving up.

She crawled out from under the bush and hurried along a nar-row path she recognized that led back to her grandmother's cottage. The air around her seemed to thicken, and it almost sounded as though someone or something stalked her again. She whirled and stared into the encroaching darkness. Her knees were barely sup-porting her as the adrenaline raced through her body. The only sound that came to her ears was the waterfall behind her. She forced her feet forward.

A twig snapped behind her, and she whirled again, her heart pounding loudly in her ears and her breath was labored. The soft, furtive noises seemed deliberate—and full of malice. She wished she could convince whoever was pursuing her that she knew nothing about Koma's secret.

Her feet moved forward again of their own volition. She wanted to break into a run, but she knew she didn't dare. Panic would overtake her, and besides, it was too dark and the path too treacherous to run along it in the dark. She'd fall and break something. She wished she had a weapon. Anything. Her gaze swept the dark ground. A stout stick would do, but all she saw were twigs and branches too small to inflict any damage. A couple of sharp-edged rocks lay along the side of the path, and she stooped and grabbed them up. These would be better than nothing. Hefting a rock in each hand, she hurried as fast as she dared down the hill toward home.

She felt rather than saw the attack when it came. A wind of movement rushed past her, and she heard the rustle of leaves as someone propelled toward her. She turned and raised the rock in her left hand to defend herself, but a hard body rammed into her and drove her to the ground. She fought with the calloused hands that wrestled her. The scent of decaying leaves and moss enveloped her, then she smelled tobacco and mint on the man's breath as he leaned over her and pinned her hands to the ground above her head.

"You're a wildcat," he panted. "I'm going to have to hurt you if you don't lay still."

She redoubled her efforts, but he was too strong for her. A gash caked with blood marred his forehead, and she recognized his face but couldn't place it. "I'll do worse than cut your head if you don't let me up." She tried to bite his wrist, but he jerked it out of the way, releasing her right hand. She brought it up and smashed the rock against his cheek.

He yowled, and both hands flew to his face. She managed to get her knee up and jammed it into his groin. He uttered a screech that would have been funny if the situation weren't so desperate. With him incapacitated, she scrambled out from under him and tried to get to her feet, but he grabbed her ankle and jerked her back.

"I'll teach you," he growled.

"Logan, that's enough." The second man moved into view. Though it was too dark to see him clearly, he exuded authority and menace.

Before Leia could make another attempt at escape, he trussed her hands and feet together. The first man grabbed the rope around her wrists and jerked her to her feet. "I can't walk like this," she said. She'd lost a slipper in the struggle as well.

He grunted then leaned over and hefted her across his shoulder. Her head hanging upside down, she watched the path recede as the men carried her into the jungle.

Twenty-one

Deep in the magma chambers, heat glowed in a red-hot pool. The pressure grew and forced the molten rock up through the crevices, where it found a passage along a weakened fault line. Instead of following a previous path, this lava forced its way through a crevice and raced upward as far as it could. A few feet below the surface, its strength waned, and so it waited for the necessary pressure to build and assist it through the last bit of resistance.

Bane had been wandering aimlessly, looking for Leia and the men who had taken her. He stopped and got out his cell phone, and had a signal this time. He quickly dialed Ipo, but the call was dropped before it could go through. He walked a few feet, but it still didn't come in. He realized he was in Koma's yard. Maybe he could get a signal on the tree platform.

He squinted in the moonlight, but it was so dark that he stumbled several times over things Koma had left in the yard. He got to the tree and stood looking up into its dark branches. He clambered up to the platform and took out his phone again. There was a signal. He dialed Ipo's number again. It seemed to ring forever before Malia's voice answered. "Malia, it's me. I need you to call Detective Ono. Some men took Leia."

There was a long pause. "What men? Where is she?"

"We found the treasure, but two men showed up. They took it and Leia. I've been searching for her, but there's no trace."

Malia gasped. "I've been feeling antsy all evening. Eva called too, all upset that some monster was going to hurt Leia. We have to find her. We'll be right there. *Tûtû* is in bed, and I'll just let her sleep."

"No! Someone needs to stay with her. Get Ono and send him out. Tell him I'm at Koma's cabin. Tell him to bring flashlights. You and Ajax stay with your grandmother." Bane ended the call, then tried to call Mano. He lost the signal again. Groaning, he tossed the phone to the floor of the tree stand. Stupid technology anyway. It was useless on this island.

He saw the chest Leia had mentioned. He opened it and saw the bones. It was too dark to tell what kind they were, and he didn't relish touching them, but he had to wait for Ono anyway. A large calabash with *nenes* carved in the side held some dried leaves. A cloth caught his attention. Just to the side of the bones, it was rolled carefully. He touched it and recognized the feel of *kapa*. He unrolled it and found a *nene* carved from koa wood inside the cloth. He picked up the *nene* and looked at it. It was obviously hand-carved, and by an unskilled hand. Why would someone use a valuable *kapa* to wrap up a worthless carving? It didn't make sense.

He turned it over in his hands, but it was too dark to see clearly. Maybe there was a lantern in Koma's cabin. That might be of some use in looking for Leia. He hurried to the edge of the platform and lowered himself to the first limb, then climbed down to the ground.

He stepped to the cabin and went inside. Just to the right of the door stood a table that held a kerosene lantern and matches. He struck one, then breathed a sigh of relief when the wick sputtered and caught fire. He trimmed the wick and lifted the lantern in his hand. Holding it aloft, he went back outside and down the pathway again. Though the lantern wasn't a floodlight, he was able to see much more of the path. His eyes strained for anything out of the ordinary as he walked along. He came to a bend in the trail and stopped. Nothing. As he moved forward, his foot struck something. He glanced down and saw only tall wire grass.

Kneeling, he moved the vegetation aside and found a slipper. Leia's slipper.

He cupped his hands around his mouth. "Leia, where are you?" He didn't expect an answer, but he hoped. And prayed. The only answering call was that of an owl. He held the lantern aloft and began to look for clues. The grass rustled, and he stopped and peered into the darkness. A movement came to his left, and he flinched back.

Hina sprang from the grass and began to coil herself around his legs. "Dumb cat." He stooped to pick her up, but she hissed and darted away. A few feet from where he found the slipper, he found a flattened spot on the grass and a few drops of blood. Leia's? The thought left him weak.

He couldn't let himself panic. Leia needed him to keep a clear head. He took a deep breath, then another. Maybe there were more clues. He began to look again, but there was nothing he could see in the dim glow of the lantern. A shout caught his attention. The voice gave him a shot of hope, then he saw Ono running up the path. He was alone, so Malia must have stayed with Ipo.

"Anything?" he asked.

Bane shook his head. "But I found one of her slippers. It looks like there's been a struggle here." He showed the detective the flattened grass.

"I'll get some floodlights strung up out here and see if we can figure out what this is all about." Ono had dropped the joking manner. "You two used to be engaged. Did you have a falling-out? A big fight?"

Bane saw where the detective was heading. "We were working on our relationship. Look, you're chasing a rabbit trail by suspecting me. We'll waste valuable time trying to figure out who took her. She already told you we surprised an intruder the other night, and she found out she was the target. I'd say those two men she overheard under the tree came back for another try."

"Could be." He eyed Bane. "But dirty work is easily hired out."
Bane tried again. "I wouldn't hurt Leia. I love her. We have to find
her, and we're not going to do that by standing around discussing your
harebrained idea. Let's get some lights out here and find her!"

Bane knew the detective wasn't convinced, but the man nodded
and turned to go back down the trail. "I'll get the lights," he said.

*L*eia's neck throbbed from her scuffle on the ground. They
entered a building, and she smelled damp and mold. The odor
reminded her of Tony's grave, and she shuddered. The closest captor thrust her to the dirt floor. Her elbow struck the ground and
began to throb. She sat up, and she looked around. Though the
place was dark, she saw enough in the moonlight to recognize the
cabin where Koma said Ku lived.

"Stay put, or you'll be shark bait," her attacker growled. "No
smart comments or I'll gag you."

He lit a kerosene lamp, and the weak glow pushed back the stark
terror Leia had been feeling. She had to stay strong. She wanted Bane
here with a desperation that surprised her. She'd tried to be self-
sufficient, but maybe she was fooling herself. Her arms felt tingly,
and she couldn't feel her fingers. She wrestled with the bonds at her
wrists, trying not to let her captors see. Flexing her fingers, she tried
to think. They couldn't let her go. She'd seen them. One was probably the man who had killed Jermaine. "What do you want with me?"

"We want the real treasure. If the old lady turns it over, we'll let
you go." The one she'd injured withdrew a cigarette from his pocket.

"We dug where my grandmother told me. You got all that was
there."

"There has to be more." The one who carried her sat on an
upturned five-gallon bucket and watched her like Ajax watched
Hina. He almost had a trace of fear in his face. "Your dad gave it to
the old lady. We know that much."

What were these guys talking about? Her dad didn't know anything about the Spanish treasure. She shook her head. "Could you loosen these ropes? My feet and hands are asleep."

He regarded her for a long minute, then stood and leaned over her. His breath smelled of fish. He untied her, then retied her feet but left her hands unbound. He pulled a revolver from his back pocket and checked the chamber. "Don't try anything, or this is liable to go off. It's going to be a long night if you don't cooperate."

"No guns," Logan said. "Put it away before someone else gets hurt."

"This is all your fault, just remember that, Logan. If you hadn't shot the old man, we could have found the right cave with the treasure. So don't tell me what to do."

"It was an accident, Moe," Logan flared. "I was just trying to scare him."

Moe snickered. "You're a lousy shot, Logan. That's why I've got the gun."

His brief smile made her shudder. She had to get away. And soon. She was fresh out of good plans though. Almost too tired to think, she wanted to pillow her head in her arms and sleep. "Please, you've got to believe me. My dad knows nothing about the galleon. He's never had any interest in that kind of thing."

Moe sighed. "Don't try that with us. We don't care about a few lousy coins and trinkets. We want the cave artifacts, and we mean to get them. We know your dad took them. Your family has them stashed somewhere."

Cave artifacts? Karshmer Cave? "My father wouldn't steal a pack of gum, let alone Hawaiian artifacts. You're wrong."

Moe stood and brushed the dirt from his hands. "And we know you've got them. Our boss doesn't like to be kept waiting."

Something skated at the edge of her memory, something she could use to fool them. "Okay," she said. "I'll take you to them." She could lead them to Koma's cabin and give them the old bones she'd found in the monkeypod tree. They wouldn't have any idea the trunk was just full of a bunch of animal remains. If she was lucky, Bane would have managed to get Detective Ono out to help look for her, and she'd lead these two right into the hands of the police. "You want to go now?"

Moe stared at her, but she must have managed to look contrite enough, because he finally shook his head. "First thing in the morning. It's too dark to see tonight." He rose and tossed her a blanket. "Remember, I've got the gun," he warned. "I don't have anything to lose by shooting you. And don't try any tricks tomorrow. If you don't lead us to the artifacts, we can snatch the old lady or your dad."

"Why grab me in the first place? What made you think I'd know anything?"

"We didn't," Moe said. "But the old lady is loony, and your dad would be harder to handle. Besides, if you didn't know, all we'd have to do is call your dad and threaten to kill you. He'd do anything for you. As it is, we were right, and you know all about it. All the easier for us."

She had to maintain the deception. "Smart. I admit I'm impressed. No one else has even suspected *Makua* has the artifacts."

Moe's eyes narrowed. "Don't try to butter me up." He went to the pile of sleeping bags on the floor and pulled one out. "Logan, tie her to something so we don't have to stay awake and watch her."

Logan. Leia stared at the man, finally figuring out why he looked vaguely familiar. He was the redheaded seaman who was so afraid of Hina. He saw her staring and averted his head. She'd only seen Logan standing in the doorway once and hadn't paid any attention, but it might be the same man.

Logan grabbed a coil of rope from the corner, bound her hands behind her, and anchored the other end of the rope to the table leg. Still not looking her in the eye, he grabbed the other sleeping bag and spread it out. Leia watched him crawl into it before she shuffled around on the blanket and closed her eyes. The terror gnawing at her insides would never let her sleep.

Twenty-two

Bane pulled into the driveway of the Kahale home. He and Ono had searched the jungle until the trail petered out. While Ono went to find volunteers to search more, Bane knew he needed to talk to Leia's parents. They had taken Ipo home with them and cleaned out the cottage.

Ingrid greeted him at the door. "Why didn't you grab the shovel or something?" Ingrid whirled in a graceful movement and walked to the window. Her shoulders were rigid. "Bane, you're a big guy. You could have made mincemeat of the thief. Now it's all lost, and Leia is missing."

Bane winced. He was already dealing with the guilt of failing to protect her. "I'll find her, Mrs. Kahale." He checked the time on his watch.

"Now, Ingrid, don't hammer the boy." Akoni spoke from the chair by the door. "He did the best he could. They're going to find Leia. I'm going out to help search too."

Ingrid frowned and nodded toward the window. "Looks like Candace heard the news."

Bane stood and went to the window. With tears streaming down her face, Candace came flying up the walk. Bane pinched the bridge of his nose. He was so tired of failing everyone around him. "I'll talk to her." He left the living room and hurried to the door as the bell pealed repeatedly. What could he say to the young widow? The truth was going to hurt.

Candace was leaning against the doorjamb when Bane opened the door. "Is it true?" she demanded, swiping the back of her hand across her cheek.

"If you're talking about Leia's disappearance and the stolen treasure, I'm afraid so." Bane stood back to allow Candace to enter. "Ono is gathering volunteers to help look for Leia."

"Did you look at mug shots?" Candace continued to stand outside.

Bane glanced at his watch. "I didn't see him. Ono has shut down the airports and the ferries, but the guy could have his own boat."

"I can't believe this. All that treasure, just gone." She groaned. "You can't let anything happen to Leia." She rubbed her stomach.

The stolen treasure would have fixed everything for her and her baby. "I'll find Leia. I wish I could say the same about the booty."

"The money would have been nice, but as long as Leia is all right, that's the important thing. I don't know what I'm going to do, but I'll figure out something."

"Just so you know, there was hardly any treasure in the chest, just a sprinkling of jewelry and some coins. I doubt it was worth more than maybe a hundred thousand dollars." While that sounded like a lot, it wouldn't have lasted Candace more than two years—if that—with the cost of living in Hawai'i.

Candace dropped her hands. "You're kidding. I thought it would be worth millions."

"If the chest had been full, it would have. But it wasn't much of a treasure, as treasures go." He looked at his watch again.

"Could more of it be still buried—or on the ship?"

"Maybe."

"So all hope isn't lost." Hope buoyed Candace's voice. "You may find the real bulk of the treasure on the ship. At least we now know it's more than a myth."

"I wouldn't put all my hope on that," Bane warned. "I'd guess someone took bits and pieces of the treasure out of the chest over the centuries and sold them off. What we found is probably all that's left." He glanced at his watch. "I've got to get out of here. I'm meeting Ono and the others at Ipo's house."

Ingrid came to the door as he spoke. "Candace, you look exhausted. Come inside. I just put some tea on."

He left Candace with Ingrid and ran to his car.

M̄ove. We don't have all day." Logan jerked Leia to her feet and shoved her toward the door.

Leia's feet tingled, and she felt clumsy and awkward as she shuffled barefoot through the door into the early morning light. The sun was barely up, and the light was still murky. "Um, I need to use the outhouse," she said, her face burning.

Logan nodded. "Around back," he said. He marched her in front of him to the outhouse.

"I'll need my hands free," she said.

Logan glanced around. "No tricks," he warned. "Look, just so you know, I didn't want any part of hurting anyone."

"You work for Ron, don't you?"

"Ron who?" He wasn't meeting her eyes.

"Why did Moe kill Jermaine? I can't see you doing it."

He raised his head then, and his gaze held defiance. "The treasure was ours. I guess the boss hired him to keep an eye on Tony, but he had no business going off on his own."

"Where is his body?"

Logan shrugged. "We tipped him over the cliff. He's fish food by now, and no one will find him." He gestured toward the outhouse. "Take care of business. We need to get going."

Rubbing her sore wrists, Leia nodded and ducked inside the outhouse. It had only one small, high window that let in a trickle of light, but it was too small for her to squeeze through, even if she could hoist herself up to it. She heard a beep and realized Logan had dialed his cell phone. He was talking. She craned her head to listen at the tiny window.

"She's taking us to it now. We should have it by midmorning. We had to kill another guy who was on the trail. Didn't you trust us to find it, Mr. Westerfield?"

Westerfield. Bane had suspected Westerfield was behind the sabotage of the plane. It appeared he was interested in more than sunken ships.

There was silence from Logan, then he finally spoke again. "I'm sorry to doubt you, sir. I'd appreciate it if you could pay me as soon as possible. My wife needs another treatment soon." He paused and listened. "Thank you, sir."

She didn't want to feel any pity for Logan. He'd chosen his path in spite of what sounded like unfortunate circumstances. She quickly used the toilet, then went back outside when he ended the call. Maybe Logan would forget to tie her hands again.

Blood had clotted along the cut she'd inflicted on him. He looked her up and down, but he didn't say anything, and he didn't tie her hands again. While she didn't trust either man, she felt safer with Logan. Glancing at her watch, she saw it was later than she'd imagined—nearly six in the morning. Bane and the police were probably long gone from Koma's cabin. She had no one to depend on but herself. And God. She pushed away the thought of God. He wouldn't help her now. She moved slowly and tried to plan what to do. If she climbed the tree herself and left them below, was there any way she could get high enough to get out of range of Moe's gun? She wouldn't know until she got there.

They moved single file through the forest. Moe's gun prodded her back occasionally, and Leia picked up her pace. It was going to be at least seven by the time they got to Koma's cabin. "I need to stop and rest a minute," she said, leaning against the rough bark of a macadamia tree. Her lungs burned, and so did her legs where brambles had torn her skin. Her bare feet felt like they were encased in cement.

"No time. Let's get this over with." Moe took her arm and shoved her forward.

Leia staggered but couldn't maintain her balance. She fell face forward into the thick vegetation. Inhaling the scent of the wildflowers, she protested when Moe hauled her to her feet. "Please, I can't go on. I have to rest."

He swore and let her fall back to the ground. "Fifteen minutes."

It was bliss to ease the tension from her muscles. Her mouth was dry, but she was too tired to ask for water. She needed to think, to plan. She shouldn't waste these precious minutes on unconsciousness, but it was hard to wrap her mind around any possible solution to her dilemma. One thing in her favor was she knew the area. If she could get away from the men, they would have trouble following her through the forest. Her eyes closed.

Moments later she was jerked to her feet. "Time's up," Logan said.

She nodded and began to move forward. She had to recover her strength. Praying as she dodged the thick trees and shrubs, she came to the path that led to Koma's cabin. "This way," she said.

"That leads to where the old man lived," Moe said. "We've come back to where we first took you."

"We should have made her tell us when we were here before," Logan grumbled. "I just want to finish this and get out of here."

"We're here now. Just shut your yap so we can get this over with. I can't wait to get back to civilization."

Leia's steps lightened now that the end was in sight. She hurried along the path. From here she could see Koma's cabin. It looked deserted. She stepped around the edge of the cabin. "It's back here."

"You're getting smart now. No games," Moe said.

Leia was practically running by the time she hit the backyard. She didn't want to be alone with either of the men. While they hadn't made any advances, she didn't like the way Moe looked at her. She reached the base of the tree where Koma had built his meditation platform. She put one foot in the fork of the tree and began to climb.

"What are you doing?" Moe grabbed her arm and yanked her back. "I told you—no funny stuff."

"It's in a chest in the tree stand," she said. "I'll get it for you."

"Do you expect me to believe that?"

"It's there. Look, what do you have to lose? Just let me get it so I can go home." His green eyes, as clear as glass, locked with hers. She found it hard to believe a man with such beautiful eyes could be all evil. "Please, I just want to get this over with."

He dropped his hand. "Logan, go up with her."

"I can get it. I don't need any help." Leia's hope began to slip away. With someone up there with her, she had no chance of escape.

"You're too eager to give us what we want. I don't trust you." Moe jerked his head toward the tree. "Get going, both of you."

Leia closed her eyes briefly, then turned and began to climb the large monkeypod tree. She easily scrambled to the top. Logan grunted as he hauled his bulk from branch to branch. She glanced around and saw the chest. At least it was still here. She would have been in a lot of trouble if it had been missing. Logan clambered onto the wooden floor and lay gasping on his stomach. Leia heard a meow and looked up. Hina jumped to her shoulder. A rush of joy flooded her. At least she wasn't alone anymore, even if it was just her cat.

Logan sat up. "Keep that thing away from me. I hate cats."

It wasn't just dislike she saw on his face, but pure terror. Maybe she could use it. He backed away, his gaze riveted on Hina. With a sudden movement, Leia scooped Hina up and tossed him at Logan. The man threw up his hands and stumbled back as the cat extended her claws. Logan shrieked like a woman and batted at the air, and the cat fastened on his shirt, then released her claws and dropped to the floor of the platform. Logan took another step back—this one into thin air. With a scream, he disappeared from view.

Leia winced when she heard him thump on the ground. "*Mahalo*, Lord," she whispered. She rushed to the edge and peered over. Moe was kneeling over his unconscious partner. He glanced up at her and brandished the gun. "Get down here with those artifacts."

She ducked back so he couldn't see her and scooped Hina into her arms. Her pulse was pounding, and her mouth went dry. He could easily shoot up through the boards, and he just might hit her. She looked around for branches that would allow her to climb higher or would mingle with those from another tree so she could travel through the treetops, but the ones above her head looked too spindly to support her weight. Her gaze landed on an object at her feet. A cell phone. She picked it up with two fingers and looked at it. How did it work? She examined the tiny buttons. Praying for a signal, she flipped it open and looked at the display. It made a beep and dots appeared on the tiny screen. She dialed 911 and prayed. Gingerly holding it out from her head an inch or so, she listened. It was dialing! A miracle straight from God.

A dispatcher answered, and Leia cupped her hand over the phone. "Send help to Koma Hamai's old cabin. Hurry." A shot ricocheted off the underside of the floorboards. Another splintered the wood and erupted near her feet. She dropped the phone and moved as quietly as she could to another part of the tree stand. The dispatcher continued to talk, and Leia could hear the voice from here. Probably Moe could as well, because he continued to fire into the wood near the phone. A bullet connected with the phone, and it finally fell silent.

"Look, come on down. No hard feelings," Moe called.

Leia could hear him circling below her, then his voice moved away. He went out far enough to look up into the tree stand. She clung to a twisted branch and tried to blend in with the leaves. The thick foliage must have been hard to see through, because he went back under the tree stand, and she heard him grunt as he began to climb the tree. She was trapped here. In spite of his comment about no hard feelings, she knew she was in for big trouble if he reached her. Looking around for a weapon, she went to the chest and opened it. In the bright light of day, she realized the bones inside were human. She hadn't taken time to look closely before.

Had she accidentally been right? Was this box full of the stolen artifacts? She didn't want to believe that her father would have taken something so valuable, but the real possibility was staring her in the face. She thought back on what had been taken. It would take something much larger than this small chest to hold it all. The thought comforted her. She didn't know what this chest contained, but it couldn't be the missing artifacts.

Moving the bones out of the way gently, she looked for something to use to keep Moe from reaching the tree stand. A *lā'au pālau* lay in the bottom of the chest, surrounded by dry leaves. The club was a short one—only about two feet long—but it would do. She grabbed it and rushed to where Moe's hands were even now grasping for purchase to haul himself onto the platform. She could try stomping on his fingers, but her bare feet would inflict no damage. Holding the club aloft, she warned him first. "Climb back down, and I won't hurt you, Moe. I don't want to hit you, but I will if you don't let go."

Moe's face tipped up, and he fumbled for the gun at his waist. She had no choice. Praying for strength, she brought the head of the stone club down on his fingers. He yelped but managed to hang on, though one finger began to swell, and she saw drops of blood where the stone had cut his flesh. She bit her lip at the sight but reminded herself he would kill her if he reached the platform. She raised the club again and brought it down on his fingers. He howled again, and this time he loosened his grip and began to slide back down the tree. His momentum accelerated, and he plummeted to the ground to join Logan, who was still prostrate on the wire grass.

Leia knelt on her hands and knees and peered at the two men. Moe lay motionless on the ground for several moments, then began to stir. He rolled onto his back, nursing his injured hands. His gaze connected with Leia's, and she suppressed a shudder at the menace in his face. If he got his hands on her, he would kill her.

He fumbled with his gun, and she ducked out of sight. "I called the police, Moe. They're on their way." Her gaze fell on the club she'd used. The stone head had broken loose from the handle. It would be useless to her now if he tried to come back up.

A bullet cut through the branches above her head. He'd moved out from under the platform and was firing wildly. She scooted on her backside to a large branch and put as much of her body behind it as she could. Bullets continued to rain around her, then finally stopped. She peeked out from behind the branch, but she couldn't see anything from here. She listened. She wouldn't give a quarter for her chances of surviving the day. Her gaze fell back on the chest. Listening for furtive sounds from below, she scooted toward it. Maybe there was another weapon inside. The scent that rushed up to meet her when she opened the lid was that of tea. The dry leaves in the bottom were loose tea. She thought of her grandmother's chant. Loose tea in the treasure chest.

The club she'd used on Moe suddenly looked familiar. She told herself that most clubs looked alike. The one stolen from the museum had a *pakololio* symbol on it. The shieldlike symbol was one that invoked the power to control the wind. The club lay on the platform floor. She'd know the truth if she picked it up and checked, but did she even want to know? She wished she could go back to yesterday morning, when things seemed so much more clear. Biting her lip, she reached out and picked up the club. The rock was smooth and worn on this side with no symbols. Running her hand over the worn wooden handle, she flipped it over with a decisive movement. The symbol almost seemed to glow on the head of the club.

She dropped it, and it thudded on the platform. It couldn't be true. Her father couldn't be a thief. She thought of all the things she'd been taught growing up—morals built on the foundation of the Scriptures. Truth, honesty, love for others. Had it all been a sham? She heard a sound and whirled to see Moe beginning to climb onto the platform.

Twenty-three

hat was Ono. Leia called in. She's at Koma's cabin." Bane slammed the phone back into its cradle. Ipo's kitchen held most of the people who cared about Leia: her parents, Ipo, Malia, Eva, Mano, and Annie. "I'm going out there. Ono is on his way, but it will be nearly an hour before he can get here."

"I'll go with you." Akoni followed him.

"Wait for me." Mano jogged after the other two men.

Bane barely acknowledged the other men. His focus was on getting to Leia. She had to be okay if she'd called in, right? He tried to reassure himself. What was she doing back at Koma's cabin?

"Did Ono say anything other than that she'd called?" Mano asked, his breath ragged as he ran to keep up with Bane.

Bane hadn't wanted to say all of it in front of the women. "The dispatcher heard shots in the background, and the line went dead."

Akoni put on a burst of speed and jogged ahead. His face was white and set. Bane had often admired the relationship between him and his daughters, but days like this showed how vulnerable love made a person. Was he ready for that? He suppressed a rueful sigh. It was too late. He was a goner and had been since the day he first met Leia. He'd paced the night away, and the turmoil had left his emotions cartwheeling all over the place. Until last night, he hadn't been certain which was worse—a life without Leia or one without children. Now he was certain that an existence without Leia wasn't worth living.

The three men didn't say another word as they rushed along the path to Koma's cabin. As they neared the clearing, Bane put on another burst of speed, but Mano grabbed his arm. "Wait. There's no way Ono could have gotten here yet. If there were gunshots fired, the guys who got her may still be around. If we go rushing in there, we may put her in more danger."

Bane didn't want to stop to think and be cautious. He wanted to see Leia's smile, but he knew his brother was right. He slowed and stopped. Just over the rise, he could see the roof of Koma's house. "We probably should have brought some kind of weapon."

Akoni didn't say anything, but he stepped into the forest and bent over to pick up a stout stick. "I used to be proficient with one of these when I was young. I think I can hammer someone in the head with it."

Bane nodded, and he and Mano found their own sticks. "We'll spread out and find her. Mano, you circle around the front. Akoni and I will circle to the back. I'll take the west side, and Akoni, you can take the east."

The older man nodded and held the stick in both hands in a warrior stance. Bane wouldn't want to meet him in a dark alley. He imitated Akoni's grip on his stick and moved cautiously around the side of the house. He passed the outhouse, then backtracked and peered inside. Empty. He resumed his trek into the backyard. He caught a glimpse of movement and whirled to see Akoni stalking around the other side of the house. They nodded to one another and continued to scout out the terrain.

The jungle marched along the property about thirty feet from the back side of the house. Bane heard a sound and peered around the corner. He stifled a gasp when he recognized Logan's red hair. No wonder Westerfield knew everything they were up to. Logan sat on the ground gazing up into the tree, and Bane spotted another man's boots at the top as the guy struggled to pull himself onto the platform. He heard Leia scream. Without thinking, he launched himself into the backyard. Bellowing, he reached the base of the tree. He scrambled up the ladder and grabbed the man's ankle.

The man swore and kicked out at him. Bane hung on, pulling down on the man's foot. He heard Leia scream again. Looking up, he saw the man had hold of her leg and was dragging her back with him. "Kick him in the face," Bane yelled.

Leia scooted back, then her free foot connected with the man's nose. The guy yelped and let go of her leg. Bane gave another tug, then he and the man both fell back to the ground. Bane lay winded, but Mano pounced on the man. Akoni towered over Logan, who cowered on the ground.

The other man pulled a gun from his waistband. "Back off," he ordered Mano.

Staring at him, Bane realized the man was the diver who had come at him with a knife in the underwater cave. He recognized the vivid green eyes.

The man gestured with the gun. "Help him up," he told Akoni. Akoni hesitated, then hoisted Logan to his feet. Mano put his hands in the air and took a step back. The other man struggled to his feet and began to back away. "Get down here, or I shoot your boyfriend," he yelled.

"Don't do it, Leia," Bane said. "Stay back." He glared at the man. "She's not coming down."

The man swore. "Get going," he told Logan. Logan limped toward the trees. The other man turned and ran into the jungle behind him. Mano started to go after him, but Bane grabbed his arm. "Don't risk it, not with that gun in his hand. Let Ono go after him."

Mano nodded, and the men looked into the tree. Bane saw Leia peering down at him. Her face was scratched and streaked with dirt, but he'd never seen a more beautiful sight. He wanted to rush up the tree and grab her, but he forced himself to stay cool. "Rapunzel, Rapunzel, let down your hair."

Her eyes widened, then she smiled, and her dimple appeared. "I'm too tired to hoist you up. But come up here. I want to show you something."

He'd never been much for climbing trees, but he wanted to touch her, to know she was all right. He scrambled up the tree faster than he would have imagined possible. He rolled onto the platform and bounded to his feet. Looking behind him, he saw Akoni putting his foot in the fork of the tree to follow. Leia opened her mouth to say something, but he swept her into his arms and held her against his chest. "I thought I'd lost you," he murmured into her hair.

She clung to him, burying her face against his shirt. Her tears soaked through the fabric, and he realized she'd wanted to stay strong, but his appearance had stripped her defenses.

"You're my hero," she gulped. "I had nothing left to fight him with."

"You're okay," he said, hugging her tight. "I've got you." He heard a sound behind him. "I was hoping to get a kiss as my reward, but your dad is climbing up," he whispered, pressing his lips against her brow. "But I'll take a rain check."

She grew still, and her heaving sobs stopped. She pulled away, wiping her face with the back of her right hand. "*Makua* is here?" she whispered.

His hands were still on her shoulders, and he could feel her trembling. He frowned. Was that dread on her face? He turned. "He's right here." Akoni's hand grasped the last branch, and he practically rolled onto the platform. Lines of concern and love etched his face. He held out his hand to his daughter, but Leia took a step back. Bane's gaze swept back to her. He didn't understand her reaction.

"*Keiki*, you're all right." Akoni rushed to grab his daughter, but she held up her hand.

"Wait, *Makua*. Don't touch me. You have some explaining to do." She made a sweeping motion with her hand toward a rough wooden chest.

Akoni stared. He opened his mouth, then shut it and wet his lips. "I can explain," he said.

*L*eia stared at her father. She'd thought she knew him so well—from his strength of character to his faithfulness to his family. Now she was looking at a stranger. The dark eyes that stared back at her were filled with desperation. And love. She couldn't look at the love on his face. Was it even real? "These are some of the artifacts that were stolen under your watch. Where are the rest?"

Her father dropped his gaze. "Buried in an underwater cave."

"Why, *Makua?*" she whispered.

He raised his eyes to meet her gaze again. "I found out they were going to be sold to Westerfield. He would split them up and sell them off. I couldn't let that happen. They deserved to have a decent burial. Even the display at the museum always bothered me. The remains should never have been taken from their burial site to be gawked at."

"Why not just take the bones and bury them? You could have left the other things for display."

"I thought about it. The curator would have suspected me right off though, because I argued against selling the remains. I had to take it all or none. It needed to stay together anyway."

Leia digested his explanation in silence. It tilted everything she thought she'd known growing up. Her father had taught her the truth was always best, that character is something built on a daily basis. His character had always been the example she strove to model. His motive was good, she couldn't deny that. But the cost to her family and to his own integrity had been huge. "Does Mama know?"

"No. She wouldn't understand."

"Neither do I, *Makua*. Not fully. I understand your reason, but you trampled everything you taught me to believe in. Honor, truth, character. Was it all a sham?"

He shook his head vigorously. "I know it looks that way. Maybe when my character was put to the test, I failed. I had to do what I thought was right for the situation."

She was going to have to think about this when she was alone.

She couldn't catalog it with him looking at her. She glanced at Bane. "Are the police coming?"

"I think I hear the helicopter now. Do you know who grabbed you? I recognized Logan. Who was the other man?"

She heard the chopper too, now that he mentioned it. The *whop-whop* of the propeller blades grew louder. "Logan called him Moe. Somehow they knew my father had the artifacts. Westerfield hired them."

"I should have told Ono to investigate him. I didn't have any proof he sabotaged my plane, but I should have passed my suspicions on to the police." He glanced at Akoni. "Any idea how Westerfield knew you had the artifacts?"

Leia looked at her father. "I always thought he was so upset with you because the robbery happened on your watch. Now you're saying he was furious he lost out on the chance to buy them. What's the real story?"

Her father's head hung even lower. He put out his hand and slowly lowered himself to sit on the platform bench. "He suspected all along I took the artifacts because I was against the sale. His was the most vocal voice accusing me. He never gave up on getting at the truth."

"Why are these bones and artifacts not buried?" Bane asked. "Did Koma know where you buried the artifacts?"

"Yes, he arranged for his nephew to help him take them down. The boy got transferred to O'ahu before the final box could be taken to the cave."

"A submerged cave?" She had to raise her voice to be heard over the helicopter as it came in for a landing. "You have to give the artifacts back, *Makua*. You know that."

"I can't, Leia. It would kill your mother for people to know what I've done."

"You have to. It's the right thing. We have to trust God to turn this out for the best. That was your mistake in the first place. You

didn't trust his sovereignty." It was getting too loud to talk now. She
motioned for them to go down. Her father went first. When she
would have followed him, Bane took her arm and leaned in close
to speak in her ear.

"You need to practice what you preach. Where is your trust in
God to work things out for the best in your life?" He pulled away
and searched her face.

She stared back at him. The police were shouting for them
now. There was no time to talk about this, but he was wrong. She
wasn't going to gamble with a child's life, and that's what he
wanted. Shooting him an annoyed look, she went down the tree.
She couldn't tell the police about the artifacts. Her father needed to
be the one to come clean. If she could talk him into giving up the
artifacts, he might not get into too much trouble. Maybe he'd get a
suspended sentence when it came out that he had the best inten-
tions for what he'd done.

Hina leaped from the tree behind her, and she picked her up.
The helicopter rotors had quit turning, and she hurried to where
Ono stood with her father.

The detective turned toward her, his mustache quivering. "Are
you all right, Pilgrim?" Though he still called her the nickname, his
eyes were sober.

"A little shaken up, but I'm not hurt."

"What happened?"

She launched into the explanation of how the men had seized
her and where they'd taken her. "I talked them into coming here
because I hoped you'd all still be here looking for me."

"What made them think your father had stolen the artifacts
when he had been cleared of any wrongdoing?" Ono was writing
everything down in a small red spiral notebook.

"I don't know. They seemed to have been hired by someone
else. They referred to Mr. Westerfield." At least the detective wasn't
questioning her father's guilt.

"We got back the autopsy on Tony," Ono said. "He died of puffer-fish poisoning, so it was evidently accidental."

"You can't believe that with everything else going on!"

"Coincidences happen now and then."

She caught Akoni's eye, but he turned away, and she knew he wasn't going to come clean. She swallowed and looked over to Bane. He must have sensed her anguish, because he stepped closer and put his arm around her.

"I can tell you about Westerfield, Detective. Let Leia get some rest. She's exhausted, and I'd like to get her back to her family. They're all waiting back at Ipo's house for word." He told the detective all he knew about Sam Westerfield. "My boss, Ron Pimental, can tell you more."

Ono nodded. "I'll give him a call. I'm sure we'll have more questions, but that's enough for now. Get some rest. We'll head out to the cabin you mentioned and take a look around. If they've been staying there, we might find some clues." Ono walked off to talk to another policeman.

Leia leaned against Bane. Fatigue had caught up with her, and her eyelids felt heavy. Hina meowed and reached out to touch Bane's arm. "I forgot to tell you—Hina saved me today." She couldn't help the smile that curved her lips.

He dislodged Hina's claws from his T-shirt. The cat licked his hand. "This fur ball? I can't see her saving anything but another trip to her feeding trough."

Leia covered her smile with her hand, her fatigue lifting.

"Ajax needs lunch," Bane grumbled.

"Hina would have him for lunch. He's terrified of her."

"With good reason. She's a psycho."

"You're just jealous."

He glanced at her as they walked toward her grandmother's cottage. "Maybe I am. I'd like you to look at me with the same love you do the cat. I'm not giving up, Leia. Almost losing you made me realize even my desire for children isn't as strong as my love for you. A life without you is no life at all." He stopped and turned her toward him. "We were meant to be together."

She looked away from the love in his eyes. She loved him too much to let him make that sacrifice. Mano and her father hurried to catch up with them, and the moment was lost when they could have talked. Maybe it was for the best.

"*Mahalo* for not giving me away," her father said, his voice low and strained.

It hurt to hear the shame in his voice. Leia was used to seeing him stride around with a confident walk and a booming laugh. When she was growing up, she thought he was the biggest man in the world. He seemed shrunken and diminished in her eyes now. She needed his help to figure out who was coming after them. Moe and Logan would be back. "*Makua*, can you think of anyone else who might have figured out that you had the artifacts?"

"I've been wondering about that ever since you told me. The investigation cleared me of suspicion."

"How did you manage that?" Bane asked.

"Luck, really. I staged the break-in to happen when I was on duty. I put the artifacts in the back of my van. Coincidentally, security cameras caught another man slipping out the back door at about the same time, and it obviously wasn't me. So I was cleared."

That sounded ominous. Leia paused and put her hand on her father's arm. "Who was he, and what was he doing going out the back door?"

"I've never figured it out for sure. I didn't recognize the man, so I know it wasn't Westerfield. That same night we had some things come up missing from Queen Liliuokalani's palace as well. I think the thief might have been the same. The camera didn't get a good look at him. He had a stocking over his face."

"I wonder if it could have been Moe or Logan. Describe his build and anything you can remember about him," Bane prompted.

"He was a big guy. Broad shoulders, big feet and hands." Akoni shook his head. "Sorry, that's all. He was dressed in black and the stocking distorted his features. I couldn't even tell what color hair he had."

"Moe is a big guy. It could have been him," Leia said.

"He was like a tank when he attacked me at the cave," Bane said. "We'd better decide what to do with the artifacts we left back in the tree before those two come back."

"I want to put them with the other things." Akoni started down the path again. "I'll go back after them when the police are gone."

"No, *Makua,* we have to give them back. They don't belong to you."

He turned on his heel. "They don't belong to anyone. How would you like people gawking over your poor remains three hundred years from now? It's not right, Leia. You know it's a disgrace to the bones of our ancestors. It's bad for the *mana* in them."

"I do understand, but sometimes we have to trust God to work things out." Listen to her, what a hypocrite she was. Bane was right. Trusting in God was the last thing she'd been doing.

Akoni pressed his fingers at the bridge of his nose. "Maybe you're right. I don't know what's right and wrong in this situation anymore. But I can't stash the artifacts anyway. I don't dive. Koma took them to the ship for me."

"I'll go get them," Bane said. "What ship?"

"The Spanish galleon." He looked away. "The cave is right behind it."

Leia wanted to pummel him. "You've known all this time where the galleon was?"

"I didn't think anyone would ever find it, and the bones and artifacts would be mingled with the others who died there. The other boxes are in a small cave just off the ledge where the ship sits, and we planned to set off an explosive and seal the mouth of it."

"That's going to be hard to reach. We'll need special air and equipment to work that deep. I bet Ron already has some lined up though," Bane said. "I'll go down after it."

"How did Koma dive that deep? I got narced in just a few minutes."

"He didn't seem susceptible to it, but he'd been a diver a long time. He used to even free dive." Her father looked back toward the tree. "It will take several trips to bring everything up. There is quite a lot."

"I'll go get it," Bane said.

Leia shook her head. "You can't do it alone. It's not safe to dive alone, especially that deep."

"Koma and his nephew did it," her father pointed out. "It took them three trips, but he knew the area well."

"It's too dangerous. I can't let him go alone."

"I'll go too," Mano said.

"Your blood-sugar levels have been unstable," Bane said. "I can't let you go down."

"We could do it right after my insulin shot."

Bane was still shaking his head. "I think it was an hour after your shot you had your last reaction. You're in no shape to do any diving right now."

She couldn't let Bane go by himself. It was too dangerous. Of all people, she knew just how dangerous it could be. "I'll go with you." Bane and her father began loud protests, but she held up her hand, then turned and continued down the trail. "You can't change my mind. I'm going with him."

Eva washed the ink from her hands. She liked her job at ARC, and today's duties were her favorite—stuffing envelopes with a newsletter for a local business. Her neck and shoulders hurt though. She and Lani had stuffed lots of envelopes today. Probably a billion, Lani said. Eva thought her friend was right.

"What are you going to do tonight?" Lani stuffed her lunch box in her backpack.

"Maybe scuba!" Eva bounced on the balls of her feet. "Maybe Bane will take me. I'm going to ask him. And I want to see Leia. I had a bad dream about her."

"Can I come?"

"You don't know how to scuba," Eva pointed out. She didn't want to be mean, but it made her happy that she could do something Lani couldn't do. Lani's fingers were thinner and could stuff things easier than Eva could. At least Eva could scuba.

"I could learn." Lani scowled and went toward the door.

Eva felt bad. She was being selfish. Jesus didn't like her to be selfish. "I'll ask Bane about it."

Lani's smile came back. "Call me!" she sang out as she ran out the door.

Eva grabbed her own backpack and put her crumpled box of Cheetos into it. She touched the penknife Hotshot had given her. It made her happy to see it. Stepping into the sunshine, she started toward home.

"Eva."

She turned. "Hey, Hotshot, where you been?" He looked funny today, kind of glum. Eva wished she could cheer him up.

"You remember I told you I would need your help one day?"

Eva straightened and nodded. "I remember."

"Today is the day. We need to get your dad out of trouble. He took something that doesn't belong to him, and he needs to give it back. I thought he might have put some of the stuff in the sled he was making, but there were no compartments. So we have to help him."

"My dad wouldn't steal." The idea made Eva mad. Her dad was good. The best man she knew.

"It was an accident," Hotshot said. "He didn't know it belonged to me. But he'll be in trouble if we don't help him. You're the only one who can save him."

Eva's chest swelled at her friend's words. Sometimes she dreamed she was Luke Skywalker about to save the world, but in her real life she knew she was lucky to have her job. Lots of people didn't hire girls like her. "What should I do?"

"I need you to write your dad a letter. Then you need to come stay with me awhile until he does what he needs to do."

"Stay with you? Mama will be mad if I don't come home on time."

"I'll explain it to her. It will be okay." Still smiling, Hotshot pulled out a notebook. "Just write what I tell you. When you're done, we'll go diving."

"I love diving!" Eva said. Hotshot offered her a pencil, and she took it, touching it to the tip of her tongue to wet it. "Okay."

Twenty-four

The ship rocked in the waves. Leia was shivering, and she wasn't even in the water. The trade winds blew across her exposed flesh, but they felt cold to her, though she knew they were as warm and balmy as usual. She began to pull on her wet suit. Might as well get this over with. Bane already had his gear on and stood with Mano looking out over the water from the bow of the *Pomaik'i*. Ron was on the island rounding up some more equipment, though he'd managed to get enough for today's dive. She was thankful he hadn't asked too many questions.

Annie was helping her gear up. She stood and shaded her eyes with her hand. "Hey, is that your dad?"

Leia looked up to see her father speeding toward them in his small dingy. From the whine of the motor, she figured he had it opened up all the way. She waved, and he motioned wildly, a frantic movement that made her rise and hurry to catch the towrope he tossed her way. "What's wrong?"

"It's Eva. She didn't come home after work, but we got this note." He stepped aboard and handed her a folded piece of paper.

Bane and Mano joined them. Ajax pressed close to Bane's leg. Leia took the note and unfolded it. I'M OKAY, BUT YOU HAVE TO DO WHAT HOTSHOT SAYS. GIVE HIM BACK HIS STUF. DON'T CALL POLISE. EVA. Leia's fingers tightened on the paper until it began to crumple. Eva was so trusting, so easily taken in by anyone who was nice to her. She looked at her dad. "Hotshot? Who's Hotshot?" Her father's gaze was fastened on her face as though he hoped she held the answer. "And what stuff does he want?"

He took back the note. "I have no idea who he is. I'd say the stuff is the artifacts."

"Does Mama know? Eva talks to her a lot."

"She's heard her mention him, but she thought this Hotshot was one of Eva's coworkers. We called Laura Gallagher, but she's never heard of him."

Laura was Eva's supervisor at ARC. She kept a tight rein on the employees. Whoever this guy was, he had made sure no one saw him with Eva. Leia curled her fingers into her palms.

"Did you call Detective Ono?" Bane asked. He held out his hand for the note, and Akoni gave it to him. He grunted as he read it.

Akoni hesitated. "I was afraid to call when the note said not to. I'll just turn over the artifacts and get my daughter back. I can't run the risk that the guy would hurt her."

Leia rubbed her palm over her face. "I don't know what we should do. I don't want them to hurt Eva."

"You think there's more than one?" her father asked.

"I wonder if it's the same two men who grabbed me. The big guy, Moe, could have a nickname like that."

"Let's get the artifacts up top before we call the police. We'll see what they want to do once the items are in our possession." Bane held on to his mouthpiece and jumped into the water.

Leia started to follow him, but her dad grabbed her arm. "I'm sorry, Leia. Sorry I've made such a mess of things. I should be protecting my family, and instead, I've put you all in danger."

Leia put her hand over his. "We'll figure it out. We're Kahales, after all."

His answering smile was strained, and he dropped his hand. "I'll be praying for you."

"I'll take all the prayers I can get." She moved to the edge of the boat, held her mouthpiece, and jumped into the blue water. She grabbed the line attached to the cargo basket and brought it with her. The warm caress usually relaxed her, but every muscle tensed as she plunged down after Bane. The strange taste of the specially mixed air made her tongue tingle.

They'd called Nani as they were setting out, and the dolphin met her as she entered the water. Leia grabbed Nani's dorsal fin and let her pull her down to where Bane floated. The drop-off grew closer, and she resisted the impulse to turn and swim back to the boat. Bane couldn't do this alone. She flipped on her halogen light, and the bright illumination reassured her.

She let go of Nani, and the dolphin nosed rocks near the drop-off. Leia realized she was breathing too fast and made a conscious effort to control her air. It had to last. Bane saw her and motioned for her to come with him. He disappeared over the side into the blue hole. She kicked her fins and propelled herself after him, though every muscle in her body wanted to shoot for the surface. She hesitated at the edge and peered over. There was no floor in sight.

She moved downward. Nani kept up with her. When Leia paused, Nani bumped her hand with her nostrum. Leia rubbed the dolphin, and the action settled her excitement a bit. She checked her dive computer. She was at one hundred fifty feet. Another fifty feet to go. She could see Bane from here as he approached the cave where the boat sat.

Leia studied the cave. It was more of an overhang than a real cave, but they had to find the one that held the artifacts. While Bane searched the right side of the overhang where the fish hovered, she finned herself forward, toward the back of the cave. Her father hadn't been certain where the cave was, because he'd never been down here. He'd only reported what Koma had told him. She swept her light over the wall and down to the floor. The hole sprang into relief, and before she could react, Nani shot through it. Leia turned around and looked for Bane. He was looking her direction, so she motioned to him and waved her light back and forth over the opening. He propelled himself toward her. Peering inside, he then stuck his head in, kicked his fins, and disappeared.

Her ears were ringing a bit, but she didn't feel narced. The special mix of air was helping delay the effects. Exhaling a stream of bubbles, she put her head through the opening. The fit was tight, but she could make it if Bane could. Gritting her teeth, she kicked firmly with her fins. Maybe on the other end of this tunnel-like entrance, it would get bigger. She knew it was her imagination that her air tasted more stale and tight. The walls around her gradually expanded, then she found herself in a cave about twenty feet in diameter.

Bane was already swimming back toward her with a load in his hands. He pointed behind him, and she saw more floating boxes tethered by ropes that wrapped around a natural pillar of coral. She pulled out her knife and cut the ropes to the nearest box. It weighed practically nothing in the water. She moved back to the opening and joined Bane as he maneuvered the boxes into the basket. They secured the boxes, then swam back to the cave.

Leia was getting her stride back. She now noticed the fish zipping by her mask and admired the bright coral that grew along the bow of the ship. A moray eel zipped back into its hole, then poked out its head to watch them pass. She went first this time and swam to the last of the artifacts. There was only one more box, a small one. Bane's eyes behind his mask were warm with approval as he took the box from her, and then turned to head out.

Nani bumped into them. She darted back and forth in a frenzied water dance. Leia paused to try to figure out what had upset the dolphin when she noticed rocks beginning to slide on the slopes of the cave around them. It seemed hotter all at once. She glanced at her dive computer and looked at the temperature gauge. At first she thought the temperature had remained the same, but then she realized it had skyrocketed ten degrees. That wasn't possible. She showed the computer to Bane.

He gripped her arm, then pointed. Pillow lava was dripping

over the front of the cave. They had to get out. She started for the cave opening, but the water got hotter, and the lava was dripping so quickly there was no room to get by without being burned. Bane pulled her back. It was too late. They were trapped. His eyes held a terrible awareness that they were going to die. He pulled her into his arms, and she listened to the sound of his regulator. It would soon stop. He would run out of air before she did because he was a big guy and pulled a lot of air.

Leia didn't want to die yet. There was so much she wanted to experience, and she realized she wanted that life to include Bane. While she looked forward to heaven someday, she'd never thought that day could come so soon. Her gaze locked with Bane's. She tried to tell him with her eyes how much she loved him and how sorry she was for everything. Bane opened his arms, and she moved into them.

*E*va didn't like this place. The corners held spiderwebs with dead bugs hanging in them. Hotshot had promised they'd go for diving, but she didn't see gear around. They were just in this dumpy cabin that took forever to walk to. Hotshot had brought her here and told her he'd be back later. When he left, she'd tried the door, but it was locked.

Eva had tried to open a window and crawl through, but they were stuck shut. It was hot in here too. She wanted to go home and watch *Home Alone* again. She watched it every day. Sometimes she felt like Kevin in the film—invisible enough that she could be forgotten by her family. At the same time, the film gave her hope that she could be a hero too.

She was tired of sitting on the cot. She wished she had a book to read—maybe *Black Beauty*. She stood and walked around the room. On the old table she carved her name, then something scraped at the front door. She sprang to her feet and faced the door. Maybe Hotshot was back with his diving gear. She rushed to

the door as Hotshot entered the cabin. His hands were empty. "No
diving gear?"

"Not yet." His smile widened as he took a lock of her blonde
hair and twisted it around his finger. "You've sure got pretty hair,
Eva."

There was something about his smile that she wasn't sure
about. It made her feel funny, excited, and icky all at once. She
backed away. "I think I should go home now."

"Not yet," he said, kicking the door shut behind him. "We
have lots to do yet."

They floated heart to heart for a few seconds, then Leia realized
the dolphin was trying to drive them apart.

Nani swam in circles around them. She bumped against their
legs, and Nani rolled over then zipped to a rock that stuck out into
the cave. She disappeared behind it. Leia hadn't realized there was
enough space back there to hold the dolphin's body. Gesturing to
Bane, she led the way to see what Nani had discovered. Leia's light
caught a small opening near the floor. Nani must have swum into
it. Could there be another way out?

Bane pushed her toward the opening. She swam into it. Nani
must have brushed the sides, because it was nearly too tight for Leia
to negotiate. Phosphorescent plankton glowed along the way,
swirling in the current. Wait, there was actually a current? She
watched and realized it was true. This water was flowing somewhere.
Nani hadn't come back either. Her light picked up starfish and
translucent shrimp clinging to the walls. It almost looked like stars.

Stars. Eva had said something about stars. In her dream, she
said Bane followed the stars out of the cave. Hope resurrected, and
she looked back to smile at Bane. He looked puzzled, but he smiled
back, though she could see the resignation in his eyes. She paused
and swept her hand through the plankton. Her motion made him

frown, then he watched the plankton flow at a fast clip away from them. He took her arm in an excited grip. Nodding forward, he gave her a gentle push. She kicked off with her fins, moving faster now. Her light played along the ceiling with the glow of starfish. The corridor turned vertical, and she looked up into a tunnel that seemingly had no end.

She turned to glance back at Bane. Right behind him came a column of pillow lava. She pointed. He turned and saw it, then grabbed her arm and shoved her upward. She shot up through the tunnel, moving as fast as she dared. They might need to find a hyperbaric chamber when they got out of here. If they got out. Bane was right on her heels, but thankfully, the pillow lava didn't seem to be billowing after them. She paused to decompress a bit. Bane enveloped her in his arms again, and they floated like that for several minutes.

Leia had been so concerned about the lava and the water temperature that she hadn't checked their bottom time. She glanced at her computer and realized she had only fifteen minutes. If she had fifteen, Bane probably had only ten, maybe five. She pulled away from Bane and shot upward again. Bane followed after her. Starfish still glowed in the light of her lamp. The tunnel began to widen as they raced upward, then they were through the tunnel and in another cave. Leia checked her gauge, and the temperature had increased another couple of degrees. They had to find a way out of here. She glanced back at Bane and realized he had hardly any bubbles coming out of his regulator. He was almost out of air.

She grabbed her octopus regulator and thrust it at him. He spit out his mouthpiece and slipped her auxiliary one into his mouth. In sync, they swam farther into the cave. With both of them using her tanks, they had less than five minutes to live. Her light picked up Nani swimming toward them. The dolphin slowed, and Bane grabbed her dorsal fin. Nani flipped her tail and drew them with her as she moved through the water toward an opening in the cave wall. Once they were through, Leia recognized where they were.

The cave they'd just exited was the cave Bane had wanted to explore. The crack leading from the cave to a seamount at the edge of the blue hole had widened, and through the ash swirling in the water, she saw a red glow deep under the masses of pillow lava. It was about thirty feet away, too close for comfort.

Nani shot up through the water as though she understood her human friends had little time left. Leia was beginning to suck hard on her regulator, and she knew Bane must be having the same difficulty. She took another breath, and there was nothing there. Her initial reaction was to try to hang on to her last lungful of air, but she knew she had to exhale as she rose or risk the same fate as Tony. Exhaling slowly, she kicked her fins with the dolphin, trying to shoot up faster.

Dots began to cloud her vision. She was blacking out. She peered through the haze of her fading vision at Bane and realized he was almost unconscious as well, barely hanging on to Nani. Then her head broke the surface of the water. She spit out her regulator and drew in the sweetest air she'd ever breathed. She gasped in another lungful as Bane did the same. They clung together and filled their bodies with oxygen.

"The chamber," Bane sputtered. He waved feebly at the ship, which had moved away, probably to avoid the danger presented by the lava. The ash in the water could foul the engines. Mano kicked off his shoes and dove into the water toward them. Annie threw two life preservers after him, and Mano swam to them, towing the preservers with him. Leia got one arm through the life preserver, and Bane managed to get an arm through the other. They had both expended nearly all their strength.

"We need the chamber," Bane gasped. "The bends."

Leia wasn't feeling them yet, but she knew it was only a matter of minutes before the excruciating pain set in.

Mano didn't waste time with talk. His strong arms towed them to the ship, and the crew helped haul them aboard. "They need the chamber," Mano barked. "Get their clothes off."

"The basket, get the basket raised," Bane gasped out.

"Already done." Mano began to jerk off Bane's wet suit.

Before Leia could think, Annie hustled her into a corner, stripped her of the wet suit, and wrapped her in a warm robe. Annie rushed her into the hyperbaric chamber as Mano was shoving Bane toward it as well. Bane grabbed a thick beach towel from a hook as he passed and wrapped it around himself. His lips were blue, and Leia could see he was shaking as much as she was. The pain was starting, and Leia didn't resist the rush. There was no time to lose. A bubble of nitrogen could hit her brain or her lungs. Bane stepped aside to let her in first then followed. Mano shut them in and began to pressurize the chamber. She just hoped they were in time.

Twenty-five

Bane leaned against the wall of the hyperbaric chamber. He didn't know how long they'd slept. The air hissed through the vents in a comforting concert. Leia was sleeping. He studied her face, the planes and angles, the high cheekbones. He'd never seen a more brave and beautiful face.

He'd been poking her about accepting God's sovereignty, but he realized as death had stared him in the face that he hadn't taken his own advice. God had created him the way he was—poetic parts and all. He'd been trying to be Mr. Tough Guy all his life. If there was any problem, he would handle it and squelch all the softer feelings he had inside. Or at least that's what he'd told himself. Who said he shouldn't let people get too close? No one in his family. His own fear had made him put on a mask and hide the real man inside. He closed his eyes and promised God he'd try to take the chains off his heart.

Leia stirred, and he opened his eyes. "How are you feeling?" he asked her. She had a blanket wrapped around her where she huddled on the bench a few feet away.

"Okay. No pain or anything. I'm sleepy. I can't believe it, but I am. There's too much to do to even rest."

"We can't do anything until we get out of here anyway. You might as well rest. We'll have our work cut out for us when we're done decompressing." He shuffled on the bench. What was happening outside? He could hear the throb of the engines under his feet as the ship headed to another destination.

"I wish we knew if the artifacts had been damaged, and if my dad has heard any more from Eva."

"One way to find out." He leaned over and pressed the inter-com button. "Mano, you out there?"

His brother's worried face appeared in the round porthole window. "I'm here." Mano's voice sounded crackly in the speaker. Annie peeked over his shoulder into the window too.

Bane stared into his brother's face. He'd never been able to tell Mano or any of his family how much he loved them. Instead, he'd told Mano what to do, criticized his every move, and held him to standards no one could live up to. Mano had never called him on it—he'd just continued to do what he thought was right and to be there for everyone in the Oana family. Bane didn't deserve a brother like him. Things needed to change.

Bane spread his palm on the window. "Thanks for saving me out there. I love you, man."

Mano put his hand on the other side of the window. "Hey, I need you around to keep me in line. I love you too." His voice was husky, and he blinked rapidly.

There was nothing like a close brush with death to see things clearly for the first time. He'd never even been able to tell Leia clearly how he felt. He'd stumbled around like a schoolboy with his first crush. Maybe he could do better now.

Leia leaned toward the window as Mano stepped away. "What's going on out there? Is this a major eruption?"

Annie moved closer to the intercom. "Not major, no. Similar to Lo'ihi, though not as large yet. The lava is oozing out, so it's not an explosive event, though it will make swimming and diving in this area very undesirable for a long time to come. Can you tell me what you saw down there?"

Leia shuddered. "It was awful, Annie. We were trapped in a cave when the lava began to pillow over the entrance. It grew so fast, we couldn't get out. Then Nani found a way through to the higher cave and got us out. She's the real hero."

"I'll let Kaia know her dolphin saved the day. Again." Mano's worried smile turned to Bane. "How are you both feeling? Any pain?"

"No. How much longer do we have to cook?"

Mano glanced at the gauges by the door. "Another few minutes."

"What about my dad? Any word about Eva?"

Mano nodded. "He was here. He got a phone call telling him where to take the artifacts. He's gone there with them."

"No!" Leia sprang to her feet. "He can't go alone. It isn't safe."

"We tried to tell him that, but he wouldn't listen. He lit out of here as soon as he knew you were going to be all right."

"Where was he going?" Bane curled his hands into fists. He needed to get out of here.

"He wouldn't tell me. He mumbled something about a fishpond, then he shut up."

"The cabin near the abandoned fishpond," Leia said. "I've got to go after him."

"You can't yet. You're not done cooking." Bane put his arm around her. She was trembling, and he gave her a reassuring squeeze.

"We have to go! Something will happen to both of them." She pulled away and tried to go to the door. "You have to let me out, Mano. Please."

The desperation in her voice made Bane capitulate. "Let us out, Mano. Surely we've been in here long enough."

Mano was frowning. "I don't like it. Get back here if you get any symptoms." He began to twist the handle, then the door creaked open.

Ajax ran to Bane's side. Bane rubbed the dog's ears, then they rushed to get dressed. Ron stopped Bane by his locker. "The ship is gone, isn't it?"

"I'm afraid so, Ron. The lava got it," Bane said. A piece of history gone forever, and a lot of money down the toilet.

Ron slammed his fist against the wall and swore. "This project has been bad luck from the start. You'd better get going. You need backup?"

"I think we can handle it. Mano will come with us. We'll take the boat to the dock in Kalaupapa and get Leia's cycle. You got a cell phone I can borrow? I dropped mine somewhere."

Ron dug in his pocket. "Here."

"Thanks." Bane pulled on shorts and a T-shirt, then went to the dingy. Leia and Mano were already aboard. "Where's Annie?"

"Calling the observatory," Mano said. "They'll want to send more scientists out to take a look. This is big."

Bane told his dog to stay on the ship, then Mano started the motor, and the dingy pulled away from the *Pomaik'i*. Bane hoped they were headed in the right direction. There was no guarantee Akoni had gone to the old fishpond.

*E*va stood by the door. Her mother always told her she was too old to cry, but that's what she wanted to do. Hotshot wasn't fun anymore. He kept following her around, touching her hair, and she didn't like it. When her parents or her sister caressed her hair, it felt good. Why did she feel funny when Hotshot did it? Maybe Leia would know. She would ask her when she saw her.

"Sit down a minute," Hotshot said. He took her arm and guided her toward the smelly cot.

She tried to pull her arm from his grasp, but he was too strong. "I'm tired of sitting. I want to go outside. It stinks in here."

"Well, you can't." He pushed her toward the cot.

Eva was wishing more and more she'd never come with him. She thought he was her friend, but he wasn't acting like it. Leia said friends helped one another. Hotshot wasn't helping her at all. "I want to go home and see my dad."

"Your dad will be coming to get you soon." Hotshot drew the back of his hand across her cheek. "It's too bad you're a dummy, Eva. You're so beautiful."

Eva's cheeks got hot. "I don't like it when people call me a dummy. Leia says people who call others names are weak themselves and are only doing it to make themselves think they're bigger than they are." Hotshot's face got red, and his eyes got all squinty. He squeezed her arm hard enough to make her cry, but she gritted her teeth instead. She wouldn't cry.

"Why don't you just shut up?" He shoved her away, then stood and stomped to the window. When he turned back around, he was smiling his normal smile. "Here comes your dad now. Earlier than I expected, so it's a good thing you weren't as affectionate as I'd hoped."

Eva's eyes widened when he took a gun out from behind the waistband of his shorts. "What are you doing with a gun? They're bad."

"They're useful. Just sit down and shut up."

Skylarks warbled in the trees around the clearing. The ancient fishpond was dry of water-and of people. Rushing up the path from her grandmother's cottage where they'd left the bike, Leia hoped to see her father soon. "Let's try the cabin," Leia suggested. She ran ahead of Bane and Mano along the path to the old cabin.

"Slow down." Bane rushed to catch her and grabbed her arm. "We can't go rushing in like a Swat team. There's too much at stake. Your father and sister both might be in danger."

She knew he was right, but nervous energy strummed along her veins, hurrying her steps. The urgency she felt clouded her thinking. "Just hurry." She caught sight of Mano's face. Beads of perspiration dotted his forehead, and he was pale.

"I'm so stupid," Mano admitted. "I was so worried, I forgot breakfast. I remembered a few minutes ago, but I don't have anything with me, not even glucose tablets."

"I don't have anything for you to eat either." Leia often carried hard candy in her purse, but she had left it behind on the ship. She had no homepathics with her either. "We cleared the food out of

my grandmother's house, but the clinic will have glucose tablets.
Go there and get some."

"Call someone else to go with you. You need backup." Mano's
voice was anguished.

"There's no one to call. We'll be all right."

"I'll rush back as soon as I eat. Call me in half an hour."

"Can you get back by yourself? You don't look good," Bane said.

Leia wondered the same thing. A hypoglycemic reaction was
nothing to fool around with. "You'd better go with him, Bane. I'll
just go watch the cabin. I won't go in until you get back."

"I'll be fine," Mano insisted.

Bane took another look at his brother's face. "No, you're not.
She's right." He turned to Leia. "You should be the one to go with
him. I don't know anything about medicine. I'll wait for you."

She started to protest, but he held up his hand. "I'll just observe
from the trees. I promise. I'll call Mano's number in half an hour to
see where you are. Try not to worry. I've got it under control."

"We'll hurry." Everything in her wanted to shout no, but she
knew it made sense. Mano was probably feeling bad enough without a temper tantrum from her upsetting him even more. She
watched Bane disappear into the forest, then she and Mano went
back down the trail toward town.

"Sorry, Leia. I'm such a dork."

"No, you're not. It was an upsetting morning. Let's just get you
feeling better." Were his hands trembling? She picked up her pace
when she realized his hands had a slight tremor. He was a big guy.
If he passed out on the path, she wouldn't be able to cart him to the
clinic. They passed the rest of the trek in silence.

They reached her grandmother's yard. Mano was sagging
against a tree. Sweat ran down his face in rivulets, and the tremors
in his hands were more pronounced. She grabbed his arm and
started to help him to the sidecar. He collapsed into the seat and
closed his eyes. She slung herself onto the bike and drove to town

at seventy miles an hour. A nurse met her at the clinic door and rushed for some glucose tablets. She ran back to the sidecar and gave them to Mano.

"Mahalo," Mano muttered. His head lolled back, but she could see the effort he was making to stay conscious.

"I could help you manage your diabetes with homepathics, Mano. When this is all over, I'd like to show you." With the offer, Leia realized she had to take the residency in natural medicine Dr. Kapuy had told her about. She wanted to cure people, not just treat the illness. Leia waited for the tablets to work, turning to look out over the sleepy town. Not many tourists here today. A familiar figure caught her eye, and she waved at Candace. Leaving Mano to recover, she advanced a few steps to meet her friend. "What are you doing here?"

"A guy chartered the boat to come out here today. He was willing to pay an outlandish price, so I couldn't refuse. He just wanted to wander the place and take pictures. I guess his great-grandfather died out there. I thought you'd be out on the ship. How's the excavation going?"

"It's a bust." Leia hated to burst her hopes even more. She told her about the morning's events. Candace closed her eyes and sighed. "Try not to worry," Leia said, pressing her hand. "It will work out. You'll see. God has it under control."

Candace opened her eyes. "I don't think so, Leia. I think I'll have to move to the mainland, find some way to support us."

Leia hated to see Candace so discouraged, but the minutes were ticking by. Mano should be recovered in another few minutes. The cell phone in her pocket rang, and she opened it gingerly and held out a few inches from her head. "Bane?"

"Yeah, it's me. I just got to the cabin. How's Mano?"

"Recovering. I'll meet you at my grandmother's, and we'll figure out where to go from there."

"Is something wrong?" Candace wanted to know.

"We're looking for Eva. I thought she might be at the old cabin up the trail from my grandmother's. Bane went to look, but she's not there."

"I could help you look," Candace offered. "The guy said he'd be here a couple of hours and I have nothing else to do."

Leia glanced at Candace's attire: slim-fitting sundress and high-heeled sandals. Not suitable for hiking through the jungle. "It's okay, we'll find her." She tried to keep her tone light and unconcerned. Word about what her dad had done couldn't be allowed to get out, not even to friends.

Twenty-six

Mynahs squawked from the trees, and Bane looked up. He wished he had a clue where to go. A fishpond. No other places came to mind. Kicking ajar the unlocked door, he stepped inside the empty cabin. Its dampness enveloped him. It didn't feel as if anyone had been inside recently. He prowled the room, looking to see if anything appeared different from when he was here last. His gaze settled on the old table. EVA had been carved in block letters on the surface.

He touched the lettering. She had been here! He dug out his cell phone and dialed Mano's phone again. When his brother answered, Bane told him what he'd found. Mano told him they were at Ipo's cottage and could be at the abandoned cabin in minutes. Bane shut his phone and continued his search. He checked the cabinets, the rusting metal cooler, and the heap of sleeping bags in the corner. He pulled the blankets from the bed, but there was nothing under them but stains. He tossed them back onto the cot and looked around. He'd checked everywhere. His gaze fell on the cot again. Except for under the mattress.

He dragged it from the metal frame and hit pay dirt. A small yellow Big Bird backpack he'd seen Eva tote around forever was pushed under the cot, clear back to the wall. He tossed the mattress off to the side and pulled the cot out from the wall, then grabbed the satchel. It was heavier than he'd thought. As he unzipped it, he heard Mano's voice calling him. "In here," he yelled.

Mano and Leia rushed through the door. He held up the bag. "It's Eva's, isn't it?"

Leia nodded wordlessly. She held out her hand and walked toward him. He gave her the bag. "Look inside and see if there are any clues to who has her, anything unusual."

"She usually carries her paper and watercolors in it. And anything else that's important to her." Leia went to the dusty table and set the bag down and began to rummage through it. Bane and Mano stood behind her and looked over her shoulder. She drew out a snorkel mask and fins, then drawing pads and colored pencils. "Her *honu*." Leia held up a rock that looked like a sea turtle. Leia picked up the sketch pad and began to flip through the pages. "I haven't looked at her drawings in a while. Maybe she did a picture of the guy she's with. She likes to draw people best of all."

Bane nodded and watched her turn the pages. Eva's talent shone in her attention to detail and the colors she chose. His gaze landed on the landscape scene Leia was about to pass over. "Wait, I know that place. Dirk took Tony and me to that cabin once to go fishing. There's an old fishpond there, now that I think about it. I knew there was some old pond that I couldn't remember. It's been driving me crazy."

"Dirk? Could he have anything to do with this?" Mano asked.

"I don't know," Bane said. "Dirk said the cabin was owned by his grandfather, but it's rarely used. Maybe someone just took advantage of its accessibility."

Leia was still looking at the sketch pad. "Look here." She showed him a picture of a man Eva had drawn. It was clearly Dirk Forsythe. *Hotshot* was written under it. "Dirk has her."

*E*va held her father's hand as Hotshot made them walk along the narrow strip of sand. She'd been here before, snorkeling with Hotshot. *Makua* gave her hand a squeeze that made her feel better, and she held on to it with all her strength. With her father here, she wasn't as scared, but she still wanted to go home. "Mama will be worried," she told him.

"We'll see her soon." They climbed a small hill and soon reached the cabin where she'd changed into her suit when she snorkeled before. It was nicer than the other one. There was no dust on the tables here, and no mouse doo-doo. "Now what?" her father asked Hotshot. "You have what you wanted—why don't you just let us go?"

"Cooperate with me and you'll be freed. I know there's more."

"There isn't," her father said.

His voice boomed in a way that usually scared Eva, but Hotshot didn't seem to flinch. Eva huddled closer to her father, and he put his arm around her. She watched Hotshot's face and wondered why he looked so mad. Her dad had been nice to him and had even brought him some boxes of stuff. It didn't look very interesting to Eva: old broken pottery and creepy bones. It made her shiver to look at them.

"I read the list. I know one of the items is a priceless *lā'au pālau*. I want it."

Her father's eyes widened. "I forgot. There is one small box of things that Koma didn't get down to the cave before he broke his hip. It's in the tree stand at his cabin. I meant to get it yesterday, but when you took Eva, I forgot about it." He stared defiantly at Hotshot.

Eva began to hum. She didn't want her dad to make Hotshot mad. She'd seen him knuckle a boy's head once when he got an attitude. It was Joe Leoki, and he had cried. Joe was a big boy, so she knew it hurt. She didn't want Hotshot to hurt her dad. She tugged on his arm. When he looked at her, she shook her head. "Don't make him mad," she whispered.

"Your daughter is smart. Don't make me mad. Sit." He pointed to two blue camp chairs against the wall. Taking out his cell phone, he punched in a number and spoke into it. "The rest of the stuff is in the tree stand at Koma's. Get it, and come here." He listened, then grunted and hung up. "If it's not there . . ."

They decided the easiest and fastest way to get to Dirk's cabin would be to hike back to the cottage, get Leia's bike, and drive to the boat. They could take the boat to the beach near the cabin. The plans went without a hitch until they raced to the dock and got into the *Eva II*. The engine wouldn't start.

"It's got plenty of gas," Mano said, wiping the grease from his hands after trying to tinker with the engine. "I don't know what's wrong."

Leia's gaze landed on Candace's boat. "Let's take Candace's boat."

"Can you find her to ask her?"

"I don't want to traipse all over the village looking for her. She said she'd be here awhile." Nodding toward the old man casting nets from the pier, she started toward him. "I'll tell Jeb to tell her we'll be back as soon as we can. Maybe he can get this boat going and use it to run her customer back." He promised to keep an eye out for Candace and tell her Leia had taken the boat. He got his tools and headed toward the Kahales' boat.

When she got back, the others had already boarded Candace's boat. She untied the rope, threw it to Bane, then hopped onto the boat. Mano started the engine, and the craft pulled away from the dock. She looked back, hoping to see Candace and wave an apology, but her friend was nowhere to be seen. It was probably just as well. At least she knew Candace wasn't going to need it anytime soon.

Bane directed Mano on where to head the boat. Fatigue hit Leia, and she felt shaky. She sat down on the seat. Maybe if she had something to eat she'd feel better. Leia began to rummage through the cabinets in search of food. She found some Cheese Nips and grabbed a handful. They were stale, but she ate them anyway. As she put the box away, her gaze fell on a weight belt. It was damaged, the cut edges sticking up in the air. She picked it up and looked at it, then flipped it over. A red label bearing Tony's name was still attached.

She made a sound, and Bane looked up. "What's wrong?"

Wordlessly, she held out the belt. "It's Tony's. The one we couldn't find."

He absorbed her words in silence, then took the belt from her fingers. "How would she get this? She wasn't even down there."

"Dirk uses this boat too."

"That means . . ."

"That Dirk not only has my sister, but he also killed Tony. He's probably got my dad too," Leia finished for him in a choked voice. "We've got to find him! He's capable of killing them. This proves it."

Bane went to tell Mano what they'd found. Leia held the weight belt and tried to figure out where this all led. Dirk wasn't with the divers. How had he killed Tony? He'd been at Candace's house when she went to offer her condolences to Candace the night Tony died. Candace was the usual pilot of the boat, and she hated to let anyone take the boat out without her. If Dirk was onboard, so was Candace. She glanced at Bane and saw the same doubt in his eyes.

Bane's eyes widened. "I'd say Candace is involved too, Leia."

Leia didn't want to believe it. Could all Candace's tears about Tony's death be hiding the heart of a black widow? "I don't believe it, Bane. She's been just crushed by all this. Maybe Dirk is trying to implicate her."

"Maybe. But consider this—Candace was an actress. Tony was always bragging about how good she was."

"That's true," Leia whispered. "But she wasn't down there that day."

"Neither was Dirk," he pointed out. "What if she was having an affair with Dirk and got sucked into the whole thing?

"I'd like to believe that she never intended Tony harm, and that Dirk did it. But how? He must have taken a separate boat out and waited for Tony."

She nodded. "He was handling the shop that day. He could have closed it a few hours, gone out to kill Tony, and gotten back."

"He would have had to tell her about it." Bane picked up the belt. "Otherwise, this wouldn't be here."

He had a point. At the very least, she was an accomplice after the fact and had helped hide his guilt. At the worst, she'd been in on it from the beginning. "Should we go back and confront her? Make her tell us where Dirk has Eva and my dad?"

He shook his head. "It's all speculation. She may know nothing, and we'll have wasted valuable time. At least we have an inkling of where to look right now."

She was beginning to feel hopeless. "I hope you're right."

"I think I can find this place."

She looked up to see the boat heading for shore. The barren stretch of beach held no sign of habitation other than a rickety pier that jutted into the heavy surf. "I don't see the cabin."

"It's up the hill, in the trees. You can't see it from here."

The engine throttled back, and Mano brought the boat alongside the pier. Two other boats were anchored there. Bane jumped out and secured the rope. "We need to hurry. The surf is high today, and the rope may not hold for long." He helped Leia navigate the pitching deck until she was on the pier. Mano hopped nimbly after them. "It's up this way." Bane charged up the hill.

Leia followed, and he stopped to help her clamber over a pile of black lava rocks. With every step, her hope surged again. She wanted to grab her sister and hug her tight. The world would be deprived of a wonderful light without Eva. Leia almost physically ached at the thought of losing her sister. Eva was way too trusting, but that was part of her charm. The thought made her realize that she couldn't blame God for the gift of Eva. He'd known what he was doing all along. Eva was special, and her dream about the starfish had helped save them today. Maybe God had known what he was doing with the things Leia had gone through as well.

She stopped to catch her breath at the top of the hill. "Listen! I think I hear Eva." The voice came again. Though she couldn't make out any words, the stress in her sister's voice traveled through the trees loud and clear. "Hurry!" As they rushed through the path covered with wildflowers, Mano pulled out his gun.

They reached the clearing, and Bane held Leia back when she would have charged to the cabin. "Let's circle around the back and see if we can tell what's going on. Mano, you stay here and watch the front. Leia and I will be right back."

Eva's voice had stilled, and Leia couldn't tell where it had come from. They crept around the end of the house, following the scent of Japanese honeysuckle. Both windows in the back of the two-room cabin were open, so they would have to be quiet. Leia was tall enough to peer in the window, so she leaned forward and peeked around the honeysuckle to the inside of the cabin. Eva and her father sat in camp chairs. Dirk stood over them waving a gun angrily. None of them were looking toward the window.

Leia ducked back down again. "He's got a gun."

"I saw. We need to distract him." He took her hand, and they slipped back to the trees. He motioned to his brother, and Mano joined them at the front-left corner of the house.

"We're going to have to draw him out." Bane motioned for Mano to lead the way. "You've got the gun, buddy."

"I've got the brawn, you've got the brains, is that it?" Mano grinned but stepped out with his gun ready.

They ducked under the window and crept to the door. "Stay here," Bane whispered.

Leia shook her head. No way was she waiting out here. She wanted to touch Eva and make sure she was all right. Her father too. She tiptoed behind Bane and Mano toward the front of the cabin. Bane motioned for her to get behind a large monkeypod tree, and she moved to the safety of its gnarled branches. Bane and Mano slipped to the front of the cabin.

Mano held his finger to his lips, then picked up a rock, moved to the side of the door, and banged the rock on the outside of the cabin. Stepping behind a bush, he brought his gun up. Leia heard a muffled oath from inside the cabin. The door eased open, and Dirk's gun poked out. His eyes squinted and his gaze sweeping the landscape, Dirk stepped outside.

"Freeze!" Mano shouted. Dirk whirled, bringing his gun up. Before he could fire, Bane jumped him from behind. Dirk thrashed under Bane as Mano leaped to help his brother. He wrested the gun from Dirk's hand and stuck both it and his own gun in his waistband.

Leia rushed to the cabin door and entered. She grabbed Eva, who jumped to her feet as Leia came through the door. Leia inhaled the essence of her sister—ginger shampoo, some musty odor she couldn't identify, and the salt of her tears.

Her father came up behind her and embraced both of them. "I knew you'd find us. You're like a pit bull."

Bane and Mano hustled Dirk into the cabin. Leia turned to face Dirk. She whipped out Tony's weight belt and shook it in Dirk's face. "You killed Tony, didn't you? Why? He was your friend—he trusted you. He had nothing to do with any of this. Why did you kill him?"

Dirk's face turned a mottled red as Bane shoved him into a chair. "Where'd you get that? You can't prove anything."

Leia realized they couldn't. It had been found on Candace's boat. Candace would be the one to go down for it, though with his kidnapping of Eva, he was in plenty of trouble.

Eva lifted her head from Leia's shoulder. "I saw that in Hotshot's bag when I was looking for candy."

Leia turned to her sister. "Why didn't you tell me? You knew we were looking for it."

Eva dropped her gaze. "He said it was Candace's."

Leia hugged her. "It's not your fault." She glared at Dirk. "All for money." Events of the past few days began to bubble to mind. "You worked for a security firm on O'ahu. Was the museum one of your clients? Is that how you figured out my dad had the artifacts?

There was something on one of the tapes, wasn't there? You figured you could get it from him, so you hid the tape from the police. When did you plant the belt on Candace's boat?"

He shrugged. "Sounds like you've got it all figured out, Sherlock." He jutted out his chin.

"Did Candace know about this? Did she fall for your charm?" Bane asked.

Leia raised her brows and shook her head so Bane would see her. She wanted to keep Candace out of this. It was obvious Dirk had set her up. Dirk didn't answer Bane's jibe, but Leia saw the flash of triumph in his eyes. Her gaze went back to Bane. He'd been right about Candace working with Dirk. She felt sick. Candace knew about it and had shielded a murderer. Her friend would be arrested too.

Bane pulled out the cell phone. "I better call the cops." He stared at the phone, then put it away. "No signal here."

Eva was crying now, and Leia looked down into her sister's exhausted face. "*Makua*, you'd better take Eva home. Take one of the boats and send the police back here. We'll stay here with Dirk until the cavalry arrives."

"I think I'll go with them if you can handle it," Mano said. "I want to check on Annie and her volcano. She's probably harried with all the media attention. You want my gun?"

Bane shook his head. "I've got Dirk's gun. Besides, he's trussed up good and tight. We'll be fine until the police arrive."

Leia hugged her sister and father and thanked Mano for all he'd done, and the three headed to the beach where they'd left the boat. Now all they had to do was wait for the police. Once Mano could use his cell phone, he would summon help.

"We might as well get comfortable." Bane pulled out a camp chair for Leia, then dropped into one himself. "You think the money was worth it, Dirk?"

"You don't know anything," he said. He clamped his mouth shut and turned to stare at the back wall.

His posture changed in some indefinable way that put Leia's senses on alert. She turned to look out the window, but there was nothing there. She told herself she was jumping at shadows, but the skin on the back of her neck continued to prickle. "Is there water in the cooler?" Dirk didn't answer, so she stood and went to the cooler on the table. It was full of soft drinks and bottled water. "Want something, Bane?"

"I'll take some water," a soft voice said from the doorway. Leia wheeled and stared down the barrel of the gun Candace held in her hand. Her other hand held the small box of the artifacts that had been on the tree stand at Koma's. "Surprised?" Candace asked with a gentle smile. "Toss me the gun, Bane."

Twenty-seven

I wondered when you'd get here, babe. Untie me." Dirk twisted so she could get at his bound hands, but instead of going to him, Candace shut the door behind her and strolled toward Leia to take the bottle of water from her hands. The gun never wavered. She picked up the gun Bane had shoved toward her.

Leia kept her gaze on Candace. The beautiful face still held no trace of evil or guile that she could see. The cornflower eyes had a disingenuous smile in them. The full lips were curved in what seemed to be genuine joy. She managed to smile at Candace. "Are you here to rescue us, or him?"

Candace uncapped her bottle of water and took a swig, but the gun didn't waver. She set the bottle down with a deliberate motion. "Neither, I'm afraid." She picked up a hank of rope and tossed it to Leia. "Tie up lover boy. Good and tight. I'm going to check your work." Leia hesitated, but Candace's beautiful mask slipped as her lips thinned, and her nostrils flared. "I've always liked you, Leia, but I forget those kinds of details when I'm mad. Do it now, or I'll have to shoot him." She gestured at Bane with the gun. "Sit down."

Leia carried the rope to where Bane sat. She knelt in front of him, and he held out his hands.

"Hands behind the chair, idiot." Candace strode across the floor and pointed the gun at Bane. "I'm losing my patience here."

"Untie me, babe," Dirk said again. Candace didn't look at him, and he began to bounce in his chair.

"Shut up, Dirk," she said. "I don't want to have to shoot you too."

Leia glanced at him in time to see his jaw drop. What was going on? She finished tying up Bane, then stood behind him. Candace's perfume, a heavy floral scent, overpowered the room with a nauseating effect.

"Bring me the rope." Candace pushed a camp chair in front of her and motioned for Leia to sit.

She didn't seem to notice the tiny penknife Eva had dropped into the chair. Leia quickly slid into the seat and grabbed the knife as she sat so Candace didn't catch a glimpse of it. Candace began to lash her hands together behind her back. Leia's gaze met Bane's. Candace finished her task and stepped back. Leia tipped her head to look up at her. "Why, Candace? Tony loved you."

Candace gave an elegant shrug as she walked toward the propane stove. "He was getting suspicious about me and Dirk. Besides, I thought with him dead, you'd be quick to help me out, and I could use you to force your dad to give up the artifacts."

"Did you feed him puffer fish?" Leia asked. Another incident floated to her memory. "It was in his fish oil capsules, wasn't it? The ones you gave him before we went diving."

Candace shrugged. "I had to time the effects. Once the poison took effect, all Jermaine had to do was cut the weight belt."

"Jermaine? I thought he was one of Westerfield's men."

Candace smiled. "Jermaine was young and rather smitten. He wanted to please me."

"There's not really a baby either, is there? It was all a ploy to get my sympathy." Leia knew her voice dripped with disgust, but it still didn't match the level of contempt she felt.

"Candace, cut these ropes." Dirk's voice rose, and he thumped his feet on the floor.

She glanced back at him as she picked up the lighter. "You haven't figured it out yet, have you, Dirk? I want it all. The money, my freedom. There's going to be a convenient accident with the propane stove. Such a tragedy while you were waiting for help to arrive." A smile played around her perfect lips. "But the murderer has been caught and deserves to die in the fire. I can play the grieving widow a few more weeks, then move to the mainland when I can't make a go of the shop by myself."

"No!" Dirk began to struggle against the bonds. "We're going to be together."

"You seemed so brokenhearted," Leia murmured to Candace. She was actually sorry for Dirk.

"You mean like this?" Candace's lips began to quiver. Tears made her eyes look luminous, and one rolled down her cheek. She dashed the tears away with the back of her hand and began to smile. "Tony was right about one thing—I was good enough to make it in Hollywood, but I never got the breaks. Maybe I will now. I've certainly had enough practice."

"How—" Leia couldn't finish.

"How can I cry at the drop of a hat?" Candace smiled. "I just remember how I felt the night my sister was crowned homecoming queen. That brings on the tears every time."

Leia remembered what Dirk had said about Candace's family. "Your twin and your parents died in a fire."

"Fire is handy. It cleans up so many details." Candace was watching her like Hina watched Ajax. Like she was just waiting to pounce. "The treasure hunt was all Dirk's idea, but he was useful for that much."

"That's a lie," Dirk shouted. "It was all her idea. She was the receptionist at Marks Security. She moved here and married Tony, then called me and told me Akoni lived here, and she had a plan to get the artifacts."

"Why did you marry Tony?"

"He was useful," Candace said, still smiling in that chilling way. "And he was fun. Besides, he knew your family well, and I needed an inside track to figure out what your dad did with the artifacts. And I thought there was at least a shot he might know where that ship was. That would have been a bonus if I'd been able to get both treasures."

Leia shuddered. "I never knew you at all, did I, Candace?"

"I wish I could let you live, Leia. You were always good to me. But I have plans that I've worked on a long time. I can't go soft now." She disconnected the propane line from the stove, and it began to hiss. Candace walked to the door. "So long. Sorry it had to end this way."

She didn't look sorry. Her face was bright with color, and her eyes gleamed with exhilaration. She'd won, knew it, and relished it. Leia squirmed and tried to get the little knife in her hand to open, but it resisted her efforts. One by one, Candace carried the three boxes of artifacts out of the cabin and to an ATV that Leia could see parked in the jungle. With the last box, she shut the door behind her with a decisive click. Leia could hear her humming as she walked away.

"I've got Eva's knife. Help me get it open, and I can get us loose." Bane thumped his way over to her. She bounced as well, and they managed to get their backs to one another. "Hurry, the gas odor is getting thicker." Bane's fingers were strong, and he got the knife open, then began to saw at the bonds. The movement caused the rope to burn into her wrists, but she didn't care. If they didn't get loose, she wouldn't be feeling much of anything in a few seconds.

"They're getting looser." She twisted her wrists, and then they were free. She leaped to her feet and grabbed the knife from Bane's hand. "Come on, come on," she begged. The knife sliced a little deeper, then moments later, he was free too.

"Get out of here. I'll get Dirk." He took the knife and rushed to where Dirk sat.

Glass tinkled onto the floor, and Leia wheeled toward the window. Candace had thrown a flaming stick through, then run off. "It's going to blow!" She dashed for the door and threw it open. Maybe the fresh air would buy them a few seconds. She darted a glance behind her and saw Bane and Dirk running for the door. She raced through. Just as Bane and Dirk reached the doorway, something behind them rumbled. A massive *whump* impacted Leia's eardrums, more with pressure than with sound, as the propane tank blew. The explosion tossed Leia high in the air. She grappled for something to grab hold of to break her fall but found nothing. The ground rose up to meet her, and she slammed facedown into the dirt. She groaned and sat up. Where was Bane? Her vision blurred as she tried to focus on his face. He and Dirk were moving where they'd fallen too.

She turned to look at the cabin. Flames were shooting out the windows and door of the cabin. The heat from the fire shimmered in the air. Ash and smoke made her cough as she struggled to rise. The acrid odor of smoke burned her nose and landed on her tongue.

Bane lifted her to her feet, then grabbed Dirk as he was trying to run for a boat. "You're not going anywhere. We'll just wait down here for the police." He yanked some vines from a nearby tree.

"What about Candace?" Leia asked.

"Let's see if we can catch her and get those artifacts back." Bane tied Dirk to a tree with the vines, then took Leia's hand and ran.

*L*eia had always prided herself on being a good judge of people, but the evil that lurked behind Candace's beautiful face had rocked her. She'd thought they were friends, but Leia didn't know if Candace was capable of real friendship. At least Tony had died never knowing he'd been duped.

Her lungs still burned as she and Bane ran toward the beach. "She can't get away," she told Bane.

"There she is!" Bane pointed.

Leia could see her now. The wind whipped Candace's blonde hair around her face as she struggled to shove her boat into the waves. The abandoned ATV sat with its tires half-submerged in the water. The tide was coming in, and the high surf hampered the vessel's movement. The other of the two boats that were anchored here had floated away in the tide. Candace must have tossed its mooring line off the pier.

Leia put on an extra spurt of speed. Her slippers came off in the soft sand, but she didn't stop to retrieve them. Bane ran beside her. Candace saw them coming and jumped into the boat. She tried to start the motor, but it only coughed. Leia wasn't going to let her get away. She threw herself into the water. The shock of submersion cleared her head of the smoke. Bane hit the waves beside her. A wave slapped her in the face, and she swallowed a rush of warm seawater. She spat it out and began to swim in the surging tide. Bane's strong arms sliced the waves beside her, and he pulled ahead. He reached the boat first, but Leia was only a stroke behind him. He grabbed the bow of the boat as Candace tried the engine again. It started this time, but Bane's weight dragged the hull into the sand, and the boat was unable to move.

Leia grabbed the side and pulled herself over. She lay on the deck and looked up to see Candace scrabbling for her gun. Leia rolled to her knees and flung herself toward the other woman. The two collided, and the gun slipped away from Candace. She sprang toward it again, and Leia tackled her. The two fell to the deck with Leia on top. Candace bared her teeth as she fought to free herself, her fingers still reaching toward the gun, but Leia had six inches on her and was more muscular. She straddled Candace's body with her legs and grabbed her wrists, pinning her to the deck.

"Let go of me," Candace spat.

Leia pressed down on Candace's arms. Bane clambered aboard the boat as well. Candace's gaze went past Leia's shoulder to Bane, and she finally quit struggling.

"You're hurting me," Candace said in a plaintive voice. "Let me up. Please."

Leia moved off the other woman and released Candace's arms. She stood and stepped closer to Bane as he dropped his arm over her shoulders. "Get up, Candace," Leia told her.

Candace sat up and rubbed her arms. "You didn't have to be so rough." She rose and went to a box of artifacts. "Hey, we could split these." She leaned over the box and brought out a piece of *kapa*. "I bet you'd like this, Leia. It's worth a lot of money. Take a look at it."

Leia's gaze fell on the *kapa*. It was the most exquisite piece she'd ever seen. Her fingers itched to touch it, to unfold it and examine the pattern. She held out her hands, and Candace laid it in them. The cloth was just as soft as it looked. She unfolded it with a reverent touch. The pattern was flawed from age with a few holes here and there, but it was still the most beautifully designed piece she'd ever laid eyes on. She could only hope to be so talented some day. Her gaze fell on the tiny *honu* at the bottom. Her ancestors had often stitched a sea turtle like it on the *kapa* they'd made. Could this be the *kapa* her grandmother had talked about? If so, it wasn't part of the artifacts. She'd have to ask her dad.

"It can be yours," Candace said in a coaxing voice. "Just let me go, and give me a head start before you sic the police on me." Her head jerked up at the sound of the sirens on the two Coast Guard boats speeding toward shore. "They can't take me into custody. I was in jail once, and I swore I'd rather die than go back." Her voice deepened and took on a note of desperation.

Bane squeezed Leia's shoulder, and she tore her gaze away from the cloth. Staring into Candace's face, she didn't know if she could believe the uncertainty and fear lurking in the other woman's eyes. "Who are you really? Is your name even Candace?"

"Of course it is." Candace held her gaze for several moments before looking away.

She was lying. Even Leia could tell now that Candace was so close to being arrested. "I suppose the police will find out who you really are. How could you carry off such a full-scale lie for so long?"

Candace looked away. "Don't preach me any sermons. I did what I had to do. Look at me, Leia. Look at this body, this face. Men turn to look wherever I go. All I did was use what I was given, and yet you judge me for that? You would do the same thing in my shoes. You use what you have."

"You used people. That's the difference." She looked to wave at the police boats, and while her back was turned, Candace plunged over the side of the boat and into the water. The woman slogged to shore through the waves. "She's getting away," Leia screamed. She started to go after Candace, but Bane went over the side first.

Candace raced to the ATV. She turned the key, and the engine roared to life. The sound of the engine whining traveled over the water, but the vehicle didn't seem to be moving. The tires were sunk in wet sand and waves. Bane reached the shore. Candace looked up and saw him, then jumped off the ATV. She ran toward the jungle, but Bane was faster. He caught Candace, and she flailed and screamed obscenities at him as he pulled her arms behind her.

The police boats reached Leia. She motioned for them to help Bane, and two seamen jumped overboard and hurried to shore through the waves. They took Candace into custody, and nearly two hours passed before they'd asked all their questions and left with Candace and Dirk under arrest. They took the boxes of artifacts with them. It was all Leia could do to let them cart off the *kapa*.

The truth would come out now. She didn't know how her mother would handle it.

Twenty-eight

Every time Leia closed her eyes she could see and smell the *kapa* cloth. She could feel the texture of it in her hands, the smoothness and strength of the fabric, the scent of sandalwood. For the first time she realized the struggle her father had to have faced with what was right to do with the artifacts. The situation was out of her hands anyway, but the truth still haunted her. She knew craftspeople like her could benefit from studying the works of beauty created by masters of the past. She tried not to think that the lost *kapa* might belong to her grandmother.

She hadn't found any time to spend with Bane for several days. A flurry of publicity over the volcanic activity and recovery of the artifacts had struck the quiet island. Reporters camped outside her parents' house, and Leia had to run a gauntlet of paparazzi every time she left her cottage as well. They followed her when she jogged on the beach or when she worked in the clinic. They snapped pictures of her and Eva picking up seashells for Malia's leis and crouched behind her bushes when she picked flowers in the yard. Her father had been arrested but was now out on bail. Pete had turned over the bones he'd found when it was confirmed that they belonged among the recovered artifacts. What would happen to them was still up in the air.

Leia had thought about going to see Candace, but she couldn't bear the thought of hearing more of her former friend's excuses for what she'd done. At least Shaina would likely get what was left of Tony's estate for her daughter. Leia contented herself with doing things around *Tûtû*'s house, getting it ready to sell. After living with her eldest son and wife for a few days, her grandmother had finally consented to moving to an assisted-living facility as long as her son took care of Pua.

Leia was yanking out cat's claw by the fistfuls from her bed of orchids when a shadow fell over her face. She jerked up, expecting to see more reporters. Instead, she saw Bane's smiling face. He was holding a bouquet of white ginger in his hand. Ajax sat at his feet. Her gaze went to the *kapa* over his arm.

Hina had been digging in the dirt with Leia, and the cat meowed when she saw Bane and leaped into his arms. He held her at arm's length in one hand with the flowers in the other. "I was kind of hoping for that reaction from you," he told Leia with a wry grin. "You're a little dirty, Hina." Her paws were covered with rich black soil. He put her down, and the cat gave a plaintive cry. "Here, these are for you." He thrust the mass of fragrant flowers into her hands.

Ginger was her favorite flower, and Bane had hit on her soft spot. "I'll put them in water." She wanted to ask about the cloth over his arm, but she had a feeling he wanted to wait to talk about it. He followed her into the cottage. She sensed him watching as she got a vase out, filled it with water, and arranged the flowers in it. She stuck her nose in the bouquet and inhaled the sweet aroma. There was stillness about him, a contemplative attitude. With a last poke of a flower into place, she turned to face him. "What's wrong?"

"I just talked to Ono. He's found out quite a lot about Candace. Her real name is Elizabeth Howard. She was married before. Her first husband drowned while swimming, but it was never investigated. He's also arrested Sam Westerfield and his cohorts. He was the one who had hired the two men who abducted you."

Leia absorbed the information. "I know the Bible says we're all born wicked, but I don't think I ever really believed it until now. I never really knew Candace. It makes me wonder if we ever know another person and what's in their heart. Will they reopen her first husband's death?"

He nodded. "That's the plan." He studied her face again. "I've been doing more thinking about you and me. Coming so close to losing you really shook me. I want to marry you, Leia, no matter what the conditions. But first we have to talk about some things."

She focused her gaze on the *kapa*. Its perfection mocked her. Every detail was beautiful—and perfect. Bane might not understand now, but she needed to do what was best for him. She loved him too much to let him settle for second best. She turned away without answering and went to the living room, where she scooped Hina into her arms and sank onto the couch. He followed Leia and sat beside her. His nearness made it hard to think rationally. Was that his intention?

He put his arm over the back of the couch behind her head. "I think you love me, Leia. You're just being stubborn."

There was something in Bane's voice that made her take a sharp look at his face. He didn't sound perturbed or frustrated. Her gaze went to the *kapa* again. She longed to touch it.

"You still haven't accepted the fact that God is sovereign, have you?" He removed the cloth from his arm and began to unfold it. "Beautiful isn't it?" he asked, laying it across her lap.

"It's exquisite." She ran her hand over it and inhaled the scent of sandalwood. "Why do you have it?"

"I got it from Ono. After conferring with the list of missing artifacts and talking to your grandmother, he realized it belongs to your family. Your grandmother asked me to bring it to you."

"It's perfect." And fragile, lovely, and remarkable. She'd never seen anything like it.

"Not perfect. It has some burn marks and some imperfections in the weaving of it." He pointed them out to her. "It's really worthless. I'll throw it away." He stood and began to gather the cloth in his arms.

She caught at his arm. "Are you crazy? It's priceless!"

"It's flawed." His intent stare pinned her in place.

"I see where you're going with this. You're saying I'm valuable even though I was born with birth defects. I know that. I'm grateful for my life, thankful for the medical advances that have allowed me to live a normal life, but I mean what I said: I don't want to have children who would go through what I did."

"This *kapa* is more beautiful because of the years it was used, the lives it enhanced. Everything we go through makes us stronger and unique. Every life has value, Leia. God has a reason for everything he sends. If he chose to send us a flawed child, at least flawed the way the world looks at it, we'd love it anyway, just like he does. But he might choose to send us a healthy baby. It's not our choice. You know what? Even if we had our own children, I'd like to adopt a child with special needs. That child would have been brought into the world through no fault of ours. You would be a great mother to a child like that. I see the way you love Eva."

The thought held more appeal than she'd imagined it could. Before she could think about it, Bane fully unfurled the cloth. He wrapped it over her and tucked it under her chin with gentle hands. "Think about it. I'll go now. Are you coming to the festival tonight?"

She tore her gaze from the *kapa*. "I'd planned on it. I hope you're going to beat Pete, and I want to see how my *kapa* did in the judging."

"You're going to win. I'll play better with you there."

"It's always surprised me that you play the ukulele with such passion. You don't seem the artistic type. You're a military man."

He looked at his feet. "There's a lot I've tried to change about myself because of my fears about being left."

He didn't like to talk about his childhood. "Maybe you don't stop to think of the ways your experiences as a child have shaped you into the man you are. You're strong, dependable, and as constant as the tide," she told him.

"I've realized it lately. And I've decided to stop letting those experiences change who I am inside." He smiled, a wry but gentle grimace. "I tried to become who I needed to be and buried some things. Things God has shown me I need to let out. It's going to be hard, but I'll try if you will."

She stared into his earnest face. She loved this man with all her heart. Too much to promise something that would hurt him in the end. "I don't know if I can make that promise. And you might not want to wait. I've decided to do a residency in natural medicine."

His expectant look turned solemn. "I'll wait for you forever, Leia. But I could go with you, you know. Pray about it, Leia. Promise me that much."

"Okay," she said after a long pause. "But God and I aren't on the best terms right now."

"That's the first thing you need to fix."

She chose not to answer and rose to lead him to the door. Carrying the *kapa,* because she couldn't bear to lay it aside, she showed him out.

"Be sure to come tonight. I might surprise you." His smile held a trace of mischief and promise. "I've decided to let the real Bane Oana come out to play. For all the world to see, in fact."

Her pulse jumped at the look in his eyes. What did he mean? She couldn't wait to find out.

Bane had no idea if his plan would work. Leia could be stubborn when she thought she was right. In this case she was wrong, totally wrong, and he had to figure out a way to prove it to her. He could only hope and pray she listened to God if she wouldn't listen to anyone else. In the meantime, he was going to proceed with the evening he'd planned, even if the prospect terrified him.

He parked outside her parents' home. Several reporters stood on the front walk with cameramen aiming their equipment at the house. One of them started toward his car. He'd have to hurry to avoid her. "We're here, Ajax." His dog cocked his head and whined.

Bane felt like whining himself. His palms were sweating, and he rubbed them on his shorts. "Come on, boy." He let the dog out, and Ajax ran into the yard. Slamming the door behind him, Bane crossed the yard. The reporter didn't follow. Evidently, she'd been warned not to trespass.

Pua came running to greet them. She saw the dog and hissed. "Easy, girl." He didn't have anything to feed her, so she stalked off in a huff. Her indignant squawk made him grin. The front door seemed bigger than he remembered. He knew Ingrid would be happy to see him, but Akoni had withdrawn from everyone. Inhaling sharply, he squared his shoulders and stepped forward and rang the doorbell. From the heavy tread, he realized Akoni was going to be the one answering his summons.

The door swung open, and Akoni's scowl changed to a surprised smile. "Aloha, Bane. Is Leia with you?"

"No, she's at her cottage. Could we talk a minute?"

"Sure." Akoni stepped aside to allow Bane and Ajax to enter. He rubbed the dog on the head as he passed. "Is anything wrong?"

"It depends on Leia." Bane said. He went down the hall to the living room. "Is Ingrid here too?"

"No, she's at the hospital. Working is her sanity right now." Akoni lowered his stocky frame into the rocking chair. "So what's up? What did you mean about Leia?"

Bane sat on the sofa. "I'd like you and the rest of her family to come to the ukulele festival tonight. With your permission, I'm going to attempt to give her an engagement ring."

"Attempt?" Akoni smiled. "You're not sure?"

"You know how determined she can be. She doesn't want to marry anyone. Because of her birth defect, she's got it in her head that she doesn't want kids and can't deprive a future husband of children. She had genetic testing done, and the odds aren't good."

Akoni answered slowly. "I had no idea." He fell silent a few moments before he spoke again. "Ingrid can be stern, but she adores her children, Leia especially. I think she saw Leia as much like herself. That's why she is always so hard on her."

Bane had never seen pride in Ingrid's face. He wondered if it was wishful thinking on Akoni's part. "I guess it's why we broke up in the first place, but I'm just now figuring it out. Will you and Ingrid come?"

Akoni looked at the floor. "I don't know, Bane. I haven't been out in public since the arrest. My presence is liable to be more of a distraction than a help. The reporters will swarm me if I go out. I don't know if Ingrid will even be seen with me. She isn't even talking to me right now."

Bane leaned forward. "I think you might be the only one who can give Leia the courage to risk a life with me. Will you come?"

"I'll have to think about it. I can't answer right now."

Bane tried not to show his disappointment. "It starts at seven. Please come."

He stood and Akoni rose as well. The men shook hands. "Good luck," Akoni said. "I wish you the best even if I don't make it."

As Bane and Ajax left the house, his hope for the evening waned, and he prayed his plans weren't about to explode in his face.

*L*eia took another whiff of the sandalwood that drifted up from the *kapa* snuggled around her body. Bane had left half an hour ago, but she still sat on the couch, thinking about what he'd said. Her heart recognized the truth he'd spoken. She thought of her sister and how much joy Eva had brought to all of them. She wouldn't change anything about Eva. Maybe for Eva's sake, Leia would like to have seen her different, just so she could live a "normal" life, whatever that was. But Eva was happy. Her smile brought delight to all of them, and even her dreams had saved Leia and Bane. If God hadn't created Eva just the way she was, all their lives would have been different.

She finally folded the cloth and carefully carried it to her bedroom, where she put it in a cedar chest to make sure Hina couldn't
get to it with her claws. Her gaze fell on her Bible. Bane had asked
her to pray. Picking up her Bible, she began to leaf through the
pages. She'd read Psalm 139 before, and it had angered her, but she
turned to it again, telling herself she'd try to look at it with an open
mind. Her gaze focused on verse 16.

Your eyes saw my substance, being yet unformed.
And in Your book they all were written,
The days fashioned for me,
When as yet there were none of them.

The truth hit her in a way it never had before. God knew every
single day of surgery she'd gone through. He fashioned the days she
would have. There was some purpose for the way he'd made her, for
the way he'd created Eva. Did she trust God enough not to know that
purpose? Tears sprang to her eyes, and she struggled to hold them
back. She'd always said she'd never cry again. Never. But the tears
refused to be blocked. They poured from her eyes in a cleansing flood
as she sank to her knees and acknowledged she could trust the Lord.
The anger and disappointment with God fell away as she prayed.

She wiped the tears from her face, her fingers lighting on the
tiny scar on her lip. This time she didn't flinch. This scar was a
badge of God's love for her. The weight was gone from her shoulders. She had a party to get ready for, though she still didn't know
how she was going to answer Bane. Did she have the courage to
reach out for her happiness? She prepared for the evening in a fog.
She hadn't worn the red sundress she'd bought on Maui last month.
It was a sarong-type that hugged her figure and fell to just above her
knees. She showered, washed and dried her hair, and dressed. Her
hair looked more lustrous tonight, her eyes brighter. Her cheeks
bloomed with color. She didn't look half bad. Slipping her feet into

sequined slippers, she went to her car. The ukulele festival was held at Kiowea Beach Park on the south shore. As she drove toward the beach, she could hear the music calling over the waves. Her gaze scanned the golden sand for Bane's tall figure. He was usually easy to find because of his height. She parked and then hurried toward the crowd gathered around the musicians.

The fragrance of flowers struck her first. She glanced around and saw masses of bouquets all around the clearing: ginger, orchids, plumeria, all her favorites. She searched until she spotted Bane. He was just getting ready to play.

His face lit up with pleasure when he saw her. He put down his instrument and came toward her. "You're just in time." He picked up something at his feet.

Leia's gaze took in the beautiful lei. It had to be Malia's artwork. Tiny seashells mingled with perfect white blossoms. Bane slipped it over her head, and the sweet scent made her senses reel. He took her by the hand and led her through the flowers and the crowd. She glanced around and stopped when she saw her father. "*Makua,* you're here?"

"Bane told me something exciting was going to happen tonight. I didn't want to miss it. And your mother insisted we come. She says we're not going to hang our heads."

"Mama said that?" Leia couldn't keep the incredulity from her voice.

"Your mother has her issues, but she's sticking by me, Leia. I'm grateful for that." Her father's smile faltered. "Your mother is over there somewhere with Eva. I was just getting her a drink." He pointed toward the refreshment stand.

Leia saw her mother's blonde head. The disappointment she'd felt over her mother's coldness began to dissipate. Her mother couldn't change her nature. God had ordained her mother's days too. It was best if Leia simply accepted what love her mother was able to show. Pressing her father's arm, she stepped into the crowd with Bane.

His family was here as well, and even Kaia and Jesse had returned. They were seated near Mano and Annie with Malia on the other side of Annie. Malia had picked *Tûtû* up from the assisted-living home, and their grandmother looked bright and alert tonight as she chatted with Luana. Kaia's color was high, and her eyes were bright with expectation. A strange smile hovered on Mano's lips. He looked almost—proud. Even Malia's smile seemed to stretch across her face. What was going on? She gave the family another glance, then followed Bane.

Several rocks jutted through the sand in the open area where the musicians were playing. Bane seated her on one, picked up his ukulele and began to strum. His fingers picked out the chords. When he opened his mouth, she was shocked. He never sang.

"*Aloha nui loa.*" His rich tenor filled the night air. The words meant "I love you very much."

Leia flushed hot and cold as the meaning of his song penetrated. Bane was private and rarely even held her hand in public when they'd been engaged. He was staring now—his gaze full of love and longing. He wasn't trying to hide what he felt from the world. The Hawaiian song spoke of his great love and longing for her and ended with a proposal of marriage. She'd never heard it, and she wondered where he'd found the song. When the chords of the ukulele echoed away, he put down the instrument and came toward her. He went to one knee in front of her. The crowd began to cheer and whistle. Leia put her hands on her cheeks, and the heat radiated up through her palms.

Tenderness radiated from his eyes. "I wrote this song for you, Leia. Did you understand all the words?"

She nodded, her throat too tight to speak. Tears hovered at the backs of her eyes. She wouldn't cry, she reminded herself.

"Well? Are you going to answer me?" he asked.

She couldn't think, couldn't decide what to do. Bane's face was turned up to her, and the love in his eyes broke through her fear.

He'd braved this crowd to reveal a softer side she'd never seen. How could she hold on to her fear in the face of such devotion? "*Aloha au ia 'oe.*" She whispered Hawaiian words for *I love you.* "I don't think I have any choice but to say . . . yes." With her surrender, the tears pushed past the walls she'd erected and flowed down her cheeks. She found she didn't mind at all.

"There's always a choice. But I've taken down the barrier I've had up, Leia. My heart is yours."

"You sound almost poetic," she said. His grip on her hand was so tight it was almost painful, but she didn't mind.

"That was the part inside I was hiding. I hope you don't mind if I bring you flowers and sing you love songs."

"I wouldn't have it any other way." She leaned forward, and their lips met in a kiss. She inhaled the scent of him along with the love in his touch. With Bane she would never feel inferior or damaged. The crowd clapped even louder, and she heard Eva's shriek of happiness, a joyous sound that illuminated life, the good, the bad, and the incredible adventure. The scars healed, both inside and out. She pulled away. "You realize Hina will be thrilled."

"I think I just became a cat lover," he said, bringing her face down for another kiss.

Hawaiian Language Pronunciation Guide

Although Hawaiian words may look challenging to pronounce, they're typically easy to say when sounded out by each syllable. The Hawaiian language utilizes five vowels (a, e, i, o, u) and seven consonants (h, k, l, m, n, p, w). Please note that sometimes the *w* is pronounced the same as *v*, as in Hawaii.

a–ah, as in car: *aloha*

e–a, as in may: *nene*

i–ee, as in bee: *honi*

o–oh, as in so: *mahalo*

u–oo, as in spoon: *kapu*

Dipthongs: Generally, vowels are pronounced separately except when they appear together:

ai, ae–sounds like *I* or *eye*

ao–sounds like *ow* in *how*, but without a nasal twang

au–sounds like the *ou* in *house* or *out*, but without a nasal twang

ei–sounds like *ei* in *chow mein* or in *eight*

eu–has no equivalent in English, but sounds like *eh-oo* run together as a single syllable

iu–sounds like the *ew* in *few*

oi–sounds like the *oi* in *voice*

ou–sounds like the *ow* in *bowl*

ui–an unusual sound for English-speakers, sort of like the *ooey* in *gooey*, but pronounced as a single syllable.

Words Used in This Book

'ae (EYE): yes

aloha (ah-LOW-hah): hello as used in this book. Aloha is a wonderful word though. It's a blessing of love, mercy, and compassion bestowed on the receiver.

aloha au ia 'oe (ah-LOW-hah OW EE-uh OY): I love you

aloha no (ah-LOW-hah NO): oh no!

aloha kakah'aka (ah-LOW-hah kah-kah-HAH-kah): good morning

aloha nui loa (ah-LOW-hah NOOEY LOW-ah): I love you very much

a'ole loa (ah-oh-lay LOW-ah): certainly not

ha'iku (HI-koo): flower

haole (ha-OH-lay): white person, any foreigner

he'e holua (HAY-ay WHO-lah): lava sledding, an ancient Hawaiian sport

ho'olohe (HO-oh-low-hay): listen to me

honu (HO-new): sea turtle

hula ku'i Moloka'i (WHO-lah KU-ee MOW-low-kye): an ancient, fast dance with stamping, heel twisting, thigh slapping, dipping of knees, and fist doubling as in boxing, vigorous gestures of such pursuits as dragging fish nets, and unaccompanied by instruments

imu (EE-moo): firepit for cooking luau pig

hahuna (hah-WHO-nah): expert

kala mai ia'u (CALL-ah my EE-ow): excuse me

kapa (KAH-pah): Hawaiian bark cloth, the finest textured of all *tapa* (bark cloth made in other parts of the world)

kapu (KAH-poo): taboo

keiki (KAY-kee): child

konane (koh-AH-nee): ancient Hawaiian board game

kope (KOE-pay): coffee

kua kuku (KOO-ah koo-koo): wooden anvil for beating
    tapa

kupuna (kah-POO-nah): grandparent, ancestor

lâ'au pâlau (LAU puh-LAU): ancient Hawaiian club

mahalo nui loa (mah-HAH-low NEW-ee LOW-ah):
    thank you very much

mahalo no (mah-HAH-low NO): thanks but no

mahalo (mah-HAH-low): thanks

makua (mah-KOO-ah): nickname for father

makuahine (mah-KOO-ah-HEE-nee): mother

makuakane (mah-KOO-ah-KAH-nay): father

malo (MAH-low): loincloth for male

mana (MAH-nah): spiritual power

nene (nay-nay): endangered Hawaiian goose

'ohana (oh-HAH-nah): family

'ohelo (oh-HAY-low): a small native Hawaiian shrub in
    the cranberry family

'ohi'a (oh-HEE-uh): mountain apple tree

pakololio (pah-koe-LOW-lee-oh): a Hawaiian symbol
    used to bring control over the wind

pau (POW): women's skirt or sarong

pehea 'oe (pay-HEY-ah OY): how are you?

pomaik'i: good fortune

pupus (POO-poose): appetizers

tûtû (TOO-too): grandmother

tûtû kâne (TOO-too KAH-nay): grandpa

tûtû-man (TOO-too-MON): grandfather

wahine (wah-HE-nee): woman, wife

Acknowledgments

Aloha! I've grown very fond of that word in the writing of this series. Aloha means so many things: everything that is full of love, mercy, goodness, and friendship. The Hawaiian people are some of the friendliest on the planet, and they've opened their hearts to us every time we've gone to the islands for a research trip. A special blessing of aloha on Malia Spencer's head for reading my manuscripts and helping this *haole* navigate the writing waters to make sure I got right the culture I love so much. Her father, El Captain, as we call him, Bruce Spencer, gave me much-needed advice about Moloka'i and the world of boats. *Mahalo nui loa* to both of you!

Mahalo nui loa to Robin Miller for reading the final draft to make sure I didn't leave any plot holes. If I did, blame her. Seriously though, Robin, you were a great help, and I appreciate your friendship so much!

Mahalo nui loa to my best friends and critique partners: Kristin Billerbeck, Denise Hunter, and Diann Hunt. Your e-mails and constant support make the journey worthwhile!

My great agent and friend, Karen Solem, has been by my side through thick and thin. Mostly better since you came into my life, Karen. I call a blessing of aloha from God on your head for all you've done for me.

My editor, Erin Healy, is a source of envy among my writing friends. They are ready to steal her away, but I'll never let her go. She's a fabulous editor, and she makes me better than I can be. *Mahalo nui loa*, Erin!

I'm blessed beyond measure by my publishing family at Thomas Nelson. When *Black Sands* arrived, publisher Allen Arnold included some tissues because he knew I always cry when I hold a new book in my hands. That's the kind of publishing family I have: one that really knows and loves me. It's a partnership I never take for granted but thank God for every day. *Mahalo nui loa* to the fabulous team: Ami McConnell is the best editor I've ever met. I love her like my daughter, and I've adopted her kids as my grandchildren, because my own children are slow in providing them. Thanks also to Amanda Bostic, my editorial assistant who keeps us all on track and makes me smile while she does it; Caroline Craddock, my beautiful and fabulous publicist; Jennifer Deshler, my incredibly creative marketing guru; and Lisa Young, my friend and Allen's assistant, who is always there with a quick hug to pick me up. Allen Arnold is wonderful and amazing. He has taken the Fiction imprint and launched it into the stratosphere. He charges up a room just by entering it and makes me think I can do more than I ever dreamed. Thanks for letting me share the journey, my friends.

My family is my wonderful blessing from God. No more supportive husband ever walked the earth than my David. He tells people about my books, reads them before they go to the editors, and keeps me on track. My children, Kara and Dave, bring me joy every day. I'm blessed beyond measure by what God has done in my life, both personally and professionally. *Aloha nui loa.*

And most important, *mahalo nui loa* to the One who made it all possible and who has lavished every blessing on me. *Aloha nui loa.*

Dangerous Depths

COLLEEN COBLE

READING GROUP GUIDE QUESTIONS

---

1. Tony was obsessed with finding the treasure. How do you think it affected his life for good or bad? Is obsession ever good?

2. Leia was self-conscious about her so-called "defect." Is there some aspect of your appearance that makes you feel awkward? What can you do to get over it?

3. Leia didn't tell Bane the truth about why she broke off her engagement. Is there ever a good reason to lie?

4. Leia never felt unconditional love from her mother. Why do you think the way our parents show love can have such crucial effects through our whole lives? Is there a way to get over what we perceive as a lack of good parenting?

5. Bane was the family leader and felt responsible for his siblings. How did that shape the man he became?

6. Bane felt he had to hide his soft side. What kinds of expectations do we put on our sons that are wrong? What are the important things to teach them?

7. Eva was an adult even though she was mentally impaired, and was fair game to a predator. It's a difficult line to walk between giving a daughter like her enough freedom and too much. Were her parents right to let her have free time on her own? Why or why not?

8. Tûtû's mental problems caused more problems for Leia, but we've all run into problems with family members who say hurtful things. How do you handle that? How would Christ respond?

9. Why do you think Leia was so attached to natural medicine? Could there be an element of rebellion against her mother's way?

10. Have you ever know someone who was focused totally on his/her own wants and desires with no regard for other people like the villain? How do you deal with someone like that?

COLLEEN COBLE

Fire Dancer

THOMAS NELSON
Since 1798

thomasnelson.com

AN EXCERPT FROM

Fire Dancer

$\mathcal{D}$ust settled around the Jeep as Tess parked in front of the old adobe-style ranch house. A familiar ache started under her breastbone and moved up her chest in a suffocating pressure. She'd loved this house, yet it looked hostile to her now. The curved windows seemed to peer back at her like eyes slitted with malice. Why had she agreed to come? She should have insisted Stevie tell her what this was all about over the phone. She let her squirrel scamper out, then slammed the Jeep's door behind her and wiped her dusty hands on the seat of her jeans.

"Some things never change," a deep voice behind her said. "You're still running late."

She sometimes heard that voice at night in her dreams (or more accurately, nightmares). Tess pinned a fake smile to her lips and forced herself to turn. "Hello, Chase," she said, determined to sound carefree and natural. If it were up to her, he would never know how much he irritated her even still. Her gaze ranged from his dusty boots up the faded denim jeans and T-shirt, then lingered on the strong-jawed face under the tan cowboy hat. The fierce Arizona sun hadn't managed to wash out his vivid blue eyes. "You've got a new hat."

Sheesh, could she say anything more lame? She wished she could spit the dust from her tongue, but it wouldn't be ladylike, and while she hardly considered herself a girly-girl, she wasn't about to let Chase Huston sense even an ounce of weakness. Why didn't he say something? He stared her down as if he was trying to look under her skin and into her soul, a knack he'd always had, unfortunately. Tiny new lines crouched at the edges of his eyes, and she spotted a weary droop to his lips. Maybe she could hold her own against him this trip, especially no longer than she planned to be here.

She took a step toward him, but he didn't move. If she dared, she'd stick her tongue out at him. "Are you going to hug me or just stare?"

He unbent then, pulling his hands from the pockets of his jeans. They exchanged a brief hug, but it was like trying to embrace a saguaro cactus. She probably should have kept her distance, but she couldn't resist the desire to unsettle him just a little.

"I'm surprised you showed your face," he said. "I had a bet going with Whip that you'd make some lame excuse at the last minute and not show up. You're late."

"I took a wrong turn."

"More likely a shortcut that got you lost. When will you learn shortcuts are of the devil?" He flashed white teeth in a grin.

He knew her too well. She stepped away from him. "Would you turn Wildfire out into the pasture?"

"Sure. I see Dooley hasn't deserted you yet." He watched the squirrel run along the edge of the driveway and pick up something in the dirt.

"He still rules the roost. Stevie in the house?"

"Yeah. In her bedroom. Your parents' old room," he amended.

Tess took two steps toward the house before his words sank in. "In bed? At eleven in the morning? What's wrong?" She didn't wait for an answer but stepped into the shade of the overhanging portico. Hummingbirds flitted away from the feeder as she passed, and the air movement stirred the brilliant cardinal flowers that attracted the hummers. She'd forgotten how the hummingbirds flocked around the porch. Her mother had loved them. She clamped off the memory before it could hurt her.

Crossing the threshold onto the terra-cotta tile felt like going through a time portal. The scent of the pine boughs Stevie and their mother liked hanging around the house brought all the memories of home rushing back. Tess closed her eyes and swayed. In her mind, she heard her mother's voice call. Everything in her wanted to turn and rush out the way she'd come. She opened her eyes and forced herself to take a few deep breaths, then took a moment to glance around the large open living space. Dead pine needles lay littered around the bough on top of the TV, and a dry odor of decay began to insinuate itself past the fragrance of pine. The place was usually spotless. What was going on here?

"Stevie?" Tess ran down the hall lined with pictures of her and her sister from birth through high school. It was as if the air itself pushed against her and slowed her movements until she reached the bedroom door. An invisible barrier seemed to guard the oak door. When she was a little girl, she used to crawl in bed with her mother. Her dad was usually up and out the door by the time she and Stevie woke up. Her mom would fix him breakfast then go back to bed for a little while. When Tess poked her head in, her mom would throw back the covers and open her arms, and Tess would scramble into them.

There would be no welcoming smile from her mother today. Tess could almost hear the crackle of the fire that night so long ago, almost smell the smoke. She looked at the closed door. Her hand hovered over the doorknob. What would she find inside? Stevie never stayed in bed past six. Even after Abby was born, Stevie had been in the kitchen fixing breakfast by six.

She cleared her hoarse voice and tapped on the door. "Stevie? It's me. Are you awake?"

"Tess, get in here so I can hug you."

Her sister sounded normal, and the pressure pushing Tess away from the door eased. Tess twisted the doorknob and peeked inside. Stevie lay propped against the pillows with her Bible in her hand. A gray pallor pinched the color from her cheeks, and she looked like she'd gained at least twenty pounds. She put down her Bible and held out her hands. "Come here right now."

The room looked nothing like it had when her parents were alive, and Stevie's smile welcomed her. Tess flew into her sister's embrace. In spite of the heat in the room, Stevie's skin was cold and dry to the touch. She held Tess in a fierce hug that brought tears surging to Tess' eyes. She'd stayed away too long. Tess hung onto Stevie even after her sister let go.

Stevie grasped Tess' shoulders and pushed her away to look in her face. "You look marvelous, Tessie. I'm so glad to see you. Abby will be thrilled. She's in the back meadow with her dad."

"I can't wait to see her." She sat on the edge of the bed and took her sister's hand. "What's wrong with you, Stevie?" she asked, keeping her voice soft.

Stevie's fingers tightened on hers. She licked her lips. "I'm going to be fine, Tessie. Don't look so scared. We've had few rough weeks, but it's getting better. I'm not dying or anything."

"You're still not saying what it is. Is it—" She couldn't say the word *cancer.*

"I'm fine. Really." Stevie gave Tess's fingers a gentle squeeze. "I've got lupus. Isn't that just my luck—a disease that hates heat when I live in Arizona."

"Lupus?" Tess wasn't sure what it was, though she knew she'd heard of it. It was some kind of autoimmune disease, wasn't it?

"I know I look like the Pillsbury Doughboy, but it's the steroids they have me on. I'm feeling much better, but fatigue still knocks me down at times. I'd hoped to meet you at the door." Stevie's eyelids were half closed, and she was beginning to slur her words.

At least it wasn't cancer. Tess consoled herself with the thought. Her sister was the one thing stable in her life, even if she didn't get to see her as often as she liked. Tess patted Stevie's hand. "You need to sleep for a while. I think I'll go see Abby and Rory."

Stevie's eyes popped open. "Did you see Chase?"

"Briefly. He was his usual charming self, though he did agree to pasture Wildfire for me. Are you sure you don't mind me bringing him home for a while? It seemed reasonable since I was going to be living so close."

"I don't know why you resent Chase so much." Stevie's lids drooped again.

You mean other than the fact he took my place? Tess didn't say the words. She tiptoed from the room and closed the door behind her. Backing away from the door, she bumped into Chase in the hall. She skidded on the tile and began to fall, but he steadied her with a hand on her arm. Jerking away, she crossed her arm and glared up at him. "Why didn't you tell me she was so sick?"

His blue eyes held disdain. "If you'd been any kind of sister, you would have seen it for yourself, just like the rest of us did. But you were too busy running to take time for family."

Though his words stung, she lifted her chin and managed not to flinch. "It's not like I was goofing off, Chase. Do you have any idea how many fires I've fought, how many lives I've helped save this year?"

"Tess Masterson, super hero. You still don't get it, do you, Tess? Sometimes the bravest thing we do is get out of bed in the morning and do our duty by the ones we love. It's easy to run away from responsibility."

"I never ran away!" Conscious of her sleeping sister, Tess lowered her voice. "You won, isn't that enough for you, Chase?" She stomped past him and headed for the front door. She heard his boots clicking on the tile as he came behind her.

Quickening her pace, she flung open the screen door and ran to her Jeep. She clicked the lock as he put his hand on the door. He pounded on the window, and hoping to irritate him, she flashed a victory smile as she drove away in a plume of red dust. Why did he bring out her childish side? She should be bigger than that, able to rise above his jibes. Another reason to hate him.

THOMAS NELSON
Since 1798

thomasnelson.com

Alaska
Twilight

COLLEEN COBLE

Alaska
Twilight

COLLEEN COBLE

THE ALOHA REEF SERIES

THOMAS NELSON
Since 1798

thomasnelson.com

9 780785 260448